The Koreans sprinted forward, Bolan and their leader trailing

As the leader touched the button to close the elevator door, Bolan commented, "I saw smoke coming out of one of the shafts."

"We blew the other cables, but not this one," the leader said in halting English, "in case a strategic retreat was called for."

"Who are you," Bolan asked, "and what do you want with me?"

"We've been watching you, American. We hunt the same quarry." Not so much as a hint of friendliness was visible in the man's face. "We will compare notes, as you would say. You will tell me who you work for and why you are after Sin Mak-Fang."

"If I refuse?"

"I would not recommend it. The last person who refused to tell me what I wanted to know was found floating facedown in the Yellow Sea."

DON PENDLETON's
MACK BOLAN®

EVIL ALLIANCE

A GOLD EAGLE BOOK FROM
WORLDWIDE®

TORONTO • NEW YORK • LONDON
AMSTERDAM • PARIS • SYDNEY • HAMBURG
STOCKHOLM • ATHENS • TOKYO • MILAN
MADRID • WARSAW • BUDAPEST • AUCKLAND

First edition November 2000

ISBN 0-373-61475-6

Special thanks and acknowledgment to
David Robbins for his contribution to this work.

EVIL ALLIANCE

Printed in U.S.A.

This is no time to speak of the hopes of the future, or the broader world which lies beyond our struggles and our victory. We have to win that world for our children. We have to win it by our sacrifices.

—Sir Winston Churchill
November 10, 1942

The sacrifices I make to wage Eternal War against evil may seem high, but I make them of my own free will. At the end of the road, my only regret would be that there was still so much left to do and not enough time.

—Mack Bolan

PROLOGUE

San Diego, California

Bob Walker ran a comb through his neatly clipped brown hair one last time, then set the comb on his dresser and stared at his reflection in the mirror. His moon face was much too round and babylike to suit him. Just as his body was too plump, his hands too pudgy, his double chin an abomination.

Walker would much rather have the handsome features of a movie star and the build of a weightlifter. But life had treated him cruelly. He liked to blame his looks on poor genetics, on his parents, which didn't jibe with the fact his father was a broomstick and his mother a petite brunette.

"What does it matter tonight?" Walker asked aloud, smoothing his suit, and grinned. For once his appearance was of no consequence. Where he was going, they wouldn't care what he looked like. They wouldn't giggle behind his broad back, or mock him with whispers, or point and sneer.

Scooping up a set of keys, Walker hurried out, locked the door and excitedly barreled down the stairs. In the parking lot he slid behind the wheel of his van.

Purchased just two months ago, it still had that new smell he liked so much.

Gunning the engine, Walker headed for his date with destiny.

He was tingling with excitement. He was about to embark on one of the most thrilling escapades of his life, thanks to Barney Fedelston in the electronics division. From a pocket he took the index card on which Barney had scribbled the address, placed it on the dash and patted it.

Finding the place, though, proved harder than Walker anticipated. It was out toward La Mesa, on a quiet residential street. The high brick wall and wrought-iron gate were exactly as Barney had described them.

Walker received his first surprise of the evening when he pulled up to the gate and a dour Oriental fellow in dark clothes materialized next to his window as if out of thin air. Walker nearly jumped out of his skin. Rolling down the window, he mustered a nervous smile. "You startled me."

"Token?" the man said.

"Oh. Yes. Sorry." Walker fished in his pocket again and produced the cherry-red token Barney had given him. On both sides Club X and a naked woman were imprinted in silver.

The Oriental fellow vanished without another word. Walker heard a hum, and the gate swung inward. He followed a winding drive to the three-story stucco building, mildly disappointed there were no garish lights, no skimpily clad women waiting with enticing smiles. For a den of iniquity, Walker mused as he parked the car, it left a lot to be desired.

He thumped the heavy brass knocker on the stout

oak door. Almost immediately the door was opened by another Oriental man in dark clothes. Walker showed his token again, and the fellow motioned for him to proceed down a short corridor.

It was at that point Walker almost turned and left. Barney had warned him the club was a bit cloak-and-dagger. But it was more than the gate and the guards that made Walker uneasy. He didn't like the feel of the place.

But he had decided to undertake this adventure, so he squared his rounded shoulders, advanced to a door and lifted his hand to rap. Suddenly it opened. Bright lights, the drone of voices and tantalizing fragrances assaulted Walker's senses. He blinked, then felt a slender arm encircle his. A ravishing Oriental woman in a clinging red dress steered him toward a mahogany bar.

"Good evening, sir, and welcome to Club X." The woman's English was impeccable.

"I'm Madame Rhee. From this minute on, your every wish is our command."

Walker was mesmerized by the sight of eight lovely women seated on plush sofas or chairs. Now, this was more like it! he told himself. He held out the token. "Barney Fedelston gave me this—" he began to explain.

"You may keep it," Madame Rhee said pleasantly, and indicated a jar on the counter half-filled with more. "Take a few extra. Give them to acquaintances you trust, to those who crave the tasty delights my unique establishment offers. Have them mention your name, and you'll receive ten percent off your next visit."

"Ten percent?" Walker repeated. He hadn't intended to come more than this once, but one-tenth off was quite an inducement. The bartender, he noticed, was Oriental like the other men and Madame Rhee herself.

As if she could read his mind, she said, "I am South Korean. So is most of the staff.

"My mother was married to an American serviceman stationed in Seoul. They passed on years ago, and I have been making ends meet as best I can."

Walker admired their plush surroundings. "You've done quite well, I'd say."

"Thank you." Madame Rhee had brown, twinkling eyes and a perpetual smile Walker found disarming. "Now, before we order a drink and you select your escort, I must make the ground rules clear. Drunkenness and violence are not tolerated."

"I would never—" he began, but she didn't let him finish.

"I run a clean, orderly establishment. My girls are the best money can buy. They are ladies, not gutter trash. So I expect all our customers to behave as gentlemen." Madame Rhee lowered her voice a trifle. "As for your privacy, you need never fear on that score. Your visits and all matters pertaining to them will be handled with the utmost discretion."

"That's nice to know," Walker said, envisioning the fit his mother would throw if she ever found out he'd cuddled with a prostitute.

"Payment is required at the time services are rendered. All major credit cards are accepted. You pay by the hour. Drinks and meals are extra. There is also a small charge for the loan of accessories such as whips and chains.''

''Whips and chains?'' Walker blurted, and regretted it, afraid his inexperience was showing and he'd come across as a total boob.

''Now then, as for your entertainment—'' Madame Rhee gently squeezed his hand ''—what would you like to drink? And what type of young lady are you most interested in?''

The next sixty minutes were all Bob Walker had hoped they would be. He ordered a Scotch whiskey on the rocks, then selected his escort from among the assorted beauties.

The blonde guided Walker up to a lavish bedroom on the third floor. What happened next was too incredible for words. He was nervous at first, but she seemed to sense as much and knew just what to do to put him at ease. She brought his wildest fantasies to life, doing everything he had ever wanted to do, and more. At the end of the hour he was spent but supremely content. In a blissful daze, he allowed her to lead him downstairs.

Madame Rhee was at the bar. ''Now then, young sir, how would you like to pay?''

Barely aware of what he was doing, Walker handed her a credit card.

Madame Rhee walked him to the foyer. ''Thank you for your patronage. I do so hope you will stop by again sometime.''

''You can count on it,'' Walker said. He would revisit the brothel as often as he could. It was heaven on earth, or the closest thing to it. Whistling to himself, Walker ambled off.

MADAME RHEE SMILED and waved, watching until the outer door closed behind him. Then her smile withered, and she crossed to the bar to retrieve the credit-card receipt. With this in hand, she opened a door to the left of the counter and entered a small room that contained a chair and table, a computer and a bespectacled computer operator.

In their native language Madame Rhee said, "You should have seen this one, Kim. He was a typical soft, flabby American, a child pretending to be a man. I doubt he will amount to much, but we never know. Run it."

Nodding, Kim took the slip, adjusted his glasses and typed at the keyboard. It didn't take him long to run a routine credit check using the credit-card information, as he had done countless times on countless patrons.

In short order the monitor flashed with the information Madame Rhee needed, and she stood at Kim's elbow to read it. "'Robert J. Walker. Age, twenty-seven. Place of residence, the Wilshire Apartments on Hawthorne Street. Place of employment, Omnitronics, Incorporated.'"

"They do contract work for the Department of Defense, don't they?"

"Yes, indeed." A new sort of smile twisted Madame Rhee's thin red lips, a perversely wicked smile that would have shocked Bob Walker had he seen it. "I'm intrigued. Do a complete check. I want everything there is to know about our flabby young friend."

Madame Rhee waited at the bar. She greeted several more customers, her demeanor as cheerful and polite as ever. No one would ever suspect who she really was or take her for more than she seemed to be. Which was exactly as she wanted it.

At last Kim emerged and handed Madame Rhee a printout of the results. She ran her finger down the first page, speed-reading. An evil little chuckle escaped her. "So! Mr. Walker is a graduate of MIT. A design engineer, employed at Omnitronics since graduation. He earns one hundred and twenty thousand dollars a year, has no wife, no children. I daresay he is ideal."

"For all we know, he designs fireproof sprinkler systems," Kim said, referring to a previous customer who had been a monumental waste of his time and effort.

"Let's see what our kitten learned." Madame Rhee gave Kim the printout, and they went out the rear of the computer room and down a hallway to a door that was always kept locked. Kim opened it for her, then sank into a chair in front of a large console topped by a dozen monitors. Some were lit, showing women and men in various stages of undress and intimacy.

"Which room?" Kim asked.

"Number 5," Madame Rhee said. "He was with Gloria." The blonde had been at Club X for the better part of a year. Her big doe eyes, healthy farm girl looks and a body that wouldn't quit had endeared her to many of the johns. No one would guess she had taken the job to support her way through secretarial school.

Neither Gloria nor any of the other fallen doves suspected their every encounter was videotaped.

Kim hit the appropriate button, rewinding the tape to room 5, then punched the start button.

Madame Rhee suspected it had been Robert Walker's first time. The young man was exceptionally shy. When he undressed, he turned his back to Gloria, then scooted under the covers as if afraid to have Gloria see him naked. Little was said until after they were done, lying arm in arm, when Gloria started to make small talk, as she had been instructed to do.

"You were marvelous, handsome."

Walker beamed like a kid given cotton candy. "Really? I mean, well, you weren't bad yourself."

Gloria stroked his temple. "I hope I'll see you again, Bob. You're different than most men. You know how to make a woman feel special."

To Madame Rhee's amazement, the young American blushed.

"Why, thank you."

On the tape, Gloria pecked Walker on the cheek. "If you don't mind my asking, what do you do for a living, Bob? I'll bet you're a big business executive or something like that."

"Goodness, no. I'm an engineer."

"I'll bet it's awfully complicated."

Her flattery had the desired effect. "You could say that. I design sophisticated systems for military hardware."

Walker placed his lips close to the blonde's ear and whispered something Madame Rhee couldn't quite catch. "Rewind and amplify the sound," she directed.

Kim's deft fingers flew over the console.

"Don't tell anyone—" Walker's voice was now crystal clear "—but at this very moment I'm involved in a highly classified project for the United States government."

Gloria's doe eyes widened. "You don't say? Top secret or something, huh?"

"Have you ever heard of the stealth sub?" When Gloria shook her head, Walker said, "Well, all I can tell you is that it's the undersea equivalent of the stealth bomber. And I'm responsible for designing some of the most critical systems."

"What kind of systems?"

"Sorry, I'd like to tell you but I can't. It could get me in a lot of trouble."

The rest was small talk, of no interest to Madame Rhee. She ordered Kim to turn off the tape. "Contact our master. Inform him we have hit the jackpot, as the Americans say. Advise him I will send a detailed follow-up as soon as Mr. Walker pays us another visit."

Kim rose. "I take it Mr. Walker is to receive special treatment the next time?"

"Yes," Madame Rhee said, her wicked smile in full bloom. "Very special treatment, indeed."

CHAPTER ONE

Japan

The war went on.

Sometimes it seemed to Mack Bolan that for every drug lord and arms dealer he put out of business, half a dozen lurked in the wings ready to take his place. But that didn't stop the soldier from waging his endless fight on any and all fronts. It didn't stop him from going wherever he was needed and doing whatever was necessary to stem the dark tide that threatened to mire his beloved country in the muck of drug addiction and social decay.

So it was that the Executioner found himself in Yokohama, Japan. To most Americans, Yokohama was a picturesque port situated on the west shore of Tokyo Bay. Vacationers visited its many parks and gardens, its bustling wharf, unaware that under the tranquil surface thrived an illegal trade in opiates.

Mack Bolan knew. Much of the heroin funneled into the United States came out of the Golden Triangle in Southeast Asia and was transported through either Hong Kong, Taiwan or Japan. Japanese authorities were diligent in their efforts to stop the flow, but they couldn't stem all of it. So Bolan took it on himself to plug the leaks. And one of the biggest at the moment was Hideo Koto.

Intelligence reports suggested Koto had his fingers in many pies. It was believed he had links to the Yakuza, that although he wasn't a formal member, he handled large heroin shipments for them, the infamous Red Hand and other sources. According to the Feds, the previous year alone Koto had smuggled tens of millions of dollars' worth into America.

Bolan was in Yokohama to insure Koto never smuggled in another ounce.

A light mist dampened the docks. Out on the bay a tug's horn blared. The smell of salt water and fish was heavy in the air as Bolan catfooted across a night-shrouded rooftop that overlooked a particular section of the harbor. Clad in a combat blacksuit crammed with the lethal tools of his trade, the Executioner dropped onto his stomach and crawled the final few yards to the roof's edge.

Stealth and silence were crucial. Under no circumstances could Bolan do anything that would bring local police to the scene. Not while he was there, at any rate. His mission wasn't officially sanctioned by the U.S. government. Were he to be caught, all knowledge of him and his activities would be disavowed. His plan was to get in, dispose of Hideo Koto with extreme prejudice and get out before Koto or Koto's underlings knew what hit them. All with as little fuss as possible.

To that end, Bolan was armed for up-close-and-personal work. His Beretta 93-R rode leather under his left armpit, and he carried a Mini-Uzi fitted with a folding stock and a Wilson Arms sound suppressor.

Ironically, the suppressor was about as long as the Uzi itself and rendered it far less compact, but without it Bolan would attract gunners like a hound dog attracted fleas. The Mini-Uzi hung from a sling under his right arm and could be employed with a flick of his wrist.

Bolan's piercing blue eyes narrowed as he studied the warehouse. If the intel relayed by the Feds was correct, a large shipment of heroin was due to be loaded onto the freighter berthed at the adjacent dock. But the warehouse was dark and quiet, and no activity whatsoever was visible. He wondered if the intel was wrong.

No sooner did the thought cross the soldier's mind than a bus rounded a corner several blocks to the south, followed by a limousine. The two vehicles braked at a gate in a chain-link fence. A man climbed from the bus, unlocked a padlock and swung the gate aside. After the vehicles went through, he locked it again.

Nineteen more men filed from the bus after it parked near huge double doors on the south side of the warehouse. The doors were promptly slid open, and the limousine drove inside.

Bolan didn't move until the doors were pulled shut. Gliding to the right, he climbed down the same rickety ladder that had gained him access to the roof, then sidled along the wall until he reached the corner.

The fence across the street was only six feet high, and it wasn't topped by barbed wire. Nor were there any guards or guard dogs to contend with. In fact, Bolan saw no deterrents at all to keep him or anyone else from breaching the perimeter.

Hideo Koto, evidently, didn't want to attract undue

attention by turning the warehouse and its environs into a fortress. Not that he really needed to, when the intimidation factor was considered. Koto had a well-deserved reputation for being as vicious as a rabid dog. A long string of brutal murders was chalked to his credit but went unpunished because Koto's money bought tremendous political influence and judicial clout.

No one in his or her right mind would dare stand up to Hideo Koto, or dare trespass on his property.

Bolan looked both ways. At that time of night the narrow street was deserted. He started to cross, but a metallic clatter less than a block away caused him to duck back again. As immobile as a statue, the soldier searched for the source. Movement registered, and a four-legged shape padded in his direction. It was a mongrel dog, nosing into every nook and cranny in search of scraps to eat. Not much more than knee high, it posed no threat except in one important regard. If it spotted him, it might make so much noise that Koto or some of Koto's men would notice and investigate.

Bolan backed into the alley and squatted behind an empty trash can. He gripped the Mini-Uzi, not intending to use it, but keeping it ready as a precaution. He heard the clack-clack-clack of claws, then loud sniffing.

The mongrel was at the alley's mouth, its head tilted, nostrils flaring. It had a mottled coat and short ears, which were pricked forward.

Bolan hoped it would move on. He had no desire to kill it, but neither could he let the animal compromise his mission. When it took a step toward the trash can, he gripped the Uzi's cocking handle. But the mongrel went no farther. It sniffed a few more times, then trotted off, oblivious to its close call.

A full minute after the clicking claws receded in the distance, Bolan rose and surveyed the immediate vicinity. All of the high warehouse windows were now lit but their glow didn't extend as far as the street. Crouching, he sprinted to the fence and vaulted upward. His outstretched hands closed on the top links. They sagged under his weight but they didn't buckle. In another heartbeat he was up and over.

Landing as lightly as a cat, Bolan slanted to the left, toward the opposite side of the building from the double doors. Pallets stacked high with crates and metal drums offered concealment.

Once among the pallets, Bolan unzipped a pocket and pulled out a spare magazine. From a smaller pocket he produced a metal clip, which he used to attach the spare magazine to the mag already inserted in the Mini-Uzi. He attached it near the bottom, at right angles, resulting in an odd L-shaped configuration underneath the SMG. But it had a purpose.

Bolan could now replace the magazine in the Uzi, when it was spent, with the other one attached to it, all in the blink of an eye. It effectively gave him sixty-four rounds instead of thirty-two. In addition, he'd found that the marginal extra weight helped a bit in countering muzzle climb.

Extending the stock, he adopted a two-handed grip, then straightened.

Except for a row of windows at the top of the warehouse, the north side was plunged in gloom. Bolan threaded through the pallets to the corrugated metal wall. Muffled voices and the whir of machinery emanated from within.

Seeking a way inside, the soldier moved along the wall to the corner nearest the bay. Off to the left fishing boats were lined up four and five deep. Most doubled as homes for the families that relied on them for their livelihood, families who had long since turned in for the night.

Bolan eased around the corner, his senses primed. He had taken a single step when a pinpoint of light flared at the end of the dock that flanked the south side of the building. Crouching, he spotted two men, one of whom had just lit a cigarette.

The pair was gazing out over the harbor and talking in subdued tones. As one man laughed and gestured toward the water, the submachine guns slung over their shoulders were clearly visible. They were sentries. Strolling along in the shadow of the freighter as if they didn't have a care in the world, the gunners reached the warehouse and bore to the right.

Bolan raised the Mini-Uzi, tucking the stock to his shoulder. They were coming straight toward him. As careless as they were, in another ten to twelve feet they were bound to spy his hunkered form. Several more strides was all he allowed them. Then he smoothly stroked the trigger twice, unleashing short bursts.

The sentries were caught flat-footed. Three 9 mm Parabellum rounds cored their chests, punching them to the ground in disjointed heaps, shock etched on their faces.

Before moving out, Bolan waited to gauge the reaction, if any, from within the warehouse and on the freighter. Only when he was assured the deaths had gone unnoticed did he warily rise. Swinging the Mini-Uzi behind him, the soldier dragged the bodies back around the corner to where they would be less apt to be discovered.

Their subguns, Bolan discovered, were Shin Chuo Kogyo models, manufactured in Japan. He'd never fired one, but he had heard they were sturdily constructed and dependable. Strangely, he noticed that the company had incorporated a grip safety attached to the magazine housing instead of the grip itself, an unusual feature shared by only two other subguns Bolan could think of—the Italian TOZ and the Madsen.

More cautiously than ever, the Executioner crept to the front of the building. The enormous double doors were still closed. Nearby, a gangplank linked the dock to the freighter. No one was visible either on the gangplank or the deck above.

Bolan needed to see into the warehouse, but the windows were too high and cracking open the doors was out of the question. It would make too much noise. Thwarted, he was debating whether to shimmy up onto the freighter to gain a higher vantage point when headlights blossomed out by the gate. The driver leaned on the horn.

Within moments one of the huge doors creaked on rollers in need of grease. Five men emerged, all in suits. Their wariness and posture suggested they were Koto's personal bodyguards. One jogged forward to admit the vehicle.

A late-model sedan drove onto the premises. It stopped next to the bus, and the driver got out. He was dressed in a black chauffeur's uniform that clung to his lean, muscular frame like a second skin. His appearance was striking, not because of the uniform, but due to his great height.

Bolan estimated the man had to be seven feet tall, if not a bit taller. All the more remarkable, given that Orientals were, on average, shorter than Caucasians.

The chauffeur opened the rear door, and out slid an expensively attired young man with a mane of black hair and a cocky attitude. Smiling smugly, he strutted toward the warehouse.

Something about them nagged at Bolan's mind, something he couldn't quite peg until the newcomers halted in the rectangle of light spilling through the doorway. Then he realized what it was. The men weren't Japanese; they were Korean.

Why would two Koreans visit Hideo Koto? Bolan asked himself. There had been nothing in any of the intel gleaned by various agencies to suggest Koto had any dealings with the South Korean underworld. Yet here was apparent proof right in front of Bolan's eyes.

A short, squat and bull-shouldered man exited the warehouse. His bushy, beetling brows were crowned by a balding pate; his face was like that of a hairless gorilla. It wasn't the kind of face one easily forgot. Bolan had seen it in the file he'd studied before committing himself to the operation—Hideo Koto.

Koto welcomed his younger visitor with a formal, stiff bow. They smiled and shared pleasantries as if they were long-lost brothers, but a certain coolness marked their manner, a certain reserve, as if neither fully trusted or liked the other.

The giant chauffeur stood to one side, seemingly at ease. He didn't appear to be armed, yet Koto's bodyguards repeatedly bestowed nervous glances on him, as if his mere presence inspired fear.

Bolan's fluency in Japanese was limited. He caught a few of the words, but not enough to get the gist of the conversation. He did gather that Koto was a bit surprised by the young man's visit.

A commotion in the doorway heralded a flurry of movement up the gangplank and onto the freighter. Workers began to transfer crates from the warehouse to the ship's hold. Two forklifts were employed.

Koto and the young Korean moved to one side to continue their discussion. Unfortunately for Bolan, they moved to the other side of the open door, so the steady stream of workers passed between him and his target. He brought the Mini-Uzi to bear but didn't fire.

He wouldn't until he was sure of a kill.

No one had realized the sentries were missing. The workers were busy at their tasks, the bodyguards were focused on the tall chauffeur as if fearing he would sprout hair and fangs, and Koto was preoccupied with the young Korean. But Bolan couldn't count on their oversight lasting forever. Sooner or later someone would wonder where the two men had gotten to, and launch a search. He had to get close enough to Koto before that occurred.

But how? Bolan couldn't very well waltz out into the open. Nor would crawling along the base of the wall do any good. By now the freighter was ablaze with lamps and lanterns. He wouldn't get ten feet before he was detected.

Then some of the workmen began to stack crates just outside the warehouse for the forklift operators to convey up the gangplank. As the stacks grew in number and size, they cast lengthening shadows toward the bay and the corner where the Executioner was concealed.

Flattening, Bolan bided his time until no one was looking in his general direction.

Then he scurried like a crab toward the crates. Between his blacksuit and the combat cosmetics smeared over his face, he felt warranted in taking the gamble.

Someone yelled up on the ship. Bolan froze and twisted, prepared to battle his way out, but the yell had been directed at a worker on the forward deck by a crane operator who was lowering pallets into the hold. Bolan resumed crawling and rose onto his knees when he was next to a stack.

When voices rose, raised in anger, Bolan stood to peer between two crates. Hideo Koto and the young Korean were arguing, over what he couldn't guess. But whatever it was, Koto was extremely upset. Gesturing sharply, the drug lord poked his visitor in the chest.

What happened next surprised Bolan as much as it did Koto's bodyguards. The tall chauffeur moved with dazzling speed, his right arm lancing out, his oversize hand as rigid as a board. His fingers sheared into Koto's ribs, and the Japanese doubled over, grunting. Belatedly, the five bodyguards galvanized to their employer's defense and leaped at the tall Korean. They never laid a finger on him. In a blur the chauffeur reacted, his limbs a whirlwind of force and precision. All five dropped to the tarmac. One clutched a wrist, another a kneecap, a third gagged and sputtered, his hands over his throat. None had been slain, but they were in tremendous pain.

Most of the workers paused in what they were doing, but they didn't intervene. They awaited word from the drug lord.

Koto was livid. Recovering, he railed at the young Korean. Several times Bolan distinctly heard the word "Fang." He wished he could understand more. As if to oblige him, the very next second the young Korean addressed Hideo Koto in mildly accented English.

"I will spare you further loss of face, Koto-san. Speak in English so your men will not understand. What I have to say next is for your ears, and yours alone."

"You have already said too much, damn you," Koto responded. "How dare you treat me in this fashion! I am no petty thief or common thug, Cho-Hee!"

Cho-Hee remained calm. "Then stop acting like one, Hideo. You are the one who lost his temper, not I."

"What did you expect?" Koto was practically beside himself, his face scarlet with suppressed rage. "I greeted you as an equal! I thought your uncle sent you to finalize the arrangements. Instead, you tell me they have been changed. That now my percentage is less than you promised, yet I must make delivery in half the time!"

"You are quibbling," Cho-Hee said.

It was the last straw. Koto launched himself at the young Korean but never laid a hand on him. The tall chauffeur intercepted him with a lithe bound, one hand gripping Koto by the throat, the other hooking into his belt. Wheezing and flailing, Koto was lifted off his feet, raised until he was above the chauffeur's head. The chauffeur said something in Korean.

Cho-Hee answered, and the tall Korean lowered Koto as gently as if he weighed no more than a feather.

"You really must control yourself," Cho-Hee advised. "Kon-Li would have split your skull like rotted fruit. Sometimes he does not know his own strength."

Koto rubbed his raw neck and glared at the chauffeur. "He is a freak, an abomination."

"Be thankful he doesn't speak English," Cho-Hee stated. "He was trained from infancy for one purpose. Attack me again, and I will not accept blame for what he does."

Koto glanced at his bodyguards, three of whom were still on the ground. Defeat showed in the set of his features, the slump of his shoulders.

Bolan was genuinely surprised. Given Hideo Koto's reputation, he wouldn't have thought the man would back down to anyone. He wanted to learn more about these Koreans; who they were, what the reason for their visit was.

The young Korean draped an arm across Koto's squat shoulders. Koto plainly resented the familiarity but didn't object. "Believe it or not, I do respect you, Hideo. I have told my uncle many times that you can be depended on. But this childish display of yours has given me doubts."

"Forgive me," Koto said, dipping his chin to his chest.

"I already have," Cho-Hee said suavely. "As the Americans are so fond of saying, let us forgive and forget, shall we? In return for your apology, I promise not to mention this incident to my uncle. You can imagine what he would do should he hear of it."

Bolan saw Koto's Adam's apple bob. The implied threat terrified him. Who *was* this uncle? What sort of man was he that he inspired such fear in a vicious brute like Koto?

"Let us put things in perspective," Cho-Hee continued. "You are a powerful man in Japan, a man of respect, of authority. But my uncle operates in many countries, in Korea, China, Vietnam, Laos, Russia, Canada, the United States and others. So I ask you. Which of you is more influential in the greater scheme of things?"

"Your uncle," Koto admitted.

"While you have maybe sixty men in your organization, my uncle has six hundred. Where you deal in millions of dollars of illegal goods, my uncle deals in hundreds of millions. All he need do is snap his finger, and your entire operation would be wiped off the face of the earth as if it had never been." Cho-Hee paused. "Is this not so?"

"It is so."

"Then keep your famous temper in check. I will only tolerate so much." Cho-Hee removed his arm. "Next we should consider your complaints. First, the cut in your percentage—"

Koto interrupted. "It is most unfair. You asked me to reserve half the holding capacity for the goods you wish to transport to America. You told me I would be entitled to five percent of the street value. But now you tell me that your uncle needs an entire ship, and you wish to reduce my take to three percent."

Cho-Hee brushed a hand across his hair. "Perhaps you should invest in a calculator. I hear that your countrymen are noted for their fine electronics."

"Are you mocking me?"

"Not at all. But tell me. What is five percent of ten million dollars?"

Koto's brow knit. "Five hundred thousand."

"And what is three percent of twenty million?"

There was a pregnant silence. "Six hundred thousand." Hideo Koto bowed from the waist. "I am utmostly sorry, Cho-Hee. I did not stop to think. I thought your uncle was trying to take advantage of me. Please forgive my rudeness."

"Never apologize for the same mistake twice," the young Korean said. "My uncle values your friendship too much to impose on you. He knows you are doing him a favor by interrupting your shipping schedule to reserve one of your three freighters for him. Which is why he is being so generous."

Bolan wished that one or the other would say the uncle's name.

"The *Nagaoka* will arrive in two days," Koto said. "We can begin loading that evening if your shipment arrives by then."

"The *Petra* is already en route from Bangkok. It will dock here tomorrow."

"It's already on its way?" Koto said. "Your uncle must have been confident I would agree to his proposal."

"One way or another, yes," Cho-Hee said. "This venture is of the utmost importance to him. The shipment must be switched to your freighter and reach San Francisco by the specified date."

"We have plenty of time. It's not typhoon season. And the *Nagaoka*'s paperwork is all in order. The permits have all been obtained. American customs will have no reason to be suspicious.''

"Let's hope not, for both our sakes.'' Cho-Hee crooked a finger at the chauffeur. "I have taken up too much of your time. You have my number should any problems arise.''

"Will I hear from your uncle directly?'' Koto inquired.

"Why should you need to? Unless something goes drastically wrong, all contact will be through me. My uncle only becomes involved in extraordinary situations.'' Cho-Hee walked to the sedan, trailed by Koto. The chauffeur opened the door but the young Korean, about to slide in, paused. "I have your personal assurance that nothing will go wrong?''

Bolan barely heard the question over the sound of the forklifts and the racket raised by the workers.

"Yes, indeed. I have not gotten where I am today by making mistakes.''

"I will relay the news to my uncle. He will be most pleased.''

Koto stood and watched the sedan depart. When the taillights faded into blackness, he pivoted and stalked toward the warehouse. Despite his claims to the contrary, he simmered with fury. Barking orders at his bodyguards, he stopped to survey the loading operation.

Mack Bolan had a clear shot. A head shot, no less. But although he had elevated the Mini-Uzi and had a bead on the drug lord, he hesitated.

The soldier had an important decision to make. He had flown to Japan to end Hideo Koto's illicit dealings, and he could do it now with a single stroke of the trigger. But if he terminated the Japanese hoodlum, he would never learn who those Koreans were or whom they worked for. And based on what he had overheard, it was obvious that, compared to Cho-Hee's uncle, Hideo Koto was small potatoes.

It made sense for Bolan to use the little fish to catch an even bigger one, for him to let Koto live long enough to glean a clue to the identity of Cho-Hee's uncle. He started to lower the Uzi, intending to slip off into the night, but fate decreed otherwise.

Without warning, a worker appeared at the end of the crates, saw Bolan and shouted an alarm.

CHAPTER TWO

Mack Bolan knew how important it was to never let his mind stray. In firefights beyond number, from the paddies of Thailand to the steaming jungles of the Congo, from the frigid wastes of the Arctic to the verdant banks of the Amazon, the soldier had waged the good fight against those who would spread evil. Staying sharp and alert had become second nature to him. He seldom suffered a lapse. Seldom, but it did happen. Every once in a rare while Bolan let his focus waver, as he had done just now, and in each and every instance he came close to paying for his mistake with his life.

The big man had been concentrating on Cho-Hee and Hideo Koto and what he intended to do rather than on the swirl of activity around him. Now a worker about to slide a crate onto a forklift had caught sight of him.

The worker's hand stabbed under his shirt and came out flourishing a pistol. Bolan cored the man with a short burst, then backpedaled, firing as he retreated, first at a worker on the freighter who popped a shot at him, then at one of the bodyguards who recklessly charged the crates.

Koto's underlings were shouting, cursing, diving for cover. Koto himself was being hustled into the warehouse.

Lead hornets buzzed the warrior, some smacking into the corrugated metal with a sound like hail hitting tin. Bolan answered in kind, dropping two gunners. Reaching the corner, he indulged in firing random bursts to discourage the opposition, then wheeled and bolted.

At the next corner Bolan glanced back. Dark silhouettes were framed against the backdrop of the freighter. Fireflies sparkled, and he narrowly evaded a lethal swarm by racing around the corner. Now he was on the north side of the warehouse, shrouded in shadow and misty rain. He could head west, to the street, but to reach it he had to cover a lot of open space. To the north, though, were the fishing craft, scores and scores at berth, a virtual maze in which to lose himself.

Veering toward them, Bolan ran flat out. He was almost to the chain-link fence when his pursuers spotted him and opened fire. But in their haste they missed, their rounds thudding into the soil or pinging off the fence.

The soldier never slowed, never broke stride. At the right split second he hurtled upward, snagged the top and levered himself over. He was in among the boats before the gunners could steady their aim. Bounding across the deck of the first craft, he leaped to the next, and then to the one after that.

Broader and lower to the water than Chinese junks, the Japanese fishing boats were packed like sardines in a can. All were of the same general size but of varying deck designs. Most of each deck, though, was broad and flat, enabling Bolan to pour on the speed without having to worry about the danger of a misstep. His pounding feet, combined with the rocking motion of the boats he leaped onto, sufficed to awaken many of the occupants. Some hollered, while others went on deck to see what was going on. The general racket and confusion benefited the soldier.

Looking back, Bolan saw Koto's men were still after him. But so many people had come up onto the decks that they couldn't make much headway. Irate fishermen and their angry wives railed at them, protesting the intrusion. The gunners had to force their way through, which made the people angrier. The resultant uproar woke up even more, who, in turn, added to the general bedlam.

Bolan slowed. He doubted Koto's underlings could still see him. Moving toward shore, he leaped from the last craft onto the dock and hastened to a narrow street. He hid in an inky, recessed doorway and waited. When five minutes went by with no sign of further pursuit, he slung the Mini-Uzi behind him and made off through the streets toward the house where he was staying.

It wasn't a typical residence. Maintained by the U.S. government for clandestine ops, it was primarily used by espionage agents and others who needed to keep a low profile while in Japan. Only recently, a dissident Chinese scientist who had defected to the West was kept there for a week while appropriate papers were prepared that allowed him to be flown to the U.S. on a commercial airline. Under the protection of federal agents, of course.

Bolan was able to use the safehouse thanks to the help of his longtime friend, Hal Brognola. Brognola, the director of the ultrasecret Sensitive Operations Group, was one of the most important, influential and powerful men in Washington.

In the unending war waged against the invisible evil empires that thrived worldwide, there was a critical need for seasoned warriors like Mack Bolan to carry the fight to the enemy. There was also an equally critical need for planners and coordinators like Hal Brognola, men who had access to all the sensitive intelligence reports Congress and the media never saw, men who made things happen from behind the scenes with no thought to their own reward.

Hal Brognola was one of the few people on the planet the Executioner trusted completely and unreservedly. The big Fed was his best link to intelligence data he would otherwise be denied. So the first thing Bolan did upon arriving at the house was to use the secure phone to place a direct call to Brognola's office. By his watch it was about 1:00 p.m. in the U.S. capital.

Brognola's deep voice was tinged with warmth. "Striker? How did it go?"

"It didn't."

"What happened?"

Briefly, concisely, Bolan related his encounter.

"I think you did right in not eliminating Koto," was Brognola's quick assessment. "The important thing now is to uncover the identity of this mysterious Korean, and Koto is our only link. I'll have an interagency check run on the name Cho-Hee and get back to you as soon as I can." He paused. "It could be you've stumbled onto something big. If what you overheard is true, this Korean has to be a major player, and a damned clever one if I've never heard of him.''

The big Fed said his goodbyes, and Bolan hung up the receiver.

Brognola's point was well taken. He had his finger on the pulse of the global intelligence network, as it were. Each day he waded through reams of reports, including capsule summaries from all the major intel-gathering organizations. If it was worth knowing, Brognola knew it.

But whoever this Korean was, he had successfully cloaked his activities. No mean feat, in light of the constant scrutiny by those who made it their business to uncover every little dark secret in every little dark corner of the world.

Shrugging, Bolan stripped off the blacksuit and headed for the bathroom. A shower and a meal were in order. His raven hair and vivid blue eyes presented quite a contrast in his reflection in the mirror over the sink. He wiped off the combat cosmetics, set hot water spewing from the shower nozzle and stepped under the spray.

Bolan could feel the tension drain from his limbs and body. It was always this way after a mission. No matter how many times he put his life on the line, no matter how many risks he took and how many dangers he overcame, the tension was always there. And that was as it should be. The day he started to take his work for granted, the day he let his mental edge dull, would be the day they buried him.

After showering, the soldier donned chinos and a navy-blue shirt and went down to the kitchen. The refrigerator was well stocked with a variety of cuisines. There was Chinese food—left over, no doubt, from when the Chinese scientist stayed there—barley soup, pigeon eggs and duck, among other things. There were boxes and jars of Japanese food—frozen raw fish, soybean curd and paste, and seaweed.

Bolan passed all that up in favor of some good old-fashioned hamburger, which he molded into patties and cooked on the small stove. A can of string beans and potatoes completed the meal, which he washed down with several cups of strong coffee.

It was close to dawn, the time when most people were just getting up to greet the new day, when Bolan finally turned in. He slept with the Beretta under his pillow and the Uzi hanging from the bedpost.

BOLAN AWAKENED at 4:00 p.m. He treated himself to more coffee out on the small deck that ran around the outside of the house on the first-floor level. Since the house was situated on a hill, he had a fine view of the city and the harbor beyond. Yokohama was a mix of urban sprawl and scenic splendor. To the north the industrial suburb of Kawasaki separated it from metropolitan Tokyo.

Bolan saw a large freighter sailing into port and wondered if it might be the one Cho-Hee mentioned, the *Petra*. The name suggested a Russian registry, but that was far from certain. Going back inside, he took his duffel bag from a closet, rummaged in it and found the Weaver scope he was looking for.

The ship was indeed the *Petra*, and it headed straight for the dock adjacent to Hideo Koto's warehouse. The freighter that had been there the night before was still there, and Bolan watched as the new vessel berthed alongside it. Two freighters now, and the arrival of the *Nagaoka* in a couple of days would make it three.

Bolan finished the coffee, pondering. He didn't want any of the ships to make it out of port again, not loaded with drugs and arms and whatever other illegal articles they carried. A few strategically placed packets of C-4 would insure they never did. But he didn't want to make a move until Brognola came through.

As if on cue the telephone jangled.

"Striker," Brognola began without preliminaries, "you sure know how to pick them."

"How's that?"

"I've spent all day contacting everyone I can think of who might have information on our mystery Korean, with no results. And an extensive computer check of the name Cho-Hee has turned up absolutely nothing."

"Then I'll wait until the *Nagaoka* docks. Maybe the files in the captain's quarters will give us a clue."

"I haven't given up hope," Brognola said. "Nigel Williamson hasn't gotten back to me, and if anyone has heard of this Korean, he'd be our man."

"Who?"

"Sorry. He's with MI-6. Nigel is their Far East expert. I'll contact you the minute I hear from him."

Bolan never had been fond of twiddling his thumbs. The hardest part of his self-appointed purpose in life was the waiting between missions. When he was at Stony Man he could always indulge in specialized training, everything from weapons' acclimation to hand-to-hand combat. But out in the field, like now, all he could do was sit around and wait.

To occupy himself, Bolan sharpened his Ka-bar fighting knife and a few throwing knives he had brought. He broke down the Uzi, cleaned and oiled the appropriate components and reassembled it.

The phone, at long last, rang again. The soldier was quick to scoop it up. "Any news?"

"Yes and no," Brognola elaborated. "Nigel Williamson returned my call about fifteen minutes ago. The name Cho-Hee didn't ring a bell. He has heard fairly substantial rumors, though, of a new criminal kingpin who operates along the Pacific Rim."

"But nothing concrete?" Bolan didn't try to mask his disappointment. "Nothing we can use?"

"O ye of little faith," Brognola quipped. "Be patient a moment. The MI-6 cell in Hong Kong did uncover intel suggesting this new player is North Korean, not South Korean."

The revelation intrigued Bolan. North Korea was so tightly controlled by the state that organized crime was virtually nonexistent. The country's Communist overseers saw it as decadent, and stamped it out wherever it was unearthed. South Korea, with its laxer government and greater freedom, was another story. Opportunists in drug and arms dealing were all too common.

"Once I heard that, I called the CIA's Far East specialist. He checked his database and, lo and behold, the name Cho-Hee popped up."

Bolan was all interest.

"It's not much to go on, but Cho-Hee is connected in a small way to an opium-smuggling operation. Acting on a tip, last month South Korean officials boarded a trawler about to dock at Inchon. On board they found a record amount of opium. No documents were uncovered, and the crew was tight-lipped. Even an offer of immunity from prosecution wouldn't get them to tell what they knew.''

"So where does Cho-Hee fit in?''

"The trawler was owned by a firm called Fisheries Unlimited. They have a small fleet of twenty or thirty trawlers that range all along the Asian coast.'' Brognola's voice acquired a hint of excitement. "The owner of Fisheries Unlimited is one Sin Cho-Hee.''

"It might be a coincidence,'' Bolan speculated.

"I know. Then again, you'll be interested in learning that Fisheries Unlimited has an office in Japan.''

"In Yokohama, by any chance?''

"Give the man a cigar.''

It was worth checking out, Bolan mused. "Do you have an address?''

Brognola did. Not only that, but he mentioned that the report filed by the South Koreans made note of a company emblem painted on the side of the trawler. It consisted of a lobster, a tuna and a sea bass piled one on top of another with a triton speared through all three, pinning them to the ocean bottom. "While you're checking at your end, I'll delve into Fisheries Unlimited and see what I can uncover. Five will get you ten the trawlers are mainly used for smuggling, and they only bring enough fish into port to avoid arousing suspicion.''

"Is that all?'' Bolan asked.

"Not quite. A quick check of North Korean records we can access turned up no one named Sin Cho-Hee. So maybe the rumors are wrong.''

"We'll know soon enough,'' Bolan commented.

"Be careful, Striker. We don't know what we're

getting into here. It could be a simple smuggling operation. It could be much more. Whatever the case, there's only one way Cho-Hee's uncle could have stayed hidden in the background so long.''

Bolan didn't need to ask what that was. Loose lips, as the Navy had it, sank ships. The most effective means of keeping those ships afloat was to silence the lips of anyone and everyone who posed a threat. ''I'll watch my back.''

MACK BOLAN WASN'T an espionage agent. He wasn't a spy. He was a warrior, conditioned by training and temperament to engage the enemy head-on and do whatever was necessary to get the job done. But that didn't mean he wouldn't perform field work. On those occasions when a little snooping around was required, Bolan was more than up to the task.

At one in the morning the big man was again down by the wharves, this time a mile or better from Koto's warehouse. His goal was directly across the street.

Earlier in the evening Bolan had taken a cab to the waterfront and gone for a stroll that took him past the building housing Fisheries Unlimited, which was nestled among other businesses having to do with exports, imports and the fishing trade.

Bolan had taken a seat in a small corner restaurant and ordered a meal, keeping track of the comings and goings in the building. After an hour, as he reached into his pocket for the money to pay the bill, he spotted a giant of a man strolling down the street.

It was the tall Korean, but now he wore a tailored suit instead of a chauffeur's uniform and cap. He towered chest, shoulders and head above everyone else.

Many of the usually discreet Japanese gawked openly. Children pointed and marveled.

Those in the giant's path scurried to move aside, and Bolan couldn't help thinking that more than politeness had something to do with it. The tall Korean radiated menace much as the sun radiated heat. It wasn't that he perpetually glared or scowled. Quite the contrary. His features were expressionless, as blank as a slate. But he had a unique quality about him, something in the catlike way he moved, in his dark, unblinking eyes, in his very posture, that sparked an undercurrent of fear in those who beheld him.

The giant arrived at the building that housed Fisheries Unlimited. His huge hand closed on the knob. Then, for no evident reason, he turned and slowly, deliberately scoured the street.

Bolan turned away. Somehow, the man had felt his eyes on him. Call it a sixth sense, possessed by those who lived on the raw edge of human existence. Bolan had experienced the same thing a number of times. After a minute he glanced over his shoulder.

The Korean had gone in.

Six hours later the soldier was directly across from the same entrance. He was dressed in black but not the combat blacksuit. Instead he had chosen a sweatsuit and a windbreaker. He'd attract much less attention. If the police stopped and questioned him, he could claim to be a simple tourist out for a late-night jog. As long as they didn't frisk him or look under his windbreaker and find the Beretta leathered under his right arm or the small kit of special tools in his back pocket, he could bluff his way out.

This part of Yokohama wasn't as isolated as the

warehouse district. Despite the lateness of the hour, many people were abroad. Lovers linked arm in arm, people on their way home from the movies or theater and some who were out for a late bite to eat.

Bolan stood in the doorway of a closed shoe store waiting for the right moment. It came when vehicular traffic momentarily died and only a few pedestrians were in sight and moving in the other direction. He quickly crossed the street, removing the kit from his back pocket as he did.

The lock was fairly standard. Bolan didn't qualify as a master thief or locksmith, but he could pick most ordinary locks fairly quickly.

Inserting a long, thin serrated sliver of metal, Bolan worked it up and down a few times, then twisted. No luck. He tried a second pick, and a third.

Footsteps approached. Bolan turned the pick harder, almost hard enough to break it, and was rewarded with an audible click. Slipping inside, he pulled the pick from the lock and closed and locked the door, then ducked low. Not three seconds later an elderly couple strolled by.

Bolan replaced the pick and slid the kit into his pocket. The building was as still as a tomb and as dark as the inside of a coffin. He removed a pencil flashlight from his windbreaker. A press of a button and its slender beam spiked into the darkness. Bolan played it over the directory at his elbow, which listed all the businesses and their respective floors. Written in Japanese, the list might as well be ancient Greek. But beside one of the names was a small logo or emblem depicting a lobster, a tuna and a sea bass all pinned to the ocean floor by a triton.

Bingo, Bolan thought to himself. It had to be Fisheries Unlimited, and the company was located on the uppermost floor.

His right hand on the Beretta, Bolan moved down the hall to a stairwell. His soft-soled shoes made no sound as he climbed. He passed the second landing and was midway to the next when muffled sounds brought him up short. He heard voices, speaking in Japanese, then soft music.

Bolan finally reached the third floor and checked to the right and the left. A soft, diffused glow rimmed a door on the right, and the voice came from the room behind.

The soldier exercised all the stealth at his command. He didn't draw the Beretta, not when it might be a janitor or someone working unusually late. The office had a window, and the blinds had been drawn but not quite all the way. At the bottom was a quarter-inch crack.

Bending, Bolan saw desks and file cabinets and a computer facing the window. The computer had been left on, its monitor aglow, and it was the light from the monitor that had caught his eye. The voices and music were explained by a small radio on the same desk as the computer.

Someone had left work in a hurry and hadn't bothered to turn either off. Or so Bolan assumed until a door at the rear of the office opened and out pranced a middle-aged man in his underwear and a woman half his age, probably his secretary, as naked as the day she was born. They were giggling and tickling each other.

The big man's mouth quirked upward. Some things

never changed from country to country, culture to culture.

Retreating to the stairwell, Bolan ascended to the fourth floor and went from door to door, stopping at the fifth. It bore the familiar emblem. Sinking to one knee, he retrieved his lock pick and opened the door.

Bolan slipped inside and shut the door. His flashlight revealed an office little different than the one on the third floor. Desks, a typewriter, a couple of computers, all presented the illusion that Fisheries Unlimited was no different from any of the other businesses in the building.

The soldier stepped over to a computer to turn it on. It was unlikely Sin Cho-Hee was foolish enough to leave incriminating documents lying around, but there might be files on the hard drive he could download. Or, better yet, he could send them via fax or as an e-mail attachment directly to Brognola. But Bolan never had the chance.

Sounds drew him to the window. He parted the blinds and saw Sin Cho-Hee and the deadly giant heading down the hall toward Fisheries Unlimited.

CHAPTER THREE

The Executioner darted to the door and turned the lock so Cho-Hee would find nothing amiss. Then he whirled and hurried through an inner doorway. A large painting of the company emblem, probably the original artwork, hung above an oak desk. On the desk sat a framed photo of Sin Cho-Hee. Neither interested Bolan as much as a door, which he pulled open to find a storage closet. There was barely enough time for him to slip in, crouch besides boxes of computer paper and close the door again before muted voices reached his ears.

Light appeared at the bottom of the closet door. Bolan heard the tread of shoes, the scrape of a chair. Sin Cho-Hee was at the desk not three yards away.

The younger man and the giant Kon-Li were speaking in Korean. Bolan had no idea what they were saying. After a bit he heard what he took to be a tapping sound, but then realized it had to be a finger punching numbers on a telephone. A lot of numbers, indicating it was a long-distance call.

Cho-Hee's tone implied it was someone he was fond of. The conversation went on for a quarter of an hour, then the young Korean hung up and dialed another long-distance number.

Bolan lucked out. Whoever Cho-Hee phoned spoke English.

"Mr. Lucca? Good to talk with you again.... Yes, it is late here. There's quite a time difference between Japan and America." Cho-Hee paused, apparently listening. "That's good to hear. Your performance continues to impress me, and when I am impressed, my uncle is impressed."

Again a mention of the man behind the scenes. Bolan mentally crossed his fingers that the young Korean would let a name slip.

"Our arrangements are proceeding according to schedule. We expect the freighter to leave port within three days, at the very latest.... Yes, yes, exactly the quantity we previously quoted you." Again Cho-Hee paused. "That would be most unfortunate." His tone had acquired a flinty edge. "We began these dealings in good faith. We expect you to do as you promised."

Bolan thought he heard a soft sound close to the closet and wondered if it was the giant.

"Problems are obstacles we must overcome, Mr. Lucca," Cho-Hee said gruffly.

"You agreed to a specified amount. We anticipate that you will have the funds on hand when delivery is made."

Whatever the man in America replied made Cho-Hee angrier. "Allow me to put this to you another way. My uncle will be severely upset if you fail to hold up your end of the bargain. And you know what happens to those who upset him." He paused once more. "No, that is not a threat, Mr. Lucca. Although, were I you, I would take it as a word to the wise. Isn't that the expression your countrymen use?"

Pressure against the closet door caused it to creak. Bolan wrapped his fingers around the butt of the Beretta, thinking Cho-Hee's bodyguard was about to open it. But the knob never turned. As best he could figure, Kon-Li was leaning against the door.

"I suggest you do whatever is necessary to have the money on hand when the freighter docks. Use whatever persuasion is necessary…. No, no, I leave that to your discretion. Surely someone as inventive as you are supposed to be can come up with a creative way of convincing them?" Cho-Hee chuckled. "Sleeps with the fishes? No, Mr. Lucca, I haven't heard that one before. We have a saying in North Korea that applies. Roughly translated, it would be, 'Bones can't talk.'"

Cho-Hee muttered in Korean, which made Bolan suspect he had a hand over the receiver. Kon-Li answered in his deep, gravelly voice.

"Very well, Mr. Lucca. I will call you again when the ship departs. And I will expect good news from your end…. Yes, I will…. No, I have never been to your illustrious city, but I have always wanted to visit the Golden Gate Bridge…. Yes, yes. Until then. Good night."

The phone smacked down. Cho-Hee, without thinking, spit in English, "Americans! They think the sun rises and sets for them alone! Mafia or no Mafia, if he fails to keep his word, I will personally see to it he sleeps with the fishes, as their quaint expression goes."

The Mafia? Bolan let the full import sink in. Whoever these Koreans were, they were establishing ties with criminal organizations from Asia to the U. S. The implications were staggering. There had never been a global network linking all major crime cartels, but it appeared these North Koreans were in the process of setting one up. Bolan remembered Cho-Hee saying they already operated in half a dozen countries. It was more important than ever that Bolan learn who headed the organization and where to find him.

The young Korean was placing yet another long-distance call. "May I speak to Madame Rhee, please. Tell her it is her cousin. She will know."

While waiting, Cho-Hee spoke quietly to Kon-Li in Korean. The soldier was sure he heard Cho-Hee mention "San Diego."

"Ah, Madame Rhee!" the younger man said, then launched into a lengthy chat in his native language.

The door creaked as the pressure was removed. Bolan stared at the knob, but the giant had merely walked away. As Cho-Hee rambled on, Bolan mulled his options. He would like nothing better than to terminate both men. But in doing so, he would sever his only link to Cho-Hee's uncle, who would undoubtedly go so deep into hiding that tracking him down would be next to impossible.

As Brognola had noted, Bolan mused, he had stumbled onto something big. Until—and if—the Feds came up with valuable intel, Bolan was on his own. He had to wing it, adapt to situations as they presented themselves and make the best judgment calls he could. At the moment, as much as it rankled him, his best bet was to let Cho-Hee go about his business for the time being.

Reluctantly, the soldier removed his hand from the Beretta.

Another five minutes passed before the young Korean hung up. His chair scraped, then Bolan heard him go into the outer office. Kon-Li made a comment that elicited a long response. Finally, the outer door rattled open and closed.

Bolan never took anything for granted. He didn't open the closet until several minutes of perfect silence convinced him the men were really gone.

Searching both offices took more than an hour. Few of the drawers were locked. Those that were fell easy prey to Bolan's lock picks. From one he confiscated seven computer disks; from another he took a small address book in Korean. He added a handful of manila folders, stuffing everything into a briefcase he found by Cho-Hee's desk. Whether any of it was information that could be used remained to be seen.

Bolan left everything exactly as he found it. If all went well, days might go by before the disks and files were missed.

Time to go. The soldier checked the hall, then quickly slipped out. At the landing he peered into the depths of the stairwell but saw no one. Taking the steps two at a time, he hurried lower. He was a few steps shy of the next landing when a door slammed and someone giggled. Spinning, Bolan sped to the landing he'd just left.

Laughing and tittering, the philandering businessman and his paramour appeared.

They walked arm in arm, acting like teenagers in love. He kissed her cheek, her neck, and she cooed giddily. They took their sweet time descending, stopping frequently to embrace.

As silent as a specter, Bolan followed.

At the entrance the businessman pinched the woman's posterior, and she laughed merrily. Suddenly becoming serious, the man scoured the street, then gestured. He went one direction; the woman went the other.

Bolan pulled up his jacket collar, switched the briefcase to his left hand in case any nasty surprises awaited and ventured out. A few pedestrians were across the street, but they didn't give him a second glance.

It was a long walk back to the safehouse, but Bolan didn't mind. He had been cooped up all day and craved activity.

The house was in an affluent residential neighborhood. Few of the homes were lit at that hour. A night bird chirped as the soldier wound along a gravel path that led past neatly tilled gardens. Once a week a caretaker came to work on the grounds and trim the strip of grass that was the lawn.

A few yards from the ground-floor platform, Bolan dipped a hand into his pants pocket for the keys. Abruptly, he halted. He couldn't say exactly why, but he had the sensation he wasn't alone. His senses, honed to the sharpness of a sword by years of living on the raw edge, probed the darkness and turned up nothing.

Still, he didn't discount it out of hand. Intuition had saved his life before. Something wasn't as it should be, something a part of his mind perceived but that he couldn't quite place. Setting the briefcase on the platform, Bolan palmed the Beretta and opened the front door. Peace and quiet reigned. He made a circuit of the main room and the kitchen, and although a tiny voice deep inside warned him to stay on his guard, everything seemed to be in order.

Bolan wasn't prone to jitters or a case of nerves. His combat-forged instincts had seldom failed him, but it appeared he was concerned without cause. He holstered the Beretta, then brought in the briefcase, deposited it on the kitchen table and headed upstairs without turning on the lights.

The rooms had been Westernized to the extent that few strictly Japanese features remained. There were no sliding paper screens between rooms, and the floors weren't covered with straw mats, or *tatami*. But the living room did have a nook, or alcove, typical of many Japanese homes. Known as *tokonoma,* this one had a scroll hanging in it, with a floral arrangement in front.

Bolan had to pass the alcove to reach the stairs. As he walked by, he idly glanced at the scroll and an electric shock spiked through him. It was tilted at an angle—yet it hadn't been when he left.

The soldier slowed, and the instant he did the wide floral arrangement in front of the nook surged to life. Or, rather, the man hidden behind the flowers did. Dressed in black, including a black ski mask, he made no outcry as he attacked.

In pure reflex Bolan snatched the Beretta from its holster and sought to level the pistol. A metallic object flashed, and a stunning blow to the Executioner's right wrist sent the Beretta flying toward the kitchen. Bolan didn't go after it; exposing his back to his attacker would prove too costly. Pivoting to the right, he ducked as the metal object the man wielded whizzed at his head.

It took Bolan a few seconds to realize what it was. His assailant was armed with a *nunchaku,* a weapon that had acquired great notoriety in the West after being featured in several martial-arts movies. Street gangs were quite fond of them. And a few police departments had issued them to their officers instead of traditional batons or nightsticks.

Bolan had seen demonstrations of the *nunchaku*'s use. He'd even practiced with one a few times. But he'd never included one his personal arsenal. To him it fell into the same category as throwing stars, *sai, katanas,* three-sectioned staffs and the many other exotic weapons martial disciplines relied on. In the hands of a master it was undeniably deadly, but in his opinion had little place in real-world combat. No matter how skilled a person might be with a sword or staff, all it took was one shot from even a small-caliber gun to render all their skill worthless.

The man in black was highly skilled. Flailing his *nunchaku* with blinding speed, he pressed his attack. Unlike most *nunchaku,* which featured basically two hardwood handles connected by a length of cord or rope, his handles were metal, and linked by strong wire.

Bolan wasn't quite quick enough in skipping aside and received an agonizing blow to the left leg, just below his knee. It staggered him. Had it struck the kneecap, he wouldn't be able to stand.

The soldier's duffel bag, with his personal arsenal, was upstairs. To reach it he had to get past the man in black. He tried by feinting right and going left, but a glancing strike to the arm drove him back.

Bolan didn't wonder who the man was or why the man had been sent to kill him. Those were considerations for later, provided he survived. He feinted to the right again, then started to go left to make the man think he was trying the same ruse. Instead, he dived straight at his adversary, springing off the ball of his good leg. His shoulder slammed into the man's chest, and they both went down.

The soldier wound up on top. He rammed a fist into the man's jaw, which snapped the man's head back. But where others would have been dazed by the punch, Bolan's foe merely redoubled his efforts.

At close quarters the *nunchaku*'s handles could be used to strike, block, choke and paralyze. Bolan was reminded of this when he cocked his fist to slug the figure again but the man in black executed a double upward thrust, spearing both ends of the handles into Bolan's ribs. Anguish seared through him, but the soldier ignored it and drove an elbow at the assassin's throat, only to have the man jerk aside.

In retaliation, the would-be assassin smashed the handles against his temples.

Bright pinpoints of light filled Bolan's vision. The room spun and bounced. He needed a few moments to clear his head, and to gain those moments he hurled himself away and rolled up onto his knees.

The man in black flipped agilely onto his feet and adopted a cat stance. He wove the *nunchaku* in a lightning figure-eight pattern, swinging it wide to either side to keep Bolan from reaching the front door or the stairs. Whoever he was, he was a pro. He hadn't uttered a word, hadn't slowed his onslaught one iota. Nothing short of death would stop him, Bolan's or his own. A twist of his wrist sent the *nunchaku* sizzling at the soldier's face.

Bolan flung himself backward, into the kitchen. His leg bumped against a chair and he pretended to slip. The other man took the bait and leaped in close, the octagonal handles of his weapon glittering dully in the gloom. Gripping the chair with both hands, Bolan swung it like a club. It smashed into his adversary, bowling him over.

Bolan looked around for the Beretta. In just that brief instant the man in black was up and at him again. A knee gouged into the Executioner's back, and the thin wire looped around his neck. He felt it dig into his flesh, felt searing pain and the dampness of his own blood.

There were only heartbeats in which to do something. The man in black would pull harder and harder, digging the wire deeper and deeper. Bolan wasn't about to let that happen. Rather than pry in vain at the constricting wire or tug at the *nunchaku*'s handles, the soldier threw himself under the table, barely clearing the bottom edge.

The man on his back wasn't so lucky. Table and assassin collided. Nearly dislodged, the killer tried to firm his grip on his weapon.

Shifting, Bolan arced an elbow into the man's midsection, not once but three times, and at the third blow the man in black tottered toward the stove. Shoving upright, Bolan faced his enemy.

In the close confines of the kitchen the assassin couldn't use the *nunchaku* to its full advantage. The table on one side and the stove on the other hampered his movements. Since he couldn't whip the metal handle, he snapped it, like a cowboy using an extremely short bullwhip.

Again and again the weapon rained at Bolan's arms, chest and head. He deliberately retreated toward the kitchen counter, to a drawer filled with cooking utensils. Reaching behind him, Bolan gripped the small knob in the center of the drawer and wrenched it open. With his other arm he warded off the *nunchaku* as best he was able, taking a terrible bruising.

The night before, after Bolan finished his meal, he had washed off the silverware and stuck it back into the drawer. When he did, he'd noticed a long carving knife that lay on the left side. The same knife was now clasped in his callused hand.

Its blade was ten or eleven inches long and half as wide as a bowie. Keeping it low against his leg, Bolan intentionally put himself at risk by stepping into his adversary's next swing. The *nunchaku* caught Bolan high on the shoulder, and he doubled over as if in anguish. Seeing an opening, the man in black pounced, going for the choke hold again.

The soldier slashed the carving knife up and around, drilling it into the man's abdomen, slicing through fabric and skin. Inner organs spilled out, like chunks of stew spilling from a can, and the assassin cried out, the first sound he'd made. Pressing splayed fingers over the wound, he grunted, planted his legs and swung the *nunchaku* again. It was an act of desperation more than anything else, and Bolan easily avoided it.

Dropping the weapon, the man clutched at his abdomen and sagged against the stove. Like molten wax he melted to the floor and sat wheezing noisily. He made no move to defend himself.

Bolan saw the Beretta lying nearby. Retrieving it, he tossed the knife into the sink and pointed the pistol at the man's ski mask. "Who are you?" he demanded. "Why did you try to kill me?"

"K'ah-chih."

The word or name meant nothing to Bolan. "Do you speak English? Who sent you?"

"K'ah-chih."

Holding the Beretta back so the man couldn't grab it, Bolan gripped the top of the ski mask and tugged. It slid off, revealing yet another in a seemingly unending series of surprises. The assassin wasn't Japanese, nor Korean. "You're Chinese?"

"K'ah-chih," the man said a third time, so weakly his lips barely moved. A crimson puddle was spreading outward from his hips.

Bolan saw the killer's fingers creep toward a pocket. Bending, he jerked the man's wrist to one side, then carefully removed the pocket's contents himself. It was a throwing dart with a red tassel. The tip was discolored and gave off a slight odor. Poison, Bolan guessed.

"Was this what you wanted? Nice try."

The man glared, then slumped to one side, dead.

The Executioner scoured the house from bottom to top, satisfying himself there had been only one assassin. He left the body where it was and picked up the phone. The big Fed answered on the second ring.

"Glad I caught you," Bolan said.

"Problems?"

Bolan briefly detailed his clash. "I have no idea why he jumped me. All he would say at the end was 'K'ah-chih.'"

"That's the name of the Chinese scientist who defected a couple of weeks ago," Brognola said, and swore. "They've been after him ever since. My hunch is they learned about the safehouse and sent your playmate to take care of K'ah-chih. They don't know we'd already shuttled him to the States." The Fed sighed. "We can't use that house anymore. I'll make a call and have a clean-up crew on-site within the hour."

"There's more," Bolan said.

"You've fallen for a geisha and don't intend to come back?"

The soldier chuckled, then recapped his visit to Fisheries Unlimited. He left out the part about the businessman and the secretary.

"The more we learn about these North Koreans, Striker, the more I don't like what we're learning. The only Luccas I can think of off the top of my head are Don Angelo Lucca, head of a San Francisco Family, and his son, Anthony."

"I can't see Cho-Hee treating the Don the way he treated the man he called," Bolan said. "It had to be the son."

"Whichever it was, this puts a whole new spin on things. Whoever Cho-Hee's uncle is, he's in the process of setting up a drug network that stretches from the Golden Triangle to the Golden Gate Bridge. We have to take him down."

"You read my mind."

"I'll have a courier pick up the disks and files and

we'll get you situated somewhere else. How much longer do you plan to stay in Yokohama?"

"The *Nagaoka* is due into port tomorrow. Tomorrow night they'll probably switch the drugs from the *Petra*'s holds to the *Nagaoka*'s." Bolan had been doing a lot of thinking on his way back from Fisheries Unlimited, and he had come to the conclusion new tactics were called for. "I think it's time I threw a monkey wrench into the works."

"How big a monkey wrench?"

Bolan explained what he had in mind. "To pull it off, I'll need a small inflatable raft, enough C-4 to do the job right, det cord and timers."

"I'll have it delivered by tomorrow afternoon," Brognola promised. "In the meantime I'll continue to shake the intelligence tree and see what falls out. We'll run a computer check on anyone using the name Madame Rhee." He paused. "You don't think she could be a real madam, do you?"

"Anything is possible."

"I should let you know that I've been on the phone with my South Korean counterpart. Within a day or so he is supposed to get back to me with whatever intel he can glean on Sin Cho-Hee, but he was rather skeptical Cho-Hee is a North Korean."

"Communism and ill-gotten gains don't mix, is that it?"

"More or less. Oh, there's a black market for drugs and other illegal goods in North Korea, but it's piddling compared to other countries. He called it inconceivable that a North Korean is the head of a major new drug ring. And I have to admit he has a point."

"Unless Cho-Hee's uncle was born in North Korea and slipped out of the country years ago."

"Find out where this wolf has his lair and we'll have the answers," Brognola stated. "I'll be of any help I can."

TRUE TO THE BIG FED'S WORD, a clean-up crew arrived before sixty minutes were up. They asked no questions. Quickly, efficiently, they went about the business of removing the body in a body bag and cleaning up the gore and blood.

Bolan packed the duffel and was ready to go when the courier arrived about forty-five minutes after the clean-up crew left. The courier was a Japanese woman, smartly dressed, as businesslike in her way as the clean-up crew had been. After accepting the disks and documents, she placed them in a special-issue briefcase.

"Now, if you will be so kind, sir, come with me and I will show you where you will be staying until your work here is done."

The new safehouse, it turned out, was almost in Kawasaki. It meant Bolan had to travel a lot farther to reach Hideo Koto's warehouse, which wasn't to his liking. Evidently, his slight frown when he stepped out of the car gave it away because the woman, whose name was Kiri Tanaka, bowed and said, "I am most sorry if these lodgings are not agreeable. This is the best we could manage on such short notice. The only other house we have available is in Tokyo, and my superiors were quite specific in instructing me to keep you as close to Yokohama as possible."

"You've done fine."

"Here are the keys," Tanaka said, handing them over. "I will return tomorrow with the items you have requested." She tossed him a second set of keys and pointed at a Toyota. "That is yours. A rental, so try not to damage it, if you can."

She had to be more than a simple courier, Bolan reflected. But just as she hadn't pried into his background, he didn't pry into hers. It was enough to know that Brognola had sent her. "I'll be here."

"Will there be anything else you require? Any particular food? Or beverage? Books to read? Movies to watch? Or perhaps a companion for the night?"

"No, thank you." Bolan watched her walk off, so prim and professional in her smart outfit, yet every inch a full-bodied woman with an alluring sway to her slender hips. He let out a sigh. The life he had chosen could be a lonely one at times, but he had no regrets. Well, maybe a few. Dwelling on them, though, was pointless.

As long as he had breath in his body, the soldier would go on waging war against those who preyed on the innocence and weaknesses of others. Like the mysterious North Korean. When the time came, Bolan was going to bring the mystery man down. Bring him down hard.

CHAPTER FOUR

San Diego

Bob Walker hadn't intended to return to Club X so soon, but he couldn't help himself. Every waking moment he thought of Gloria, exquisite Gloria, and the things they had done. Her fragrant scent seemed to cling to him, and in his idle moments he swore he could feel the touch of her velvet skin against his. He yearned to be with her again.

Walker had tried to hold off, but just that morning at work he had been daydreaming of her and made an elementary mistake on a schematic that took him half an hour to correct. So he figured another visit was in order. It would help get her out of his system, he told himself.

Cranking the volume on his favorite rock station, Walker sped through the city streets as if he were taking part in the Indy 500. A storm front was moving in. Ominous dark clouds spread rapidly eastward. Thunder boomed, although he saw no lightning. The weatherman had been predicting thunderstorms were in store, and for once he was right.

The promise of bad weather, though, didn't dampen

Bob Walker's soaring spirits one bit. While the elements raged outside, he would be snug and happy in Gloria's arms. He grinned in keen anticipation.

He was so happy that it didn't bother him at all when he pulled up to the gate and an Oriental fellow popped out of nowhere, just as before. "Hi. Better find yourself an umbrella. You'll need one soon," Walker bantered.

"Token."

"Oh. Sure." He reached into his pants pocket, where he was certain he had put one, but it wasn't there.

"Token."

Panic gripped him. He frantically groped every pocket he had, afraid he had forgotten it and wouldn't be permitted to enter. "I have one. I know I do. Madame Rhee let me take several the other night." Walker hadn't taken her suggestion and passed them on to anyone else yet, however. The thought of his coworkers being intimate with Gloria wasn't to his liking.

"Token."

Walker glanced at the swarthy Oriental. Hadn't Madame Rhee mentioned her staff were largely Koreans? "What are you, a broken record? I have one, I tell you." He reached inside his jacket, into the last pocket, and nearly yipped with relief. "Here, my good man," he said, holding it for the man to inspect. "Told you, didn't I?"

The gate buzzed and opened, and Walker wheeled up to the parking lot. The Korean at the front door admitted him with no problem, and he was whisked along the corridor to the parlor. Eagerly, he scanned the lovelies relaxing on the sofas and chairs and those at the bar. Gloria wasn't among them. A cold fist enclosed his heart and he whined like a distraught puppy. "Please, no," he said under his breath. He had to see her. He just had to!

"Why, Mr. Walker. This is a pleasant surprise. I hadn't expected you back so soon."

He saw Madame Rhee emerging from a hall off to the right. Smiling broadly, she warmly clasped his hand. "Hello," he said distractedly.

"Is something the matter? You appear upset."

"I was hoping to find Gloria here." Another woman and a customer were coming down the stairs, and it occurred to him that Gloria might be busy. The thought sickened him.

"I'm sorry, but she works only four nights a week," Madame Rhee explained. "This is one of her days off." She swept an arm toward her girls. "But, as you can see, you have many beautiful ladies to chose from. Take your pick."

"I wanted Gloria."

Madame Rhee regarded him for a moment. "Why don't I treat you to a drink? You look as if you could use one."

Walker absently nodded and dutifully let her lead him to a stool. Out of habit he ordered a Scotch whiskey.

"So you are smitten by our Gloria, are you?" Madame Rhee said good-naturedly, placing a hand on his knee. "I don't blame you. She is a popular girl. Four or five men have even asked her to marry them."

Walker took a gulp and winced as the liquor warmed a path to his stomach. He had been a fool to get so excited about seeing her again.

"She will be sad when she learns she missed you," Madame Rhee commented.

"She will?" He wondered why that should be. To Gloria he was just another customer, one of many who lusted after her. She wasn't his fair princess. Once again he had let his fantasies carry him away.

"Oh, yes. I know for a fact she is fond of you. She said so, that night after you left."

The cold fist enclosing his heart melted under a fiery blaze of happiness. "She did? She said she likes me?" It was too good to be true.

"Would I lie to you, my friend?" Madame Rhee said, squeezing his knee. "Gloria has never said that about anyone else. You must have made quite an impression."

"Could I—?" Walker began, and hesitated. He wasn't all that knowledgeable about brothel etiquette and didn't want to offend Madame Rhee by stepping over the bounds.

"Could you what? Don't be afraid. I won't bite."

"I was hoping…that is, I mean, I was thinking that maybe you could give me her phone number or her address."

Madame Rhee was most understanding. "Would that I could, Robert. You wear your feelings for her on your sleeve. But, so sorry, it is against policy. Please don't take it personally. Plainly, you are a fine, decent young man. But when my girls come to work for me, they do so under a promise of anonymity. We never use their real names, we never give out private information."

"Gloria isn't her name?" The disclosure seared Walker like a laser. He'd been toying with the idea of paying her a visit at her home, but how could he without a single shred of information to go on?

"Please, Robert. Try to understand. Put yourself in their shoes. My girls wouldn't have a moment's peace if our customers knew who they were and where they lived. They would be pestered night and day." Madame Rhee's smile was angelic. "Not all our patrons are as kind as you."

"Oh."

"Now then, might I suggest someone else for tonight?" Madame Rhee pointed at a shapely minx in a skimpy nightie. "You seem to have a preference for blondes. Marcy there is about your age, and she is great fun, I have heard."

"I don't know…" He'd had his heart set on Gloria and Gloria alone. To go upstairs with someone else would be a betrayal of his feelings.

"Trust me. Marcy is just what you need to snap you out of your doldrums." Sliding off her stool, Madame Rhee beckoned and the blonde bounced over.

"Yes, ma'am?"

"My dear, I would like you to escort this young gentleman upstairs. Treat him with special care."

Marcy leaned toward Walker and teasingly whispered in his ear. "Come along, lover. We'll make this a night you'll never forget."

Walker almost said no. He almost got up and left. But Marcy smelled so sweet and fresh, just like Gloria, and the feel of her bosom when she pressed against him sent sensual ripples through his body. To fortify himself, he downed the rest of the whiskey, then smacked the glass onto the counter as a he-man would do. Gloria would forgive him, he thought.

AN HOUR AND TEN MINUTES LATER a weary but supremely contented Bob Walker was led back downstairs. Marcy pecked him on the cheek, thanked him for a wonderful time and went to rejoin her friends. He walked to the bar to pay. Madame Rhee wasn't there, but another Korean fellow he couldn't recall seeing before was.

"Mr. Walker! I have been waiting for you."

"You have?"

"I am Kim. If you would be so kind, Madame Rhee would like to see you in her office. Follow me, please." Without waiting for a reply, Kim headed toward the hall to the right.

"What does she want?"

"I do not know. I am only relaying her request. Please. Come along."

A string of possible reasons flashed through Walker's mind. Maybe there was a problem with the credit-card company. Maybe she just wanted to chat. Or maybe she had changed her mind and she was willing to give him Gloria's name and address. He couldn't wait to find out. When Kim opened a door for him, he hurried in.

Madame Rhee's office was spacious and elegantly furnished. It had plush carpet, a Corinthian leather sofa, braided drapes, the works. A single lamp provided less than adequate lighting. He saw Madame Rhee at a mahogany desk, writing on a notepad. Looking up, she smiled. "Please have a seat, Robert. There is something we must discuss."

Hoping he was right about it being Gloria's name and address, Walker sank into a chair in front of the desk. In his excitement over Gloria, he didn't pay much attention to the fact the chair was solid metal, with no padding or cushioning of any kind, the sort of chair one might find in a factory or a prison. Certainly not in a lavish office. "I'm all ears."

"It's about your job," Madame Rhee said, sitting back and making a steeple of her fingers with their long painted fingernails.

"What about it?" Walker was puzzled. He didn't see what his place of employment had to do with anything.

"You work at Omnitronics, Incorporated, which is a primary contractor for the United States government. To be specific, you design systems with sensitive military applications."

Profound unease made him fidget. "Where did you learn that?"

"We ran a credit check on you, Robert. It's standard procedure with all our customers. We wouldn't want someone to kiss and run, as it were." Madame Rhee grinned at her little joke.

Walker didn't share her amusement. He didn't know how much information a typical credit check provided, but he was positive it wouldn't include the exact nature of the work he did. Something wasn't quite right. "Who did you run this credit check through? A credit agency?"

"That is unimportant," Madame Rhee said. "Our concern now is whether you are willing to share the sensitive secrets you have had access to for substantial sums of money?"

"Come again?" Walker couldn't have heard correctly. It almost sounded as if she were trying to bribe him into betraying his country.

"Enough money to set yourself up in luxury for the rest of your life," Madame Rhee elaborated. "Think of it. A fine house, the newest car, whatever you desire could be yours for the asking. Why, you would be able to give Gloria anything she desired."

"You're asking me to sell you classified secrets?" He almost pinched himself to see if he was really awake or still lying up in Marcy's bed, dreaming.

"The individual I work for is very interested in the new stealth submarine, which you have been helping to design. It would be easy, would it not, for you to sneak certain documents from Omnitronics? I will make copies, and you can put the originals back where they belong before anyone is the wiser."

"You're serious?" Walker gazed around the room, hoping the dream would dissolve in a blur. That was when he spotted a man in the shadows along the right wall. A glance to the left revealed another. Twisting, he saw that Kim was behind the metal chair. A swarm of butterflies fluttered in his stomach.

"I have never been more serious in my life, Robert. Acquiring detailed information about the stealth sub would be a feather in my cap, as you Americans like to say. My superior will be tremendously pleased." Madame Rhee rested her elbows on the desk, her chin on the back of her hands. "So how shall we do this, the easy way or the hard way?"

This couldn't be happening to him. Madame Rhee was a *madam*, not some kind of spy. She ran a brothel, for crying out loud.

"Robert?"

"I'm sorry. I can't believe you've asked me this. I signed an oath of secrecy. I gave my word I'd never divulge classified information." He started to rise. "Now, if you'll excuse me." He wanted to get out of there, to leave and never come back.

"Kim," Madame Rhee said.

Strong arms wrapped around Walker's chest, pinning his arms to his sides. He struggled to break free, but the other two Koreans came out of the shadows and roughly forced him back into the chair. They each gripped a wrist and pressed it against the chair's arms.

"Let go of me!" Walker ordered.

They did no such thing. Kim quickly wrapped what appeared to be wide black Velcro strips around the younger man's forearms, strapping him in place. Then Kim did the same to his ankles.

Until that moment Walker hadn't really been scared, but he was now. Raw fear chilled him to the core. His mouth went dry and his palms grew damp. The whole horrid truth washed over him in a tidal wave of comprehension. "You're all enemy agents!"

"More or less," Madame Rhee cheerfully admitted. Opening a drawer, she removed a leather case, which she placed in front of her, then opened.

"I won't tell you a damned thing!" Walker declared. Inwardly, he wasn't so sure. He had a low tolerance for pain. If they tortured him, he might crack.

"Yes, you will, Robert." From the case Madame Rhee took a hypodermic needle and a small vial containing a greenish fluid. "I had hoped to spare you this. Sometimes there are painful, if minor, side effects."

Walker's legs began to tremble uncontrollably. He tried to rip his arms free, but the straps held him securely. The three Korean men ringed the chair, standing at attention like soldiers. "What is that stuff?"

"A mixture of thiopental sodium, amobarbital and other chemicals. It was developed as part of our ongoing program to find the perfect brainwashing medium." Madame Rhee slowly inserted the needle into the vial's stopper. "It is ten times more potent than simple sodium pentothal."

"You're going to inject it into me?"

"I am certainly not going to inject it into myself."

Fear and horror nearly overwhelmed Walker. He had never in his life been in a situation like this. Terror clawed at his mind like a ravenous wolf seeking to devour him.

"I wouldn't worry overly much, Robert. Very few have adverse reactions." Madame Rhee worked the plunger, drawing green fluid from the vial into the barrel of the hypodermic.

The woman rose, pressing the plunger just enough for a drop of green fluid to form at the needle's tip. "Feel free to shout for help if you want. My office is completely soundproofed. No one will hear you, even if they walk by in the hall."

Walker glared at her. Hate such as he had never experienced welled up within him, hate so potent he wanted to lash out, to hit her, to pound her into the carpet. She had no right to do this to him!

"Would you do the honors?" Madame Rhee asked, giving the syringe to Kim.

"Yes, my wife."

Walker struggled against the straps again, in vain. He sought to rock the chair and discovered it was attached to the floor. Kim stepped around behind him, and his skin crawled in anxious dread.

Madame Rhee bent so they were practically nose to nose. "There will be a slight discomfort, Robert, as the needle is inserted into your brain—"

"My brain!"

"Yes. We have found the serum is much more effective that way. The effect lasts about an hour, depending on the individual."

"I'll go to the police! To the FBI!"

Madame Rhee laughed. "How naive you Americans are. How juvenile. You will not report us to anyone, Robert, because you won't remember any of this after the serum wears off."

"What?"

"While you are under its influence, you are suggestible to my every command. You will do whatever I tell you. When I order you to reveal all you know about the stealth submarine, you will do just that. And later, when I direct you to forget this ever happened, you will wipe it from your mind and walk out of here with no memory of the brainwashing."

"You bitch!"

Madame Rhee frowned, and nodded at Kim. Walker felt a prick and fleeting pain at the base of his skull, then his brain seemed to be enveloped in molten lava. He opened his mouth to scream, but if he did, he never heard it.

South Korea

HALF A WORLD AWAY, a high-ranking official in the Research Department for External Intelligence, North

Korea's primary agency responsible for collecting foreign intel, otherwise known as the RDEI, entered a room as lavish as Madame Rhee's in a building in Inchon, South Korea.

Chang Do-Young had been spirited across the DMZ two nights ago by a crack squad of North Korean soldiers for the express purpose of seeing the man who stood by a window gazing down at the traffic far below. Chang didn't mince words. "You are being recalled. The Central Committee requires that you accompany me back to North Korea."

The man at the window turned slowly. He was in his late forties, with rugged features and high cheekbones. His stocky frame was clothed in the most expensive apparel money could buy. On three of his fingers were glittering diamond rings, and his gold watchband was inlaid with the gems. The stickpin in his tie sported another. Instead of answering, he sighed.

"Did you hear me?" Chang demanded.

"Why did they send you?" the man inquired.

"Need you ask?" Chang rejoined. "You have ignored repeated summons, both by phone and by messenger."

"No, that is not what I meant. Why you, Chang? Why didn't they send someone else? I have always liked you."

"Which is exactly why they chose me." Chang walked over to him. "What has gotten into you, old friend? After working so long and so hard to get where you are, why are you risking the wrath of the Central Committee in this reckless fashion? What can you hope to gain?"

"I have already gained it," the bald man said. "Come. Let me show you." He stepped to the wall at the head of the room and pressed a button. A large panel slid down, uncovering a computer screen and a keyboard. The bald man flicked a switch, and the screen crackled to life. At the press of a few keys a map of the world appeared. Bright dots marked many of the countries along the Pacific Rim. "My empire," he said with pride.

"*Your* empire?" Chang said. "You forget yourself. This entire operation was the brainchild of the RDEI. The initial funds were supplied by us, and we have guided you every step of the way."

The bald man folded his hands behind his back. "The RDEI has advised me from time to time, true, but I, and I alone, am responsible for the scope of my enterprise."

"Why do you keep calling it that? It is a front, a means of gathering intelligence data using avenues otherwise not open to us. It was set up for that express purpose."

"I have done my duty, Chang. I relayed more important intelligence to the Central Committee in the past year than they have gathered in the past ten. My brothels in America, Japan, Hong Kong and elsewhere have provided us with a wealth of information."

"There you go again," Chang said in exasperation. "They are not *your* brothels. You, Sin Mak-Fang, are just a cog in a machine. And because of you, that machine is not running smoothly any longer."

"So the Central Committee wants to recall me and install someone else in my place," Sin Mak-Fang said bitterly.

"Perhaps not. At this point they merely want an explanation. They want to know why you have not responded to their summons. They want to know why you had several of your own operatives terminated. They want to know why you have set up a Swiss bank account in your own name. And much more."

"They know about my Swiss account, do they?" Sin Mak-Fang smiled, but it was a smile without warmth. "You would think they would have figured it out by now."

Trying to be patient, Chang said, "Figured out what?"

Sin Mak-Fang faced his visitor. "That I am severing my ties to the Central Committee, to North Korea, to communism. Those operatives I killed were working undercover for the Committee, spying on me, as you well know." Sin Mak-Fang slid a hand into a pocket.

"I have found that I like wielding power, Chang. I like having money. Lots and lots of money. The empire I have set up is no longer theirs to direct as they see fit. It is mine, and mine alone."

Chang was too shocked to speak.

"I will be more specific. From now on all the money I reap goes into my own account. I will do as I wish, when I wish. If the Committee wants access to the information I gather, they must bid on it on the open market like everyone else."

"This is an outrage!" Chang found his voice. "It is blasphemy against the Party! Against all you were taught! When I report this, the Central Committee will sanction your elimination!"

"Regrettably, they won't hear your report." From

his pocket Sin Mak-Fang drew a North Korean Type 64 pistol fitted with a stubby silencer.

"No!" Chang said.

Sin Mak-Fang fired four shots at point-blank range. Then, frowning, he said, "You were my best friend once, Chang Do-Young. I thought I would feel a twinge of remorse, but all I feel is contentment. I have burned the last bridge. No one can stop me now."

CHAPTER FIVE

Japan

Yokohama was a major port. Even late at night ships and smaller craft crisscrossed its choppy waters. The Executioner had to keep that in mind as he stroked the small paddle belonging to the inflatable raft Kiri Tanaka had provided. He was dressed as he had been on his first clandestine visit to Hideo Koto's private pier, in his blacksuit, with combat cosmetics streaking his rugged features. The Beretta, as usual, was leathered under his arm. In addition, instead of the Mini-Uzi he had an M-16 A-1.

This time Bolan has also brought a backpack containing C-4, detonation cord and timers so he could set the plastic explosive to command detonation electrically.

Bolan wasn't so much infiltrating an enemy position as going into battle.

Above all else the soldier was a consummate tactician. He seldom did anything unless guided by solid strategy. Devising tactics to deal with enemies was his forte, and like all the best tacticians, Bolan was flexible. His decisions weren't carved in stone. He wasn't like a few field commanders he had known who devised strategy and then stuck with it as if it were the holy writ of war, often at the cost of their men's lives and their own. When Bolan saw a tactic wasn't working, when a new one was called for, he immediately adapted. He did whatever it took to get the job done, even if that meant switching currents in midstream.

The penetration Bolan was engaged in was a case in point. He wasn't going in specifically to terminate Hideo Koto, although that was a secondary goal. He was going to turn up the heat, literally. No more holding back. He had a twofold plan to flush Sin Cho-Hee's uncle into the open.

An analogy had occurred to him the night before as he lay in bed thinking. The mysterious uncle was like a man-eating tiger, a scourge that must be destroyed. But the devious tiger was safe in its hidden lair. No one could find him. No one could stop his attacks. Hunters who relied on stealth and woodcraft failed, not through any fault of their own, but because the tiger was wise enough not to leave tracks. But where stealth wouldn't work, maybe beating the bush for the tiger would. Raising enough noise and smoke and commotion might draw the angry man-eater into the open where the hunter could end its rampage with a well-placed shot.

Such was Bolan's plan. Earlier, when Brognola phoned, the soldier had outlined his change in tactics.

Brognola had been all for it, especially since official channels were one dead end after another. "The identity of Sin Cho-Hee's uncle is the best-kept secret on the Asian continent," the big Fed had remarked.

"Cho-Hee's uncle only becomes involved in extraordinary situations,'' Bolan quoted the young Korean. ''So I'm going to create one.''

''You know, Striker, it just hit me. Cho-Hee is bound to give his uncle a call. I'm going to have a bug planted in Fisheries Unlimited.''

''I can do it,'' Bolan volunteered.

''No, you have enough to do. And there isn't much time, which precludes going through official channels. I'll have Ms. Tanaka handle it.''

Bolan had known many competent female operatives over the years, but he didn't like the idea of Tanaka sneaking into Fisheries Unlimited in the dead of night. As Cho-Hee had demonstrated, there was no telling when the nephew and the giant might show up. ''Isn't that a little risky?''

''Relax. She's a big girl. She's done work like this for me before, and she's quite resourceful.''

The soldier had let the matter drop.

Now, hours later, their talk was forgotten as Bolan approached Koto's shipping operation from the south, moving parallel to shore and a hundred yards out from the battery of bobbing fishing boats at berth for the night.

Common sense told Bolan that after the firefight at the warehouse Koto would post more sentries along the fence and dock. They would be on their guard against a perimeter breach, but from the landward side. They might not expect anyone to be reckless enough to come at them across the open waters of Tokyo Bay.

Or so Bolan hoped. He had a quarter of a mile to cover. Over the tops of the fishing boats the darkling silhouettes of the three freighters lined up at Koto's dock loomed like prehistoric creatures. Lights were ablaze on two of them. Crates and boxes were being switched from the *Petra* to the *Nagaoka*. All was going according to the elusive uncle's plan.

The toot of a ship's horn made Bolan swivel on his knees. A midsize vessel was leaving a wharf behind him. He didn't give it much thought since he figured it would head straight out for sea. But a minute later, as he tirelessly continued to smoothly stroke the paddle, the horn blared again, closer, and he looked back to find that the ship was also sailing parallel to the shoreline, and about the same distance out into the bay as he was. Unless it angled off across the harbor, in a couple of minutes it would overtake him.

Bolan kept one eye on the approaching ship. As it drew nearer, he saw it was a coastal freighter, a smaller version of the oceangoing freighters Koto owned. He still figured it would make off across the bay at any moment. But as the distance narrowed to where he could see white froth at its bow, he realized it wasn't going to. Unless he got out of the freighter's way, and quickly, it would crush him under its massive bulk or maybe chew him to bits with its huge propellers.

The nearest safe haven was in among the fishing boats. Bolan turned the raft and bent his whole upper body into each stroke. The drone of the small freighter's screws rose in volume. It was gaining speed. Bolan heard hissing caused by the metal hull slicing through the water.

Even a small ship was gigantic to someone in a rubber raft. The coastal freighter hove out of the night like a dreadnought. Bolan, stroking for all he was worth, glanced back. He was clear of the vessel, but he didn't stop paddling. There was another factor to consider.

The ship began to head for open water. Its wake rippled and churned, spreading outward, and caught the raft when it was still ninety feet from the fishing craft.

To Bolan it was as if an invisible hand rose from under the sea, gripped the raft and propelled it forward. Froth churned around him as he tried to slow the raft, but his paddle was no match for the force generated by the freighter.

The fishing boats swept toward Bolan like a wooden wall. At the speed he was traveling, he could easily break an arm or leg. He plunged the paddle into the water, seeking to use it as a makeshift rudder, but he might as well have tried to steer a bobbing cork. The rear of the inflatable lifted and canted at a steep angle, threatening to pitch him into the drink. He had to grip the sides, all pretense at control gone.

Just as rapidly as it had formed, the wake began to subside, its momentum weakening. But was it soon enough? The fishing boats were thirty feet away. As the raft began to level off, Bolan stroked in reverse, seeking to bring it to a stop. He wasn't quite successful.

Still moving several knots faster than it was designed to do, the raft hurtled in among the wooden craft. Bolan saw a high stern and braced for impact, but the raft missed it by a whisker and passed between two of the fishing boats into a narrow, murky gap not much wider than it was.

Bolan was jarred when his vessel bounced against the fishing boat on his right, careened off and struck the one on the left. Neither impact did any damage. Within seconds he had slowed to a crawl. Thrusting the paddle against the left-hand boat, he brought himself to a complete stop.

Backing out of the gap, Bolan resumed his northerly bearing. As he neared the southernmost of the three freighters docked at Koto's wharf, he scanned the harbor from end to end to insure no other vessels were in his vicinity. Then he veered farther into the bay in a wide loop that would bring him up on the warehouse from due east.

The wind picked up and the waves grew choppier. Bolan had to exert himself more than he preferred. It wouldn't be wise to go into a firefight tired. He conserved his energy as much as he could and in due course came within a stone's throw of the north end of the dock.

Directly ahead was the warehouse. The huge double doors were open, but he was too low in the water to see what was transpiring. To the left of the warehouse was the freighter that had been there on Bolan's previous visit. It lay quiet and dark under the myriad of stars. Berthed next to it was the *Petra*, the ship that belonged to Cho-Hee, or rather, to Cho-Hee's uncle. Its hold contained millions in drugs, which were at that very moment being transferred to the *Nagaoka*, the vessel that was going to transport the drugs across the Pacific to San Francisco.

Or so Koto and Cho-Hee's uncle planned.

Bolan let the lapping waves carry him the final dozen yards to a wooden ladder that led from water level up onto the dock. He secured a short rope from the raft to the bottom rung, shrugged into the backpack over his back, slung the M-16 over his right shoulder and climbed. He went slowly, aware of voices and the grind of machinery. He had a couple of rungs left to go when soft footsteps warned him someone was right above him. He froze.

A shadowy shape was outlined against the canopy of sky. One of the gunners was gazing out over the bay. All the man had to do was glance down and he would spot the soldier. But after a few moments he moved away.

Cautiously, Bolan rose up high enough to see over the top. He counted three gunners between the shore and the warehouse. Other guards roved the fence, two pair were up near the street and two more along the section that flanked the rear of the building.

As Bolan had predicted, Hideo Koto had left nothing to chance. Boarding the darkened freighter from the dock by way of the mooring lines wasn't feasible. Climbing back down, Bolan carefully dropped into the raft, untied it and quietly paddled into the inky gloom at the base of the freighter. The gap between the great ship and the dock wasn't much wider than the gap between the fishing boats had been.

The ship's name was bathed in light from the warehouse. It was called the *Kraken*.

Moments later Bolan spotted the huge chain to the starboard anchor. He fastened the raft to it, then, hand over hand, his legs wrapped tight, he shimmied upward. Darkness shrouded him until he was almost level with the dock.

Stopping, Bolan craned his neck. Most of the activity swirled around the other two freighters, although a forklift was carrying a pallet heaped high with containers into the warehouse. Two of the gunners he had seen minutes earlier were moving toward the back of the building.

Bolan quickly clambered to the top of the anchor chain. Bending his legs, he braced his heels against it and straightened high enough to get a grip on the gunwale. No shouts of alarm rang out as he pulled himself up and over. He didn't spot any guards on deck.

Drawing the Beretta, the soldier glided in search of a companionway. He listened at the first set of stairs he came to but heard no unusual sounds from below. Resorting to a powerful pencil flashlight, he ventured into the freighter's bowels, proceeding with his customary wariness.

Most ships were built according to general design. Those constructed in Japan were little different from those constructed in America. The number of decks might vary, the superstructure wasn't always the same, but by and large one ship was pretty much like the other. Which made finding the holds simple for someone who knew his way around.

Bolan had no reservations about what he intended to do. The *Kraken* was owned by Hideo Koto, a vicious drug lord. The men on the dock and in the warehouse were Koto's underlings. No innocents would be harmed.

Taking off the backpack, Bolan took out a packet of C-4, the roll of detonation cord and the other items he needed. When it came to setting the timer, he paused. How much time should he give himself? That was the all-important question. Too little, and he might be caught in the blasts. Too much, and there was always the risk of someone stumbling on one of the charges and having the time to defuse it and all the others. Granted, the prospect was slim, but he had to take every possibility into account.

Bolan gave himself seventy minutes. That should be enough to place all the charges and get out.

The soldier repeated the procedure in each hold, setting the timers so they all would go off simultaneously. After planting four in the *Kraken*, he hustled up onto deck.

One ship down, two to go.

Running to the gunwale, Bolan peered over the side. Two gunners were at the warehouse door but they were watching the forklift operator and had their backs to him. No one else was close enough to pose a threat. He eased over the side and descended to the raft.

Once in the vessel, Bolan untied the line and paddled aft. He hugged the shadows, working his way around the *Kraken* to the *Petra*. It wasn't necessary that he go on board to disable the second vessel. He was counting on a chain reaction from the *Kraken* to spread from ship to ship, but as added insurance he set another packet close to the waterline, above the vessel's props. He did the same with the *Nagaoka*.

By Bolan's watch he had twelve minutes left when he placed the empty backpack in the raft and moved toward the southernmost end of Koto's pier. Just as he couldn't rely on the chain reaction to cripple all three ships, he couldn't take it for granted Hideo Koto would die in the conflagration.

Some things a man had to do for himself.

Past the end of Koto's private pier, past the chain-link fence, was a large concrete abutment that separated Koto's domain from the massed fishing craft.

The square abutment had no ladder or handholds, but there was a railing at the top to keep the careless from falling off.

The soldier secured the raft to a pylon, unzipped a pocket on the raft's ring, and took out a grappling hook and forty feet of coiled line encased in a watertight sheath. The grapple's prongs were collapsible. Snapping out all four so they locked into position, Bolan swung the hook in a small circle, letting out the line gradually until, at the apex of a swing, he released the nylon and the grapple shot upward to latch on to the rail.

The rope was knotted. Bolan scaled it effortlessly, stopping when he could see over the abutment. Beyond the fence Koto's crew busily moved cargo from one vessel to the other. The place was lit up like a Christmas tree. Right away Bolan spied Koto, on the foredeck overseeing the operation.

Sliding up over the rail, the big man lay on his belly and unslung the M-16. He pulled the charging handle all the way to the rear and released it. Since the range from the abutment to the *Nagaoka* was well under three hundred yards, he didn't adjust the M-16's sights. Those familiar with the rifle knew that its battle sights were more than adequate at that distance. The prearranged settings allowed a shooter to hit combat-sized targets under three hundred yards without so much as a tweak.

Bolan took aim at Hideo Koto. He had a clear shot, but as he had done at the warehouse, he held off. Temporarily. He was waiting for the C-4 to be detonated, for the noise and confusion to mask the sound of the

M-16. A check of his watch indicated only five minutes remained.

Moments later a sedan braked at the front gate and honked for admittance. Bolan raised his head to see who it was. It looked like the same sedan Cho-Hee drove. Sure enough, when it stopped at the warehouse, out jumped Kon-Li, who held the back door open for Sin Cho-Hee. The young Korean snapped his fingers at the giant, who stepped to the trunk and opened it.

Bolan wondered what was going on, but he didn't wonder long. The giant bent, reached into the trunk and pulled out someone who had been lying inside.

They had a captive.

Bending the person's arm, Kon-Li hurried to catch up with Cho-Hee, who was heading for the *Nagaoka*.

The Executioner recognized their prisoner, and frowned. Sometimes even the best-laid plans went awry. Only four minutes remained before the freighters and their cargo would be blown to kingdom come. Four minutes before Koto and all those on the dock would be wiped off the face of the earth.

Including the young woman in Kon-Li's iron grasp—Kiri Tanaka.

KIRI TANAKA HAD ALWAYS considered herself born under a lucky star. Her parents were both well-to-do, so much so that she had been privileged to attend the best schools in the U.S. She had grown into an intelligent, athletic, lovely young woman with a keen curiosity about other countries, other cultures. She was also deeply patriotic. So it was only natural she developed an interest in working for the U.S. government overseas.

At the bright age of twenty-one Tanaka had joined the diplomatic corps and was assigned to several foreign embassies before what she liked to call her "lucky break."

It came in Ankara, Turkey, one wintry night when a trio of leftists broke into the embassy intent on wiping out the staff as a message to the rest of the capitalist world. They drove up to the gate disguised as groundsmen and killed the Marine guards, but not before one of the Marines wounded two of them as he went down. Undeterred, the three charged into the embassy hurling epithets and bullets. Another Marine slew one and was himself wounded.

At that juncture Tanaka blundered onto the scene. Her father, a black belt in *shotokan* karate, had instilled a love for the art in her at an early age, and she had gone on to become skilled in her own right. When she rounded the corner and saw the stricken young Marine and a bearded fanatic about to shoot him in the head, she had acted without thinking.

Two weeks later Tanaka had been called into her superior's office. He had introduced her to an imposing man from the Justice Department, and left. It seemed her high IQ and stellar performance evaluations, capped by her courage against the terrorists, had brought her to his attention. He wanted her to occasionally do a little side work for him. The pay wasn't that great, but she would be doing a great service for her country.

Tanaka said yes on the spot.

For the most part her duties consisted of routine embassy work. But every now and again she would be contacted by her liaison to perform special tasks.

Sometimes she did courier duty. Sometimes she helped hide defectors.

Then there was Tanaka's work with those she called the shadow men, those who operated in the dark corners of government and did the dirty deeds no one else would or could do. Those like the big man at the safehouse, the man whose name she had never learned, the one whose eyes were like magnets, whose presence made her think of a lion about to pounce.

Tanaka hadn't been the least bit surprised when she got another call. They needed her to plant a listening device at a place called Fisheries Unlimited. Routine work, really, but she left nothing to chance. For an entire day she watched the building, noting who went in and who came out. When the two Koreans she had been told about left, she went up to the fourth floor to the company's office. Knocking, she had poked her head in the door, all smiles, and asked about another business farther down the hall, giving the impression she couldn't find it. Her real purpose was to get a look at the office and memorize the secretary's features.

The next evening, after she saw the secretary leave, Tanaka pulled up in a fake delivery truck and carried a large bouquet of flowers inside. Most of the businesses were still open, but no one questioned her. Why should they? It was a public building, and she was just a uniformed delivery woman.

Tanaka knew Cho-Hee and the giant were gone. She had been parked down the street for hours and had seen them leave. Now that the secretary had called it quits for the day, Fisheries Unlimited was deserted. She could do as her liaison wanted and be out of there within minutes, no one the wiser.

On her previous visit Tanaka had noted the type of lock. A master key admitted her, and she went straight to the back office. Turning on the light, she contemplated where to secret the first of three bugs. Behind the company emblem was too obvious.

A favorite spot of hers was underneath a drawer. The first device, no bigger than a watch battery, was easily taped in place. The second went inside a wall clock after she unscrewed the back to drop it in. As she was hanging the clock up again, she sensed she was no longer alone, and spun.

Framed in the doorway was the tall Korean, Kon-Li.

Fear spiked into her, but she fought the fright down, mustered her most charming smile and scooped up the bouquet from the desk. "So sorry," she said in Japanese. "Is this the Komoto Tea Company?"

A cold voice from behind the giant snapped, "Subdue her."

Pretense was useless. Tanaka flung the flowers at the giant as he advanced, hoping to distract him for the split second she needed to set herself and deliver a *Kansetsu-geri* that would have taken him off at the knees. The blow landed, but it did more harm to her than to Kon-Li. Her foot felt as if she had kicked solid steel.

The giant stopped and regarded her a moment, then grunted and adopted a forward stance common to many martial arts. Since he was Korean, the woman assumed he was proficient at tae kwon do, which she had seen demonstrated on occasion. She thought she knew what to expect. She couldn't have been more wrong.

Going low had been ineffective, so Tanaka went high, arcing her other leg in a roundhouse kick, using the ball of the foot. She had knocked one of the terrorists out using that kick and had every hope of doing the same to the tall Korean. But all he did was lift his forearm just enough to catch the brunt on his wrist.

Again Tanaka suffered terrible pangs, clear down her leg to her hips. Confused, growing anxious, she launched into a flurry of hand and foot blows that would have disabled most any man alive. Yet the Korean absorbed it all without so much as flinching.

Cho-Hee was in the doorway now, and he was upset. "Damn it, I said subdue her, not toy with her!"

Kon-Li's right leg moved. At least, she *thought* it was his right leg. The next she knew, she was on her back with the giant's knee gouging into her chest. Evidently she had been knocked unconscious because Cho-Hee was beside her, holding the open wall clock in one hand and the bug in the other.

"What have we here, woman?"

Tanaka's stomach cramped into a ball.

"Who are you? Who do you work for?" Cho-Hee tossed the clock onto his desk and thoughtfully fingered the device. "Not talking? You will, though. Before Kon-Li is done with you, you will tell me your life's story. Why not spare yourself such unpleasantness and cooperate?"

"Never," she rasped, her throat and mouth as dry as a desert.

Cho-Hee leaned over her, leering. "Never is the same as forever. Can you tolerate torture that long? I think not."

The giant reached for her.

CHAPTER SIX

Precious seconds were ticking away.

Mack Bolan never hesitated. He didn't stop to consider the fact that in less than four minutes the entire dock was going to go up like a Roman candle, vaporizing everyone caught in the blast radius. He didn't try to justify doing nothing by telling himself Kiri Tanaka was a grown woman who knew the risks of the trade, and if she died, well, that was how things worked out sometimes. He didn't put his own life before hers.

The instant the soldier saw her, he was in motion.

Bolan hurried down the rope to the raft and pumped the paddle in a fury. Urgency, not panic, spurred him on. He propelled the raft to the south end of the dock, where a wooden ladder led up from water level just as one had at the north end. He climbed swiftly, the timers and the C-4 uppermost on his mind. As he stepped onto the dock and unslung the M-16, his internal clock warned him he now had less than three minutes.

No one caught sight of him at first. All the workers were busy at their assigned jobs, moving crates, loading pallets onto the hoist, lowering cargo into the *Na-*

gaoka's holds. The gunners, and Hideo Koto, had eyes only for the two Koreans and their prisoner. Cho-Hee and Kon-Li had passed the vessel's bow and were almost to the gangplank that would take them up to where Hideo Koto stood.

Between Bolan and Tanaka were half a dozen workers preparing pallets for loading. There were also two guards, watching the Koreans.

Bolan broke into a run. He was almost to the workers when one looked up and shouted an alarm. Koto's workers were armed, and they went for their guns just as the guards did. The Executioner cut loose, triggering short bursts, dropping hardmen right and left, never slowing as he threaded through the pallets toward Tanaka. The element of surprise gave him an initial edge. He neutralized the two guards and the nearest workers before any could snap off a shot. Then the men on the freighter and those farther down the dock were galvanized to action.

A guard with an SMG appeared atop the *Nagaoka*, only to be chopped at the waist by Bolan's autorifle. A worker on the gangplank fumbled under his jacket for a revolver and had his sternum punctured by 5.56 mm slugs for his trouble.

Cho-Hee and Kon-Li had halted. The young Korean said something and both men turned to flee, the giant pulling Kiri Tanaka, who dug in her heels.

Bolan's magazine was empty. In a second he replaced it and fired, deliberately aiming low to avoid hitting Tanaka. Cho-Hee flung his hands out as if to ward off the hot lead, then bellowed at Kon-Li. The giant shoved the woman to the dock, spun and loped off at Cho-Hee's side.

Tanaka was on her knees, battered and bruised and bloody, yet she marshaled a crooked smile as Bolan rushed up to her. "I never thought—" she croaked.

"Not now!" Rotating, Bolan sent a searing hailstorm at the deck of the freighter. Several men went down, while others scurried for cover. Somewhere out of sight, Hideo Koto was roaring orders.

"Run!" Bolan shouted, gripping the woman's arm and shoving her toward the end of the dock. "Run like hell!"

She tried, but whatever the Koreans had done to her had left her weak and hurting. The best she could do was a limping shuffle, a grotesque imitation of an Egyptian mummy from an old horror movie.

Bolan was firing nonstop now, squeezing off burst after burst, doing his best to keep the gunners pinned down long enough for her to reach safety. All the while, the seconds continued to count down. He guessed they had two minutes left, if that.

Tanaka reached the pallets and leaned on one to rest, but Bolan couldn't let her. "Keep going!" he urged, switching magazines for the second time by pressing the release button with one hand while fluidly whipping another magazine from a pocket in his blacksuit. He pressed the head of the bolt catch on the left side of the lower receiver and was ready to rock, all so fast there was hardly a break in his firing.

A gunner on the freighter saw him reloading and popped up to get off a shot. But the man didn't pop up quickly enough.

Shots zinged from behind Bolan now, from the vicinity of the fence. Whirling, he punched lead into a pair of onrushing guards, pulverizing their faces. As he swung back around, he saw Tanaka on one knee, blood oozing from her side. She had caught one. A bound brought Bolan to her, and he hooked his left arm around her slender chest.

"Leave me," she said, the words hardly audible.

Bolan didn't waste breath answering. He backpedaled toward the bay, firing with one hand, the rifle's butt jammed under his right arm. Triggering one short burst after another, swinging the muzzle toward any and all immediate threats, he held Koto's underlings at bay. He was only a few feet from the end of the dock when the magazine went empty again, but this time he didn't reload. Slinging the M-16, he scooped Tanaka into both arms and jumped off into space.

The gunners on the *Nagaoka* and those along the dock who had been pinned down by the soldier's devastatingly accurate fire now rose up en masse and unleashed a deluge of searing slugs.

A swarm of hornets buzzed over Bolan's head as he and Tanaka plunged toward the cold waters of Tokyo Bay. They cleaved the water neatly, feetfirst, and Bolan clasped her to him and angled away from the freighters, away from the packet of plastic explosives he had set on the stern of the vessel. A minute remained, if that.

Bolan had to forget using the raft. It was too slow, too cumbersome. The only thing that would save them was distance, as much distance as they could manage in under sixty seconds. Which wasn't much. Hampered by his clothes and having to support Tanaka, he seemed to be moving at a snail's pace.

The woman clung to him, kicking as best she was able. In the dark water Bolan couldn't see her face.

He couldn't tell if she had realized why they weren't making for the surface. She'd learn why soon enough.

The blast, when it came, was everything the soldier had known it would be.

Even twelve feet down, the *crump* of the charges in the *Kraken* were audible. Then those attached to the other two vessels detonated, setting off the chain reaction Bolan had hoped for. Louder explosions rocked the night, one after the other, and the water lit up as if it were the middle of the day.

A glance showed Bolan two huge fireballs roiling heavenward. He held Tanaka closer. Seconds later the concussion slammed into them like a tidal wave, and they were hurled through the water like living torpedoes. Bolan half expected they would go tumbling out of control, but they didn't. They traveled dozens of yards in a twinkling. The force gradually lessened, but they couldn't break loose from its grasp.

Their lungs were running out of air. Bolan kicked and kicked, trying to arc to the surface. Kiri was thrashing wildly, desperate to breathe. Wrenching upward, bending his spine so far back the pain was almost unbearable, Bolan knifed up out of the deep into the muggy night. They trod water and sucked in needed breath.

"You—you—" Tanaka gasped.

"Not now," Bolan said, turning so he could see Hideo Koto's dock.

The three freighters were ablaze. The *Kraken* had sustained massive damage. Her hull had crumpled in three places, and fire gushed from her ruptured holds, spewing thick columns of smoke. Both the *Petra* and the *Nagaoka* were listing, the former to starboard, the latter to port.

Their sterns were in ruin and taking in water at prodigious rates. Whether either could be salvaged was questionable.

The dock itself was a raging inferno. Fiery debris had rained on the warehouse, but the corrugated metal had withstood the flames, if not the explosions. A third of the building looked as if a tornado had reduced the walls to so much scrap.

Screams and shrieks pierced the bedlam. Men were running every which way. Some were burning alive and swatting at their blazing clothes in vain.

Bolan saw no trace of Hideo Koto, but he did spot the sedan belonging to Cho-Hee, out near the gate. The young Korean had his head out the rear window.

The two roiling fireballs coalesced into a giant firestorm that swept higher and higher, forming a towering pillar. Suddenly, its base was blistered by new, lesser blasts, explosions emanating from the hulls of the *Kraken* and the *Petra*. Apparently, drugs weren't the only cargo. Illegal munitions were included, and now the incendiary heat was igniting the explosives. Popping sounds, like a thousand kids using cap guns simultaneously, were added to the din. Tracers streaked into the sky.

Tokyo Bay mirrored the pyrotechnics. The harbor was lit for half a mile or more, and caught in the light, bobbing like two corks in a bouncing sea, were Bolan and Tanaka. They had wound up hundreds of feet from Koto's vessels and sixty yards from shore.

"Must—must tell you," the woman said faintly through chattering teeth. Her whole body was quaking.

"It can wait," Bolan assured her as he stroked toward land. In her weakened state the cold water might induce hypothermia. He had to get her somewhere dry and warm, and quickly.

Again Tanaka tried to speak, but her chin folded against his chest. Bolan could see nasty welts and bruises on her face, neck and shoulders. She had been brutally beaten. Since it was unlikely Cho-Hee would soil his hands, Kon-Li had to have inflicted the punishment. The soldier made a mental note that before he was done, there would be an accounting.

Sirens wailing, emergency vehicles sped to the scene from many different directions, their red-and-blue lights flashing. Fire engines, ambulances, the police, all were on their way.

The thunderous pandemonium had awakened the families on the fishing boats. Hundreds were crowded on the decks of their craft, gaping and gesturing.

No one saw Bolan wade onto a short strip of isolated shore carrying Kiri Tanaka. Drenched to the skin, his own body chilled to the marrow, Bolan sought the sheltering darkness of the side street where he had parked the Toyota.

Lights had come on all over. Men and women were poking their heads out windows and doors to observe the goings-on.

Tanaka mumbled to herself as Bolan gently eased her into the front passenger seat, then slid behind the wheel. She needed to be in the hospital. But for him to waltz into an emergency room with her in his arms was to invite hours of endless questions before Brognola could get him released.

Bolan made for the house out near Kawasaki. It was

the best they could do under the circumstances. He broke every Japanese speed law, but with all the emergency vehicles and others racing to and fro, no one gave his car a second glance.

Once inside, Bolan placed the woman on the sofa and made a quick call. Brognola wasn't in, so he left word with the big Fed's secretary, an efficient woman who knew just what to do.

His next priority was to fill the bathtub with warm water. Bolan didn't undress Tanaka; he simply lowered her in, clothes and all. Sparing her possible embarrassment wasn't the reason. She needed to be warmed up. Immediately. Her body was icy to the touch and her lips were blue.

Soaking a washcloth, Bolan applied warm water to her face and neck. The bruises were darkening. Her lower lip had been split, and her right ear would take weeks to heal from a ragged gash. Bolan was too seasoned a professional to let emotion affect his judgment, but he couldn't help experiencing a deep, simmering resentment at how she had been mistreated. Kon-Li had concentrated on nerve centers and pressure points to heighten her agony.

After lowering the soft cloth into the warm water, Bolan wrung it out to apply it to her forehead. When he looked up, he was surprised to find she had revived.

"Where—?"

"Don't talk," Bolan said. "Don't even move. You're probably busted up inside, maybe bleeding internally. As soon as you stop trembling and your lips are their normal shade, I'm stripping you and tucking you into bed until a medical team arrives."

"Must tell you something," Tanaka said, every word an effort.

Bolan had already silenced her twice. Whatever it was, it had to be important. He laid the cloth on her cold brow. "I'm listening."

"Third bug—" she began, but even that was too much and she winced in anguish, then groaned.

"You really should keep still."

"Important," Tanaka said, stubbornly persistent. She grit her teeth, then spit it out in a rush, "Cho-Hee found the bug I put in his clock and the one under his desk drawer. But I planted a third. Let them know." She broke off, in too much torment.

"Cho-Hee caught you in the act, was that it?" Bolan meant the question to be rhetorical. She wasn't supposed to answer.

"Yes. Kon-Li...did things...to me. I slipped the last bug I had into his pocket."

Bolan had to hand it to her. She'd endured a beating that would have killed most people, yet she had completed her assignment under the very noses of the pair torturing her. "I'll pass on the word."

Tanaka nodded once, smiled thinly, and was out like a light.

TEN MINUTES LATER the call from Brognola came through. Bolan had just tucked the young woman under the covers. He filled in the big Fed on the latest developments, ending with, "If this doesn't lure Cho-Hee's uncle out of the woodwork, we're back to square one."

"An ambulance will be there inside of half an hour to transport Ms. Tanaka to a private facility," Brognola said. "And now that we know one of our little electronic ears is in place, an around-the-clock monitor team will be set up."

"Did you ever hear anything from your South Korean counterpart?"

"An hour ago, as a matter of fact. He came up empty-handed like everyone else. But his sources north of the border have been instructed to ferret out whatever they can."

"So it's a waiting game again," Bolan observed.

"I do have some pertinent news. We did some checking. According to sources close to the Lucca Family, they're expecting a big shipment from overseas. No one knows what kind of shipment, but Anthony, the Don's son, was overheard bragging that soon his Family would have the money and firepower needed to set themselves up as kings of the West Coast. An exact quote."

"He'll be one unhappy puppy when he learns what happened to their shipment." Especially, Bolan mused, after Cho-Hee had given Anthony such a hard time about raising the money on time.

"We're on the cusp of a big one, Striker," Brognola said. "I can feel it in my bones. I'll have a pilot and jet waiting to take you wherever you need to go next. My money is on San Francisco."

Bolan didn't take his friend up on the bet, but he should have. Four hours after Tanaka had been whisked off in an unmarked ambulance, and only half an hour after Bolan had stretched out to try to catch some sleep before the new day dawned, the big Fed phoned with an update.

"I hope your bags are packed. You have forty-five minutes before you leave for South Korea."

"Kiri's sacrifice paid off?"

"Big dividends. Cho-Hee is fit to spit nails. He went straight to his office and has been placing calls to his people all over Asia and Malaysia. Hong Kong, Bangkok, Taipei, Manila, Ho Chi Minh City, you name it. His organization is bigger than we suspected."

"His uncle's organization, you mean," Bolan corrected him.

A smile crept into the big Fed's voice. "How would you like to meet that uncle, up close and personal?"

"An early Christmas present?"

"One of Cho-Hee's calls was to Inchon, South Korea. We've got the uncle's voice on tape."

"And a name to go with it?"

"You would think so, wouldn't you? But Cho-Hee never used a name. It was 'uncle' this, or 'sir' that. Whoever he is, the uncle wasn't pleased with his nephew's performance. He demanded Cho-Hee report to him immediately."

"I can take them both down at the same time, then," Bolan said. And Kon-Li, he reminded himself.

"I think you'll have this wrapped up in another day or so," Brognola predicted. "Then why don't you head back to Stony Man for some R&R?"

Bolan shared his friend's optimism. The end to his quest was near.

South Korea

INCHON, SOUTH KOREA, was one of that country's major ports. Located on the Yellow Sea twenty-four miles to the southwest of Seoul, it was the site of one of the most dramatic events of the Korean War when the United Nations forces staged a crucial landing.

The Executioner arrived in Seoul on a private flight from Tokyo. He couldn't very well use a standard airline. As a general rule, commercial carriers discouraged passengers from carrying on board enough weapons to stock an armory. Thanks to Brognola's influence, he was able to bypass customs. He went straight to the rental-car booths and rented a station wagon.

By noon Bolan was on his way to Inchon. The streets of Seoul were thronged with traffic, so it wasn't until close to one that he left the last of the sprawling city behind. The Korean countryside was as picturesque as ever, a clash of modern and ancient, much like Japan.

Bolan had received another update from Brognola on the flight across the Sea of Japan, via a satellite link. A trace on Sin Cho-Hee's call from Yokohama to Inchon had revealed he phoned a business known as Diversified Industries, Incorporated. It was a name that meant little in and of itself until the Feds did some digging and established that Fisheries Unlimited was a subsidiary of D.I.

Diversified Industries would bring Bolan one step nearer to Cho-Hee's uncle. But whether it was the final step, and whether it would result in the outcome Bolan wanted, remained to be seen.

The address Bolan had been given was outside Inchon proper in an industrialized suburb within sight of the Yellow Sea. From a rise of land Bolan enjoyed a panoramic vista of seafaring vessels and smaller craft similar to the scene from the hilltop house in Yokohama.

The maps he had been provided were in English, with the exact location of Diversified Industries circled in red. As he neared the general area he noticed a skyscraper that towered eight to ten stories above everything else. He came to the avenue where D.I. was supposed to be located and cruised along it, reading off the numbers.

The skyscraper *was* D.I.

Several blocks to the west Bolan found a parking lot. Getting out, he opened the trunk and removed a pair of binoculars from his duffel. He trained them out to sea first to give the illusion he was interested in the comings and goings down at the harbor, then he slowly pivoted until the skyscraper filled both lenses. It was a modern building, sleek and streamlined like a needle.

Bolan had to admit the discovery was troubling. The intel had made it plain that the uncle's wheelings and dealings extended all along the Pacific Rim, but Bolan never counted on anything like this. Illegal drugs, illicit munitions, front companies, a corporate headquarters—it suggested a complex organization that required a complex mind to run it. Since Cho-Hee hadn't shown any great streaks of brilliance, that left the uncle.

In his far-flung travels Bolan had gone up against every type of criminal under the sun. Drug lords, Mafia Dons, traitors, gang leaders, enemy agents, bureaucrats on the take, warlords, pimps, rogues—he had met them all. And it had been his experience that the ones who were the most deadly were the ones who relied more on their brains than on their brawn.

The uncle struck Bolan as being just such a man. Mr. Mysterious had carved out an underground empire that spanned half the globe without the world's best intelligence agencies being any the wiser. And what did it say about the man's cunning, to say nothing of his ego, that he had chosen to base his operation out of a skyscraper?

Bolan got into the car and shoved the binoculars under the seat. A room had been registered in his name at one of the best hotels Inchon offered. Ironically, from his balcony he had a clear view of Diversified Industries. He ordered a meal and sat watching the shadows lengthen and twilight claim the land.

When the phone rang, Bolan snatched it up. "About time."

Hal Brognola was in a testy mood, too. "Don't blame me. I haven't had a minute to myself all day. The Japanese suspect someone acting under the American banner of covert ops is involved. They're not dummies. The only thing that saved it from blowing up into an international incident was the fact no civilians were hurt. The death toll stands at thirty-seven, all with known ties to Hideo Koto."

"And Kiri Tanaka?"

"Doing nicely, thank you. She'll be out of the hospital in a week to ten days."

"She deserves a break. Do you have anything I can use?"

"Until an hour ago the bug Kiri risked her life planting was a gold mine of information."

"What happened then?"

"We think the giant changed clothes. We were able to listen in on everything Cho-Hee said from the time they left Yokohama until shortly after they landed at Seoul. I've also been in touch with Mr. Park, my South Korean counterpart, and this time he was more helpful. He gave me all they have on Diversified Industries."

Bolan sat on the edge of his chair. "Did it include the uncle's identity?"

"Wishful thinking. The head of the company is listed as Sin Cho-Hee, and I know what you're thinking. If I didn't know any better, if we didn't have the uncle's voice on tape talking with Cho-Hee, I'd be skeptical the man even existed."

"Break it down for me."

"D.I. was incorporated three years ago. One of the company's first acts was to buy one of the tallest buildings in Inchon. Their offices occupy the upper four floors. The lower twenty are rented out, which means more innocent bystanders to watch out for."

Bolan had hoped differently. It altered his whole strategy when he had to take civilians into account. His insertion must be planned with a minimum of collateral damage.

"Mr. Park delved into their tax records and the like and they came up smelling like a rose. They are as clean as clean can be. And the South Koreans won't go barging in without just cause."

"Where does that leave us?"

"Caught between the proverbial rock and a hard place. You know D.I. is dirty, and I know D.I. is dirty, but we can't step out of line or we'll get the South Koreans as mad as the Japanese." Brognola let a few seconds go by. "Now that I've been such a big help, how soon do you plan to go in?"

Mack Bolan did something he rarely did. He laughed out loud.

CHAPTER SEVEN

It was more like a throne room than an executive's corporate office. Inches-thick red carpet covered the floor, matching the red curtains and red leather upholstery. The initial impression when visitors walked through the ornate doors with their brass trim was that the spacious chamber had been smeared in fresh blood.

The man who sat in the thronelike chair at the head of the gilt table liked the effect. Red was his favorite color, just as diamonds were his favorite gems, and tailored clothes the only kind he would wear.

Sin Mak-Fang had risen high in life. He had come a long way from his humble beginnings as a farmer's son in a remote region of North Korea. There were days when he couldn't quite believe his good fortune, balanced by days when he thought it was his rightful due.

He had worked hard to get where he was. By his guile and his strength he had risen into the elite of the RDEI, North Korea's premier intelligence agency. Along the way he had done things, terrible things, and never felt the prick of conscience.

The Central Committee had been proud of his accomplishments. He was their golden boy, the operative who could do no wrong. What better person, then, to put in charge of their special covert op? The RDEI had laid out all the groundwork before Sin Mak-Fang was chosen. All he had to do was step into a role that fit him like a new suit.

The only thing was, Sin Mak-Fang had grown to like the role, to cherish it, to want to continue in it indefinitely. And now, by slaying Chang Do-Young, he had taken the last, irrevocable step in severing his ties with his former masters. From now on, Sin Mak-Fang was his *own* master. He would decide his own destiny. If the RDEI dared to retaliate, if they sent assassins to dispose of him, he would unleash a hit team of his own.

Or so Sin Mak-Fang mused, until the opening of the gilt doors ended his reflection. In came the pair he had summoned twelve hours earlier. "Nephew," he said with a bob of his bald head. He didn't greet Kon-Li.

Sin Cho-Hee, ever courteous, ever respectful, bowed, then came to take his customary seat on his uncle's right.

Kon-Li moved to a corner and stood as rigid as a tree, awaiting orders.

"I am not happy," Sin Mak-Fang bluntly stated.

"I do not blame you, sir," Cho-Hee said, tucking his chin low. "I have failed you. I am unworthy. Do with me as you will."

Sin Mak-Fang's dark eyes glittered like those of a rattler about to strike. But he didn't. His nephew was the one human being on the planet he completely trusted. He had taken the boy under his wing years ago, helped Cho-Hee rise through the ranks and given him an important position in his new organization. He had a lot invested in the younger man. One day, years away, his nephew stood to inherit his empire.

"Tell me what you know," the uncle commanded.

"Very little, I am afraid. Someone hit Hideo Koto. Three freighters were destroyed, including one of ours. We lost the entire shipment."

A rap at the door interrupted them. Sin Mak-Fang glanced up in annoyance that evaporated when he saw who it was. "Yes?"

"My apologies, Mr. Fang," his secretary said, extending a cellular phone. "You told me to put this gentleman through to you immediately whenever he calls."

Sin Mak-Fang snapped his fingers, and she hastened to give the phone to him. "What news?" he asked. After the person at the other end gave a short report, he said, "I will be in touch." He gave the phone back to her and motioned for her to leave. Then he sank deeper into his chair, disturbed by what he had just learned. He became aware of his nephew's quizzical stare. "Yes?"

As if caught with his hand in a candy jar, Cho-Hee averted his gaze. "It is nothing, sir. A trifle."

"I will decide what is and isn't important. Speak."

"I have often wondered, Uncle, why you use your given name as if it were your family name, is all."

Fang understood why his nephew was puzzled. Koreans were usually addressed by their family names, just as in English-speaking countries. The only difference was, in English usage family names were written or spoken last. They were called Mr. Smith, or Mr. Jones. In Korean it was the opposite. Family names were always spoken first. Sin was his last name, Fang his first name.

He had never given the matter much thought until his foreign language studies at the RDEI academy. It greatly amused him to learn that in English, the language of his country's most bitter enemies, his first name, Fang, referred to a long, sharp tooth by which prey was seized and torn. On the other hand, his last name, Sin, had something to do with a silly Western concept of falling from the grace of a nonexistent deity.

So Fang had developed the habit of using his first name as Westerners used their last names. He liked the drama of it, the fear it instilled. In all his overseas dealings he was known as Mr. Fang, not Mr. Sin.

"I will explain some day," Fang told his nephew. "For now, we have a much more important matter to discuss. That was my contact at the NIA." The South Korean National Information Agency was the equivalent of the American CIA. "It seems the illustrious Mr. Park has been nosing into our affairs."

"First Koto, now this. Do you think they are connected, Uncle?"

Fang sighed. His nephew was undeniably loyal but not always the brightest of individuals. "Think, Cho-Hee. Think. The biggest smuggling deal we have ever set up goes up in flames. Then we learn that someone is investigating Diversified Industries. What does this suggest to you?"

"Someone is out to destroy us?" Cho-Hee said.

"Excellent. Now the question you must ask yourself is who. Could it be the North Koreans? No, they would not dismantle an organization their money helped build. The South Koreans? Unlikely, since they would not dare risk Japan's anger by causing so much destruction. The British? What do they care about Korea.'' Fang smiled slyly. "Who does that leave, Cho-Hee? Who treats all other countries like doormats? Who would not think twice about blowing up the three freighters? Who could put pressure on Park to investigate our front businesses?"

"The Americans!"

"You are learning, Cho-Hee." Fang drummed his fingers on the arm of his chair. "My contact at the NIA tells me that an American assassin is here in South Korea expressly to terminate me."

"Then we should terminate him before he can get you in his sights."

"My wishes, exactly. Get hold of Jun-Han. I want our best men to handle this. We must leave nothing to chance."

"How many should be in on the hit? Two? Maybe three?"

"Didn't you hear me? We are up against a trained American assassin. Say what we will about Americans, one thing they know how to do is kill. Have Jun-Han take six or seven men along."

"How will we find this Yankee?"

"My contact has told me where he is staying."

"Do you want him alive or dead?"

Fang made a *tsk-tsk* sound. "Just when you were doing so well, you go and ask such a stupid question."

Cho-Hee rose. "It will be done as you wish, Uncle. The American dog is as good as dead."

BOLAN HAD ENJOYED a good night's sleep, his first in three days. He'd eaten breakfast at a nearby restaurant, then returned to the hotel to await word from Brognola. Now, shortly before noon, he was seated in the hotel lobby near a wide window that afforded a fine view of the port, studying the skyscraper that promised to be his next battleground.

The soldier never committed himself without a plan, if he could help it. Brognola had promised him diagrams of the building along with whatever other helpful information the South Koreans had. Information Bolan needed to plot his strategy.

"Mr. Randall Brown?"

Bolan turned from the window. Brown was the alias he was using. A nattily dressed Korean male in his mid- to late thirties stood a few feet away, holding an attaché case. "You would be?"

"Bon Chae-Ku, sir, at your service. The desk clerk pointed you out to me. I am an assistant to Mr. Park, with whom I believe you are familiar."

"Yes." Park was South Korea's equivalent of Hal Brognola. Bolan rose and they shook hands.

"Forgive my showing up unannounced, but I was instructed to deliver these documents promptly, in person." Bon tapped the attaché case. "Is there somewhere we can talk in private?"

"My room will do."

They were the only ones in the elevator on its way up so Bon felt free to say, "More information has come to our attention since you last talked to your superior in Washington. Diversified Industries is but the tip of a malignant cancer that must be excised from my country."

Bolan wondered if Bon was a field operative or a

desk jockey. He'd wager money on the latter. "Does anyone else know about my being here?"

"No, sir. Only Mr. Park and myself. He was quite explicit about that." Bon's eyes mirrored intense curiosity, but Bolan didn't volunteer anything. "All I know is that I am to do whatever you ask of me. I am your official liaison. Until you leave our country, think of me as your shadow."

The last thing Bolan needed was an eager-beaver bureaucrat tagging along. But he held his peace for the moment.

"The man you are after, Mr. Fang, is like an octopus. He has tentacles everywhere. When you see what we have uncovered, I think you agree he is most clever."

"Mr. Fang?" Bolan said.

"Oh. Forgive me. You have not heard, have you? We finally learned the identity of Sin Cho-Hee's uncle. His name is Sin Mak-Fang, but he likes to be called simply Fang. Why that should be, I cannot imagine."

Fang. The name seemed to echo in the recesses of Bolan's mind like a shout echoing out of a deep mine shaft. It had a ring to it, and it certainly fit a man who was the head of an evil empire that spanned continents. He was about to ask for more details when the elevator door opened.

"Once we learned his identity, we tapped into a wealth of information," Bon said softly as they walked down the corridor. "The NIA has a file on him from his days with the RDEI in North Korea. He was one of their star operatives."

"Wait," Bolan cautioned.

A woman had emerged from a room ahead. It was a maid, and she smiled sweetly as she went by.

Bon grinned like a ten year old. "Ah. Cloak-and-dagger. Is that not the expression you Americans use?"

"Save the rest until we're in my room," Bolan advised. Once they were, he sank into a chair while his liaison set the attaché case on the edge of the bed and opened it. The case was crammed with folders and papers.

"All that is for me?"

"Yes, sir. It is everything we have. Including detailed information on the Diversified Industries building, which I was led to understand was very important to you." Bon held up a binder three inches thick. "This has wiring diagrams, plumbing schematics, air ducts, all that you need."

If nothing else, the man was thorough. "Let's start with the background intel on Sin Mak-Fang."

Bolan was a firm believer in the axiom, "know your enemy." What he learned as he read the first file convinced him that his new adversary was as formidable as they came.

Born to a poverty-stricken farmer out of Sakchu, Fang had demonstrated a keen intellect at an early age. At the state-run elementary school he'd scored at the top of his class.

He was also good at sports. His ability came to the notice of the RDEI, which was always on the lookout for bright new recruits.

Bon Chae-Ku was standing to one side and craning his neck to see what Bolan was reading. "Someone in the RDEI must have taken Fang under their wing," he commented. "A mentor, perhaps. It is the only explanation for his rapid rise up through the ranks."

Which was an understatement. Fang had shot to the top echelon of North Korea's most feared intelligence agency in a third of the time it normally took. He was made a foreign operative, and bounced from country to country. A list was appended to the bio. "Japan, Hong Kong, the Philippines, Thailand," Bolan read aloud. He saw a pattern emerging.

"Mr. Fang is very well traveled, yes," Bon said.

Then, according to the file, about five years ago Fang vanished off the face of the earth. The South Koreans lost all trace of him. "Five years," Bolan said, remembering that Diversified Industries had come into existence about that time.

"It was rumored he had gone back to North Korea," Bon mentioned. "But after years went by and nothing more was heard of him, his file was downgraded from active to inactive status. It was presumed he was dead."

A description was included. Fang was six feet two inches tall and weighed in at a muscular 210 pounds. Big for a Korean, but nowhere near as big as Kon-Li. Under distinguishing features Bolan learned that Fang had a hereditary hair disorder that rendered him bald by the time he was fourteen.

"Try the green folder next," Bon suggested. "I think you will find it the most interesting of all."

It contained a dossier on Diversified Industries, Incorporated. As Bolan had already learned, Diversified Industries was a front, a corporate umbrella for over a dozen smaller companies, one of them Fisheries Unlimited. What drew Bolan's interest now were references to overseas firms.

Bon chatted on. "We are still piecing together all the details, but it appears an Asian-wide network of drug and arms smuggling has been set up. All within the past several years."

Bolan saw no mention of companies in America, yet he distinctly recalled Cho-Hee saying the Sins had business interests there. "No companies in the United States?"

"Not that we know of yet, sir, no. Your Mr. Brognola is working on that at his end. He's in a much better position to track it down, after all."

Under Hong Kong Bolan noticed something that caught his eye. "The Palace of Pleasure?"

"A brothel, sir. It is our understanding Mr. Fang owns a string of them." Bon smirked. "Places to indulge his animal passion, I expect."

Or was there more to it? Bolan had encountered men like Fang before. They never did anything without a reason. Opening a whore house for the fun of it was as likely as Fang building an amusement park.

"The yellow file has important information, too," Bon remarked.

It contained information on five South Korean subsidiaries of Diversified Industries. "What exactly do all these businesses do?"

Bon coughed. "Um, we're not quite sure. They really don't seem to do much of anything. Mr. Park feels they are more front companies. Although that last one, Allied Electronics, is promising."

"In what regard?"

"They import and export electronic equipment. We

are in the process of acquiring their shipping manifests to learn exactly what kind of equipment they deal in and where they ship it to.''

"It could be a relay center," Bolan conjectured. "They funnel in drugs from, say, the Golden Triangle, then relay it on to the States or somewhere else."

"Mr. Park would like to raid Allied Electronics and every other business on that list," Bon Chae-Ku said. "But he has deferred to your Mr. Brognola in this matter. We will not make a move until Mr. Brognola says." Bon looked at his wristwatch. "I am supposed to call Mr. Park with word of your plans. What shall I tell him?"

"I'll be done here by tomorrow afternoon."

"That soon?"

Bolan nodded. Now that he had all the intel he needed, he could get on with the job. He would spend all afternoon and evening poring over the binder's contents and be ready to go by midnight.

"I will make the call and be right back," Bon Chae-Ku said.

Bolan didn't want the man hanging around. He didn't like being saddled with watchdogs, and when all was said and done, that was exactly what Bon Chae-Ku was. Park had sent Bon to keep tabs on him. Maybe Park had learned of the incident in Tokyo Bay and was leery of a similar incident in Inchon. "How about if we get together tomorrow morning to compare notes?"

"You want me to leave, is that it? I am sorry, sir. Mr. Park was quite explicit. As your liaison, I am to stay with you until you depart South Korea."

Bolan saw that a talk with Brognola was in order.

"Come to think of it, I need to put through a call of my own."

Bon wasn't the complete stooge he gave the impression of being. "Complaining to your superior about me won't do any good, sir. When in Rome, if you see what I mean."

"You're not coming with me to Diversified Industries tonight."

"Rest easy, sir. Before I became one of Mr. Park's assistants, I did field work. I'm versed in firearms and unarmed combat. I'm more of an asset than a liability."

Here was another sterling example of why Bolan liked to work alone, of why it was better to keep local contacts to a minimum. Locals couldn't help meddling. But he had an ace in the hole in Hal. Usually the big Fed could get pests like Bon off his back. "Why don't we each make our calls?" he proposed.

A knock at the door intruded. Standing, Bolan placed the files on the dresser. "Expecting anyone?" he inquired quietly.

"No, sir."

Neither was Bolan. Unbuttoning his jacket, he slipped a hand under it and curled his fingers around the Beretta. "Who is it?" he called out, sidling along the wall.

"The maid, sir. Forgive me if this is a bad time. I have new towels and washcloths."

It was the same maid Bolan had seen earlier. Admitting her, he stood by the door while she scooted into the bathroom. He heard a drawer open, heard a rustling noise and the drawer closed again. She came out carrying folded washcloths and towels.

"So sorry. So sorry," she said. "I did not mean to disturb you."

"It's no trouble at all," Bolan said. As she nervously went by, she glanced at Bon Chae-Ku. Bolan closed the door and took a step toward his chair, then was struck by just *how* nervous she had been. It was almost as if she had been afraid of him—or had something to hide.

"Hold on a minute," the soldier told Bon. He walked into the bathroom. Draped over the tub were the washcloth and towel he had used that morning. In a tidy pile close to the sink were what seemed to be the same spare cloths and towels that had been there that morning when he picked the two he used.

Bending, Bolan opened both of the drawers. In the first were complimentary packets of shampoo and lotion. The second was empty, left for guests to fill as they saw fit. Why had the maid opened one? To put in more packets? She'd claimed she was there to change towels. Yet if that was the case, why hadn't she taken the used towel and washcloth?

The questions spurred Bolan into hurrying to the door. Cracking it open, he peered to the right, the direction she had gone. Near the elevator was the maid and three Korean men in suits and sunglasses. As he looked on, one of the men pulled a wad of bills from a pocket and handed it to her.

They had paid her to verify he was in his room.

Closing the door, Bolan hurried to the closet and took out his duffel bag.

"What is the matter, Mr. Brown?" Bon asked politely.

"We have company."

"Who?"

Bolan slipped a hand under the strap and slung the duffel across his back. "Some of Fang's men, I would guess."

Bon Chae-Ku chortled. "That is quite impossible. How would he know who you are or why you are in the country? We are not even sure *he* is. We know the nephew arrived by private jet last night, but that is all."

"Do you have a gun?"

"No. I do not normally use one in my day-to-day administrative duties." Bon moved past the soldier. "Permit me to see for myself."

"No." Bolan gripped the South Korean's arm. "We'll do this my way."

"Really, sir. I must protest. I realize you Americans are paranoid by nature but this is carrying it a bit too far." Bon sought to pry off Bolan's fingers. "You are in a luxury hotel in the heart of a major city in the middle of the day. What do you honestly think Fang would dare do?"

Another knock shut Bon Chae-Ku up.

"Who is it?" Bolan demanded, forcing the liaison to one side.

"It is the maid again, sir."

Her voice was different this time, thinner and reedier and strained as tight as barbed wire. "What do you want now?" Bolan moved close to the right-hand wall and drew the Beretta. At sight of it, Bon Chae-Ku's eyes grew wide.

"I forgot something, sir," the maid said.

Bolan glanced at the balcony. They were three floors up, so jumping wasn't feasible. "I'm getting undressed. I'm just about to take a shower," he stalled. "Come back later."

"It will only take a moment. I neglected to check the soap dish."

"I was just in there. I have plenty of soap." Bolan gestured for Bon to move farther back so he would be out of the line of fire, but the man was as dense as a brick and shook his head.

"Please, sir. It is part of my job. I will be fired if I do not do it."

"Didn't you hear me?" Bolan countered. "Have your boss call my room. The soap is fine. The towels are fine. Now go away and leave me alone." He had the part of the disgruntled tourist down pat. But would the three gunners fall for it?

After a few seconds the maid tried another tack. "Will you at least come to the door and take the fresh bar of soap I have and put it in the bathroom for me? Will you at least do that much?"

"This is silly!" Bon Chae-Ku declared. "Why do you not do as the poor woman wants?" So saying, he started to do so. "Hang on, young lady! I will let you in!"

The soldier lunged, snagging the liaison's jacket, and yanked him back. But it was too late. The harm had been done. In a violent shower of slivers and chips, the door dissolved under a blistering hailstorm of autofire.

CHAPTER EIGHT

The gunners on the other side of the door made two mistakes. First, they opened fire without being sure of where their targets were. Second, instead of waiting to gauge the reaction to their initial bursts, they threw their shoulders into what was left of the door and smashed it open. In their haste to finish the job, they rushed headlong into the grave.

Mack Bolan had shoved Bon out of harm's way and flattened against the wall just as the space they had occupied sizzled with the passage of lead. Then the door was struck with a resounding thump and buckled under the impact. When the hardmen poured in, Bolan was ready, the Beretta out and level in a two-handed grip. Before the trio could get off another round, he shot them, slamming them to the floor in a crimson tangle.

Movement beyond them, in the hallway, caused Bolan to whirl.

It was only the terror-struck maid, the money the killers had paid her still clutched in her left hand. She gaped at them, then at the Beretta trained on her. Fear overcame her and she fled, screaming.

Bon moved toward the bodies as if his own were

being jerked by an invisible puppeteer. "You shot them!" he bleated, astounded at the turn of events.

Bolan didn't know what else the man expected him to do. "Grab everything you brought. We're getting out of here."

"What?" Bon couldn't take his eyes off the broken figures seeping scarlet.

"Put all the documents in the attaché case," Bolan directed. "We have to leave immediately."

"What for?" Blinking, Bon turned toward the nightstand and the telephone. "What we must do is notify the police. I must also let Mr. Park know what has happened."

Bolan took two long strides and clamped his hand on the liaison's arm. "Not now! Phone him later." He pushed Bon, none too gently, toward the bed. "Gather up all the files and the binder."

Out in the hall voices were being raised in query and alarm. Bolan strode to the doorway and peered out. Two more men in suits and sunglasses were stepping off the elevator. "Hurry," he snapped.

Bon was obeying, although reluctantly. "This is most irregular! I could get into a lot of trouble by leaving the scene of a shooting. So can you. Your special status doesn't make you immune to our laws, you know."

The two suits had pulled hardware and were warily advancing, one on either side of the corridor. Doors were opening up and down the hall, then slamming shut again when the occupants spotted the armed duo.

Bon wasn't moving fast enough to suit Bolan. Hurrying over, he threw the last of the files into the attaché case, slammed it shut and shoved it into the man's arms. "We're not out of the woods yet." He hauled him to the doorway. "Run to the left. Stay low and keep going until you reach the stairwell. I'll be right behind you."

"What do you mean by 'not out of the woods'? You have killed the men Fang sent to dispose of you."

Now it was Bolan who blinked, but he recovered his composure before the other noticed. "They weren't alone," he said, and barged into the corridor, pulling Bon along with him. He gave the Korean a hard push even as he fired at the gunners. One dived flat. The other, within reach of a door, kicked it in and ducked inside to the accompaniment of shrill shrieks.

The stairwell was only fifteen yards away but it might as well be miles, as slow as Bon was moving. Rapidly backpedaling, the soldier sent several rounds in the direction of the gunner on the floor, who responded in kind.

Only when lead smacked into the wall almost at Bon's elbow did a spark of apprehension spur him into racing the final few yards and barreling onto the landing.

The gunner on the floor started to jack up onto a knee and was flipped backward by Bolan's next shot.

That left the gunner who had ducked into the room. He wasn't about to make the same blunders his companions had. Poking his hand out, and only his hand, he sprayed lead at random.

Wild shots were no less fatal than those that were precisely aimed. Bolan backed into the stairwell door, still firing, only to find that Bon had let it close. The magazine cycled empty as he shouldered the door open and headed down, taking three steps at a time.

"Come on," he shouted at the liaison, who was still on the landing. "Unless you think they'll spare your life."

Gnawing on his lower lip, Bon glanced at the door just as slugs drilled into it. His decision was made for him. Muttering in Korean, he followed, moving with surprising speed.

Bolan couldn't begin to guess how many gunners Fang had sent. Maybe it was just the five. Or there could be more waiting in the lobby. He reached the next landing and paused to replace the spent magazine.

"I really must get to a telephone," Bon said as they continued down. "Mr. Park will want to send his own people to handle this. It is beyond the scope of the police." When Bolan didn't say anything, he went on. "I must thank you for saving my life. Please forgive my blundering about. I had forgotten how terrifying it is to be shot at."

Bolan, always careful not to take his eyes off the man for more than a second or two, wondered if that was the real reason Bon had been dragging his heels.

The liaison chuckled nervously. "This will give me something to tell my friends at the agency, will it not?"

The click of a latch above them brought Bolan to a stop. A face adorned by sunglasses jutted over a rail. Bolan brought up the Beretta, but the man skipped back. "Stay close to the wall," he told Bon, and did the same himself the rest of the way down.

At the door to the lobby the soldier paused.

"You have a hole," Bon said.

"A what?" High overhead feet scraped on the stairs. Bolan debated lying in wait for the fifth gunner and decided it was smarter to get out of there before more showed up.

"You have a hole in your bag."

Shifting, Bolan saw there was indeed a bullet hole in the duffel. A quick check established the round had gone clean through. Later he would check whether anything had been damaged. Cracking the door open an inch, Bolan scanned the lobby.

Word of the gun battle had reached the front desk. The assistant manager who had been on duty when Bolan checked in was now on the phone, talking excitedly, most likely to the police. Guests were milling about, anxious but not panicked, casting worried glances at the elevators. Bellboys were scurrying about trying to calm everyone.

Bolan pulled the door open wider, then tensed. Two more dark suits with sunglasses were on the other side of the lobby by a plate-glass window. That all Fang's men dressed the same didn't strike him as odd. Gangs in the States did it all the time. Here, it was a way for Fang's men to readily pick out one another in, say, a crowded lobby.

Bon Chae-Ku put his hand on the soldier's shoulder. "Please, sir, let me by. The sooner I contact Mr. Park, the better for both of us."

"There are more," Bolan said.

"More killers?" Bon tried to see past him. "How many? Maybe we can reach the front desk without them noticing us."

"They already have."

The shorter of the pair had glanced toward the stairwell, then poked his friend. Both slid hands under their jackets and began wending their way through the growing crowd.

"My car is right outside in the parking lot," Bolan said. "You're welcome to come with me, if you want." Without waiting for a reply, he headed out. Rather than cut across the lobby, he kept close to the wall, moving briskly but not so fast as to draw attention.

It worked. The gunners didn't spot him until he was almost to the entrance. By then they were halfway to the stairwell and hemmed in by the crowd. They couldn't resort to their weapons, but they did bull their way toward the soldier, shoving aside anyone who failed to get out of their way quickly enough.

"They're after us!" Bon exclaimed. He was a step behind Bolan, the attaché case clutched to his chest.

The glare of sunlight made them both squint as they sprinted toward the Executioner's vehicle, parked in the foremost row. Throwing open the rear door, Bolan shrugged out of the strap and threw the duffel onto the back seat. Then he jumped behind the wheel, inserted the key and twisted it.

Bon slid into the other bucket seat. "Where are we going? What do you intend to do?"

"Wait and see." Bolan couldn't be more specific, not if he was right about the significance of Bon's remark up in the room. He tromped on the gas pedal at the same moment the two suits burst into daylight. The tall one started to draw his pistol, but the short one smacked his arm and together they sprinted toward their own car.

"They intend to chase us down." The liaison had a flair for stating the obvious.

Bolan took the exit at fifty miles per hour and sent the speedometer surging higher. Traffic was light. He skillfully weaved through it for a quarter of a mile, then bore to the left at an intersection.

"They are still after us."

That they were, in a yellow sports car, of all things. They couldn't be more conspicuous if they tried, not with all the swerving in and out of traffic and speeding they were doing to overtake Bolan's rental vehicle.

Bon twisted in his seat. "Faster. They are gaining."

Bolan was driving as fast as conditions allowed. Any faster, and he risked endangering innocents. More by circumstance than design he was heading south, and at the next junction he skidded to the right, heading westward now.

"Whoever is driving that thing is a madman," Bon said, referring to the fishtail the sports car performed negotiating the same corner.

A madman with a purpose, Bolan reflected. He pressed the button to lower his window, then placed the Beretta between his legs so he could grab it easily if need be.

"I still cannot believe this is happening," Bon said. "Fang sent seven men after you. Seven! He must not believe in leaving anything to chance."

That was one possible explanation, Bolan thought to himself. He crested a low hill and the bay unfolded before them.

"We cannot hope to lose them, not in the middle of the day," Bon said. "I recommend we find a police station. It is our only hope."

"And be detained until the next Ice Age?" Bolan responded. "No, thanks."

"I am not without influence. And if it comes to that, Mr. Park will intercede in our behalf."

Bolan veered to avoid a Jeep pulling out of a side street. "My cover would be blown. I'd have to leave the country."

Bon shrugged. "Better that than to lose your life, eh? Mr. Brognola can send someone else to finish the job. It is not as if Fang is going anywhere."

A traffic light was up ahead. It turned yellow, and Bolan stomped on the gas to get through the intersection before it changed to red. A driver on his left was just as eager to get a jump on the green. The two vehicles hurtled at each other like metal battering rams, and only Bolan's lightning reflexes prevented a collision. He spun the wheel clockwise, missing the other car by the width of a license plate, if that.

Bon recoiled, his hands in front of his face. "Look out!" he yelled, but by then they had shot past and were burning rubber along a straight stretch, toward the wharves.

The sports car had run the light and slashed their lead by half. The driver was no slouch; he could grind gears with the best of them.

"We should try to find a police station," Bon said. "I doubt these cutthroats would go anywhere near one."

Bolan, on the other hand, was confident they would stop at nothing to do Fang's bidding.

Downshifting, he turned at each of the next four intersections, first to the left, then to the right, alternating to make it harder for the gunners to keep up. The gambit enabled him to pull slightly ahead.

Then the gunner on the passenger side leaned out

and banged off several rounds from a large-caliber handgun.

"We are dead men!" Bon declared.

His ceaseless whining was an annoyance Bolan could well do without. But the soldier wasn't letting the liaison out of his sight until he learned the truth.

An open-air fish market appeared, off on the right in a large lot. Beyond the fish vendors, with their crudely painted signs and displays, was a pier. Beyond that, the Yellow Sea.

Bolan slammed a palm onto the horn even as he slewed into the lot. The car went into a skid. Spinning the steering wheel furiously, he brought the car under control and roared down an aisle, scattering pedestrians like sparrows before a diving hawk. At the end of the aisle he turned left, then left again, racing back in the direction he had come.

Bon blanched and braced his hands against the dashboard. "What in the name of heaven are you doing? You will run over someone!"

The sports car, bouncing up over the curb, careened into the parking lot. The driver sheared into a parked vehicle, then shifted and spurted forward, cutting between aisles to head the warrior off.

"He is going to ram us!" Bon wailed.

It certainly looked that way. The yellow car roared toward them broadside, the driver grinning as if he believed he had them dead to rights. The gunner on the passenger side had pulled his head and shoulders back in and had his hands pressed against the roof, bracing for the impact.

Bolan intentionally slowed a trifle, not much, but enough to make the other driver overconfident. The sports car hurtled right at them, right at Bolan's door, and for a second he locked eyes with the driver. The man laughed.

Bon screamed.

Suddenly slamming his foot onto the gas pedal, Bolan sped out of the other vehicle's path at the last instant.

The yellow car overshot the parking lot. Its engine growling like an enraged beast, it flew onto the pier. The driver applied the brakes in a desperate bid to stop, but instead the car went into a slide. Fishermen frantically ran for safety. Then, like a comet soaring over the rim of the world, the sports car soared off the pier and nosed into the bay. The splash it raised was tremendous.

"My word," Bon said.

Bolan swung around the booths and out into the street. In the distance sirens shrieked. He slowed to just under the speed limit and headed south along the shore road. Within half a mile they were in a residential area. The homes were small and frail, packed one next to the other like dominoes. Few cars were in evidence.

Past the homes the road narrowed drastically, to where Bolan had to pull over to let an elderly lady in a donkey-led cart go by.

Bon seemed to be in shock. He didn't stir or speak until five minutes later when Bolan pulled onto an isolated bluff overlooking the ocean. "What are you doing?" he demanded.

Bolan had a cramp in his calf. Getting out, he walked stiffly to a flat boulder, placed the Beretta beside him and extended his right leg.

"Why do you ignore me when I talk to you?" Bon asked, joining him. "I swear, you treat me as if I am not even here."

"I've had a lot on my mind," Bolan said, justifying his breach of etiquette. He gazed to the north, back toward the city. No one was after them. They were alone, just as he wanted. When he heard metal slide across stone, he faced around—into the muzzle of his own pistol.

Bon wore a sly mask of triumph. "Thank you, American. You have made it ridiculously easy for me."

"Does Mr. Park know you work for Sin Mak-Fang?" Bolan inquired.

Uncertainty replaced the triumph. "You know?"

"I've suspected ever since the hotel room when you mentioned those men were sent by Fang to kill me."

"But they were," Bon said.

"How would *you* know that?"

"It was a logical deduction."

"Was it?" Bolan said. "How did Fang know I was in-country? How did he know where I was staying? The only two people who did were Park and you." Bolan shook his head. "No, I realized there had to be someone on the inside. And from what I hear of Mr. Park, he's not the kind to betray his country."

Bon extended the Beretta, his nostrils flaring with anger. "You think you are so smart! But you are mistaken. I have not sold out my country."

"Then what do you call it?"

"Being practical. NIA agents do not earn a lot of money. For the most part we slave away like dogs, as you would say, for twenty or thirty years. Then we retire on a small pension, barely able to make ends meet.''

''Fang made you a better offer, is that it?'' The cramp was almost gone. Bolan casually placed both feet flat and rested his hands on the edge of the boulder.

''That is exactly what he did, yes. He paid me a visit four years ago. In the middle of the night I woke up with a gun pressed against my temple. He gave me a choice. I could work for him and earn a lot of money, or I could die.''

''You chose the money.''

''Can you blame me? What has my government ever done for me that I should give my life for it? Besides, Mr. Fang is most generous. He pays me more in one month than I earn in an entire year. And for special information he pays extra.''

''How much did you get for telling him about me?''

''Not half as much as I will receive when he learns I killed you myself.'' Bon chortled. ''It has worked out quite nicely, if I do say so myself. For a while there I thought those idiots would kill me, too.''

Bolan made no move to jump the turncoat, no attempt to wrest away the Beretta. ''They almost did,'' he mentioned.

''Only because none of them knew that I am Mr. Fang's—what do you American's call it?—his snitch.'' Bon glanced toward Inchon, then off to the south as if to insure no cars were coming. ''I never meant to put myself in their line of fire. But when Mr. Park told me to take the attaché case to you, I could not refuse without arousing suspicion. So I made the best of a bad situation.''

"By dragging your heels at the hotel in the hope they would finish me off before we could get out of there."

"Very astute. Yes. And now that you have given his men the slip, it is up to me to do what they could not." Bon closed one eye and squinted down the barrel. "I imagine I will be handsomely rewarded for squeezing this trigger. I cannot wait to tell Mr. Fang. He will probably give me the money personally, this evening."

"You might want to hold the pistol with both hands," Bolan advised.

Bon cocked his head. "Both?"

"A two-handed grip works best with a machine pistol. Flip down that lever at the front part of the slide. And a Weaver stance is best for maximum control."

"A Weaver—?" Bon's eyebrows nearly pinched together. "Why are you being so helpful?"

"I wouldn't want you to miss," the soldier said, and calmly stood.

Uttering a cry in Korean, Bon sprang back. "I knew it was a trick!" he resorted to English. Sneering, he pointed the pistol at Bolan's chest and squeezed the trigger. But nothing happened. He squeezed the trigger again, and again, disbelief and fear etching his face. "What is wrong? Why will it not work?"

Bolan reached into his pocket and held out a magazine. "Guns don't shoot without ammunition."

Bon rapped his knuckles against the 93-R. "But there is a magazine in it!"

"An empty one," Bolan revealed. "The one I emptied at the hotel."

"I saw you replace it in the stairwell!"

"I put the empty one in my pocket, remember? And I switched it again shortly before we pulled off the road."

Insight filled Bon with impotent rage. "This was a trick! A test! You put the gun down and turned away to see what I would do!"

"I wasn't completely sure you were a traitor," Bolan revealed, "so I gave you enough rope to hang yourself. And you stepped right into the noose."

Swearing in Korean, Bon hurled the Beretta at the big man's head, then bolted. In his fright he fled toward the edge of the bluff. Realizing his mistake, he stopped and spun.

Bolan had sidestepped the pistol and now picked it up. Brushing off some dust, he removed the spent magazine and inserted the full one. "Let's go. Mr. Park will want to have a long talk with you."

"Never!" Bon dropped onto his belly, thrust his legs over the side and wormed down out of sight.

In no hurry, Bolan walked to the edge. The bluff was seventy to eighty feet high. Jagged boulders sprayed by surf ringed its base. "You'll never make it," he said.

Bon was groping for handholds ten feet down. His suit smeared with dirt, his cheeks caked with dust, he cried, "Shoot me if you want! That is the only way you will stop me!"

"I wouldn't waste the bullet."

The turncoat gripped a small outcropping. "Good. Just stand there while I escape. I am an excellent swimmer, American. When I am low enough, I will dive in and swim off. To catch me you must jump in after me."

Sliding the Beretta into his shoulder holster, Bolan folded his arms. "You'll never make it. Turn around before it's too late."

Lowering a leg as far as it would go, Bon gouged and scraped with his toes, seeking a purchase. "You underestimate me. But then, everyone does. Mr. Park would never think me capable of selling out. And Mr. Fang would never think me capable of turning him in, but I will one day, after I have a big enough nest egg." He was chattering to hear himself talk, a release of nervous tension. "I have it all planned out," he crowed. "I will set a trap and have the police shoot him dead before he can tell anyone about me."

"That reminds me. I should thank you."

Bon glanced up. "What for?"

"For confirming Fang is here in Inchon."

Hatred shone through the dust and sweat. "May you die a horrible death!" Bon growled, and applied his weight to the toehold he had found. It gave way, dirt cascading from under him, and he slipped. Quickly, he snatched at a small rocky spine, but missed. In a last-ditch effort the traitor seized a clump of weeds, but it came out of the ground, roots and all.

Bon screamed shrilly. He was still screaming when his body smashed onto the jagged boulders and burst asunder like an overripe melon.

Returning to the car, Bolan headed for the city. The first skirmish had gone to Fang but their private war was far from over. The Executioner was in for the long haul, come what may.

CHAPTER NINE

San Diego

Bob Walker's life was going all to hell, and he couldn't figure out why.

For one thing, he had started to have nightmares. His whole life he'd hardly ever had any. Now he'd had nightmares three nights running. Even more strangely, it was the same one, over and over. He was trying to run away from some dark menace, but his legs wouldn't work. He was frozen in place with unmitigated terror bearing down on him.

He always woke up soaked with sweat and trembling like a leaf in a gale. The nightmares were too damned realistic! That was the problem. And they wouldn't go away.

As if that weren't enough, he started to have frequent headaches. He would find it hard to concentrate, which was all the more upsetting since his work on the stealth sub was at a critical stage.

The system Walker was currently working on tied directly into several others being designed by other engineers at other facilities. To insure all the systems melded properly, the powers-that-be had decided to grant Walker a one-time access to copies of all the applicable designs and schematics. They were highly classified, so a special government courier would bring them by and then stand around for an entire day while Walker examined them to insure his system was compatible. One day, and one day alone, that was all he had. Then the courier would whisk them back into the government's safekeeping.

In addition to the headaches, Walker started to have odd feelings, or compulsions. Each afternoon an overwhelming desire came over him to pay Club X a visit. He'd resist it, or try to, but immediately after work he would find himself driving straight there.

He never stayed long. His crush on Gloria had waned, and while he still liked her, and Marcy, he didn't look forward to his visits as much as he originally had. Why that should be, he couldn't say.

He had also noticed something else rather weird. He had grown afraid of Madame Rhee. It was silly, he knew, but whenever he saw her he would feel a deep dread he couldn't explain. She was always so kind to him, always smiling and polite, always inviting him into her private office to share a drink.

Why would he be afraid of her?

Walker was pondering that very question at his drafting table when he became aware of someone saying his name. Twisting, he nearly fell off his stool when he saw his employer regarding him as if he had lost all his marbles. "Mr. Sherman! I'm sorry. I didn't hear you come in."

"I said your name five times before you looked up," Steven Sherman mentioned. An old-school engineer in his fifties, he came across to his employees more as a father figure than a boss. "You should do your daydreaming on your own time, Bob. It's important we have the damper system designed before the courier arrives in a few days."

"I'll have it completed. Don't worry on that score."

Sherman put his hand on the younger man's shoulder. "Are you all right, Bob? You've seemed a bit distracted lately."

Walker was tempted to tell about the nightmares and the headaches, but all he said was, "I think I'm fighting off a bug. I haven't felt like myself."

"Ah." Sherman smiled. "Try mega doses of vitamin C, my boy. That's what Mrs. Sherman gives me whenever I so much as sneeze. And it's done wonders. I haven't had a cold or the flu in fifteen years."

"I'll give it a try."

"That woman is a wonder," Sherman said, going on about his favorite topic. "She has my life so regimented, you would think she was a drill instructor in the Marines."

Walker dutifully laughed, even though his boss had used the same corny line maybe fifty times since they met. "It must be nice to be married," he said without thinking.

"It is, it is," Sherman said enthusiastically. "I can't recommend it enough. The benefits far outweigh the drawbacks."

There was a standing joke at Omnitronics to the effect that if Steve Sherman hadn't become an engineer and started his own firm, he'd make a dandy Cupid. The man was always trying to get his single employees married off. Sometimes he went so far as to suggest so-and-so date so-and-so because they would make "such a nice couple" or they seemed to be "as right for each other as two peas in a pod." The man meant well but he didn't seem to realize that some people *liked* being single.

"Do you snore?" Sherman asked.

"Not that I know of, sir, no."

"Neither do I. But Mrs. Sherman does. She snores like a buzz saw. I can hear her three rooms away when I'm watching TV late at night."

That was a little more than Walker cared to know, but he grinned and bore it.

"Now, you would think her snoring would drive me nuts, wouldn't you? That I wouldn't be able to get a moment's sleep because she's always waking me up."

"You'd think so," Walker said when his employer paused.

"Well, that's not the case. Would you believe that once I fall asleep, I seldom ever hear her? And when I do, all I have to do is nudge her or shake the bed. She stops and I go right back to sleep. Now what does that tell you?"

"Um, you're hinting that you want a pair of ear-plugs for Christmas?" Walker didn't have the slightest clue what it meant.

Sherman laughed uproariously, then clapped him on the back. "You and that rapier wit of yours! That was a good one, Bob. But no, that's not what I was referring to."

Walker fought down a sigh.

"It tells you that love conquers all, my boy. Love makes us blind to the faults of those we care for. Or deaf and dumb, as the case may be." Sherman chuckled and nudged him with an elbow. "Which is why I can't recommend marriage enough. And you know, you're about at the age where you should give serious thought to a lifelong mate. I know that playing the field is the thing to do nowadays, but believe me, you'll be much happier when you finally take a walk down the aisle."

"If you say so, sir."

"Well, of course, I'm not trying to pressure you into anything." Sherman started to leave, then snapped his fingers. "I almost forgot the reason I came down here. Do you remember my niece Harriet?"

"The one with the braces?"

"That's her. You would think a young woman her age would have shed them by now, wouldn't you? Anyway, she's coming for another visit in a couple of weeks, and I'm looking for someone who might be interested in treating her to a few nights on the town."

"And you thought of me?" Walker didn't know whether to be flattered or insulted.

"Actually, I've asked every eligible bachelor in the company and they've all said they would get back to me. There's no rush in letting me know. But it would be wonderful if Harriet had someone nice to date while she was here. Someone who doesn't drink or do drugs or have any other nasty vices."

Walker envisioned Gloria and Marcy in their lacy nighties and had to bite the inside of his lower lip to keep from cackling.

"Will you consider it, Bob? As a personal favor to me?"

"Certainly." He coughed to smother a snort.

"That sounded terrible, my boy. No doubt about it. You are definitely coming down with something. Remember what I said about vitamin C." Sherman breezed out of the office.

Walker let mirth spill from him unhindered. It felt good to laugh again, to forget about his woes. Bending over the drafting table, he got back to work.

The nightmares were a fluke and would end soon. The headaches were probably brought on by sinus trouble and would go away eventually. And as for Club X, once the novelty wore off he could get on with his life.

Walker grinned. Things weren't as bad as he made them out to be.

South Korea

ALLIED ELECTRONICS and Fisheries Unlimited both had offices in Inchon, South Korea. Both were subsidiaries of Diversified Industries, but Bolan picked the former because it was closer to the skyscraper stronghold of Sin Mak-Fang.

The soldier had a plan.

At two in the morning he parked his car on a windy side street a block from Allied Electronics. Turning up the collar of the trench coat he had bought that afternoon, he headed for his next confrontation with the enemy.

The coat was a size too small, but it had to do. Finding one to fit someone as big as he was in a country where the average height was considerably under six feet had been a challenge. The clerk told him his best bet was to try stores in Seoul that catered exclusively to foreigners. But Bolan wasn't about to go all the way there and back. It wasn't that important. All he needed was a coat long enough to conceal the Mini-Uzi, which was suspended by its strap under his right arm.

So now, with the stiff wind off the Yellow Sea striking him head-on, Bolan held the Uzi close to his side, ready for instant use. He smelled moisture in the air, and in the distance lightning flashed. A storm was brewing.

At that time of night the only creatures abroad were dogs and cats. Bolan didn't spy another living soul.

Allied Electronics had half a city block all to itself. The office faced to the east on a street that ran from north to south. Behind it was a warehouse for shipping and receiving, and a loading dock. As the soldier had noted earlier when he cruised the area, the shipping door was on the north side.

He had driven by three times and not seen anyone inside, nor was anyone going in or out. The shipping door had been closed. It seemed as if Allied Electronics had gone out of business, yet according to the intel in the attaché case, the company routinely funneled electronic equipment, stashed with drugs, from mainland Asia to other countries.

Bolan had began to wonder if maybe Sin Mak-Fang was lying low. Bon Chae-Ku had to have let Fang know the NIA was investigating his empire. For all Bolan knew, Fang might have fled the country.

Then, as Bolan made one last circuit shortly before dark, he saw lights and activity. The shipping door was open, and a tractor trailer had been backed up to it.

He should have expected as much. Most of the activity at the office undoubtedly occurred after the sun went down.

It worked out perfectly.

The big man had been contemplating setting fire to the place. He needed a spectacular diversion to draw some of Fang's underlings from the skyscraper and lower the odds against him when he went after Fang.

C-4 would be better but Bolan had used up all he had in Yokohama. Hal Brognola's counterpart, Mr. Park, might be willing to supply him with some, but Bolan hadn't contacted the man. He wanted nothing more to do with the NIA or any other South Korean government agency, for the simple reason he didn't know whom he could trust. Fang might have more moles like Bon in positions of authority.

So fire had seemed his best option. The risk of it raging out of control and posing a danger to nearby structures was so great, though, Bolan was glad when he saw the men and the truck. He would try something else instead.

A few light drops of rain moistened the soldier's cheeks as he slowly approached the corner. Except for the growing howl of the wind and the far-off honk of a car horn, the city was quiet.

Allied Electronics's front office was lit up, and men were moving about inside. The tractor trailer was still at the loading dock.

According to the documents Bon had given Bolan, the owner and president of Allied Electronics was Sin Cho-Hee. All of Fang's front businesses were in the nephew's name. It was smart in one respect, in that there were no paper trails linking Fang to his evil empire. But it was not so smart in another. All Cho-Hee had to do was to bump off his uncle and he could legally take over with no questions asked. Fang either trusted Cho-Hee completely, or he was confident his nephew was too afraid to ever betray him.

Bolan hoped both the uncle and nephew were still in Inchon. He looked forward to wrapping it up and being back in the States by the weekend, but he knew better than to get ahead of himself. One step at a time. First the diversion, then the assault on the citadel.

Bolan stepped off the curb and crossed the street, hunching his shoulders so he wouldn't appear so big. He made as if to walk right by the big rig, but when he established no one was in the cab, he sprinted to the trailer and ducked underneath, then carefully crabbed toward the shipping door.

Ten men were busy loading the truck. The loading area was piled high with boxes, some with Japanese writing on them, some with Korean, some in English. Bolan saw televisions and stereos stacked halfway to the ceiling.

From the look of things, Fang was having the place cleaned out. It made sense, given that the police might swoop down on Allied Electronics at any hour. Maybe Fang had heard through his sources the authorities planned to do just that, and he was beating them to the punch by getting rid of any and all incriminating evidence.

When, after about twenty minutes, the men took a break and moved toward a row of candy and soda machines, Bolan slipped from under the trailer and through a door that separated the loading dock from the shipping office.

A portly man with glasses was bent over a ledger, writing. He looked up, into the business end of the Uzi's suppressor, and froze.

"Do you speak English?" Bolan asked quietly.

The man nodded, saying, "Little bit, little bit."

"Stand up and stick your hands in your pockets. One wrong word, one wrong move, and I'll shoot you."

As if he were made of glass so fragile it would break if he moved too fast, the Korean did as he had been instructed. "Who you be? What you want?"

"I'll ask the questions. Head for the front office."

"You make mistake, mister. Big mistake."

Bolan stepped close enough to gouge the suppressor against the base of the man's neck.

"Let me worry about that. Do as I told you."

"Please, no shoot! No shoot!"

The glass door at the end of the hall was tinted. Bolan heard voices and a strange sound he couldn't identify. "How many are in there?"

"Four."

"Do anything to warn them and it will be the last thing you ever do." Bolan reached past him and slowly turned the knob.

Two of the men were riffling desks, emptying drawers. A third sorted through a pile of folders. The last worker was feeding sheets of paper to a shredder, accounting for the strange noise.

Bolan pushed the door all the way open and shoved the portly Korean inside. The other four were caught totally unprepared. Only the one shredding paper started to reach under his jacket but changed his mind when Bolan pointed the Uzi at him.

"I want all of you on the floor, now," Bolan ordered, and jabbed the suppressor against his portly prisoner. "Tell them. Tell them they get to live if they do exactly as I say."

The portly man translated. The one who was doing all the shredding answered in Korean. "Him say you know who own place?"

"Sin Mak-Fang."

"Yet you do this?" The portly man gave Bolan a look that implied he was insane. "You die. You hear?"

The other four were lowering themselves onto their stomachs but not quickly enough to suit Bolan. Sweeping the Uzi from side to side as if about to use it, he snapped, "Hurry it up!"

No translation was needed. When all five were prone, Bolan switched to the Beretta and went from one to the other, stripping them of hardware and sliding the guns toward a far corner.

"What you want?" the portly man asked as Bolan moved to the desks.

"Keep quiet." The soldier examined the folders. The contents were in Korean, so he couldn't tell what they were. He dropped some into a trash can, crumpling papers that fell out and placing them on top.

One of the men had left a cigarette burning in an ashtray. Picking it up, Bolan pressed it against one of the crumpled sheets until the paper ignited.

"What you do?" the portly man cried.

Tiny flames began to spread. Bolan helped them along by placing the cigarette on a piece of carbon paper, which caught right away. Wispy gray tendrils curled from the trash can.

"No! No!"

One of the others suddenly leaped up and charged,

heedless of the Beretta that Bolan held down low. The pistol burped, the force of the rounds flipping the man backward. He crashed into a chair, then dropped to the floor and lay still.

"Anyone else?" Bolan asked. They all wanted to rush him. He could see it in their eyes. But they weren't fools.

The flames were rising higher, crackling and hissing as they devoured the trash. Bolan added some more folders.

"You burn place down!" the portly man protested.

Bolan hoped they would think that was his plan all along. To further convince them, he lifted a burning sheet of typing paper and dropped it on top of a pile of documents on another desk.

"Stop! You crazy person!" The portly man was wringing his hands in anxiety. Bolan nudged him with a toe, saying, "Run. All of you."

"Mister?"

"Get up! Run!" Bolan pointed at the door. "The whole place will catch on fire soon. Get out while you can."

"You not kill us?"

The man acted amazed, and truth to tell, Bolan would just as soon shoot them as let them live. They earned their livelihood at the expense of countless innocents who wound up addicted to the poisons they helped ship around the world. They deserved to be shot where they lay. But if he wiped them out, there wouldn't be anyone left to contact Fang. He needed a few alive.

"Run!" Bolan thundered.

With Portly in the lead, they fled out the door and

on up the street. They wouldn't go far, Bolan knew, but that, too, was exactly as he planned.

Smoke stinging his eyes, he retraced his steps to the loading dock. He made no attempt to hide this time. Shoving on the door, he raised the Mini-Uzi.

The ten workers responsible for loading the big rig were intent on what they were doing.

A bean pole pushing a dolly piled with cartons was the first to realize they had an unwanted visitor. Shouting a warning, he sought to whip a Tokarev from under his shirt. He was too slow.

Bolan squeezed off short bursts and ran toward the truck, felling two more. A bearded Korean abruptly appeared from out of the trailer, a revolver cradled in a two-handed grip. He rushed his shot, the slug digging a furrow in the concrete. The soldier's answering rounds chopped him at the waist and pushed him back into a column of boxes that tumbled with a gargantuan crash.

The rest were scrambling for cover, all except a cocky gunner who had produced an Uzi of his own from somewhere. Roaring like a grizzly, he rushed forward, only to be met head-on by four 9 mm slugs.

Five had gone down; five remained standing.

Bolan backed toward the trailer's rear tires. His next controlled burst stitched scarlet across the torso of a hardman who leaped up from cover not fifteen feet away. Crouching beside the big tires, the Executioner discouraged the rest by emptying his magazine at the boxes the last workers were hiding behind.

With a deft, practiced motion Bolan replaced the spent magazine with a new one.

In the sudden lull he heard shouts from the direction

of the front office. Portly and the others were extinguishing the fire before the flames could spread. That, too, was exactly what he wanted them to do.

A thatch of dark hair appeared above a mound of microwaves. Instantly, Bolan fired a burst, the Mini-Uzi's chatter was punctuated by the sound of blood gurgling in a human throat.

Ducking under the trailer, the soldier backed toward the cab. Someone cut loose with an autopistol, and lead smacked into the diesel. A revolver boomed twice, but the slugs came nowhere near him. The gunners were firing blind.

The street bordering the north side of the building was still empty. Moving out from under the trailer, Bolan placed his back against the outer wall and raced toward the corner.

Someone had propped the front door open, and smoke was seeping out. Two men stood outside. Both had taken off their jackets and were flapping them to disperse the smoke before it rose into the sky. Naturally, they didn't want it to be noticed. If the fire department was called to the scene, the police wouldn't be very far behind.

Neither was looking in Bolan's direction. He felt safe in sprinting across the street and down the block to his car. He'd left the door unlocked, and within moments he had the engine cranked over and was picking up speed.

Phase one of Bolan's plan had worked out better than he'd anticipated. But it was only the prelude to phase two, which would tax all the skills he possessed. Sneaking onto an open loading dock was one thing.

Sneaking to the top of a twenty-four-story building would be quite another.

The skyscraper loomed like a gigantic spike thrusting at the sky. Bolan leaned over the steering wheel and tilted his head to see the upper floors. Fang's lair was bound to be guarded by an army of gunners. And although the floor diagrams Bon had given to Bolan made no mention of them, there might be electronic security measures he had to deactivate.

Venturing up there would be like walking into a den of vipers. The odds were stacked against him, but the Executioner had never let the odds stop him before, and he wasn't about to let them stop him now.

In the eternal war against the armies of the night, no sacrifice was too great.

Mack Bolan's outlook on the impending firefight, as well as his personal philosophy, could be summed up in three little words: do or die.

CHAPTER TEN

Divide and conquer. It was one of the oldest tactics in the book, a time-honored stratagem that had brought success to more armies down through the ages than any other.

The Executioner was hoping it would work for him, as well. He had hit Allied Electronics to draw shooters away from the skyscraper. There was even the possibility Fang himself would rush to the scene, which would spare Bolan having to hunt him down. Or, rather, hunt him up, because Fang lived in the penthouse at the top of the skyscraper.

Bolan was parked half a block away, hunched low in his seat, only his eyes above the dashboard. From where he sat, he had a clear view of the parking lot at the rear. By his watch it had been eleven minutes since he struck Allied Electronics, and so far there had been no activity of any kind.

There were only two exits from the building. The main entrance fronted a major thoroughfare with few parking spaces, which had led Bolan to conclude that Fang's underlings used the parking lot. Nine vehicles filled random slots, including a pair of black vans that had parked side by side.

Another minute went by, and Bolan began to think his ruse hadn't worked. Suddenly, men in dark suits rushed out. Bolan counted six, seven, eight all told. And at their head was none other than Sin Cho-Hee, the nephew. They piled into the two vans and screeched out of the lot, heading for Allied Electronics.

Bolan was out of his car the instant they were out of sight. Sprinting across the lot, he cracked open the door. An empty tiled hall led toward the front.

Slipping in, Bolan padded forward. According to the diagrams provided by Mr. Park, the elevators were ahead and to the left, on the near side of the lobby. He was on the lookout for security guards or janitors or anyone else who might be abroad at that hour. If spotted, he couldn't very well shoot them. They might be perfectly innocent. Not everyone in the building was in Fang's employ.

The lobby was quiet. Bolan halted and scanned it, and it was well he did. At a desk along the right wall sat an elderly guard in a brown uniform. He had his feet propped up and was reading a magazine. Bolan couldn't tell if he was armed.

The soldier's main concern was that no alarm be sounded. Four elevators provided access to higher floors, but to reach them, he had to cross approximately forty feet of open space. The guard was bound to spot him and hit the panic button.

A distraction was called for. Pivoting, Bolan retraced his steps to a pair of bathrooms he had passed. He went into the men's. A large metal trash bin was just what he needed, and he propped the door open with it. Drawing his Ka-bar fighting knife, he cut a strip of cloth from the towel dispenser. Wadding it, he shoved the cloth down the drain of the sink nearest the door, as far down as he could, plugging it. Next he turned both faucets on full blast, the hot and the cold alike. Within seconds the small sink was half-full.

Stepping to the door, Bolan kept watch while the water level continued to rise. It spilled over the top and rapidly rippled across the floor, a minor flood in the making.

Bolan gave the trash bin a resounding kick that was bound to be heard by the guard. Darting out before the door could close on him, he ran to the women's washroom, slipped just inside and peered out.

Half a minute passed, then the guard hurried into view, his head cocked, listening. Strapped to his waist was a revolver. He advanced cautiously, glancing right and left as if in mortal dread for his life.

Bolan could hear the gushing water in the men's room, and in another few moments so did the guard. The man stepped to the door and gingerly pushed it open. On seeing the spreading pool, he muttered in Korean and dashed inside to stem the flow.

The soldier bolted toward the elevators. If all went well, the guard would chalk up the overflow to some-one's warped idea of a practical joke, to vandals, maybe. But Bolan had to be long gone before the man got done in the bathroom. He stabbed the button to the first elevator and the door pinged open. Springing to the control panel, Bolan ran his forefinger over the vertical rows of floor selector buttons. He wanted the twenty-fourth floor, but the buttons only went as high as twenty. Keenly conscious that precious seconds were being wasted, he pressed it.

The door pinged shut and the car started to rise. Bolan moved to the middle and looked up. Inset in the canopy was a maintenance hatch that also doubled as an emergency exit. Rising onto his toes, he placed both palms flat against the panel and pushed. It had to be jiggled loose. Pushing it aside, he jumped, caught hold of the edge and levered himself up onto the top of the car. The hatch went neatly back in place.

Gloom shrouded the shaft. The creak of the big cable and the whisper of the well-greased rollers in their guide rails were the only sounds.

There had been nothing in any of the floor diagrams to indicate the elevators only went as far as the twentieth. Bolan wondered if maybe Bon had left out that crucial tidbit on purpose.

It was more than likely that when the building was initially constructed, all the elevators went all the way to the top. But then Fang came along and took control. As a security precaution, he would only want one to reach the penthouse. Maybe he had also restricted the number that could reach Diversified Industries, on the twenty-first floor.

It made Bolan's search-and-destroy mission doubly difficult.

He glanced up into the shaft and heard the muted whine of the electric motor powering the pulley. Taking his pencil flashlight, he speared the beam overhead to gauge how much higher he had to go. His hunch about the elevators was borne out when the one he was on came to a stop and his beam revealed the car wasn't anywhere near the top of the shaft.

Bolan switched off the flashlight, slid it into his pocket and pressed an ear to the hatch. Satisfied no one had entered, he opened it and swung lightly down. The door opened with its familiar ping and he stepped into the hall, the Mini-Uzi tucked to his side. The hallway was deserted.

If one of the four elevators went to the top, it wasn't apparent from the outside. Bolan tried the stairwell instead. It wasn't locked, and he swiftly climbed to the next level.

Bolan looked through the small window in the landing door. The hall was dark, but there was enough light to reveal an elevator midway down, as well as a waiting area lined with chairs. He could see large brass letters but couldn't quite read what they said.

In the U.S. it was illegal to keep an emergency exit locked, and the soldier hoped the same applied in South Korea. He tried the knob and the door swung silently outward. Sidling through, he leveled the Uzi and glided along the wall until he came to the brass sign. Diversified Industries, Inc.

Through a glass door Bolan spotted a man at a desk. This one was reading a newspaper. Evidently, the security guard hadn't called up to report an intruder.

Returning to the stairwell, Bolan ascended to the twenty-second floor. Overhead lights blazed, and he saw two gunners in dark suits lounging near a candy machine. A third came out of a room and joined them.

Fang had a small army at his disposal, and it stood to reason some were on guard twenty-four hours a day. If so, it also stood to reason that Fang had to have rooms set aside where they could relax and rest when they weren't needed.

The way Bolan had it figured, the twenty-first floor was devoted to Diversified Industries. The twenty-second, this one, was where the gunners hung their guns. Anyone who wanted to get at Fang had to go through them. On the twenty-third floor, according to the floor layouts, were two large conference rooms and several small offices. The twenty-fourth was the penthouse.

Bolan continued to climb. The next corridor was a beehive of activity, men and women moving about. He suspected that his assault on Allied Electronics had stirred up a hornet's nest. He continued onward.

Before he reached the last landing, Bolan heard voices. A stocky Korean he had never seen before was addressing two others. When all three entered the elevator and it started down, he emerged and crept toward a pair of wide mahogany doors across from it.

This floor oozed wealth befitting a crime lord of Fang's stature. Luxurious paneling and carpet were complemented by paintings on the walls.

Bolan saw no cameras or evidence of alarm systems. According to the intel Bon had supplied, there was none. Yet Bolan wasn't about to take it for granted.

Halting, the soldier tried a gold handle on one of the doors. There was a soft click, and he pushed the door wide enough to slip within. He was in a foyer. Quietly shutting the door again, he took a step—and knew he had blown it. Out in the hall the elevator pinged open. Simultaneously, there was a louder click behind him. Spinning, he worked both handles and discovered he was boxed in.

Bolan pointed the Mini-Uzi at the lock, determined to fight his way out.

"I would rather you didn't," a deep, resonant voice boomed from a hidden speaker somewhere above him. "At this moment eight of my men are on the other side. They will cut you down before you can reach the stairs. Even if you did, more men are waiting on the floor below to prevent your escape."

The door at the other end of the foyer opened. Again Bolan spun.

It was Kon-Li. He beckoned and moved aside.

"Please lower your weapon," the deep voice said. "Yes, you can shoot him if you wish. But if you look past my bodyguard, you will see six other men, all armed."

Bolan had already spotted them.

"You know who this is, American," the voice said. "Just as I know you have come a long way to find me. Would you like to learn why I let you get this far without hindrance? If so, give your Uzi to my bodyguard and let him frisk you. If not, I shall give an order for all my men to rush you at once. What chance do you think you will have?"

Absolutely none, Bolan realized. Oh, he'd take some of them with him, but their overwhelming firepower would bring him down.

"What will it be, American?" Fang asked. "Would you like ten more minutes of life?"

Bolan wanted more than that. Reversing his grip on the Mini-Uzi, he extended it toward the giant.

Kon-Li passed the SMG to a gunner. Then he patted Bolan down, from shoulders to socks, relieving the soldier of the Beretta, the Ka-bar combat knife, the flashlight, his spare magazines and everything else in Bolan's pockets. His arms laden, Kon-Li grunted and walked into the next room.

Bolan's skin crawled as he followed the man. The gunners covered him every step of the way, each appearing all too eager to mow him down if he so much as sneezed. The carpet, the drapes, the upholstery were all done in red. On the right wall were monitors hooked to concealed surveillance cameras. One monitor showed the stairwell. Others displayed each of the corridors from the twenty-first floor on up.

Seated in a high-backed chair was a figure who fit the description in his dossier to a tee. Powerfully built, dressed in expensive clothes and shoes, his fingers and tie glittering with diamonds, the bald man smiled.

"Sin Mak-Fang," Bolan said.

"You have the advantage of me, American," Fang said suavely, and pointed at a smaller chair across from him.

They studied each other, Bolan's hands in his lap, next to his belt buckle. The North Korean had an air about him, a presence, an aura of keen intelligence and latent menace.

"You must be wondering why I did not have you gunned down." Fang broke the silence.

"The thought did cross my mind."

"Curiosity, American. Simple curiosity. An urge to meet you face-to-face, to take your measure."

"Why am I so privileged?"

"For the same reason a hunter watches a bear he is going to shoot before he actually pulls the trigger. For the same reason martial artists and boxers study their opponents before they step onto the mat or into the ring.''

''Or the same reason a cat toys with a mouse before killing it,'' Bolan said.

Fang chuckled. ''Exactly. You have caused me much trouble. You have destroyed a drug shipment worth millions, and set back my timetable by many months. You are a worthy adversary.''

Bolan was more interested in the telling comment Fang had made than in being praised to death. ''Your timetable?''

''The key to success in business and any other endeavor is to set goals and then strive to meet them,'' Fang responded amiably. He was totally relaxed, totally at ease, befitting someone who believed he was in complete command of the situation.

Bolan took a leap of logical deduction. ''I spoiled your plans to set up a drug pipeline into the U.S.''

''Yes. I freely admit it. But it is only a temporary, if expensive, setback. Within half a year I will be back on schedule.''

''Your masters in North Korea must be very proud of you.''

Some of Fang's good humor faded. ''You are behind the times, American. I have severed my ties with the RDEI. I outgrew them.''

''They let you walk? Just like that?'' Bolan eased his right hand onto his belt buckle and began to loosen it.

''They have no say in the matter,'' Fang said testily. ''I served them long and well. I did all they expected of me, and more. They have no cause to complain now that I have reached the point where my organization is as strong—no, stronger—than they are." Fang touched his diamond stickpin. "I dictate terms to them, not the other way around. They would not dare provoke me. My organization spans half the globe."

"And it will come crashing down when you do."

"Wishful thinking, American. Who is going to stop me? You? I think not. The South Koreans? By tomorrow night I will be far from their petty little country. When they finally get around to raiding Diversified Industries and Allied Electronics, they will find empty offices."

"You're relocating?"

Fang was as smug as only an egotist could be. "This skyscraper is but one of a hundred buildings I own. I have contingency plans within contingency plans."

Bolan had the buckle undone. Now he began to pull on the belt, barely moving his fingers so as not to attract attention. His trench coat concealed what he was doing from the gunners, but Fang might catch on if he wasn't careful.

"I must hand it to you, though, American. Were it not for you, I would have no need to shut down operations here in Inchon. Blowing up Hideo Koto's dock. Terminating my lieutenant, Hyun An-Kor. Hitting Syngman Construction this morning and Allied Electronics tonight. You have planned your moves wisely."

Bolan realized that Fang didn't know about Bon Chae-Ku yet. "I didn't terminate anyone named An-Kor, and I've never been to Syngman Construction."

He did recall, though, that the construction firm had

been on the list of front companies relayed by Mr. Park.

"Do not insult my—" Fang began, and did a double take. "You are being honest with me, aren't you?" His forehead creased. "But if not you, then who would dare—?" Again he stopped.

Suddenly, from somewhere below, the skyscraper resounded to the *whump* of a tremendous blast. The windows rattled; the chairs jumped.

On one of the monitors a group of five men clad in black combat fatigues and ski masks briefly appeared, then the monitor went dead.

Fang shot erect. "So! I am afraid I must cut this short, American. I have underestimated my former masters. In their monumental arrogance they have seen fit to challenge me." He made for the rear wall as a second explosion vibrated the furniture. "Kon-Li!" he said, and barked commands in Korean.

The giant had placed all of Bolan's hardware on a table. Without a backward glance he and four gunners formed a wedge around their boss.

Fang pressed a spot on the wall, and a door-sized panel slid aside to reveal a private elevator. Without delay he ushered his underlings into it, then glanced at Bolan. "A wise man picks his own battlegrounds," he said.

The door closed and the elevator whined downward.

Bolan glanced at the monitors again. The camera in the stairwell had been knocked out of commission. He heard autofire, then a series of blasts. A war was being waged. People were shouting. Screams pierced the din.

The two hardmen left behind were also listening, and they didn't like what they heard. One came toward him, a silenced pistol held rock steady. His intention was clear. He had been directed to finish off Bolan.

Bolan had the belt bunched in his hands. He'd intended to use it as a last resort on Fang, to wrap it around the man's neck and threaten to choke him if the gunners didn't lower their weapons. But now Fang was gone, and the oncoming shooter wasn't about to let him get close enough to apply a choke hold.

The other gunner glanced nervously at the door. He said something to his companion, perhaps telling him to hurry.

The man assigned to whack Bolan glanced back and replied. It was all the opening the Executioner needed. Surging up out of the chair, he threw his belt at the Korean's face. The gunner reacted as most people would. Not knowing what Bolan had thrown, he instinctively brought up his other hand to protect himself even as he snapped off a shot.

Bolan sidestepped, and the slug missed by a hair. Taking a long stride, the soldier launched himself at his adversary. The gunner swatted the belt aside and tried to take better aim, but Bolan was on him before he could. His shoulder smashed into the man's chest, propelling the shooter back into the second hardman. Both staggered against the wall, the second one yelping in Korean.

Pivoting, Bolan dived for the table, his fingers closing on the Beretta. Tucking into a shoulder roll, he pushed onto his knees as the two men squeezed off rounds that punched into the carpet.

With a skill honed by countless hours of practice, Bolan fired two short bursts.

The gunners died where they stood. The man on the right got off one more shot, but it, too, missed.

Bolan didn't linger. A third explosion, much closer than the previous two, spurred him into snatching up his weapons and stuffing them into whatever pockets were handy.

All the monitors were dark now except for the one that displayed the hall on the twenty-second floor. As Bolan looked on, several men dressed in loose-fitting black combat fatigues appeared. All three wore black ski masks and carried folding-stock versions of the North Korean Type 58 assault rifle, which was yet another of the many AK copies manufactured by various countries worldwide.

The trio engaged a knot of Fang's men in fierce combat. Fang's gunners held their ground until one of the trio pitched a grenade. Then it was every man for himself, and half were caught in the blast radius.

The three North Koreans moved on, chopping down the opposition relentlessly. Fang's men were no match for them. Most were ordinary criminals with no special expertise in weaponry or warfare, but it was obvious to Bolan the three North Koreans were much more. They meshed perfectly as a team, as a unit, the earmark of highly trained professionals. Commandos, perhaps. Or an elite assassination squad.

Whoever they were, they had inadvertently helped save Bolan's life.

The soldier ran to the corridor. Smoke seeped from the elevator, along with the acrid stench of burned flesh. He wondered if Fang had been caught in it on its way down. If so, it saved him a lot of trouble.

Pivoting, Bolan raced to the stairwell. The explosions were bound to bring the police to the scene, and he preferred to be long gone when they got there.

Bolan peered through the window in the stairwell door, saw no one and pushed his way through. He had taken a single step when warm metal pressed against his ear and a thickly accented voice warned, "Freeze or die!"

The soldier did as he was told, and a figure dressed in black stepped in close to relieve him of the Mini-Uzi. There was a brief moment when he considered ducking and twisting and delivering a blow to the man's throat, but it was just as well he didn't. Another commando materialized, covering him. "If you're looking for Sin Mak-Fang, he isn't here."

"How do you know?" the man who had the gun to his ear asked.

Bolan told him about the hidden elevator.

The commandos conversed in Korean. "Down the stairs," the first one ordered.

More explosions ripped the building. By the time they reached the twenty-first floor, smoke was pouring through the shattered stairwell door. The pair who had taken Bolan prisoner halted, and the one who seemed to be in charge yelled in Korean. Two others came out of the smoke, supporting a wounded comrade between them.

Bolan guessed they were the same trio he had seen on the video monitor. The one in the middle had a sucking chest wound, a bad sign.

"Keep going lower," the leader instructed him.

They descended five more floors, moving briskly despite having to practically carry the man with the wound. Stopping again, they proceeded to strip off their baggy combat fatigues and ski masks. Under their black clothes they wore lightweight street clothes. They balled up their combat garb, stuffed it into a suitcase they had previously stashed in a corner of the landing, and shoved all their assault rifles, as well as Bolan's weapons, into an oversize duffel bag.

They worked quickly, efficiently. Within ninety seconds they had effected a radical transformation, from an elite military squad to a group of seemingly ordinary civilians. They all had pistols. The leader, who took charge of Bolan, pressed a Soviet-made Stechkin machine pistol against Bolan's ribs.

"Walk slowly. Do nothing to attract attention."

One of the others opened the stairwell door. The floor they were on was lined with apartments, and the people who lived there were stumbling out in sleepy-eyed confusion, wanting to know what had awakened them.

Rather than head for the elevators in a group and perhaps incite suspicion, the North Koreans proceeded at ten-second intervals. The wounded man had to be helped, but he gamely stood as straight as he could, his teeth clenched against the pain.

Bolan and the leader were last. An elderly woman in a heavy robe pointed at Bolan and said a few words. Maybe she was asking what a foreigner was doing there. The leader of the strike team answered, and whatever he said seemed to satisfy her.

The North Koreans had the elevator all to themselves. The apartment dwellers were unaware a fire had broken out on the upper floors or there would have been mass panic. As the leader touched the button to close the elevator door, Bolan couldn't resist saying, "I saw smoke coming out of one of the shafts."

"We blew the other cables but not this one," the leader said haltingly in English. He was a muscular man with craggy features. "In case a strategic retreat was called for."

"Who are you?" Bolan inquired as the car started down. "What do you want with me?"

"We have been watching you, American. We hunt the same quarry." Not so much as a hint of friendliness was visible in the leader's face.

"That doesn't tell me much."

"We will compare notes later, as you would say. You will tell us who you work for, and why you are after Sin Mak-Fang."

"If I refuse?"

"I would not recommend it. The last person who refused to tell me what I wanted to know was found floating facedown in the Yellow Sea."

CHAPTER ELEVEN

The storm had broke in all its elemental fury. Large, stinging drops lashed the Executioner as he was ushered from the skyscraper by the North Koreans. Glancing up, he saw flames leap from shattered windows on the upper floors. The fire was spreading, but not as fast as it would without the rain. The storm was a blessing in disguise.

Sirens wailed to the northeast. Fire engines were on their way.

Bolan had seen no sign of the elderly security guard as he was guided across the lobby. He thought the man might have gone up to investigate the explosions. Then, as the North Koreans neared the entrance, Bolan glanced toward the desk the guard had been seated at and saw a pair of shoes jutting out. "That wasn't necessary," he said.

The leader gazed in the same direction. "Secondary threats on a mission are always neutralized. I could not run the risk of him alerting Sin Mak-Fang or the authorities."

"You could have bound and gagged him."

"That would take too much time. Why do you care anyway, American? What was he to you?"

Bolan didn't answer.

Now, as they hustled him toward a sedan parked at the rear of the parking lot, the soldier thought of all the tenants who might not make it out of the sky-scraper, those who would succumb to smoke inhalation or be trapped in their apartments by the sheets of flame.

The North Koreans were efficient, yes, but they were also ruthless. They had no qualms about slaying innocent civilians.

One of them threw the suitcase into the car's trunk, another took the wheel and a third hung on to the duffel.

"Into the back seat," the leader directed, gesturing. "I will be right behind you."

Bolan was wedged in the middle, and pistols were jammed against his side to discourage him from trying anything. The wounded man had to be helped into the front. Weak and starkly pale, he let his chin droop to his chest.

The leader spoke to the driver, who pulled out. It was soon obvious they weren't heading anywhere particular. Several times they reversed direction, and twice they went down the same block.

After a bit, when the leader was sure they weren't being trailed, he turned from the rear window. "We will talk, American, and I will decide what to do with you." He leaned against the door. "It is my guess you are CIA. Is this not so?"

Bolan had to marvel at how the Central Intelligence Agency was blamed for every covert op under the sun. The media, the public, even foreign governments tended to forget it wasn't the only intelligence organization in the U.S. "You're a good guesser," he said, playing along.

"And you were sent to terminate Sin Mak-Fang because your government learned about his brothel. Is that also not true?"

"How is it you know so much?" Bolan asked, hoping more would be revealed.

The leader shrugged. "Why else would they want him dead? No government likes to have its most closely guarded secrets stolen from under its very nose, eh?"

"No, they don't," Bolan agreed. Fang was stealing classified information? And it had something to do with a brothel?

"No government likes to be betrayed, either," the North Korean said. "And Sin Mak-Fang has betrayed ours."

"He mentioned something about that," Bolan remarked.

"You must be aware of the death of Chang Do-Young. He was high in the RDEI. A man of great influence in the Party. He was also the traitor's mentor, the one who helped Sin Mak-Fang rise to a position of power. And in return what did Sin do? He had Chang killed."

"You saw it happen?"

The North Korean shook his head. "No. We did not need to. We came south with Chang, across the DMZ. He was going to give Sin one last chance to submit to the wishes of the Central Committee. If that failed, we were to be sent in to dispose of him."

It wasn't hard to read between the lines. "Chang set up a meeting with Sin and never came back?"

A flash of lightning illuminated the leader's flinty countenance. "We have not heard from Chang since, no. I warned him not to go. I told him Sin could not be trusted. But he would not listen. They were old friends, Chang said. Sin would never harm him."

The man in the front on the passenger side twisted and spoke urgently. Leaning forward, the leader pressed a hand against the one who had been wounded, then frowned. "Yim is dead. Another one I owe Sin Mak-Fang."

"Your orders were to eliminate him?" Bolan probed.

"By whatever means necessary if he did not agree to accompany Chang back to our country," the leader confirmed. "As soon as it was apparent Chang had been slain, I put the plan into effect."

"Sin told me he had severed his ties with your government, that he wasn't worried because he's strong enough to hold his own."

"He said that, did he? It sounds like him. He thinks he is invincible, that one. Sin forgets who put him where he is. He forgets it was RDEI seed money that made it all possible, that it was the RDEI who set up the first brothel and chose him to run it."

Yet another reference to brothels. Bolan needed to learn how they fit into the scheme of things.

The North Korean had gone on. "At the time we did not know Sin harbored a secret ambition. It was two years before we discovered he was siphoning money from the brothels into drugs and guns. When we did, we made our next mistake."

"What would that be?"

"We did not kill him the moment we found out.

Chang thought it was wonderful his protégé had so much initiative. The RDEI was all for Sin expanding his operations. It lined our coffers with badly needed funds and was a prime source of intelligence data. Little did we realize.''

"Sin had become too big for his britches," Bolan said.

The leader looked at him. "Britches? Oh, an American figure of speech. Yes, that is precisely what happened. He let all his power and all the money go to his head."

"He's had years to build his empire," Bolan commented.

"Five years, to be exact. And he has done well. As much as I despise him, I cannot deny he has a genius for criminal enterprise." The leader glanced out the rear window at a truck that had appeared. A block later it turned, and he resumed his account. "About a year ago the RDEI began hearing rumors that Sin was selling intel on the open market, which was rightfully ours. We developed the chemical, not him."

What chemical? Bolan wanted to ask.

"Agents were sent to infiltrate his organization. But each always disappeared after a while. So finally the Central Committee summoned Sin Mak-Fang to North Korea, but he refused to go."

"So Chang took it on himself to try and persuade him."

"And now Chang has also disappeared. But Sin has outsmarted himself. He cannot defy the Central Committee any longer and live. He is a traitor, a blight on the RDEI's record. We will do whatever it takes to bring him down.'' The man paused. ''Which brings us to you.''

''I was wondering when you would get around to me.''

''We were on the roof of a building near Allied Electronics, about to move in and shut them down, when you showed up. I did not interfere because I wanted to see what you were up to. When you left, we shadowed you.''

Bolan hadn't seen anyone following him. They were pros, these North Koreans.

''It was plain to me we shared the same goal. I let you go up after Sin, thinking that while you kept Sin's men busy, my squad could sneak on in and dispose of him. But it did not work out as I planned.''

''Join the club.''

''Now the question is, what do I do with you, American?'' The leader gave it to Bolan straight. ''I should kill you. You are an enemy of my government. Your people would never know. They would think Sin Mak-Fang was responsible.''

Bolan waited. He would resist, of course, but with two pistols jammed into his ribs he would be dead before he landed a blow.

''As I said, you and I have the same goal. We both want Sin Mak-Fang dead. But achieving that goal will not be as simple as I thought. He is wily, that one. His resources are vast. It could well be that he will elude me. Or perhaps kill me before I kill him.'' The leader issued orders to the driver, who wheeled onto a side street and pulled over to the curb.

Unsure of what they had in store for him, Bolan girded himself to fight back.

"I am letting you live, American. Not because I give a damn about you, because I do not. Not because it is the right thing to do—leaving an enemy alive is never right. I am letting you live for the same reason I have told you all that I have." The man paused. "Because with both of us after Sin Mak-Fang, the better the chance that one of us will get him. Maybe it will be you who does the honors. I do not care which of us does it, just as long as he dies. Just so he pays for betraying our country and Chang's trust."

Bolan wasn't fooled. That was only part of it. Fang was an embarrassment to the RDEI, to the Party overlords who had invested so much in him only to have it flung in their faces. They wanted him disposed of before word of what he had done spread.

The leader opened his door and slid from the car, covering Bolan as he did. "Get out slowly," he said, and launched into a string of Korean.

The man on the front passenger side also climbed out. He took Bolan's weapons from the duffel, removed the magazines from both the Mini-Uzi and the Beretta and placed everything on the curb on the other side of the street.

"In case you get ideas," the leader said.

Thunder boomed overhead. Rain drenched Bolan as he unfurled and backed off, his hands out from his sides. "I won't try anything."

The leader nodded curtly and started to climb back in.

"One question," Bolan said.

"Yes?"

"I know you won't reveal who you are, but I would like to know one thing."

"Which is?"

"Your rank."

The North Korean's teeth shone dully in the downpour. "Our military bearing always gives us away, does it not? I am a colonel. You?"

"I have no rank."

The colonel's dark eyes narrowed. "Not now, perhaps, but you did once. You are a solider at heart, like me, American. I can tell. What rank have you held?"

"I was a sergeant once."

"A sergeant?" The colonel chuckled. "Leave it to you Americans to send a noncom to do an officer's job." With that, he climbed into the sedan and slammed the door. It immediately sped off.

Bolan reclaimed his weapons. He had to contact Brognola and inform him of the latest developments. Then all he could do was wait for the Feds to get a line on where Sin Mak-Fang had gone. Destroying Fang's operation in Inchon counted for little unless they could get Fang himself.

In effect, they were back to square one.

San Diego

"WHAT WAS THAT? Repeat what you just told me, Robert," Madame Rhee commanded. They were seated in her private office, Walker strapped into the steel chair as usual. Her husband, Kim, was behind it, still holding the hypodermic he had administered. Two other men were in the shadows. "This time speak clearly. Do not mumble."

Walker's face was slightly flushed, his eyes dilated, physical reactions to the potent chemicals in his system. He answered in a robotic drone, his face empty of all emotion, another trademark of the chemicals. "In three days the courier arrives."

"The one you told me about? The one who brings stealth sub systems for you to study? Including the cloaking blueprints?"

"Yes."

"Can you steal them for me, Robert? Is it possible you can bring them here without the courier knowing?"

"No."

Madame Rhee had forgotten she had to phrase her questions to elicit specific answers. Otherwise, those under the influence of the brainwashing drug tended to answer in monosyllables. "Explain please, Robert."

"The courier is not allowed to let the documents out of his sight. He must stay close to me the whole time I am studying them, and when I am done, he will take them away."

Madame Rhee glanced at Kim. "The Americans have tightened their procedures since they let the Chinese steal their most precious nuclear secrets right out from under their noses."

To Walker, she said, "Robert, can you make copies of the designs without the courier knowing it?"

"No."

"Why not?"

"The copy machine is on the next floor up. If I asked to take the documents upstairs, the courier would go with me."

"I see."

Madame Rhee motioned to her husband, who came around the desk to confer. "We must have this information at all costs. Since he can't obtain the documents or copies, we must rely on his memory.''

"The sooner he comes here after seeing the designs, the fresher his memory will be," Kim noted.

"I want a video camera set up. And have a tape recorder running as a backup. We must record everything for Sin Mak-Fang.''

"This will be a great coup," Kim said. "He will reward us greatly.''

Grinning at the thought, Madame Rhee turned to Walker. "Robert, you will do exactly as I say.''

"I will do exactly as you say.''

"After the courier leaves, you are to come straight here.''

"I will come straight here.''

Be specific, Madame Rhee reminded herself. "You will tell your employer you are not feeling well. You will leave work right away. You will get in your car and drive to Club X. Come directly to my office and knock on the door. Do you understand, Robert?''

"I understand.''

"You will tell no one what you are doing or why you are doing it. You will speak to no one on the way here. Is this also understood?''

"I will tell no one, speak to no one.''

"Excellent. Now, one last thing. When I snap my fingers, you will fall into a deep sleep. You will sleep for one hour, then you will awaken. On waking up, you will not remember any of this. You will not remember being injected, you will not remember telling me about the design systems for the stealth sub or about the courier. Is that clear?''

"It is clear.''

"All you will remember is being with Gloria and sharing a drink with me. You will remember us talking about how fond you are of her, how much you adore her, how you can't bear to be away from her."

"I will remember," Walker said in his monotone.

Madame Rhee snapped her fingers, and he was instantly asleep. She watched the rhythmic rise and fall of his chest a bit, then rose and left her office, Kim in tow. "I will be back at my desk before he wakes up. Right now you must encrypt a message to Mr. Fang. Inform him of the courier's visit and the steps we have taken."

"You are doing so well, my wife, I would not be surprised if he places you in charge of all the brothels before the year is out. He has mentioned how he needs someone he can rely on to oversee things. And from there, who knows?"

"Your ambition is showing," Madame Rhee said, and grinned. All rungs on the ladder took her one step nearer the pinnacle.

"It is unfortunate you could not lure Walker's employer here. The head of Omnitronics would be a gold mine of information."

"Based on what Walker has told me, Steven Sherman is too much of a prude to visit a house of prostitution. He is one of those who sees sex outside marriage as evil."

"Americans are so strange."

"Tell me something I don't know."

South Korea

SIN CHO-HEE WAS NOT a happy man.

His sour mood had started when he was roused from

a sound sleep by Kon-Li, who informed him that his uncle wanted to see him immediately. Cho-Hee hurriedly dressed and rushed to Sin Mak-Fang's private chambers. His uncle had gotten straight to the point.

"I have just received a call from Allied Electronics. They have been hit. I want you to go there, restore order, assess the damage and report back to me by dawn. Take however many men as you want."

As always, Cho-Hee strived his best to carry out his uncle's wishes. He had rushed to Allied Electronics. The slaughter he found had been appalling, all the more so when he learned only one man was responsible. One man! An American, too, from what the survivors said.

Cho-Hee placed a quick call to his uncle's private number and relayed the news.

He thought his uncle would be pleased by his diligence, but Sin Mak-Fang had hung up without a word of praise.

Next Cho-Hee set about restoring order. He told his men to line the bodies up in the warehouse and cover them with blankets. Those involved with shredding documents were instructed to carry on with their work. Guards were posted at the entrance and the loading-dock door.

An hour after his arrival Cho-Hee had everything well in hand. He went to the front office to place another call to his uncle and was just starting to dial when one of the men called his name and pointed to the east.

The upper floors of the skyscraper were on fire. The rain had tapered to a drizzle so there was no mistaking the blazing glow for anything other than what it was. Cho-Hee finished dialing and waited anxiously for his uncle to pick up the receiver. When Sin Mak-Fang didn't answer after twenty rings, Cho-Hee dialed the number for Diversified Industries. Someone was supposed to man the phone there twenty-four hours a day. But by the tenth ring no one responded, and he was set to hang up when finally someone did.

"Help us! Please! Help us! We're trapped! The flames! The smoke! I can barely see!"

"This is Sin Cho-Hee, Sin Mak-Fang's nephew," Cho-Hee identified himself. "Who am I talking to?"

"Sir, this is Gui Kyu-Thah." The man fell victim to a coughing fit.

Cho-Hee had to think hard to remember that Gui was a street punk hired several months ago as a lower-echelon gun. "Where is my uncle? I must speak to him immediately."

"He is gone, sir." Again Gui hacked violently.

"Gone? Gone where?"

"Word is that he left shortly after we were attacked, right before the fire broke out. Please, sir. Get help. Four of us are trapped in this office." Gui Kyu-Thah sputtered and wheezed. "The elevators will not work! And the smoke in the hall is so thick we would never make it to the stairwell."

Cho-Hee tried to absorb the news. The skyscraper attacked? His uncle nowhere to be found? "Are you sure my uncle left? Are you sure he wasn't killed?"

Gui was breathing like a bellows. "My eyes burn! My lungs hurt! Where is the fire department? Why haven't they reached us yet?"

"I am positive they will soon," Cho-Hee lied

through his teeth. "Be brave." He gazed at the flames gusting into the night. "But about my uncle—"

"I only know what I was told, sir," Gui said.

"What about Kon-Li? Have you seen him?"

The line abruptly went dead. Cho-Hee pumped the plunger to restore the dial tone and dialed the number again but this time got a busy signal. Furious, he slammed down the phone, pointed at three of his men and barged on out of the office, shouting over his shoulder for the rest to stay there until he contacted them.

Cho-Hee jogged around the corner to the vans. He planned to rush to the skyscraper, assess the situation and then decide on a course of action.

"Hurry, damn you!" Cho-Hee berated the three gunners who had just reached the corner. He ran around to the passenger side of the van he had arrived in and opened the door. To his utter astonishment, the business end of a silenced pistol was shoved into his face and he was gripped by the front of his jacket.

"Get in! Resist, and you die!"

Stupefied at the turn of events, Cho-Hee did nothing as an inky figure yanked him inside and shoved him onto the floor behind the front seats. A hand plucked his pistol from its shoulder holster. He heard the engine turn over, the squeal of tires. His own men were hollering for him to wait for them. They thought he was at the wheel! The fools!

Someone flipped Cho-Hee onto his back. In the pale gleam of the dash lights he saw a man in a ski mask. A gun muzzle was poked into his stomach, and iron fingers closed on his throat.

"Thank you for making it so easy for us, bastard."

Cho-Hee found his voice. "Who are you? What do you want?" He tried to sit up but was slammed back down. As near as he could tell, there were only two of them, the man who held him and the driver. Anger almost goaded him into striking out, but the pressure of the pistol on his gut was incentive not to do anything rash.

"We wanted you," his abductor replied, "and you walked right into our arms." The man looked out the rear window. "His men are chasing us in the other van. Go faster. Lose them and circle back."

For over five minutes Cho-Hee had to lie there, helpless, as they raced pell-mell through the night, taking corners at breakneck speed. He kept hoping his men would overtake them, but it wasn't destined to be. Soon the driver slowed to the speed limit, and shortly afterward they came to a stop.

Before Cho-Hee could think of trying to break free, the side door was flung open and two more masked men jumped in. His arms were roughly forced behind his back, and handcuffs were applied to his wrists.

"Why?" Cho-Hee demanded as they dragged him out and bodily threw him into the back of a dark sedan. All four piled in and the car took off.

"You want to know why, Sin Cho-Hee?" the one in charge asked, removing his mask to reveal a craggy, square-jawed face crowned by short-cropped hair. "I will tell you why." He drew a knife from an ankle sheath and pressed the razor tip against Cho-Hee's temple. "I am Colonel Hin. I am after your uncle, and I believe he has fled the country. You are going to tell me where I can find him."

"I have no idea," Cho-Hee said.

"Is that so? Perhaps you are telling the truth. Perhaps you are not. In any event we will know soon enough. You are going to tell us all about your uncle's organization. Every last detail."

Cho-Hee's mouth had gone dry, but he declared with more conviction than he felt, "You cannot make me talk against my will."

"Care to bet?" Colonel Hin said.

CHAPTER TWELVE

Washington, D.C.

There were days when Hal Brognola loved his job as director of the Justice Department's Sensitive Operations Group, and there were days when he hated it.

This was one of the latter.

Sin Mak-Fang had seemingly vanished off the face of the planet. The big Fed had brought the full weight of the intelligence apparatus of the United States government to bear on tracking down the renegade North Korean, with no result. All he had established was that Fang took a private jet out of Seoul shortly after the attack on the skyscraper. According to the flight plan the pilot registered, it was bound for Kyoto, Japan, but airport authorities at Kyoto insisted it never arrived.

A check of all the other major airports in Japan had proved unavailing. Where the jet had really flown to was anyone's guess.

Now all Brognola could do was twiddle his thumbs and hope for a lucky break, and on his list of top-ten things he hated, thumb-twiddling ranked up there with visits to the dentist and pompous politicians.

A knock at the door was a welcome intrusion. "It's open," the big Fed said.

In walked Agent Cliff Jeffers, a communications specialist and Justice veteran. He was currently assigned to overseeing the communications end of the search for Sin Mak-Fang.

"I hope you have good news."

"Intriguing tidbits, to say the least, sir," Jeffers responded. A short, blond man with a bulbous nose, he handed over the first of two multipage reports he held. "This just came in from the surveillance team assigned to Anthony Lucca. The audio will be relayed to us shortly if you want to hear it."

It was a transcript of a phone conversation, Brognola saw. About forty minutes ago the Don's son had received a call. Little did Anthony Lucca know his phone was being tapped. The transcript revealed the caller never identified himself, but Brognola could guess who it was. He read the exchange with increasing excitement:

Unknown Caller: "Circumstances beyond my control have delayed the shipment. I trust we can renegotiate a new delivery date."

Anthony Lucca: "You have your nerve. After your nephew reamed me a new one because we were having trouble getting up the bread, you go and pull a stunt like this?"

Unknown Caller: "It is no stunt. My shipment, and my pipeline, were targeted by certain vested interests."

Anthony Lucca: "Vested interests? What the hell does that mean? The police? Government types? Come right out and say it, for crying out loud."

Unknown Caller: "On a line we cannot guarantee is secure? You have a tendency for carelessness, Anthony, that I find most distressing."

Anthony Lucca: "Yeah, yeah. Spare me the lecture. I get enough of that crap from my old man. (Pause.) How come I'm hearing from you direct, anyway? Your nephew told me you never get personally involved."

Unknown Caller: "It could not be helped. My nephew is indisposed at the moment."

Anthony Lucca: "There you go again. Indisposed? He has the flu or something like that?"

Unknown Caller: "My nephew is unaccounted for. I have people searching for him."

Anthony Lucca: "Well, that's just peachy. As for setting a new delivery date, that's not up to me. It's up to my old man. And he's not going to like it any better than I do. We've been counting on getting that stuff. More than you know."

Unknown Caller: (Pause.) "Would your father be agreeable to a meeting?"

Anthony Lucca: "Between you and him?"

Unknown Caller: "Yes."

Anthony Lucca: (Chuckling.) "You must want to renegotiate badly if you're willing to crawl out of your cave."

Unknown Caller: "Has anyone ever accused you of having a droll sense of humor?"

Anthony Lucca: "What does 'droll' mean?"

Unknown Caller: "Speak with your father, Anthony. I would like to meet with him within the next two days. Have him choose the time and place.''

Anthony Lucca: "That soon? You must be paying the red-white-and-blue a visit, is that it?''

Unknown Caller: "I will contact you again in ten hours.''

Anthony Lucca: "Hey! Wait! Are the guns still due in tomorrow night? Some of my boys are already on their way to Eureka. If you're bowing out of that, too—''

Unknown Caller: "Our other arrangement is still in effect. Rest assured deliveries will be made on time.''

Anthony Lucca: "That's nice to hear. Nothing beats having untraceable hardware. Soon the old man and me will have enough to kick off World War III.''

Unknown Caller: "I look forward to meeting your father. From what my nephew has told me, he is an intelligent, reasonable man.''

Anthony Lucca: "And I'm not?''

Unknown Caller: "I must go, Anthony. Remember. In ten hours.''

Anthony Lucca: "Yeah, yeah. I heard you the first time. I'll buzz my old man and see what he says. But he's going to be pissed. I can tell you that up front. (Pause.) You hear me, mister? (Pause.) You there? (Pause.) I'll be damned. The snotty son of a bitch hung up on me. Me! I ought to shove his head up his—''

Brognola set the transcript on his desk, his mind awhirl with the implications. "What else do you have?"

"This was passed on to us by the CIA. It's a satellite intercept of an encrypted burst transmission from southern California. They intercepted it a couple of days ago, but it took them this long to figure out what it was."

Brognola scanned the report. "What am I looking at? What is all this technical information?"

"One of the top secret systems on the new stealth submarine."

Brognola looked up. "Is this for real?"

"So help me God. It's been confirmed, sir. Unfortunately, they weren't able to triangulate the source of the transmission. We have no idea who sent it."

The stealth submarine, as Brognola well knew, was one of America's most closely guarded secrets. Not the fact it existed, which had been reported in various trade publications, but the specifics of its construction. Revolutionary new designs were being used, and extraordinary steps were being taken to insure none of those designs fell into the wrong hands.

According to what Brognola had heard, the stealth submarine would have the most sophisticated computing system ever made. It also featured a unique near-silent propulsion system, one so quiet it could sneak up on conventional ships and subs without their knowing.

Word through the grapevine was that the stealth sub's reactor was something like twenty-five percent smaller than its predecessors and used one-third fewer moving parts, contributing greatly to its silent-running mode. The Ghost Sub, some were calling her.

Brognola tapped the report. "Which particular system is this?"

"It's a damper for the sub's electronics. Our people have been in touch with the Navy, trying to find out who was contracted to do the design work. But the Navy has been dragging its heels getting back to us."

"I'll remedy that soon enough," Brognola declared. One of the benefits of his position was the authority he had to cut through red tape, the bane of every intelligence agency's existence. "Thanks for bringing this one to my immediate attention."

Agent Jeffers grinned. "That's what they pay me the big bucks for, sir. But the real reason I brought it right in has to do with where the message was sent."

"How's that?"

"They weren't able to triangulate the source, but they do have some idea of where the transmission was sent."

"And?"

"It was Inchon, South Korea, sir."

Could it be? Brognola wondered. Was there a connection? Sin Mak-Fang had been involved with the Research Department for External Intelligence before he broke ranks and went into business for himself. Was Fang still gathering intel on his own? Was there even more to his nefarious dealings than anyone had imagined?

"Anything else?"

"Only a message for you that said 'Flyboy was picking up farmboy,' and they're en route to Edwards Air Force Base." One thing about Jeffers—he never asked questions about any of the cryptic messages Brognola received.

Flyboy was Jack Grimaldi, an ace pilot, the man Brognola relied on most to ferry Bolan and other select warriors to hot spots around the globe.

"Flyboy will contact you for further instructions when he lands," Jeffers mentioned.

"Have him put Farmboy on when he does, and pass the call through to me."

"Will do, sir." As Jeffers headed out, Brognola placed a call to the Secretary of the Navy.

Above the Pacific Ocean

THEY THOUGHT they had him on the run but that was only what he wanted them to believe.

Fang stared out the window of his private AeroStar jet as it streaked through the atmosphere high above the Pacific Ocean. The deep blue of the sea, which he usually found so soothing, did little to ease his simmering anger.

It rankled Fang, having to leave South Korea like a whipped cur with its tail between its legs, but it had been the prudent thing to do, what with the Americans and the North Koreans both out for his blood. He needed to regroup, to take stock of the adverse effects the loss of his Inchon base would have on his overall operation, and then to take appropriate steps to get everything running smoothly again.

On the way to the Seoul airport Fang had debated where to go. He owned buildings in Osaka, in Taipei, in Manila, to name just a few. But his former overlords knew of most of them and might have people waiting.

Someone once wrote that the best place to hide was in plain sight, a dictum with which Fang agreed. Since it would be suicide to try to lie low in North Korea, he was doing the next-best thing.

Where was the one place the Americans and the RDEI would never think of looking for him? On American soil, obviously. Since Fang had other business to attend to there, he could use it as a pretext for his visit and not seem to be running from those after him.

By rights, Fang knew he should be glad he had escaped with his life. The men who made up the death squad sent to punish him were the best of the best, the most efficient assassins in all of North Korea. Escaping from them was no mean feat. Yet any glee he felt was dampened by the disappearance of his nephew.

What had happened to Cho-Hee? Fang had phoned Allied Electronics from the airport and been told his nephew was gone. Three men swore on their lives that Cho-Hee had climbed into one of the vans to return to the skyscraper and rushed off before anyone else could climb in with him. The three had tried to catch up with him, but Cho-Hee had done his best to elude them, and succeeded.

It was bizarre, Fang mused. It didn't sound at all like his nephew. The only explanation he could think of at the time was that Cho-Hee, on discovering Diversified Industries had been hit, had gone into hiding. But to do so alone, without a word to anyone, was just not something Cho-Hee would do.

Fang had to face another possibility. Perhaps the same death squad that tried to snare him had snared his nephew. In that case, he could forget ever seeing Cho-Hee again. The RDEI wasn't known for its acts of mercy.

"You think of your nephew, do you not, master?"

After hours of flight time Fang had almost forgotten he wasn't alone. He had brought fourteen of his men along, but only one was permitted to share the forward section with him. Kon-Li sat across the aisle, ramrod straight, as inscrutable as a block of marble. "Is it that obvious?"

"We will find him, master. And if he is not alive, we will make those who killed him pay. This, I, Ruy Kon-Li, do swear."

It was so rare for the giant to speak without being told that Fang asked, "What is really on your mind?"

"Forgive my boldness, but I do not think it wise to go to America."

Fang was doubly astounded. For Kon-Li to disagree with him was unheard of. "Can it be that after all these years I have discovered your Achilles' heel? Can it be you are afraid?"

"You know better, master. I just feel you are taking the Americans too lightly."

"Your concern is unfounded. All our papers are in order. We are South Korean businessmen on a business trip."

"Do you bait a lion in its own den?" Kon-Li said. "It would be better if we flew to Thailand. Your estate there is the safest place you could be. It is remote, and you have most of the local officials under your thumb."

"Your advice is duly noted. But I must go to America, so your argument is moot. We will only stay four or five days. Then perhaps we will go on to Thailand." Fang turned back to the window, but his bodyguard wasn't done surprising him.

"He is still alive, you know."

"Who is? Cho-Hee?"

"The tall American. They have not found his body."

"That proves nothing. Maybe he was burned beyond recognition. Besides, what does it matter? He is one man. Even if he survived, we have seen the last of him."

"Have we? I looked into his eyes, master. They were eyes such as I have rarely seen. The eyes of a tiger. Of someone who never gives up. Who never accepts defeat. He will come after us."

"Is that what all this nonsense has been leading up to? One man has you spooked? You, who have killed more men with your hands and feet than I have fingers and toes?"

Kon-Li pursed his thin lips. "We have been together seven years, you and I. You know me as well as I know myself. So when I tell you the American is a man to be respected, you must believe me."

"What makes him so special? That he killed Hideo Koto? Because he stalked me as far as my penthouse? You forget he got that far because I *let* him." Fang thought that would be the end of it, but the giant wasn't done.

"Forgive me again, master. But just as I have trained my body to be a weapon, so have I trained my mind to measure men by how dangerous they are. It is a useful knack to have when one's life is always at stake." Kon-Li paused. "Some men pretend to be dangerous but they are braggarts and fools. Some are dangerous to a limited degree but when put to the test they break like twigs. Then there are the tigers, as I call them. Men who have the will to kill, and use that will as they see fit.''

Fang hadn't heard his bodyguard do so much talking in all the years of their association. "Like yourself," he said.

"And like the American, master."

"He impressed you that much?"

"No one I ever met has impressed me more."

The statement gave Fang food for thought for the next hundred miles. Fang still felt Kon-Li was overreacting. Even if the tall American were, by some miracle, still alive, he was just one man. And he had no inkling where they were headed.

Fang ultimately dismissed the giant's concern as petty. He had much more important matters to consider. His nephew, his deal with Don Angelo Lucca and the intriguing bit of news from Madame Rhee.

They had seen the last of the tall American. He would stake his life on it.

CHAPTER THIRTEEN

Northern California

Between Eureka and Crescent City, California, lay Humboldt Lagoons State Park. West of it, where pounding surf and land met, was Sharps Point. And south of Sharps Point, on a narrow strip of beach, prone atop a chest-high boulder close to the trees lining the sand, was the Executioner. He was dressed in his blacksuit. As always, the Beretta 93-R was snug under his left arm, and a .44 Magnum Desert Eagle was strapped on his right hip. The stock of his M-16 was wedged against his shoulder, and his right eye was pressed to the special scope mounted on the rifle.

The Starlight night-vision scope amplified existing light fifty thousand times. It could register infrared, and had a telescopic factor of four. With it Bolan was able to see in near total darkness, such as now.

Contrary to popular belief, though, night-vision scopes didn't turn night into day. Most cast the world in an eerie greenish glow. Those with heat-registering ability highlighted living creatures and other hot spots in brighter green or red.

Bolan was able to pick out a doe and fawn that

strayed into the open sixty yards away. Neither would have been obvious to the naked eye. Shifting, he swept the scope across the sky, and suddenly the heavens were filled with stars.

Satisfied the scope was functioning properly, the soldier lowered the M-16 and gazed out to sea. It was almost midnight. According to intel gleaned by the Feds, the guns the Lucca Family had bought from Fang were to be delivered in the next couple of hours right on that very strip of beach.

A vessel with a Hong Kong registry, carrying mainly legitimate goods, had already unloaded part of its shipment in Los Angeles and was now en route to Seattle to unload the rest. The captain would bring his ship to a stop about a mile off Sharps Point and send in a launch crammed to the gills with munitions for the Luccas.

Don Angelo Lucca needed guns and money, a lot of both, if he was to muscle his way to the top of the San Francisco underworld. The drug deal Bolan had nipped in the bud had set Lucca's plan back by months. Now the soldier intended to set it back even more by intercepting the arms shipment. He had been on the boulder for hours. A stiff breeze from the northwest fanned his face as he crossed his arms and rested his chin on his wrist.

It would be a while yet.

Bolan and Brognola had conferred by phone earlier. The big Fed had established that Fang owned half a dozen brothels in major cities along the Pacific Rim. Somehow they were tied to Fang's intelligence-gathering operation. Blackmail seemed the likeliest answer. Individuals with access to classified material were lured into dallying with fallen doves and then blackmailed into turning over sensitive secrets or risk having their dalliance exposed. It was one of the oldest games in the book, used widely during the Cold War.

The growl of a vehicle on Highway 101 drew Bolan's interest. The highway was well traveled, even at night, but no cars had gone by in the past ten minutes or so. Headlights flared to the south, angling off 101 and down toward the water.

Bolan's own car, a government loaner, was parked well off the highway about two hundred yards to the north.

The headlights weaved as the driver followed a winding gravel road that dead-ended shy of the sand. The vehicle came to a stop and the engine was switched off. Doors slammed; voices rose into the night.

The doe and her fawn bolted. Bolan swung the Starlight scope toward the newcomers and saw a yellow rental truck parked close to the beach, its hot engine the brightest image in the scope. Six men crossed the sand to the ocean. They were laughing and joking and talking up a storm but they weren't quite close enough for Bolan to make out what they were saying.

Swinging his legs over the side of the boulder, the soldier dropped and headed toward them. Other scattered boulders provided the cover he needed. Reaching a pile of driftwood, he went to his knees.

"—got sand in my shoes, Mario. Eighty bucks I paid for these babies, and now I've got sand in them."

"Quit your bitching, Vince. You knew what we were coming up here for. Why in hell didn't you put on an old pair?"

"I didn't think of it," Vince said. He was heavyset, with droopy jowls and a thin mustache.

"You never think, period," Mario spit. The man was tall and broad shouldered, with his black hair neatly slicked and combed. "If bricks were brains, you'd be the smartest guy in the world. Since you can't stand the sand, take off your shoes and socks and go barefoot like when we were kids."

The brief exchange told Bolan two things. First, these were Don Lucca's soldiers, and second, the man named Mario was a captain, or capo, the head of this particular crew.

Wiseguys never insulted another wiseguy. To do so was a serious breach of Mob etiquette. Insulting a superior was even worse. Any mobster who did anything to embarrass a capo or boss was never heard from again. But those in the upper ranks weren't above cutting a soldier down to size when the situation called for it.

The six hardmen stared out over the Pacific, Mario with his hands on his hips. "I hope to hell they're on time. Last shipment, we had to wait until damned near dawn. They cut it too close for comfort."

"Fang's guys didn't seem to think it was any big deal," a skinny man commented. "They acted like we had all the time in the world."

"I never have liked those damned foreigners much," another said.

"Are they Koreans or Chinese?" asked a third. "I never can get it straight."

"Dummy," Mario interjected. "Don't you know nothing? Koreans came from China way back when, so basically they're all Chinese."

The skinny man turned. "Are we taking the stuff up to the cabin or back to San Francisco?"

Mario began to pace. "Up to the cabin for now, Biagio, with the rest of our stash. The Don doesn't want any of the other Families catching on to what we're up to."

Vince chuckled. "Hell, at the rate we're storing up guns and ammo, pretty soon we'll have enough to take on an army."

"That's the general idea," Mario said. "The more firepower we have, the easier it'll be to make mince-meat of the opposition."

"Too bad the drug deal fell through," Biagio mentioned.

"It hasn't fallen through yet," Mario said. "Don Lucca has set up a meet with Fang himself."

"No fooling?" the shortest of the men spoke up. "We're going to fly all the way to Korea?"

"Yeah, right, Ray," Mario responded. "Start flapping your wings." The hardmen all laughed, and Biagio flapped his thin arms as if trying to get airborne.

"Is that a light out there?" Vince asked.

Falling quiet, the mobsters peered intently into the distance.

It wasn't one light, but nine, ranged the length of a large vessel well offshore. Bolan saw them clearly through the scope, glowing like stars close to the horizon. He could also distinguish the silhouette of the ship. It wouldn't be long now before the arms were ferried in.

"It's them," Mario declared. "As soon as they get here, hustle your butts loading everything onto the truck. We don't want a nosy hick sheriff or state trooper to drive by up on the highway and spot us.''

Ray, the short one, had something else on his mind. ''When's the big sit-down with this Fang character? No one told me about it.''

''Don't you ever pay attention to anything?'' Mario responded. ''The sit-down is the day after tomorrow. Thursday evening. The Don wanted it to be Friday, but Fang claimed he had an important meeting elsewhere he couldn't miss.''

''The Don should be the one telling Fang what to do, not the other way around,'' Vince said. ''Who the hell does this Fang think he is?''

''He's got the guns and drugs we need. So if the Don says we kiss his ass, we kiss it with gusto,'' Mario answered.

''Yuck,'' Biagio said.

The growl of a powerful outboard ended their banter. It came closer at a cautious pace. About two hundred yards out the growl dropped in pitch to a metallic purr. After several seconds a flashlight blinked on and off three times.

Mario had pulled a flashlight from his jacket. He duplicated the signal, then swung the beam in a small circle.

The motor was immediately gunned to full throttle. A launch hove out of the darkness, approaching dangerously close to shore before the motor was cut a second time. It sailed up out of the water and slid to rest with a third of its length on the beach. Instantly, one of the four Koreans manning it vaulted over the side and moved to greet the mobsters.

''We meet again, Mr. Russo.''

"Jyn-Son," Mario said. "Do you have all the stuff? Last time you were a case of pistols short."

"We have it all, even the rocket launcher and the grenades," Jyn-Son said. He was hefty of build and wore seaman's garb, including a blue cap. "You will find the manifest complete. Shall we begin unloading?"

"The sooner, the better."

For forty-five minutes Bolan watched as the shipment was transferred from the launch to the rental truck. Crate after crate was carted over and loaded onto the truck, the men grunting, huffing and puffing from their strenuous labor. Little was said, but at one point Mario Russo made a remark to Jyn-Son that merited attention.

"Did you hear that your boss is having a sit-down with our boss? It's the first time they've ever met face-to-face."

"Your boss is being granted a rare privilege. I have been in Sin Mak-Fang's employ for four years and never had the honor of meeting him in person."

"No way," Mario said.

"I beg your pardon?" The Americanism puzzled the Korean.

"How can you work for someone you've never met? For all you know, he's a scuzz who will toss you to the sharks without a second thought if his back is to the wall."

"If I understand what you are saying," Jyn-Son said, "you could not be more wrong. Sin Mak-Fang has a reputation as being a man of his word." Jyn-Son grinned. "And he pays extremely well."

"I hear that," Mario said. "I didn't become a made

man because I like the hours or the dental plan. I did it for the bread. Piles and piles of green.''

Bolan had heard the same tale before. Many mobsters were enticed into a life of crime at an early age by the lure of cold cash, and the things they could do with all that money. Fast cars and faster women were theirs for the taking. The best clothes, the best tables at the most expensive restaurants. Prestige. Influence. It was heady stuff.

"Only two more crates to go," Vince called out.

Bolan snaked around the deadwood so he was closer to the truck. The hardmen loaded the last of the armament, and three of them piled into the back and pulled the door shut. Vince and Biagio climbed into the cab.

Mario Russo hopped in, too, after shaking Jyn-Son's hand and saying, "Two months from now the last shipment is due. So I guess we'll be seeing one another again."

"I am like a milkman, yes?" the Korean said, grinning.

"A what?"

"I have heard that in America there are men who go around each morning delivering bottles of milk to people. Milkmen, they are called." Jyn-Son gestured at the truck. "I am like one of them, no? I make regular rounds, dropping off things for people." Jyn-Son walked toward the launch.

"Talk about your basic idiot," Mario muttered. Then he smiled, waved and said loud enough for the Korean to hear, "See you next month. Don't forget the milk."

Jyn-Son laughed.

Bolan made no attempt to stop the launch from leaving. The four Koreans were in for an unwelcome surprise when they reached Seattle. The Feds would be waiting to take them into custody.

The Executioner's main interest had been the shipment. His original plan was to keep the guns from ever reaching San Francisco. But now that the mobsters had let it slip they had a cache of arms secreted at a nearby cabin, a change was called for.

Mario got in on the driver's side. He ground the gears pulling out, the engine whining as the vehicle climbed the steep grade back up to Highway 101.

Bolan sprinted for his car. The truck moved slow enough that he'd be able to pace it. He thought the Lucca crowd would turn right and head south, toward San Francisco. Instead, the truck wheeled to the left.

His car was well off the highway, parked in a narrow space amid trees. It couldn't be seen from the highway unless a light was shone right on it, so it was unlikely the wiseguys had spotted it.

Backing out, Bolan accelerated quickly. Not that he was worried he would lose sight of the truck. The company it had been rented from fitted their entire fleet with governors, which prevented their trucks from doing much over fifty-five.

After going around two tight bends, Bolan spotted taillights up ahead. Rolling down his own window, he slowed, staying well back so they wouldn't suspect he was trailing them. It was close to 2:00 a.m. and traffic was extremely light.

The odometer indicated they had gone about seven and a half miles when the rental truck rounded yet another in an endless strings of curves. By then Bolan had dropped hundreds of yards behind. When he negotiated the same turn, he didn't see its taillights. Figuring the mobsters were around the next curve up ahead, he didn't think much of it until he came to a straight stretch of highway and it was empty.

Bolan sped up, doing sixty-five, seventy-five, ninety miles per hour. He squealed around one more bend, only to find the highway beyond still deserted. They had turned off somewhere! He hit the brakes so hard, the car slewed to a stop. Performing a U-turn, he raced back the way he had come to the approximate spot where he had last seen their taillights. Then he did another U-turn and prowled northward at a crawl.

Bolan hadn't seen any cutoffs, no secondary roads at all on either side. But now, as he rounded the same curve where he had lost sight of the truck, he spotted a narrow gap in the undergrowth to his right. It didn't appear to be a road, but he swung into it anyway. Lo and behold, he'd discovered a rutted track that wound off into the wilderness.

The sedan wasn't meant for off-road traveling. It bounced and swayed as Bolan went faster than any sane person would. He was constantly spinning the wheel, first in one direction, then another. The unimproved road, if that is what it was, seldom ran in a straight line for more than a dozen yards.

The soldier covered a quarter of a mile but saw no sign of the truck. Stopping, he shut off the engine, got out and listened. At first all he heard were rustling leaves stirred by the sea breeze, and the hoot of an owl. Then, faintly, the snarl of another engine, moving inland, confirmed the mobsters had preceded him.

Bolan slid back in and continued slowly. Twice he

stopped to listen and each time heard the truck. The third time he stopped, he didn't. Guessing that they had reached their destination, he left the car where it was and went on afoot. Otherwise they might hear him.

Towering pines and thick brush hemmed him in on either side, like two solid black walls. The darkness became alive with sounds, with the chirp and buzz of insects, the cries of birds, and once, something large snorted and crashed off through the vegetation, a deer, perhaps, or an elk.

Bolan hiked over a hill. Small squares of light pinpointed the cabin. The squares grew the nearer he crept, becoming an open door and two windows. The yellow truck was parked in front of a long, rustic, low-roofed structure made entirely of rough-hewn logs. An old hunting lodge, by the looks of it.

Mario Russo and his crew had backed the truck to within a few steps of the door and were busy unloading the shipment. Two of the hardmen were inside the trailer, passing down crates to two others, who in turn relayed them to the last pair in the cabin. They had no idea anyone was within miles of their hideaway.

Bolan observed the goings-on for a few minutes from behind a fir, then he stealthily worked his way to the right, seeking to get as close as he could. The wiseguys, as usual, were talking up a storm.

"—drive straight through," Vince was saying, "we can be back in San Francisco by eight."

Biagio snorted. "Do you have a race car stashed somewhere we don't know about?" He gave the truck a thump. "In this clunker, we'll be lucky if we get back by ten. And I've got to be at Abe's Tavern by eleven for the numbers pickup. I'll be pushing it close.''

"I've got a brainstorm," Ray declared. "Instead of always renting these turkeys, why don't we buy an old truck and soup it up? My cousin Tortora is a top-notch mechanic. We can look in the want ads, find a cheap clunker, and he'll fix it up so we can cruise along at eighty or ninety."

"And get pulled over by some cop for breaking the speed limit?" Mario said. "A cop who decides to look in the back when we're carrying a load?" He passed a small box down. "Some brainstorm, there, Ray."

Bolan had perfect shots at the four who were outside, but he didn't fire. Now that they had led him to their cache, there was one more thing they could do for him. The Feds hadn't been able to learn where the big meet between Lucca and Fang was taking place, and Mario or one of the others might know. When the pair inside came out, he would get the jump on all six.

Ray, who was nearest the doorway, looked inside and commented, "The pit is about full, Mario. What if we can't squeeze it all in?"

"We'd better, or we'll be digging a new pit off in the trees somewhere."

On the south side of the cabin was another window, partially covered by curtains. Bolan sidled over. The interior was sparsely furnished. A wooden table, wooden chairs and a cot were the only furniture. A fireplace, a small counter and a sink looked to be fairly recent additions.

The floor consisted of planks laid side by side. Most had been removed and piled at one end, exposing a pit nearly as long and wide as the cabin itself. Filling the pit almost to the brim were the firearms and ammunition the Luccas were storing in preparation for their war for control of San Francisco. They had enough now to virtually outfit a regiment.

Cross beams laced the gaping cavity, to support the planks when they were in place. A small ramp had been installed, leading from ground level down to the bottom of the pit, and one of the mobsters was wheeling a dolly down it.

The Feds, Bolan knew, would love to get their hands on such a huge cache of weaponry. Its loss would cripple Don Lucca's grand scheme even more than destroying the drug shipment.

Bolan crept toward the front corner. He placed each foot slowly, careful not to snap twigs or crunch pine cones and give himself away. He was almost there when the unforeseen occurred.

One of the crew stepped into view. It was Ray, and he was looking back at the others. "Give me a minute. Nature calls, boys." He took another step, then spied the Executioner. "Jesus H.!" His hand darted under his jacket.

Bolan brought up the M-16 and triggered a short burst. That close, the slugs punched the mobster backward with the force of a sledgehammer. Ray still got his pistol out, an AMT AutoMag, and although he was dead when he hit the earth, his finger tightened in involuntary reflex, banging a round into the wall.

Bolan's hope of taking them alive had been dashed by fickle circumstance. He tried anyway. Springing to the corner, he leveled the M-16 and opened his mouth to order them to drop their weapons. Two of them, though, had already unlimbered pistols. He leaped back as semiauto fire cracked in staccato cadence.

"Into the cabin!" Mario Russo bellowed.

The soldier crouched and risked a quick glance just as Biagio, the last to enter, squeezed off rapid shots from a Browning Hi-Power. The front door slammed shut.

Bolan sprinted to the window he had just looked in, thinking he still might catch them off guard. He should have known better.

"There he is!" Vince roared, and a firestorm of hot lead reduced the window and the frame to slivers in a span of seconds.

Bolan ran into the trees, circling until he could cover the front door. It was the only way in or out. None of the windows were big enough for a full-grown man to squeeze through. "You in there!" he shouted. "Do you hear me?"

Mario, as their capo, answered for all of them. "We hear you, mister. Who the hell are you? What's your beef?"

"Give up and you won't be harmed," Bolan promised. "Come out with your hands in the air."

"Fat chance!" Mario said. "Why should we? You haven't told me who you are or what this is all about."

In the eyes of the law Bolan had no legal standing, no authority to go around arresting felons. But he wouldn't tell the Lucca crew. "I'm with the federal government." Which, technically, was true.

"How do we know you're a Fed?"

"You'll have to take my word for it."

"No way."

"The place is surrounded. Surrender and make it easy on yourselves."

Mario wasn't buying it. "Like hell! You know what I think, mister? I think it's just you, and you alone."

Bolan thought he glimpsed the capo at the window on the right, but it might have been a shadow. "The only way you'll find out is to give yourselves up. You have nothing to fear. If I'd wanted you dead, I could have gunned you down while you were unloading the truck. You'd never have known what hit you."

"Says you!" Mario yelled.

"Talk it over," Bolan suggested. "You'll never make it out of there alive otherwise. Take my advice and play this smart." He mentally crossed his fingers, wanting them to give up without a fight. Dead men couldn't talk, and learning the location of the sit-down was crucial.

"Hey, mister!"

"I'm listening," Bolan said.

"Nice try, but no cigar. We outnumber you five to one, and we have enough guns and ammo in here to hold off an army. So why don't you take *my* advice and make yourself scarce before we turn you into Swiss cheese?"

The soldier pressed the M-16 to his shoulder. So much for doing it the easy way.

CHAPTER FOURTEEN

One grenade would end the clash in the Executioner's favor, but he was determined to take at least Mario Russo alive. Based on what he had overheard, Bolan was sure the capo knew where the big meet between Sin Mak-Fang and Don Angelo Lucca was to take place, and the Feds needed that bit of intel.

As a result Bolan was handicapped. He couldn't pull out all the stops to take the mobsters down quickly. He had to fight them with one hand tied behind his back, as it were, a severe drawback that gave them the edge. It helped that they didn't know they had an advantage. If they did, they would exploit it.

As it was, the wiseguys smashed out the front windows and commenced spraying lead. Bolan dropped onto his belly as three SMGs chattered simultaneously, the mobsters swinging the muzzles from side to side for maximum fields of fire. As a magazine fired empty, they replaced it and continued to spray rounds.

All around the soldier, tree trunks were perforated, branches were reduced to slivers, fragments of leaves swirled on the breeze. Once the barrage stitched a line of miniature geysers in the dirt almost at his elbow.

Abruptly, the firing ended. In the total quiet that

followed, there was a ringing in Bolan's ears. Dust settled over him and he stifled a cough. Then he put his right eye to the Starlight scope.

"Douse the lanterns, you idiots!"

That was Mario. He'd had the presence of mind to realize they would be backlit against the light if they showed so much as an arm. The cabin was promptly plunged into darkness.

Bolan swiveled the M-16 from one window to the other and back again. Part of a face appeared, and he touched his finger to the trigger but didn't fire. He couldn't tell who was peeking out. It might be the capo.

"Did we get him?" someone nervously asked.

"How the hell would I know?" Mario responded.

"Maybe one of us should go out and check," Vince suggested.

"Be my guest," Biagio said. "And if he's still alive, he'll nail you the second you step out that door."

"Keep your voices down, you lunkheads," their capo admonished. "He'll hear us and know what we're up to."

After that, all Bolan heard were faint whispers. Whether the mobsters were just talking or up to something, he couldn't say. Presently, he heard several loud thumps, then the sound of wood being splintered. He figured they were opening a crate, maybe to get more ammo. But he was only half-right.

After more whispering, Mario called out, "Hey, you hear me, mister?"

Bolan didn't say anything. It could be a trick. It could be they wanted to peg his exact position.

"What if we change our minds and give up, like you want?" the capo hollered. "What guarantees do we have that you won't gun us down if we do as you want and come out with our hands in the air?"

Not for one second did Bolan believe they were serious. He trained the scope on the windows again.

"We have enemies, you know," Mario said. "Rival Families and others who would love to whack us. Prove to us that you're the law. Show us some ID and we'll rethink this whole thing. What do you say?"

Bolan didn't say a word.

"Come on, mister," Mario persisted. "You've got us boxed in, and we're sitting on enough explosives to blow us clear to the moon. We want to work a deal. What do you say, huh?"

Russo apparently misconstrued the soldier's silence. "I knew it! I knew you weren't no Fed! You're just some wiseguy from another Family. Who sent you? Don Florio? Don Constantine? The Bauman brothers?"

Against his better judgment, Bolan shouted, "I'm not here to whack you! Surrender and you'll be turned over to the authorities."

The front door was suddenly flung open, framing a tall figure. Bolan recognized the capo. He saw something else, too, the object Mario held in both hands pointed in his general direction. Mentally berating himself for being a fool, Bolan rolled to his left, toward the shelter of a tree.

The night was rent by the *whump* and *whoosh* of the rocket launcher. The rocket itself was a molten streak. The next second the ground buckled and heaved as if from a powerful earthquake, and debris rained to the ground, clods of dirt and chunks of wood pelting the soldier like hail.

Bolan's ears were ringing in earnest now. He was unhurt, but it had been close.

The door slammed shut, and the mobsters laughed at their cleverness. "We must have waxed his butt that time!" one declared. It sounded like Vince.

They had a lot to learn. Rising, Bolan backed up a dozen feet, then jogged to the left, to the north, looping around the cabin. He couldn't recall seeing a window on the north side, but since there had been one on the south, odds were he would find one. And he did. Thanks to the Starlight scope, he also found a rock that suited his purpose. Hefting it, he moved to a pine close to the wall.

Mario and the others were enjoying themselves. "Hey, mister!" the capo yelled. "You still alive out there?" Some of his men snickered.

Bolan would give them something to laugh about. He threw the rock at the pane and was in motion the instant it left his hand, racing to the front of the building. The glass shattered under the impact.

Inside, startled exclamations and oaths preceded a firestorm directed at the north wall. The mobsters thought he had broken out the window to take a potshot at them, which was exactly what Bolan wanted them to think.

The soldier sped past the corner to the front window, already broken by the wiseguys themselves. A hardman was standing right beside it, firing an SMG at the one Bolan had just hurled the rock through.

The Starlight scope showed it wasn't Mario.

Bolan cored the wiseguy's head, rotated and

sprinted for cover. Outraged bellows greeted his ploy.
He came to a large log and dived over it just as the
clearing in front of the cabin was laced by a leaden
shower. Gunners were at both windows, firing SMGs
wildly, shooting at anything and everything in their
fury. Their emotions had gotten the better of them.

That was the thing with wiseguys. They called
themselves "soldiers," but they were as different from
real soldiers as night was from day. They lacked the
training, the discipline, the seasoned skills professional
military men possessed.

Wiseguys would kill when it was in their interest to
do so. They squeezed the trigger as readily as other
hardened criminals. But except for a few experienced
hit men, they were basically amateurs. Were a Mafia
crew to go up against a squad of true soldiers in
pitched combat, the wiseguys wouldn't stand a chance.

For more than two minutes the gunners peppered
the landscape, expending hundreds of rounds. Not until someone began to shout did the firing taper off.

"Enough! Enough, damn it!" Mario Russo fumed.
"Hold your fire, you morons!"

"He shot Louie!" Biagio replied.

"And we'll get the bastard, but we'll do it smart.
Not by wasting lead! Stay low while we get ready."

Ready for what? Bolan wondered. From where he
lay, the rental truck blocked his view of the front door.
On the off chance they'd elect to make a break for it,
he pushed up into a crouch and moved to the right
until he could see the entire front of the cabin.

Furtive movement indicated the wiseguys were indeed up to something. Bolan sank onto a knee and
braced the M-16 against a fir to steady his aim. No

sooner had he done so than the front door was flung open again and out spilled all four hardmen, all armed with SMGs, all firing on the run as they barreled toward the truck.

By a sheer fluke, one of them zinged autofire at the very tree Bolan was next to. He had to throw himself to the ground to avoid being turned into a sieve. When he looked up, Mario and Biagio were almost to the cab. He jammed the M-16 to his shoulder and spanged a short burst into the truck's door, thinking to deter them, but all that did was give the quartet some idea of where he was. Three of them swung toward him while the capo leaped for the door handle.

Bolan centered the scope on the skull of the fourth gunner and splattered the man's brains over the rental. Shifting his elbows, he fixed the scope on Vince, who was trying to eject a spent magazine from what appeared to be a Type 35 Chinese submachine gun. Vince wasn't familiar with the weapon and couldn't get the magazine out. He was tugging on it in exasperation when Bolan's next burst chewed his sternum to ribbons.

That left Mario and Biagio. Mario had the truck door open and was hauling himself up into the cab. Biagio, providing covering fire, indiscriminately spewed lead in a wide arc.

Again Bolan had to hug the sod as leaden wasps sought to sting him. When the gunfire stopped and he lifted his head, he saw that Biagio had run around the cab. Mario was already inside.

The Executioner had a clear shot at the capo. One twitch of his finger was all it would take. But he was still set on finding out where the meet would be, so he shot at the truck's engine instead. He had to keep them from driving off. The shriek of the slugs as they tore through the hood was drowned out by the roar of the engine as Mario turned it over.

Biagio was also in the cab. Bolan spotted him when he stood for a better shot.

Gears ground as Mario frantically worked the shift. Bolan fired at the hood again, finishing off the last of his magazine. Replacing it took two seconds, but in that time the truck lurched forward like a great yellow bull, lumbering toward the rutted excuse for a road that would take it back to Highway 101.

Bolan ran to cut it off. He attempted to shoot out the front tire and was positive he hit it, but the vehicle gained speed, chugging like a stricken locomotive.

On an open highway Bolan would never be able to overtake it, but the winding track through the wilderness prevented the capo from reaching full speed.

The truck was constantly slowing to negotiate sharp turns, which allowed Bolan to catch up. He was only a few yards behind the tailgate, the truck's exhaust spewing over him like toxic fumes from a smokestack, when another turn forced Mario to slow down again. Bolan raced alongside, heading for the cab. But the truck was so wide, it completely filled the road. Branches and brush scraped against it, forming a barrier that effectively foiled him.

Soon a straight stretch allowed Mario to go faster.

The soldier sprinted at his top speed, but he was in danger of being left eating dust. Then a hand strap attached next to the open rear door caught his eye. It was flapping with every bounce and sway. Exerting every muscle in his legs, Bolan took two more long strides, then jumped, arcing up into the bed of the track and gripping the strap before gravity claimed him. A sudden jolt nearly pitched him out but he held on, pressing his back against the side to brace himself.

The wiseguys didn't realize it, but they had a passenger.

Several crates hadn't been unloaded and were sliding back and forth with every turn the vehicle made. When, a minute later, the truck came to a hill and growled up the slope, the crates began to slide toward the rear—and Bolan.

He had to reach the cab. Slinging the M-16, the soldier focused on the outer edge of the roof. When Russo downshifted and the vehicle slowed, he launched himself upward, gripped the edge and flipped up and over, his shoulder muscles straining.

The truck hit a hole and tilted violently, nearly hurling Bolan off. Through sheer grit he held on to the edge, waiting for the vehicle to reach the crest. As he remembered, the top of the hill was fairly level. But he hadn't counted on the dozens of low limbs that scraped across the roof, limbs that tore and gouged at him. He felt fleeting pain in his left calf, in his lower back.

Laughter wafted from the cab. Mario and Biagio believed they had gotten clean away, and were elated.

They wouldn't be for long. The truck came to the summit and leveled off. Instantly, Bolan turned and scrambled on his hands and knees toward the front. He ducked a limb that would have swatted him off, then evaded the tapered tip of another that sought to pierce an eye. It delayed him long enough for the truck to start down the other side of the hill before he was anywhere near the cab.

Mario was gaining speed again. They shot down the incline at an ever increasing rate, like a giant yellow meteor streaking to Earth.

Bolan recalled that the road bore to the left at the bottom. Unless the capo slammed on the brakes, they were in trouble. He felt the truck shiver like a giant beast in a wintry blast and knew Mario was trying. But was it too little, too late?

The answer came in the form of squealing brake pads and grinding gears, in a piercing cry and the rending of metal.

Bolan was pitched to the right as the roof canted under him. It was as if he was on the deck of a boat being tossed by wild waves, only in this instance the smooth metal roof afforded no handholds for him to cling to. He slid to a stop at the very edge and saw a wall of vegetation loom before him.

For a moment it seemed as if the truck would level off. It began to. But then the roof canted even more and Bolan knew the tires on the driver's side had left the ground.

"We're going over!" Mario shouted.

That they were. The inky undergrowth rushed at Bolan. He was in peril of being dashed against a bole or a boulder or crushed if the truck rolled on top of him. Throwing himself at a nearby pine, he clawed for purchase. His grasping fingers wrapped around a limb, as under him, a deafening crash shattered the stillness of the forest. The limb held—but not the tree. Struck by the rental truck, it buckled like a toothpick.

Air fanned Bolan's face as the pine toppled and in

the darkness he couldn't tell what was below. His legs slammed against a lower branch. Unexpectedly, the tree jarred to a stop fifteen or twenty feet above the ground, and he was ripped loose and plummeted. Bouncing off other limbs, he crashed into a dense thicket, gashing his cheek and scratching his right ear deep enough to draw blood.

The thicket cushioned Bolan's fall but he still had the wind knocked out of him. Struggling onto his elbows, he saw the truck a few yards away, lying there like a mammoth upended tortoise, one of its tires spinning. It had nearly landed on top of him. The engine had died and the headlights were out.

"Come on, Mario! Give me your hand!"

The mobsters had survived. Bolan sat up amid thick growth that crackled with every movement he made, and twisted toward the cab.

"Hold it! I think I heard something!"

Freezing, Bolan spied the dusky form of Biagio perched above the open cab door. Picking off the gunner would be child's play except for the fact that to do so he had to unsling the M-16, or draw the Beretta or the Desert Eagle, and if he tried Biagio would pinpoint his position.

Mario spoke, too low to be understood.

"I don't know," Biagio responded. "Maybe it was an animal." Bending, he extended an arm. "Let's get the hell out of here while we still can. Whoever that guy was, he sure didn't hike all the way in from Highway 101. His car must have been hidden near the cabin. He'll be along any second now, and we don't want to be here when he does."

The statement reminded Bolan his car was only a

couple of hundred yards farther on. The keys were in his pocket but the mobsters might know how to jump-start it.

Biagio pulled the capo from the truck. Mario had an arm tucked to his side and couldn't get down without help.

"Can you make it?" Biagio asked.

"I can manage. Busted my wrist, is all." Grunting, Mario limped westward. "Let's go. We have to get to a phone and contact Don Lucca. Before noon he'll have twenty men here, and a new truck."

"The men are all we need," Biagio said. "We'll hunt the bastard down and make him pay."

"Oh, we'll do that, all right. But the guns and ammo are our main worry. We have to get all that stuff out of there. It cost the Don a small fortune. We can't afford to let anyone else get their mitts on it."

The night swallowed them.

Bolan stood, the brush crackling anew, and waded through it to the truck. His right hip was sore and his shoulder spiked with pangs when he unslung the M-16.

Staying at the edge of the road, the Executioner shadowed the pair. He wanted to take them by surprise. He thought that Mario's injuries would slow them, but he didn't see any sign of them until a flash of light told him they had found his car and opened the front door.

"These must be that guy's wheels! Get in! I can jump this sucker!" Biagio exclaimed, suiting his action to his words.

Mario shuffled around to the passenger side.

Bolan was only twenty yards away. He slanted to

the right to lose himself in the forest before they turned on the headlights, but the twin beams impaled him in their combined glare in midstride.

"Look!" Biagio roared. "It's him!"

Flinging himself into high weeds, Bolan snaked to a stump. No shots pierced the murk, which was surprising. A glance showed the headlights were still on, and both doors were open, but the mobsters were nowhere in sight. He scoured the vicinity and glimpsed movement across the road.

Relying on the skills he had honed in jungles and woodland from southeast Asia to Siberia, Bolan commenced a silent stalk. It was slow, painstaking work, with frequent pauses to look and listen. He paralleled the rutted track for about fifty yards. Then, and only then, did he venture across it, flitting to the other side before anyone could think to get a bead on him.

Bolan doubted the mobsters would stray very far from the car. It was their ticket out of there, their quickest means of getting to a telephone. So they had to be waiting for him to show himself. Their gambit would backfire, though. He could wait them out. Wait until dawn, and then take them down in the light of the new day.

Ten minutes elapsed. Half an hour. The sighing of the wind was the only sound that intruded on the serenity of the wilderness.

Bolan had to give the mobsters credit. He didn't think they were patient enough to lie in ambush that long. Every few minutes he swept the woods with the scope but never so much as glimpsed them.

The creak of the car alerted Bolan they were making their move. The taillights bounced, as they would if someone had sat in the car—or crawled up into it. Shadows rippled under the dome light. Someone was in there, all right.

Rising, the soldier catfooted back across the road. A pair of legs jutted from the driver's door. One of the mobsters was trying to jump the engine. Bolan closed in, an indigo specter. Twenty yards from the car, as he slunk past a madrone, fireflies sparkled near the front of the sedan. Slugs ripped into the madrone's trunk, and had he not sprang to the left, they would have ripped into him, as well.

Bolan didn't shoot back. It had to be Mario. Side-stepping to a wide bush, he peered through it and saw that Biagio had sat up and slid to the edge of the front seat, an SMG cocked and cradled. The Executioner took precise aim. Once Biagio was disposed of, the capo would be that much simpler to bring to bay.

Biagio ducked again.

Bolan continued eastward until he was abreast of the sedan. Biagio was on his back on the front seat, lying partway under the steering column. The wiseguy had stripped a wire with the blade to a pocket knife and was stripping another. Half a minute more and he could start the car.

When viewed through the Starlight scope, the interior was lit up like a torch. Bolan could see Biagio's flying fingers, could see the knife shear into the coating on the wire and peel it like the skin of a banana.

The crack of a twig saved Bolan's life. Pivoting, he beheld a vague two-legged shape. An SMG chattered. Automatically, the Executioner responded in kind. Reflex had taken over. He faced the car just as Biagio sat back up. Three shots in swift succession kicked the man against the opposite door, where he convulsed and vented an inarticulate cry.

Bolan ran to the right. Again an SMG chattered, the rounds almost creasing his jacket.

A waist-high boulder offered him a temporary haven.

In the car, the stricken gunsel was gurgling and whining. He had straightened enough to slump over the top of the seat.

"Biagio, how bad is it?" Mario hollered from a stand of saplings maybe thirty feet from the boulder.

The mobster raised his head and tried to answer, but all that issued from his mouth was a steady scarlet trickle.

"I'm hit, too," Mario shouted.

Bolan frowned. Losing the capo might cost him Sin Mak-Fang. "Mario!" he hollered. "Give up and I'll see that you and your friend get medical attention."

The response was predictable. The boulder and everything near it were pockmarked by enough lead to fill a bathtub.

When the firing ended, Bolan tried again. "I'm serious! You can still walk away from this! I'll take both of you to the nearest hospital." Which he imagined was in Eureka.

"Go to hell!" Mario spit.

"What have you got to lose? A few years behind bars?" Bolan bartered. "All I want is some information."

"Such as?"

"We know your boss is meeting with Fang the day after tomorrow. Tell me where the sit-down is being held."

"You expect me to break the vow I took? You should know better."

The vow the capo referred to was called the *omerta*. It was the code of silence imposed on every Mafia member. Each new inductee had to pledge, under penalty of death, never to reveal anything about the organization, even that it existed. For decades the *omerta* had hampered law enforcement efforts to close down the Mafia.

"Isn't it worth your friend's life?" Bolan asked.

"Biagio, you hear this scumbag?" Mario yelled.

The mobster couldn't answer. He had sagged lower. Only his face was visible above the dash, his mouth agape in the astonishment he had felt at his own passing.

"Damn you, mister," the capo said wearily. "I hope Don Lucca skins you alive for this." A single shot cracked, the shot of a pistol, not an SMG.

Bolan heard a thud and a groan. Wary of a trick, he charged toward the stand. The scope illuminated the twitching body and contorted lips. Lowering it, he thought he saw a gleam of triumph in Mario's dark eyes, a gleam that faded as the flame of life was extinguished. "Damn," Bolan said.

The capo never heard him.

CHAPTER FIFTEEN

San Francisco International Airport

Their perfectly forged passports and identification papers claimed they were attached to the North Korean delegation to the United Nations. Nothing could be further from the truth, but the delegation cover was a favorite of the RDEI, especially when operatives had to be sent overseas on short notice.

Colonel Hin had an anxious moment going through customs. It came when the portly man inspecting their bags asked to see his passport and then gave him a close scrutiny, just such a scrutiny as would earn a new arrival to North Korea a special visit to a special room for an interrogation by North Korean security.

"You must be proud of this one," the man commented.

"I beg your pardon?" Colonel Hin said in his best English. Fleeting anxiety gripped him, worry that the official was referring to the quality of the forged documents.

"Your photo. Most look awful, but whoever took yours actually made you look half-human." The man chuckled and handed back the passport.

"Ah. Yes. I am very pleased," Hin said, surprised that was all it had been. He was equally surprised at the cursory inspection his bags were given. You would think he was from South Korea or some other nation friendly to the United States instead of from a country that saw the U.S. as its most bitter enemy.

Americans were ridiculously naive. Hin had discovered the fact in his RDEI class on the psychology of the American mind, and subsequent experience had proved his instructor correct.

Americans were friendly and easygoing by nature, and they foolishly thought all peoples were naturally the same. They didn't like to hurt others, so they wrongly assumed no one else liked to inflict pain and suffering, either. It was no wonder they were duly shocked and outraged whenever someone appeared on the world stage who did, someone who had no more regard for human life than most humans had for insects.

They were a curious mix of traits, these strange Americans. For while they were basically gentle and gullible, they could also be fierce when aroused, fierce to the point where in the many wars they had fought, they had rarely lost. The fiasco in Vietnam notwithstanding.

Hin had learned not to underestimate them. They were easygoing, yes, but they were also unpredictable, and that very unpredictability made them formidable foes.

Childish was the word Hin thought described them best. For by and large they mainly were overgrown children. With few exceptions.

One of those exceptions had been the big American

Hin encountered in Inchon. For a reason he couldn't quite fathom, the colonel kept thinking of him. The man had made no threatening moves, had done nothing to indicate he was in any way remarkable, yet there had been something about him, an air of competence, a latent quality of menace, that had impressed Colonel Hin greatly.

The sight of the other three members of his squad waiting for him brought an end to Hin's musing. He nodded and led them to the car-rental counter. A van had been reserved, and soon they had piled their suitcases in the back and were cruising north on Interstate 280.

They took Portola Drive to Ocean Avenue. Eventually it brought them to the arranged meeting place, a parking lot that bordered John McLaren Park. In the park couples strolled arm in arm; people were jogging and riding bicycles; children tossed Frisbee disks or flew kites or played tag.

The colonel parked the van next to another, a green Volkswagen van, and climbed out. The driver of the other van was quick to do the same and dipped his chin in deference as Hin approached.

"Greetings, sir. It is a great pleasure to see you again. How long has it been since your last visit?"

Hin didn't share his contact's delight. Soh Bong-Kan was fat and slovenly, traits the colonel detested. It was hard to believe Soh was a top RDEI operative. "Nineteen months," he answered curtly.

"That long? Time flies the older we get, does it not? I would swear it had just been a few months ago."

"You have followed your instructions to the letter?" Hin asked.

"As always," Soh said. "I was not given much time, but I acquired everything on your list. The maps are in the glove compartment. So is a sketch of the grounds, the best I could do on such short notice."

"You have done well." The colonel motioned to his men, and they switched from the rental van to the one Soh had brought.

"Here is the number to call when you are done," the contact said, handing over a sheet torn from a notepad. "I will wait by the phone twenty-four hours a day until I hear from you. Then we will switch again, and you can be on your way."

Hin accepted it without comment.

"Will there be anything else, sir?" Soh inquired.

The urge was too much to resist. Hin raked the man from head to toe with open distaste. "Why have you let yourself fall apart like this, Major? I have seen your file photo. Before you came to this country, you were as thin as a broomstick. Now look at you. A blimp in jeans."

"The colonel is unhappy with my performance?"

"No. Weren't you listening? It is your appearance. A military man must stay trim and in shape at all times."

"With all due respect, sir. I am a foreign operative now. Working undercover. And we were taught, were we not, to blend into the cultures of the countries where we are assigned?" Soh didn't give the colonel a chance to respond. "I have done as my superiors in the RDEI required. To look at me, no one would ever suspect I am anything other than the computer repairman I pretend to be.''

"Even so—" Hin began.

"But to look at you," Soh went on without a break, "anyone would know at first glance that you are a soldier. The way you stand, the way you walk, you might as well have your uniform on."

Hin couldn't deny the obvious. Especially when he took such pride in his bearing and physique.

"If you have a complaint, sir, please feel free to file it with our superiors in Pyongyang. But I think you will find that they feel I am doing a fine job. My record is spotless."

"I am sure they do," Hin said brusquely. He didn't like being lectured, particularly by someone of lesser rank. And he still wondered whether Soh's slovenly appearance was less a matter of blending in and more the result of an undue fondness for American fast food and sweets.

Soh held out the keys to the Volkswagen. "The gas tank is full, and there are sandwiches in a brown bag, in case you and the others are hungry after your long flight."

"Thank you, Major." Hin would rather kick in the slob's teeth, but venting petty spite wasn't worth the consequences.

"One last thing, sir," Soh said. "I saw a lot of activity at the estate. Carloads of Lucca's men arrived. And there are guards with dogs patrolling the grounds. Penetrating it will not be easy, even for you."

"Concerned for my welfare, Major? How touching."

"No, sir. My only concern is the mission," Soh

admitted frankly. "I counted at least twenty, and there are bound to be more on hand when the meeting takes place."

"Twenty or two hundred, it will not make a difference." Hin gave the rental car's keys to Soh. "The traitor, Sin Mak-Fang, is as good as dead."

ONLY A FEW MILES to the north, in the lobby of the luxurious Bayside Hotel, the man Hin had been sent to eliminate smiled at a petite desk clerk and suavely asked, "Is there a problem, young lady?"

The brunette was gaping at Sin Mak-Fang's underlings, strung out in a long row with their suitcases in hand. "No, sir. I mean, yes, sir. When the reservations were made, no one mentioned there were sixteen people in your party. There are only two beds in our executive suites."

"Ah. But it is no problem at all." Fang, as was his habit, stroked the stickpin in his tie. "My personal valet—" he nodded at Kon-Li "—will stay with me. The rest of my party will occupy rooms adjoining mine."

"Adjoining?" The brunette glanced down at the ledger. "But most of those rooms are already occupied. I'm afraid we only have one other available near you."

"I will tell you what, then," Fang said, smiling. "I will take the entire floor. Move the people already there to other floors."

"That's impossible," the clerk said.

Fang was becoming annoyed by her incompetence. "Nothing is impossible, my dear." Fang took out his wallet. In it were six gold credit cards with limits of one hundred thousand dollars each. "And the cost is no object."

"I'm sorry," she said. "Even if you're as rich as old King Midas, I can't just throw guests out of their rooms. The best I can do is give your men adjoining rooms two floors below yours."

Fang didn't like that. He didn't like that at all. "May I speak with the manager?"

It did little good. The polite gray-haired man who emerged from an inner office apologized again and again but refused to give in to Fang's request. Fang was incensed. Most anywhere else in the world, the hotel's staff would have bent over backward to please him. He chalked it up to the inherent stupidity of Americans. Money was power. Everyone on the planet recognized the fact. Why couldn't they?

"If you like," the manager said, "I can call around for you. Maybe another hotel will have enough empty rooms on a single floor to suit your needs."

The inconvenience of driving elsewhere didn't appeal to Fang. "No, we will have to make do with what you have available. But be advised, I am most dismayed by the quality of your service."

Fang's stay in America had gotten off to a bad start. It didn't help his mood any that the executive suite, while luxurious by most standards, paled in comparison to his penthouse in Inchon.

After Kon-Li poured a drink for him, Fang dialed a special number his nephew had been given by Anthony Lucca, Don Lucca's son.

"Yeah?" someone gruffly answered on the third ring.

"This is Sin Mak-Fang. I am calling for Angelo

Lucca," Fang said, appalled the Don would have someone so crude take his calls.

"Who do you think this is? It's my private number, isn't it?" Don Lucca showed the same lack of respect the desk clerk and the hotel manager had.

Fang controlled his temper with an effort. "I have arrived on schedule. Is everything still on for tonight?"

"You bet it is, Mr. Fang," Don Lucca said. "I wouldn't miss this for the world."

Was it Fang's imagination or did he detect a note of hostility in the Italian's tone?

"I am looking forward to our meeting as much as you are," he remarked. Even more, since it was the first step in broadening his operations in the U.S. Ultimately, his goal was to supply guns and drugs to every major city in the country.

Early on, Fang had seen that gathering intelligence was nowhere near as lucrative as other criminal endeavors. The brothels brought in a lot of money, but drugs and guns brought in ten times as much. As for selling intel on the open market, it only reaped a lot if the intel was especially valuable, and gathering it was time-consuming.

"I can't wait to hear your proposal," Don Lucca declared. "Until nine, then." Rather abruptly, he hung up.

Fang was troubled. Taking his drink, he walked out onto the balcony and gazed out over San Francisco Bay. To the east was Treasure Island, to the north famous Alcatraz. He had read about them on the ride from the airport.

"Is something wrong, master?" Kon-Li filled the

doorway. In his suit and tie he could easily be mistaken for a typical businessman, were it not for his size and those flat, cold eyes.

"If I were a believer in omens," Fang said, "I would take the limo to the airport and catch the first flight to Manila."

"You distrust the Americans?"

"I have no reason to," Fang confessed, "but the Don was not as pleased to hear from me as I thought he would be." Could Cho-Hee be to blame? Fang asked himself. He had let his nephew handle the negotiations, and he wondered if Cho-Hee might have inadvertently done something to anger the Lucca Family.

Shrugging, Fang took another sip. Whatever the cause, he was confident he could smooth things over and set up a new delivery date for the drugs. And through Don Lucca he hoped to gain new contacts in other cites, new markets for his illicit merchandise.

"I have sent two men to the warehouse for weapons," Kon-Li reported. "They should return within the hour."

Fang had bought the building under an assumed name in a dummy company when he initially began doing business with the Luccas. He rarely used it, although he did keep a small cache of arms and ammo hidden there to use on his infrequent visits to the U.S.

"What about Madame Rhee?" the giant inquired. "Should I call her and confirm? Are we still going to San Diego tomorrow?"

"Why wouldn't we be?" Fang rejoined. "I want to be there in person to oversee the brainwashing session. The information on the stealth sub is too important to trust to anyone else, even her." He sank into a chair and propped his shoes on the rail. A gull flew past, then circled and wheeled overhead as if expecting a handout. Fang wished he could shoot it.

"Still no word from Sin Cho-Hee?"

"No, master. Our people are scouring Inchon but they have yet to uncover a clue to his whereabouts. I will notify you the moment I hear word."

The giant walked off, leaving his master alone with his gloomy thoughts. Fang missed his nephew. Next to Kon-Li, Cho-Hee had been the only person he trusted. The only person he truly cared about.

Coming to America hadn't snapped Fang out of the sour mood he had been in since the attack on his skyscraper, as he had hoped it would. If anything, he was more irritable, more tense. He had a vague sense that events were conspiring against him, that he had to be extravigilant from here on out.

Fang's only consolation in the recent series of setbacks was that he had disposed of the American assassin sent to slay him, and he had given the North Korean death squad and the South Korean authorities the slip.

No one knew where he was. Not the Koreans, not the Americans, not the Japanese. He was safe enough for the time being, and he would be safer still once he flew to his remote fortress in Thailand.

Fang gulped the rest of his whiskey. He should be congratulating himself on his narrow escape. He should be glad he had survived to carry on, to expand his empire, to one day become one of the most powerful men alive.

Yet all he felt was an odd sense of unease.

San Diego

BOB WALKER HAD a daily ritual. He woke up at six, showered and shaved and gulped a big bowl of sweet cereal, and was on his way to Omnitronics by seven-thirty. By eight he was at his desk. When lunchtime rolled around, he always made a beeline for his favorite eatery, Burger World on Halifax Avenue.

It was Thursday, and Sally, the pretty waitress who always worked the day shift, placed his order on the table, playfully winked and sashayed off. She liked Walker because he was a big tipper. He liked her because of how her hips swayed when she walked.

He raised the burger to take his first bite. Suddenly, a shadow fell over him and a big man he had never seen before slid in across from him. Surprised at the man's boldness, Walker said, "This is my booth, mister. Go sit somewhere else."

"We can talk here or I can have you dragged downtown," the big man said, extending a thick finger.

Startled, Walker looked in the direction the big man had pointed. Two burly types in dark suits were at the counter, watching. "What's going on here? Who are you? And who are those two men?"

"They're federal agents. As for me—" the man produced identification he flashed so quickly, Walker couldn't quite read it "—my name is Hal Brognola. I work for the Justice Department, Mr. Walker. I've come all the way from Washington, D.C., specifically to see you."

Flabbergasted, Walker didn't know what to say or do.

"It has come to our attention that you have been

passing classified secrets to enemy agents. That qualifies as treason, Mr. Walker."

"You're insane!" Walker cried, drawing quizzical looks from some of the other customers. "I'd never do a thing like that, never sell out my country!"

Brognola set his briefcase on the table, worked the tumblers to the two locks and opened it. "Recognize these?" he asked, sliding a sheaf of papers toward him.

Walker became aware of ranch dressing dribbling down his wrist. He put the burger on the plate and leaned forward to scan the first page. "This is a schematic," he said. Recognition set a butterfly to fluttering in his stomach. "It looks like one of *my* schematics, one I did for a special project I'm working on." He glanced at the big Fed. "How can this be?"

"You're an engineer, Mr. Walker, who specializes in advanced systems designs. You work at Omnitronics, Incorporated, a major government contractor. Currently, you're involved in a sensitive project pertaining to the stealth submarine. And yes, this is one of your blueprints. One we intercepted when it was transmitted to an enemy operative."

Walker's butterfly multiplied into a swarm.

"The question I need answered, Mr. Walker, is whether you divulged the information willingly or whether you were forced into revealing it."

"I've never told anyone anything about my work." He started to feel light-headed, as if he might pass out, and he gripped the table, as much for support as to convince him that what was happening was real. The man from the Justice Department studied him long and hard. "I'm telling you God's honest truth! I'm no traitor!"

"Then how can you explain your design falling into the wrong hands?" Brognola probed.

"I can't!"

"Does the name Sin Mak-Fang mean anything to you?"

"No. Should it? It sounds Japanese or something."

"It's Korean," Brognola said.

"I don't know any Koreans—" Walker began, and then caught himself, because he did know a Korean. He'd visited with her every evening for days now, and he blurted her name without thinking. "Madame Rhee!"

"Who?"

Walker hesitated. If he revealed who Madame Rhee was, he'd have to disclose how he knew about her establishment.

"Listen to me, Mr. Walker," Brognola said. "You are in serious trouble. Unless you cooperate, and cooperate fully, I will have you prosecuted to the fullest extent of the law. I guarantee that you will spend a minimum of ten years in prison."

"Prison?" Walker's skin crawled at the prospect. He'd heard about the terrible things that went on behind bars and wanted no part of it.

"We've run a thorough background check on you, Mr. Walker. We've delved into your checking and savings accounts, and we've uncovered nothing to indicate you might have come into a great sum of money recently. So either they paid you in cash and you squirreled it away, or someone is forcing you to betray the trust our government has placed in you."

Walker was going to protest his innocence again, but the big Fed wasn't done.

"You have been under surveillance since you arrived home late last night. I arrived this morning, but I waited until now to speak to you because I wanted to spare you the embarrassment of having federal authorities show up at Omnitronics." Brognola paused. "Now, shall we try this again? Who is Madame Rhee?"

"She runs a brothel in La Mesa."

"Does it go by the name of Club X?"

"You've been there?" Walker asked.

The big Fed seemed to suppress a grin. "No, Mr. Walker. We ran a credit check on you, too, and obtained a list of all your credit-card purchases for the past year and a half. Recently, you've been charging a lot of visits to a place called Club X. For entertainment, is all the receipts show. What, exactly, is the nature of that entertainment?"

Walker felt his cheeks flush crimson. "Um, I, uh, sort of, you know."

"You've been keeping company with the women at the brothel?"

"Just one. Well, okay, two. But only those two." To try to justify his visits and prove he wasn't a sex fiend, he added lamely, "And I usually have a chat with Madame Rhee."

"Tell me about these chats."

"There's not much to tell. We talk about the weather, and baseball, and the flowers she's been growing. Ordinary things."

The big Fed sat deep in thought for a while. "I would like for you to come with me," he said at last, and began to place the classified material back into the briefcase.

Walker could think of a dozen reasons why he didn't want to, but he only mentioned the foremost. "I have to get back to work. My boss will have a fit if I don't clear my backlog. Tomorrow the courier arrives."

"Courier?"

So there were things the Feds didn't know, Bob thought. Briefly, he filled in the man from Justice on the critical nature of the impending work he must do without going into explicit detail.

"I see. Then it's more imperative than ever that you accompany me." Brognola rose.

As if on unseen cue, the two agents materialized beside the booth, one placing a hand on Walker's arm. "If you would be so kind."

Icy fear sheared through the engineer. To the best of his knowledge he had done nothing wrong, but the idea of being grilled for hours on end was enough to scare anyone. "Go where?"

"To the federal building. Don't worry, though. You're not under arrest. I'll call your employer and give him a plausible excuse for your absence." Brognola nodded, and the agent pulled Walker to his feet. "I'm also going to phone a lady in Los Angeles, a psychologist at the Reed Institute. You need to see her right away. I'll have a private jet fly her down here by six this evening."

Walker's mouth was so dry he could hardly talk. "What does this woman do?"

"She's a specialist in human conditioning, Mr. Walker. One of the best in her field. I've worked with her before, with spectacular results. She'll peel back the layers of your mind and learn whether you have lied to me or whether you are being manipulated against your will.''

Grasping at straws, at anything that would get him out of the fix he was in, he asked, ''How do you know someone else didn't turn over those diagrams?''

''Because the message we intercepted was sent the same day you submitted the blueprints to your employer for final approval. No one else had time or the means to pass them on.'' Brognola guided him toward the entrance. ''When tracing a leak, Mr. Walker, I always look for the weakest link in the chain of information. And in this case, you're it.''

CHAPTER SIXTEEN

San Francisco, California

The Lucca estate was eleven miles north of San Francisco as the crow flies. From atop a low hill, the Executioner surveyed it and didn't like what he saw. The place was more an armed compound than a quaint country estate. High walls surrounded the entire ten-acre property. Floodlights were positioned at regular intervals, and sentries with dogs patrolled the perimeter.

Sneaking in undetected was a doubtful proposition.

A swirl of activity hinted the big meet was about to go down. Extra gunners had been sent to the front gate, and others had positioned themselves along the tree-lined oval parking area in front of the main house.

Headlights appeared far down the isolated road that linked the compound to the interstate. Three vehicles approached at a brisk clip.

Bolan could guess who was inside. Unslinging the M-16, he sprinted down the hill. The arrival of the guest of honor was just the distraction he needed to help him penetrate the compound.

The Feds had come through for him. They'd already

known the location of Don Lucca's estate, and thanks to a street snitch, they had learned the Don had ordered every last soldier in his Family to be at the estate by eight. Something big was supposed to happen at nine, but the snitch hadn't said what the big event was. The Feds had put two and two together, and Brognola had relayed the news.

This was Bolan's golden opportunity. He could put an end to the impending evil alliance between Fang and Don Lucca. In one fell swoop he could dispose of both men and Lucca's son, Anthony, crippling Fang's organization and leaving the Lucca Family in disarray.

All he had to do was get over that wall.

As Bolan jogged through a belt of maples and oaks, he thought about the other news Brognola had imparted. The Feds had learned the identity of the person leaking classified intel on the stealth sub, a nerdy engineer, as Brognola described him, named Walker. They had him in custody but not under arrest. According to Brognola, Walker had undergone some sort of brainwashing. Steps were being taken to counter it, but whether the steps would work remained to be seen.

The trees ended twenty feet from the rear wall, and so did Bolan's reverie. He estimated the wall's height at fifteen feet, much too high to scale unaided. The top was smooth and flat, affording no purchase for his grapple.

The soldier had to improvise, and he had to hurry. Forty yards back he had passed some saplings, and now he retraced his steps, drew the Ka-bar fighting knife and chopped at the base of a slender tree well over fifteen feet high. He heard the approaching cars when they were still a ways down the road, and heard shouts in the compound as a reception was prepared.

Bolan pressed his full weight against the sapling, the razor-sharp steel biting deeper and deeper until, suddenly, the sapling went down with a snap. Straightening, he listened but heard nothing to indicate the guards had heard. Sheathing the knife, he grabbed the tree and dragged it toward the wall.

Out on the road a car horn blared three times. For the next minute or so, all eyes would be on the front gate. Even the perimeter guards would want to be where they could witness the North Korean's arrival.

Or so Bolan hoped. Reaching the wall, he leaned the sapling against it at an angle. Then he went up, hand over hand, and when he was close enough, he lunged upward and gripped the top. Pulling himself high enough to straddle it, he kicked at the sapling so it fell.

The flood lights lit up the place as if it were noon instead of night. Bolan didn't see any guards or dogs. Sliding over, he dropped and landed lightly, then raced toward the closest building, a small shed.

The door was unlocked. Inside was a lawnmower, and a rake, hoe and shovels had been hung on the wall. He had slipped inside not a second too soon.

A pair of sentries approached, and one held the leash to a straining German shepherd.

Leaving the M-16 slung across his back, Bolan drew the Beretta. From a wide pocket on the outer thigh of his blacksuit he slid out a Wilson Arms suppressor and attached it. He was ready, should the dog pick up his scent.

The gunners and the shepherd bore to the left, the dog showing no signs of excitement as it went by.

Waiting thirty seconds, Bolan slipped back out and edged to the corner. The guards were moving along the rear wall, bearing to the east. He saw no others. Crouching, he raced toward the next building, a guest house from the looks of it. Once in the shadows, he advanced cautiously. He was halfway to the front when he smelled the unmistakable mix of water and chlorine.

An Olympic-sized pool lay between the guest house and the main residence, a sprawling Italian-style villa.

To reach the villa entailed circling wide around the pool, and Bolan would be exposed every foot of the way. In search of a less risky route, he glided along the guest house. No lights were on inside, so he gathered no one was staying there. The front door, like the shed's, was unlocked.

Going in, Bolan crouched next to the jamb. Voices reached him, growing louder. He thought it might be more guards coming around the villa but it was the lord of the manor himself, along with Lucca's esteemed guest. And they weren't alone. Anthony Lucca dogged them like a puppy. Kon-Li towered above Fang. And a phalanx of gunners, both Mafia soldiers and Fang's underlings, eyed one another with suspicion.

Don Angelo Lucca had the build of a bulldog and the notoriously surly disposition to match. Only five feet five inches, he had broad shoulders and a barrel chest. His graying hair had been slicked back from his wide, expressive face, distinguished by a high forehead, sagging cheeks and droopy jowls.

Sin Mak-Fang walked beside the Don, his hands clasped behind his back. His bald head glistened in the glow of the floodlights, his diamond stickpin sparkling. "—have done quite well for yourself," he was saying.

Don Lucca made a vague gesture. "I call it home." They came to the pool. "This extravagance you see before you was a waste of money. I had it built for my wife and son, but they hardly ever use it."

In law-enforcement circles, Anthony Lucca, the son, had a reputation for being a spoiled brat who wasn't smart enough or ruthless enough to fill his father's shoes. The Feds branded him a hothead with a tendency to flap his gums without thinking. Now the younger Lucca proved them right by snorting and declaring, "Can I help it if I never liked to swim? I wasn't born a fish, you know."

Don Lucca turned toward his offspring, and even from across the pool Bolan could see Anthony involuntarily cringe. "You must forgive my pride and joy. He's never learned to show the proper respect. A trait he acquired from hanging out with punk friends I didn't approve of when he was younger."

"The young never listen to their elders," Fang commented. "They have to learn the hard way, just as we did."

"Isn't that the truth," Don Lucca said. "Part of it, though, has to do with America, with the culture. In the old country children were courteous to their parents. They didn't talk back. They don't give their fathers and mothers lip."

Anthony didn't know when he was well off. "I

wasn't giving you any lip just now. I never liked being in water much. What's wrong with that?"

The Don glanced at Fang. "See? When I was a boy, my father would take a cane to me if I ever sassed him. I guess I've been remiss. I wasn't stern enough."

Bolan could pick off all three men from where he was, but he didn't shoot. Not with close to thirty gunners ringing them. He would never make it out of the compound alive.

"Spare the rod and spoil the child," Don Lucca remarked. "That's the saying we lived by in the old days."

"Discipline is the cornerstone to character," Sin Mak-Fang observed.

"How true." Don Lucca folded his brawny arms across his barrel chest. "You know, you're not at all what I expected, Mr. Sin."

Bolan noted that the Don had addressed the Korean properly.

"Which was?" Fang asked.

"Oh, someone less—" Don Lucca seemed to search for the right word "—impressive. I always go with my gut instincts, and my instincts are telling me that I can trust you."

"You didn't think you could?"

"To be honest, no. I had half a mind to have you gunned down the second you stepped out of your limo."

Fang was as surprised as Bolan. "I came here in good faith in the hope of establishing a long-term business relationship. Yet you considered killing me?"

They were moving toward the main house, and Bolan had to strain to hear what they said.

"The crew I sent to Eureka to pick up your last shipment never came back, Mr. Sin. One of my capos, Mario Russo, and all his men have gone missing. So has your shipment, along with everything else we've acquired from you. I sent two men up there to check when Mario didn't report in, and they discovered the cabin had been cleaned out."

"How can that be?"

"At first I thought you were to blame. I figured you had turned on me and were trying to bring me down."

"Are you serious? What possible motive would I have?"

"None. That's what changed my mind. And after what you told me out front, I realize you need me as much as I need you. So it has to be someone else."

"One of your rivals, perhaps?" Fang suggested. "From what my nephew told me, I understand that the heads of the other Families will not shed any tears if you are disposed of."

Anthony interrupted. "I'd like to see those sons of bitches try! They harm one hair on my father's head and we'll go to the mattresses! I'll gut them all and feed every last one to the fishes! So help me God."

Don Lucca made a comment, but they were entering the house and Bolan couldn't hear what it was. The giant and the rest filed in after them.

About to step out, the Executioner froze when the patter of paws alerted him a guard dog was somewhere nearby. Two sentries and another German shepherd came around the west side of the guest house. It wasn't the same pair as before, or the same dog. The animal had its nose to the ground, sniffing loudly.

Bolan eased the door shut and backed into the darkened living room. He ducked behind a sofa as the gunners and their canine passed the picture window. They halted right outside the front door, and the German shepherd scratched at it.

"What's got him so agitated?" one wiseguy wondered aloud.

"I don't know. It could be nothing, but we'd best check," his partner answered.

Bolan saw the knob turn and bent lower. A flashlight played across the room as the dog's heavy breathing grew nearer.

"Damn. He's pulling at the leash like there's no tomorrow. There must be someone in here."

"Either that, or he smells the poodle that was here last week. Remember? That friend of Mrs. Lucca's brought it."

"Oh, hell. I forgot about her and her silly pooch."

"How could you? I've never seen a dog dressed in a blouse and skirt before. You ask me, anyone who would do that to a dog is crazy."

"Some people treat their pets like the damned animals are human. I have an aunt who gives her dog a pedicure every month."

"You're kidding?"

"You ain't heard the half of it. There's this doggie beauty salon that only caters to mutts. They do all that stuff. Pedicures. Shampoos. You name it."

"What's this world coming to, Joey?"

"Beats the hell out of me. Next thing you know, people will be marrying dogs."

"That's sick, Joey. Real sick."

Chuckling, the guards departed. The shepherd

whined and scrabbled at the floor, but Joey ordered him to heel.

When their conversation dwindled, Bolan moved to the picture window. He saw them go around the main house. Wasting no time, he ventured back out and took the same route they had.

As he left the shadows, Bolan holstered the Beretta and walked in a slouch, ambling along as if he had every right in the world to be there, hoping that if any of the gunners spotted him from a distance they wouldn't realize he was an intruder.

The short hairs at his nape pricked. At any moment he expected an outcry or the blast of a gun.

Rather than go in the same door Lucca and Fang had used, the soldier searched for one on the west side of the villa. Constantly glancing both ways, he came to a side entrance that admitted him to a paneled hallway. On the left was a narrow staircase that he hurriedly ascended.

The Feds hadn't been able to obtain a layout of the house, so Bolan had to wing it. The construction firm that built the villa was a Mob front company, owned by Don Lucca. Although all the proper paperwork, including floor plans and wiring diagrams, had been submitted when the building permit was issued, everything except the permit itself had disappeared from the files.

The second floor was quiet. As far as the Feds knew, the only other person aside from the Don who lived in the big house was his wife, Lucinda. Anthony had his own condo in San Francisco.

Bolan could see his reflection in the hardwood floors, which had been polished to a mirror finish, as he sidled to a junction. Voices came from the right so he went in that direction. A larger staircase appeared before him, but as he started down a pair of mobsters emerged from an adjacent room and came toward it.

Bolan backpedaled and opened the first door he came to. He had stumbled on a library. It contained hundreds upon hundreds of older, bound volumes filling a score of tall shelves. Pressing an ear to the door, he heard the two men go by. As he waited for the tread of their steps to fade, a sharp yip sounded outside.

Thinking that it might have something to do with him, Bolan raced to the window. It overlooked the pool and the guest house, and gave him a bird's-eye view of the rear wall. Two sentries and a German shepherd were sprawled at the base, the same pair who had nearly stumbled on him in the guest house.

Perched on top of the wall were two figures in black, complete with black ski masks. As the soldier looked on, a third figure joined them, then a fourth. With military precision they lowered a rope over the side and quickly climbed down, the first one covering the others. When all four were shoulder to shoulder, the first one pumped his arm and they double-timed it toward the main house.

Bolan knew who they were. Somehow, someway, the North Korean colonel had learned about Sin Mak-Fang's connection to the Lucca Family. Somehow, someway, they had found out about the meeting, and here they were, preparing to finish what they had started in Inchon.

He didn't much care who took out Fang, just as long as the renegade was taken care of. But the colonel's timing couldn't have been worse. The North Korean either had no idea how many hardmen he was up against, or he knew and believed his unit was equal to the task.

Flying to the hall, Bolan returned to the staircase. He had to reach Fang and Lucca before the North Koreans encountered opposition and an alarm sounded. But he was still three steps from the bottom when the ratchet chatter of an SMG signaled the outbreak of a major battle.

UNKNOWN TO THE Executioner, it wasn't overconfidence or ignorance that provoked Colonel Hin to penetrate the compound. The officer had been spying on the estate for hours from a rise of land to the west. He had seen Sin Mak-Fang arrive, and smiled in anticipation. His plan was to hide in the brush across from the front gate and ambush Fang when the limousines departed, when Fang and the American gangsters were least likely to expect an attack.

But then movement caught Hin's eye and he swung his special army-issue binoculars to the rear wall where a tall figure in a blacksuit had just dropped into the compound. His smile changed to a frown. The man's features were indelibly etched in the colonel's memory, as were his quick, pantherish movements. It was the American from Inchon. The one he had let live. The soldier. The sergeant.

Hin saw the American duck into the guest house, saw the gangsters and the dog poke inside but leave without finding him.

He recalled telling the sergeant that he would let the

sergeant live to double their prospects of terminating Fang, that the important thing was that Fang die.

Hin's superiors in North Korea were determined the traitor not live out the month. Fang had turned on them, had bitten the hands that nurtured him, had shown himself to be a serpent in their midst. Even worse, Fang had the rank gall to flaunt his betrayal. He had murdered RDEI operatives. He had slain his old friend Chang Do-Young, who had been sent to bring him back to North Korea.

Such treachery wasn't to be taken lightly. And, while meriting execution, it wasn't the act of betrayal that spurred the RDEI into pulling out all the stops to bring him down. Nor was it the deaths of Chang and the others. The real reason was much more simple, more practical. Fang had to be killed as an object lesson to anyone else who might be tempted to buck the Central Committee.

The colonel was no fool. He knew that the Party wielded power through fear, that the masses, the common rabble that made up ninety-five percent of North Korea's population, was held in check by the terror their Communist overlords maintained.

The Party bent everyone to its will, from the lowliest farmer to the highest-ranking bureaucrat. They all, without exception, had to do as they were told, always, without fail. Not only that, they had to *think* as they were told to think. They weren't to harbor ideas the Party didn't want them to harbor. No dissent whatsoever was tolerated. It couldn't be. For in a land where individual will had been erased, the merest flicker of individual initiative was a threat to the status quo.

Let just one person do as he or she pleased, just one, and others might get the idea they were entitled to do the same. Before long, everyone would go around living as he or she chose, and the Central Committee's hold would be broken.

Hin had long been amused by the reaction of the Americans and other nations to the slaughter in the famous square in China. The whole world had watched, aghast, as tanks and troops crushed hundreds of college students who dared raise a banner to liberty and human rights. American newspapers called it barbaric. They tried to justify what the Chinese leaders had done by saying that the Chinese leadership hadn't really meant for the army to get so carried away.

On the contrary, the Chinese had known exactly what they were up to. They had extinguished the flickering flames of freedom before those flames spread like a wildfire across China.

The North Korean leadership would have done the same. Freedom, the very concept of it, the very word, flew in the face of every precept on which communism was based. Independent thought and action were viruses. Once let loose in the political bloodstream, they might cripple the entire body politic.

Which was why the North Korean government crushed anyone who stood up to it. Whether it was a fisherman protesting how little of his catch he was allowed to keep for himself, or an RDEI operative turned renegade who had set up a criminal empire that rivaled the Yakuza's, they had to be crushed. Crushed without mercy. Crushed so that the whole world could see the justly deserved end of those who defied their rightful masters.

That was the real reason Sin Mak-Fang had to die. The real reason his termination had been made a top priority.

Hin saw the American step from the guest house and walk boldly around the pool, in plain view. He admired the American's courage, but he had grave doubts about the wisdom of the soldier's strategy. A frontal assault on the gangsters was lunacy. Maybe the American would get close enough to Fang to put a bullet in the man's brain, and maybe not. In either event the American wouldn't make it back out alive. Not unless he was very, very good.

Hin watched the soldier stalk along the house, seeking a way in. He remembered Inchon, and how the American had distracted Fang's men long enough for his strike team to reach Fang's penthouse. Had it not been for the traitor's secret private elevator, Hin would have ended it, then and there.

Now the colonel wondered if the tall American might unwittingly aid him a second time. He saw the soldier dart into the main house, and came to an immediate decision. "On me," he said, replacing the binoculars in the case attached to his belt. Hefting his Type 58 assault rifle he jogged down the slope.

His three men followed, obedient as always, the four of them functioning as four cogs in a well-oiled machine. They had served together for years, training endlessly for their periodic assignments. No other elite unit in the North Korean military was as highly regarded or had earned as many honors.

The colonel was proud of his unit. He had worked hard to make them the best. When the current mission was over, he looked forward to finding a suitable replacement for Private Luy, who had died in Inchon.

They neared the rear wall. Hin emptied his mind of all thoughts except those pertinent to accomplishing their goal. He saw the sapling the American had used to get over the wall but made no move to use it. His men had a better way.

Hin snapped his fingers, and one of his troopers stood with his back to the wall, both hands cupped, the fingers interlocked. Another, slinging his assault rifle, placed his right boot in the first commando's hands and was boosted upward, twisting as he rose and placing his feet on the first soldier's shoulders. The third member of their unit put his foot into the cupped hands of the first, and was levered upward, into the waiting arms of the second, who hoisted him even higher, high enough for the third man to stand on the second man's shoulders.

The third trooper was now high enough to climb atop the wall. Once he did, he unfurled a slender rope, one end dropping to the ground at the colonel's feet. The trooper wrapped the other end around his waist and braced himself.

The colonel clambered up, then dangled the rope so the other two could imitate him. Before they could, a noise caused Hin to whip around.

Two gangsters and a dog had appeared. They were talking instead of doing what they were supposed to, and had not spotted Hin or the other commando.

The colonel drew a silenced pistol from the holster under his right arm. A single shot for each man and the canine sufficed. Leathering the weapon, he motioned at his two men waiting to climb, and within seconds all four of them were on top and the rope had been lowered down the other side.

Rapidly, expertly, they descended. Fanning out in a skirmish line, they advanced past a shed, past the guest house, to the huge pool.

No opposition presented itself.

Hin wasn't surprised. He had a low opinion of gangster-types, and held the widely feared Mafia in little regard. What were they compared to seasoned warriors?

Fate gave him the opportunity to find out. A second later a guard stepped around the northeast corner of the main house and opened up with a submachine gun.

CHAPTER SEVENTEEN

The Executioner sprinted behind the stairs and crouched under them just as a door farther down the hall burst open and mobsters streamed out. Six, all told, armed with various SMGs and autopistols.

In the room they had just left, Don Angelo Lucca bellowed like a mad bull. "Go see what that's all about and report back to me! Move!"

The six gunners sped past the staircase toward the rear of the house. A hubbub of noise preceded a general exodus. More mafiosos and Fang's Koreans exited the room, cramming the corridor, along with the Don himself, the Don's son and Fang.

Bolan didn't have a clear shot, though. It would in any case be suicide to open fire, since there had to be two dozen gunners. He'd be chopped to ribbons before he could take the leaders down.

A war had erupted outside the villa. Autofire, mingled with random single shots, rang out, the whole din punctuated by explosions and screams. Many of the men in the hall were talking at once, asking one another what they thought was going on and what they should do.

They shut up when Don Lucca bellowed again.

"Quiet, the whole bunch of you!" Lucca had his big hands on his hips and was glaring at anyone and everyone. He cocked his head when another explosion rocked the compound. "How dare they!" he roared. "How dare they attack my home! My family!"

"Who do you think it is?" Anthony asked anxiously. He kept glancing toward the front door as if bolting were uppermost in his thoughts.

"Who the hell cares?" his father responded. "Whoever it is, they're dead meat! The Feds, the cops, the Brunos maybe, I don't care! No one tries to whack me in my own home and gets away with it! No one!"

The Don's consuming rage cowed his son and his men, but not Fang. Fang's men, and Kon-Li, hovered close to him, their weapons out, ready to defend their boss with their life if that was what was called for.

"Pardon me, Don Lucca," Fang said, "but perhaps it would be best if I were to leave. I can return on Saturday to take up where we left off, provided you have everything under control."

"I have it under control now!" the elder Lucca responded.

As if to prove him wrong, another blast shook the villa.

"I have no interest in becoming involved in a clash with your enemies," Fang said politely. "And keep in mind if something should happen to me, you won't receive the guns and drugs you need."

As always where the Mafia was concerned, business came before all else. Don Lucca visibly got a grip on his surging emotions, and nodded. "I see your point. It wouldn't be smart to let you buy the farm." He glanced around at a shout from down the hall. "What's this action?"

Two of the mobsters sent to see what was going on came pounding back. Those protecting the Don moved aside, and the pair ran right up to him.

"Well? Well?" Don Lucca snapped. "Who the hell is it?"

"We don't know, boss," one puffed. "We looked out a window and saw some guys dressed all in black, with black masks and everything."

"Masks?" Don Lucca said.

The second man nodded. "Ski masks, boss. They have assault rifles, grenades, the works! You should see them! Our guys are trying their best, but it's not stopping them!"

"They fight like soldiers!" the first man remarked.

"What's going on?" Don Lucca said, perplexed. "It doesn't sound like the law, or anyone else I can think of."

Bolan had been watching Fang. He saw recognition register, and the quick glance Fang shot at Kon-Li.

"Whoever it is," Fang said, "can your men hold them off long enough for us to reach our limos?"

"Sure, we can," the Don said, but before anyone could move another gunner came rushing up.

"Don Lucca! We need more men! We can't hold them! We just can't hold them!"

Lucca, scarlet with fury, grabbed the man by the front of the shirt and shook him like a massive bulldog shaking a puppy. "Calm down, Benny! Calm down and tell me exactly what you saw."

Benny looked scared witless. "We're throwing everything we have at them, boss, yet they won't go down. They're good, boss. Real good. Eight or nine of our boys have bought it.''

"How many are there, Benny? And where are they?'' Don Lucca asked.

"Two of them are right out back, by the guest house, keeping a lot of us pinned down. Two others broke away. I think they headed for the front of the main house.''

In confirmation, another blistering firefight broke out at the southeast corner. Two thunderous explosions momentarily drowned it out. Then the firing rapidly rose to a crescendo again. Amid the uproar a dog howled, a plaintive wail of misery.

Anthony Lucca turned toward the front, then toward the back, and nervously licked his lips. "What's going on here, Dad? Who are these guys?''

Fang cleared his throat. "I am sorry to run out on you like this, Don Lucca, but I must try to reach my limo. I will leave half of my men to help you, though.''

The elder Lucca's features were contorted in rising rage. "We don't need any help. There are only four of these slugs, and I have thirty or more of my soldiers left. So go if you want." He angrily gestured. "Give me a call and we'll set up a new meet.''

"Very well,'' Fang said. "But I urge you to accept the help I offer. The four men in black are not ordinary killers.''

The Don's hairy eyebrows pinched together. "What makes you say that? Do you know something you're not telling me?''

Before Fang could answer, the front of the house was shaken by a gigantic boom, a detonation so powerful that a tremendous gust of hot air laced with swirling debris and dust engulfed the hoodlums and their guests. Some of those nearest the front entrance were bowled over by the concussion. Others staggered and coughed, milling in confusion.

Bolan had been idle long enough. He knew the North Korean colonel and his strike team wouldn't stop now until Fang was dead, or they were. It was time he took a hand. As luck would have it, the dust cloud parted, and the soldier saw Fang clearly. He tucked the stock of the M-16 to his shoulder, only to be thwarted when an underling blundered in front of the crime lord.

"This way!" Don Lucca shouted. "Everyone follow me!"

Bolan saw the Don barrel through the doorway and back into the room. A mass exodus resulted, and within seconds the hallway was vacant. Swatting at the dust still heavy in the air, the Executioner advanced. He heard glass break, heard jumbled yells. At the jamb he peered in.

It was a meeting chamber, a large council room with a long mahogany table and dozens of chairs. The mobsters were bunched together over by the windows, each waiting his turn to climb through one they had broken out. The Don, his son and Fang had already fled; they were nowhere to be seen.

One of the mobsters glanced over his shoulder. "Look out! Who's that?" Whipping up a pistol, he banged off six swift shots at Bolan.

The split second that the gunner stopped firing, Bolan stepped into the doorway and fired into the whole lot of them. His first burst ripped apart the loudmouth.

Then others dropped, three or four, before the rest awakened to this new danger and began to return fire in earnest. Some started toward the doorway, relying on their combined firepower to overwhelm him.

"Get him! Nail the SOB!"

Bolan ducked back again. Ordinarily, a lone shooter wouldn't stand a prayer against so many, but he had an ace in the hole. Or, rather, an ace attached to the M-16. Instead of the Starlight scope, he had fitted the rifle with an M-203 grenade launcher. Attached under the handguard on the M-16's barrel, the M-203 was a breech-loading pump-action weapon ideally suited for dealing with enemy concentrations. A quadrant sight assembly, including a range quadrant, made for reliable placement of grenades.

Bolan removed an M-397 airburst grenade from a pocket on his blacksuit and inserted it into the launcher. He had other grenades, including the standard M-406 high-explosive variety. But for this particular situation, with his adversaries massed so close together, the airburst would be doubly effective.

The M-397 was different from most grenades in that it didn't detonate on impact. Instead, when it hit, a small charge went off, propelling the M-397 four or five feet into the air. Then it exploded, the blast and fragments covering a wider area than they otherwise would, expanding the kill zone considerably.

Bolan pivoted on his heels. Several of the gunners were more than halfway across the chamber. They tried to aim, but they were a shade too slow. Bolan triggered the launcher, letting the grenade fly, then he flung himself down the hall, taking a couple of bounds and throwing himself to the floor.

The explosion seemed to shake the house.

A cloud of dust, choked with bits of wood and plaster, billowed from the council chamber. Piercing shrieks and a chorus of strangled cries fell on Bolan's ears as he rose and turned.

A mobster stumbled into the hallway. He was bleeding from a dozen wounds and his left leg was partly shredded, yet when he saw Bolan he tried to bring a Smith & Wesson to bear.

The Executioner drilled him with the M-16 and raced to the doorway. Thanks to the grenade, the mahogany table had been splintered and was on its side. Most of the chairs were broken and scattered like straw in the wind. Bodies covered the far end, some twitching, some still, some feebly attempting to rise. Only a few mobsters had survived unscathed, and they were scrambling out the windows just as fast as they could.

Sounds of fierce conflict came from the front and rear of the villa. An explosion on one of the upper floors was followed by another to the southeast.

Bolan imagined that the North Koreans were trying to keep the mobsters and Fang's men boxed in. But as skilled as they were, they were fighting a losing battle. There were simply too many mafiosi.

He ran toward the entrance, halting when he spied a group of Lucca's men huddled on either side of what was left of the entry, firing like men possessed. Shouts rose from the rear of the house, and he heard footsteps. Reinforcements were coming. If he wasn't careful, he would be caught between the two groups.

A door on the left offered an alternative. Bolan opened it and poked his head in. No one was inside.

It contained a grand piano, an ornate, full-sized harp and a number of plush chairs. A music room, evidently. No doubt Mrs. Lucca's contribution since he couldn't for the life of him envision the Don as being much of a music lover.

Shutting the door, Bolan hurried to the wide window and parted the lace curtains to scan the stretch of yard beyond. The coast seemed temporarily clear. About to raise the sash, he stiffened at a noise from within the room. Whirling, he trained the M-16 on a closet in the corner. The knob was moving!

It opened, and out stepped a terrified woman in a black-and-white maid's uniform. She was in her forties or early fifties, her terrified eyes wide, her lips quivering. When she spotted him, she cringed.

"No! Please don't kill me! Please!"

The woman would never know how close she came. Bolan's finger had started to curl around the rifle's trigger. "Quiet!" he responded. "I won't hurt you."

An exchange of autofire from the south caused the maid to raise her white knuckles to her mouth and bite them as if to stifle a scream. Tears trickled from the corners of her eyes. Suddenly moving toward him, she reached out, pleading.

"Help me! Save me!"

"You're safer in here than anywhere else," Bolan said.

"No!" She grasped his forearm. "I want to leave! Now! This minute! Take me with you!"

"Just stay in the closet and you'll be okay." Bolan sought to convince her, but at that exact moment stray slugs struck the window, high up.

The maid threw herself at him, clinging in raw

panic. "You can't leave me here! For the love of God! Whoever you are, I beg you! Please! Save me!"

Bolan could ill afford to be burdened by a civilian. Yet, judging by the rising savagery and scope of the combat, she might not be as safe in there as he'd thought. If he could get her to the trees sprinkled across the east lawn, though, she'd be well out of the line of fire.

"Please!" Her fingernails clawed into his skin and she sobbed, on the verge of hysterics. "I don't want to die!"

"Keep close to me," Bolan advised, and opened the window. It was a short drop to the ground, no more than six or seven feet. "Can you jump from this high?" he asked.

"I can fly!" the maid said, mustering a lopsided grin.

"I'll go first. When you drop, stay low and do exactly as I do." Bolan thrust a leg over the sill, gripped the side and lowered the other. A glance in both directions showed no attackers or defenders anywhere near. Pushing off, he alighted in a crouch.

"Look out!"

The maid had to have leaped out right after him. Bolan barely danced aside as she came down hard on her hands and shins, and tumbled in a flash of dress and limbs. He moved over to help her up.

"I think I sprained something, but I can still walk."

"Try running," Bolan said, and did so, pulling her along. Crouching, he zigzagged toward a wide maple that would shield her from wild shots. In her fright she pressed against him, almost making him trip.

To the north a geyser of flame shot skyward. Another explosion lit up half the compound, the blaze of light bathing a pair of mafiosis crouched beside another tree, off to the left, in its stark fiery glare.

They caught sight of Bolan at the same instant he caught sight of them. One held a MAC-11, the other a Browning shotgun. The gunner with the shotgun snapped up his weapon, but as quick as he was, Bolan was quicker. A short burst from the M-16 kicked him back against the trunk.

The second gunner rushed his shots. The MAC-11 burped, the rounds so close to Bolan that it was a wonder he wasn't hit. He went for the head, the M-16 splattering the gunner's brains on his slumping companion.

Bolan reached for the maid's hand. "Come on," he urged, glancing back—and stopped. She was on her side, her apron dotted with red-rimmed holes. Her unfocused eyes fluttered as she weakly reached for him.

"Help me! Please!"

Lifting her in both arms, Bolan hastened to the maple. He gently set her down behind it, propping her against the bole. She blinked a few times, then looked down at herself in bewildered despair.

"Oh, my."

Bolan had seen enough wounds to know which would prove fatal and which wouldn't. He wished there were something he could do, something he could say. But he had to content himself with lightly squeezing her shoulder.

The maid raised moist eyes to his. "There's hardly any pain. Why should that be?"

"It happens," Bolan said. Occasionally due to

nerve endings being destroyed, sometimes due to shock.

"It happened so fast," she said.

"It usually does." As Bolan was all too aware that in the heat of a firefight the Grim Reaper's scythe flashed quick and true.

The woman placed her hand on his and patted it as if he were the one on the threshold of dying, and not her. "You tried. I thank you for that. I guess I should have listened to you and stayed in the closet."

"I'm sorry."

"For what? It wasn't your fault." The maid coughed, then grimaced. When next she spoke, it was in a whisper. "I'd like to know your name before I go. Please. I'll say a prayer for you on the other side."

The soldier told her.

"Thank you, Mr. Bolan. I'm Rachel Petrone. It won't count for much since you don't know me, but I'm grateful. I never—" the maid's voice broke and she shivered as if cold "—I never should have taken this job. My sister warned me. She said I was asking for trouble. But the pay was good, and the hours weren't bad, and it's hard raising three kids without a husband—"

Just like that, Rachel Petrone died, her eyes locked open, her mouth slack. Bolan pressed her eyelids shut and lowered her head so her chin was on her chest, closing her mouth. He touched her head, then rose, a slight constriction in his throat.

It was true he hadn't known her, but her death had affected him. Petrone was another of the countless innocents who paid with their lives for crimes others committed. The Luccas of the world, and men like Sin

Mak-Fang, cold-hearted, scheming sociopaths who didn't care whom they hurt or who was accidentally trampled underfoot on their climb up the rungs of power. Ten or ten thousand, it was all the same to them.

What did it matter to Fang how many men, women and children became hooked on the illegal substances he pushed? What did it matter to Lucca if a passerby was accidentally gunned down in a fight with police? Or if someone crossing a street was run over in a high-speed pursuit involving his crews?

If the bodies of all the innocents who had been slain as a direct or indirect result of vicious vermin like Don Lucca and Sin Mak-Fang were to be laid out head to toe, they would stretch clear to the moon and back again.

Rachel Petrone, she had said her name was. Well, Bolan thought as he moved toward the front of the villa, he'd extract her pound of flesh.

A mobster was leaning out a second-floor window and firing at someone near the front, in the vicinity of the wide parking area. He saw the Executioner step out from under the maple and twisted, but Bolan had spotted him first.

Glass panes dissolved under a stream of 5.56 mm rounds. Bolan didn't bother to watch the gunner smash onto the ground. Sliding another grenade from a wide pocket, he fed it into the M-203. This one was a darker gold color than the airburst grenade had been, and that wasn't the only difference. The M-406 high-explosive grenade was designed to detonate on impact, spewing over three hundred fragments in a wide radius.

Another cluster of mafiosis was at the southeast corner, shooting toward the parked cars and limos. They had their backs to him until one, leaning against the wall to reload an SMG, happened to gaze back.

"Who's that?" the mobster hollered. "He's not one of ours!"

All of them turned at the same moment Bolan raised the rifle and pressed the M-203's safety forward. He aimed a little high. The mobsters were about three hundred feet away, well within the launcher's maximum effective range, so compensating for the trajectory wasn't a problem. He just wanted the grenade to do the most damage it could, and at head level the blast would be destructive in the extreme.

"Nail him!" the same gunner hollered.

Bolan fired, then dropped where he stood. He flung both arms over his head, his cheek against the sod. Through parted fingers he saw the result.

The explosion shredded flesh and bone like so much soggy paper. Those not slain outright were bowled over, some sporting jagged cavities in their chests, some with limbs missing. One was still upright, tottering stiff legged, his arms flailing rigidly, like those of a zombie from a horror movie. It would be almost humorous if not for the reason he was moving so unnaturally; his head had been blown clean off, leaving a ragged stump.

Heaving upright, Bolan raced toward an oak tree. Someone behind him became intent on stopping him. Slugs bit into the earth a whisker's width from his shoes. Spinning on the fly, he shot the M-16 from the hip and an overeager mobster took half a dozen slugs to the torso.

The firing at the rear of the villa had almost died

down, but the battle at the front was, if anything, intensifying. The gunners Bolan had just slain with his grenade were less than a third of those seeking to kill two black-garbed figures who were firing from behind the parked vehicles. Bodies sprinkled the parking area and the bordering grass. Some were Don Lucca's boys. Some were Fang's men.

Hunkering, Bolan ejected the rifle's nearly spent magazine and replaced it with a full one. It appeared the two North Koreans were pinned down, and it was only a matter of time before they succumbed. Unless a wild card was injected into the fray.

Bolan felt no great sympathy for the pair. Under different circumstances they would be his bitter enemies. It was coincidence, nothing more, that their current goal and his mission coincided. Accordingly, he was going to do what he could to take some of the pressure off them. By combining forces they stood a better chance of toppling Lucca and Fang.

The first thing to do was to level the playing field. Moving to the left, Bolan sighted on a floodlight that overlooked the parking area. A short burst, and the convex lens fractured in a shower of electric sparks.

Half the parking area was plunged into darkness. Shifting, Bolan reduced another spotlight near the gate to so much scrap. A third light, mounted on the side of the house, fared no better.

Now an acre-wide tract in front of the villa was mired in gloom, giving the two North Koreans a breather. The gunners couldn't shoot what they couldn't see, although they tried, pouring lead at the vehicles until a bellow brought their folly to an end.

"Stop shooting, you idiots! Stop, damn you, or there won't be a car left for us to drive off in!"

Don Lucca was still alive. Bolan had a hunch Fang was, as well. They wouldn't soil their own hands in personal combat, not when there was an abundance of fools willing to die on their behalf.

The soldier glided to another tree, and then another. He was thirty yards from the parking lot and about twice that distance from the mafiosi ranged near the villa. One last maple would put him close enough to the limos to reach them without being seen. Crouching low, he hustled toward it.

The firing had ceased, but the compound was far from quiet. Moans and groans from the wounded mingled with the screams of the dying to form an eerie chorus that wavered on the breeze like the demented dirge of a funeral procession.

Bolan noticed that all the cars he had seen earlier were still there, along with Fang's three limos. The North Koreans had prevented anyone from driving off. If not for them, Don Lucca and Fang would have been long gone.

The soldier reached the maple and leaned against it, gazing toward the gate. Belatedly, he sensed that he wasn't alone, that someone else had sought the relative safety of the same tree. He spun as a shadow detached itself from the trunk and extended the M-16 at the very instant the muzzle of another assault rifle appeared before his face.

CHAPTER EIGHTEEN

In a twinkling the Executioner dropped to his knees. A microsecond before squeezing the M-16's trigger he saw that the figure holding the assault rifle was one of the North Koreans.

"We meet again, American," the man whispered.

Bolan didn't shoot, but he didn't lower his weapon, either. "Colonel?"

The officer let the barrel of his Type 58 assault rifle dip toward the ground and yanked off his ski mask. A thin but friendly smile curled his mouth. "Yes, Sergeant. It seems we keep—what is the expression you Americans use?—bumping into each another."

"I saw you earlier from a window," Bolan whispered, warily rising. "Don't take this the wrong way, but you made a mistake hitting this place. There are too many of them, even for you and your men."

"So I have learned, Sergeant. I underestimated these gangsters."

Bolan glanced toward the villa. The mobsters were fanning out along the edge of the asphalt. They thought the two North Koreans were still behind the cars. Which reminded him. "Where's the soldier who was with you?"

"Private Trak is dead. So are the others, I fear." The colonel's shoulders sagged. "I am the last one left. My overconfidence cost me the lives of those who depended on my judgment. It is a disgrace I can never live down."

Bolan didn't see any trace of Don Lucca, his son or Fang. He guessed they had gone back inside. Trying to terminate them now, with the mobsters stirred up like a nest of riled hornets and Fang's men hovering around him like a pack of protective Dobermans, would be pointless. The mission had been compromised. The wise thing to do was withdraw and try again another time.

"Will you help me, American?" the colonel whispered.

"Help you how?" Bolan responded, keeping one eye on the North Korean while continuing to scour the driveway and the house.

"I must avenge the loss of my men. Honor demands it. I ask you, one soldier to another, for your assistance."

"There are too many," Bolan reiterated.

"Very shortly there will not be," the North Korean said. "Then I am going after the leader of the gangsters. And Fang, of course."

The officer was allowing his personal feelings to cloud his judgment, but Bolan couldn't blame him. In the heat of combat soldiers forged bonds of deep friendship. They shared a special camaraderie that made them one in spirit, as well as profession. All the training in the world, all the drills, the constant stressing of the fact that their objective always came first, couldn't sever those special ties. It was why soldiers often made heroic efforts to save wounded companions in the face of overwhelming odds.

"What do you mean, there won't be?" Bolan whispered. None of the gunners were anywhere near the tree so they were safe enough for the moment.

"Most of those you see out there will soon be dead," the colonel said, and crouched with his shoulder against the trunk. "I suggest you get down, Sergeant. The mine I left is quite powerful."

"Mine?" Bolan repeated, doing as the North Korean had.

"Our latest antipersonnel device. I placed it between Private Trak's legs so the gangsters would be sure to activate it when they roll him over to see if he is still alive."

When most civilians heard the word *mine,* they tended to think of the buried variety common in old war movies. But not all mines were designed for that purpose. Newer models were simply laid on the ground and were activated by trip wires or pressure-sensitive sensors. The latest versions also included a safety feature. They armed themselves thirty seconds after the primers were set, giving whoever set them time to get out of range.

"Do you know what it is like to lose men who looked up to you?" the colonel said with rising venom.

Bolan didn't respond. It wasn't the right time or place to discuss his losses. Bolan could hear the mobsters, hear the dull thuds of their rushing feet as they continued to encircle the vehicles. It wouldn't be long before the command was given for them to move in.

"I must make sure they did not die in vain," the

North Korean said. "I will not rest until this Lucca and his brat are dead."

The soldier was close to telling the officer that if he didn't shut up, they were the ones who might soon be pushing up daisies, but just then one of the Don's men gave a shout.

"Close in! Close in! Go! Go! Go!"

Bolan imagined the gunners darting in among the cars and limousines, imagined them with their weapons leveled, poking into every shadow, opening doors, peering into windows. There had been fifteen or more, and one was bound to spot Private Trak's body before too long. The man would approach it cautiously, maybe nudge the limp form with a toe or his weapon. He would bend down to turn the body over, as the colonel had figured. And then—

Even though Bolan was braced for it, the explosion was staggering. Calling it powerful didn't do it justice. There was a brief flash, then the shock wave slammed into the tree with titanic force. The trunk seemed to push against Bolan's chest as overhead limbs were shorn off and blown away like twigs in a tempest. Every window on the front of the villa, and many more besides, were shattered.

The sound was almost deafening.

Twisted metal shrieked like a horde of banshees as the vehicles were blown apart.

Some were launched into the air as if from catapults.

Bolan spun when a flaming heap of wreckage that had once been a car crashed to earth not eight feet from where he was crouched. Fiery bits and pieces arced toward him, stinging his neck and cheek.

More debris rained to the ground like molten meteors. One chunk smashed through the uppermost branches and another tumbled past the trunk, end over end. A tire, on fire, rolled by, wobbling erratically.

Bolan thought he heard the North Korean laugh. As the force of the explosion began to spend itself, new sounds arose, the screams and cries of mobsters who hadn't perished outright. One was screeching like a child.

"My legs! Oh, God, my legs are gone!"

Bolan peered around the tree. He had seen the aftermath of many mine blasts, but few rivaled this. None of the vehicles were intact. Blazing hulks of scrap were all that remained of the limos. A Mercedes and a Jaguar that had been parked farthest away were the only two that still resembled automobiles, although the Mercedes was missing its engine and the Jaguar's roof had been torn off.

Bodies, and parts of bodies, dotted the drive like so many scarlet-tinged dominoes. A gunner's torso flopped like a fish out of water, his arms and legs gone. Another had half his head missing.

Not a single one of the few survivors was in any condition to offer resistance.

Bolan slowly rose. The North Korean had already done so and stepped past the tree.

The windows in the front of the villa gaped like black holes. The entrance was a worse shambles than before, the door lying partly in, partly out of the house.

Other than the cries of the wounded, the compound was quiet.

"Will you help me, Sergeant?" the colonel repeated

his request. "There is no way for Fang or the gangsters to escape now. We must seize the initiative."

Ordinarily, Bolan wouldn't trust the commando any further than he could heave the villa. But these weren't ordinary circumstances. The colonel had spared him in Inchon, and didn't appear to be as rabidly anti-American as most in the North Korean military. Or maybe it was that they were both professionals, both true soldiers, and each had a grudging respect for the other.

"Together we can flush out Lucca and Fang and dispose of them," the colonel urged. "It is just you and I. Our governments, our ideologies, do not enter into it. What do you say, Sergeant?"

Bolan nodded. "Let's do it."

They zigzagged toward the buckled entrance, Bolan sweeping the windows and the lawn for movement. The central hallway was empty save for more bodies. Somewhere in the bowels of the house someone was groaning.

The colonel sidled along the left side, while Bolan took the right. He estimated that maybe a dozen mobsters remained alive, if that. Then there were Fang's men. Since Fang had avoided a direct confrontation, it was possible most of his underlings were unhurt. Which made for a grand total of about two dozen gunners. A far cry from fifty, but still a force to be reckoned with.

The North Korean suddenly halted and pumped his hand at a door on Bolan's side of the corridor. The soldier looked just in time to see it swing shut. He sighted down the M-16, then hesitated, thinking of the maid. The colonel looked at him questioningly, but Bolan shook his head and advanced alone.

On reaching the door, Bolan kicked it with his right foot. It thumped inward, and a figure over by the opposite wall cringed in abject fright.

"Don't shoot! Please, don't shoot!"

A plump man in a butler's uniform had both arms in the air. His balding pate and face glistened with sweat, and his eyes were rife with fear.

Bolan slid in, swinging the M-16 from wall to wall.

"There's no one else in here, mister!" the butler declared. "Honest! A bunch of them went running by a couple of minutes ago, but they didn't stop!"

"Stay in here and keep the door shut," Bolan advised. As he backed out, he nearly bumped into the North Korean, who was regarding him with an unusual expression.

"What if it had been one of them?"

"I won't kill innocents," Bolan responded, starting down the corridor.

"Your compassion will be the death of you one day, Sergeant. It is a flaw men like us can ill afford."

They shouldn't be talking, not when a mobster could pop out at any moment and open fire. But Bolan couldn't let the comment go by unchallenged. "Not if we place a premium on honor."

The colonel opened his mouth to say something, but a slight noise from the vicinity of the main stairwell silenced him.

Bolan's eyes narrowed. He had spied someone behind the stairs, where he had concealed himself earlier. The barrel of an SMG poked out, in their direction. Throwing himself flat, Bolan triggered a burst into the stairs, splintering wood from shoulder to knee height. The colonel did the same, and the next moment a mobster staggered out, his head and chest riddled. He managed two steps, then keeled over.

Neither of them spoke after that. They checked every room they passed but found no one, nor did they hear anything to indicate the mafiosi were on the second floor.

Bolan had to admit, he was puzzled. It wasn't like Angelo Lucca to tuck his tail between his legs and run off. Yet it certainly seemed as if the Don had done just that.

Then, well past the stairs, on the North Korean's side of the hall, a door was ajar. Light rimmed it, and as Bolan drew near muffled voices fell on his ears. The colonel did the honors this time, slowly pushing it wider with his assault rifle.

They had discovered another flight of stairs, only these led down, into a sublevel, possibly a basement.

Bolan crossed to the jamb and listened. From the commotion, a lot of hardmen were down there. So was their boss.

"—want a war, I give the sons of bitches a war!" the Don was snarling. "Break out the hardware, Anthony. Pass around those grenades."

Grenades? Bolan motioned for the colonel to stay put. Crouching, he crept downward, one step at a time. An overhang prevented him from observing what the mobsters were up to until he was a third of the way to the bottom.

Racks of wine lined a room that ran the length of the villa. At the south end a wide door had been opened, a door that looked as if it had been disguised to appear as part of the wall. From another, much smaller room machine guns, grenades, and more were being handed out to eleven of Lucca's soldiers by the Don and his son.

The Luccas had their own private armory. Bolan realized he should have expected as much after seeing the Don's cache at the old hunting lodge north of Eureka. He reached into a pocket on his left hip for a grenade.

"Boss! There on the stairs! Look!"

One of the mobsters had spotted him. Bolan jerked back as an SMG chattered, the rounds perforating the wall instead of his chest. Pivoting, he bounded back up and made it through the doorway well before the fleetest of the gunners reached the bottom of the stairs.

Bolan and the colonel reacted in unison, each of them dropping a target. The others, though, scrambled out of sight.

"How many are down there, Sergeant?"

Bolan told him what he had seen.

"There was no sign of Fang?"

"No."

A feral snarl rumbled from the commando's chest. "He has fled, then. Just as he did in Inchon. He is a coward at heart, as I have long suspected."

Bolan doubted it was cowardice as much as common sense. Fang was a practical man who never took needless risks. Cowards didn't carve out criminal empires that spanned the Pacific Rim. Cowards wouldn't defy their Communist overlords, or openly challenge a clandestine government entity as dangerous as the RDEI.

"Let him flee," the colonel stated. "Let him think

he has gotten away. He doesn't know that I know all his secrets now, thanks to his nephew. Sin Cho-Hee was most talkative once he lost a few fingers and toes.''

''You tortured him?'' Bolan thought it only fitting, after what Cho-Hee had directed Kon-Li to do to Kiri Tanaka. But he didn't approve. Torture was barbaric, a throwback to medieval times. It showed the true nature of those who used it, under any pretext.

''Why do you sound shocked? I think even the gentleman you answer to in Washington would agree that Fang must be stopped at any cost.''

Bolan wondered exactly how much the colonel knew about him, but he didn't get to find out. A flurry of activity below warned him the Luccas were up to something, and he glanced down the stairs as a shadow flitted across it. An arm appeared, swinging upward.

A dark object was flung toward them.

''Grenade!'' Bolan yelled, and ran. He covered twenty feet, hurled himself to the floor and glanced back.

The grenade sailed up out of the basement and struck the wall. It had an egg-shaped casing typical of standard fragmentation grenades, although its country of manufacture wasn't apparent. It bounced off the wall, landed on the floor, then rolled back through the doorway and thumped on down the stairs.

''Oh, crap!'' someone exclaimed.

It was drowned out by the explosion. A roiling cloud of dust spewed into the corridor, cutting off Bolan's view of the colonel, who had gone in the other direction and hugged the floorboards just before the grenade went off.

Bolan, swiveling, rose onto his left knee. The mobsters had outsmarted themselves. They were trapped down there. He hadn't seen any other exits. And now the only one they had might be blocked by debris.

"Boss! Carmine's been blown to bits!" a gravelly voiced hardman bellowed.

"He shouldn't have stood there like a lump," Don Lucca snapped. "The rest of you, up you go! Kill those scum!"

"But half the stairs are gone!" That sounded like Anthony Lucca.

"We can still make it up," the Don said. "Or would you rather sit down here and wait for those bastards to chuck their own grenades?"

The cloud was dissipating but not fast enough to suit Bolan. He fixed his sights on the doorway, or where it should be, and when a vague figure took shape, he fired a short burst that crumpled the silhouette like cardboard.

There were too many, though. The gunners broke from the basement en masse, spilling right and left, firing before they were clear of the cloud, spraying lead with desperate abandon. No one could withstand such a withering hailstorm.

Bolan retreated, answering their lead with some of his own. Coming to an open room, he darted inside. Just as he did, a random one-in-a-million event occurred that put him at a distinct disadvantage. Several of their wild shots smashed into the M-16, into the handguard, wrenching it from his grasp and flinging it down the hallway as if slung by a slingshot.

The soldier took a step back out to reclaim it, but four or five mobsters had other ideas.

Their combined barrage drove him back in. Unlimbering the Beretta, he adopted a two-handed grip while running toward the window.

"He's in here, boys!"

A hardman was framed by the jamb, a Type 67 machine gun cradled for action. It was another Chinese-manufactured weapon, the sort Fang specialized in smuggling. The gunner wore a smirk of triumph. He probably thought the machine gun made him invincible. He was wrong.

Bolan's three rounds punched into the mobster's face. As the man tottered, the Executioner rotated toward the window and fired again, a circular pattern that crunched the pane into hundreds of raining shards. Lowering his head and shoulders, he took four long strides, then vaulted upward.

"Stop him!"

Another machine gun burped. Heavy slugs ripped into the wall within inches of Bolan as he crashed into what was left of the window. His momentum carried him clear of the sill. He landed on his side amid a tinkling of glass. A few razor shards slashed his blacksuit but not deep enough to draw blood.

"After him. Don't let him get away!"

That sounded like Anthony Lucca. Bolan surged erect and raced toward the rear of the villa. A head was thrust out the window, the gunner making the mistake of looking in the other direction first. Bolan fired on the run, the 9 mm Parabellum rounds carving the head into sections as if it were a grapefruit.

Bolan came to the northwest corner. More bodies were sprawled around the pool, mobsters who had fallen in battle with the North Koreans. He saw one of the commandos floating in the middle. But what interested him most was a weapon next to a man face-down on the tiles.

It was an Ingram MAC-11. Not exactly the most reliable of SMGs, but this one had a 32-round magazine, and two spares jutted from a jacket pocket. Bolan leathered the Beretta and helped himself. A check showed the magazine in the Ingram was almost full.

MAC-11s were offered in a variety of calibers; this one was a .45, affording plenty of punch. Bolan extended the stock and adjusted the shoulder piece.

"This way! He went this way!"

It was thoughtful of the gunner sprinting toward the rear of the villa to advertise his presence. As the man appeared, Bolan greeted him with the Ingram. The gunner jerked and pranced like a wooden puppet on strings before folding in upon himself.

Bolan raced toward the far end of the pool. He was almost there when more pursuit materialized. He heard them before they sped around the corner. Three mafiosi—and one was Anthony Lucca, the Don's son.

Anthony and another hardman were armed with light machine guns, the same Type 67 used by the man Bolan had cut down a minute ago. They opened fire simultaneously, Anthony Lucca whooping and yipping as if he were having the time of his life.

Being armed with a machine gun—or any rapid-fire weapon—was one thing. Being able to use it, and use it effectively, was another. Hours of practice were required, before a shooter became halfway proficient. It was why the Executioners spent so much time on the range at Stony Man. Practice made perfect. Or, in this case, practice made one perfectly lethal.

It was immediately obvious neither Anthony nor his buddy had ever fired a machine gun. They held their weapons all wrong, like half-baked actors in second-rate Mob movies. Instead of firm grips and solid stances, they waved the machine guns as if they were playing with toys instead of firing in deadly earnest. So it was no great surprise, except to them, that their initial bursts missed.

Bolan made it around the pool and beelined toward the guest house. He returned fire on the fly, and because of his endless practice, his rounds struck where he aimed them. The gunner at Anthony's left elbow, his chest and throat punctured, deflated like a balloon.

Another hardman charged into sight as Bolan wheeled and smashed into the guest-house door. He came down hard on his elbows and knees, twisted, and felled a mobster racing along the edge of the pool.

Suddenly, from inside the villa, another blast rocked the night. Three of the rear windows were blown out, showering glass onto Anthony and the others, who raised their arms to shield themselves.

Bolan seized the advantage and peppered two of them. That left Anthony, who sought cover behind a hedge.

"Whoever you are, your ass is mine!" the younger Lucca roared. "You hear me, dirtball?"

Bolan heard him, all right, and now he had a fair idea of exactly where Anthony was concealed. Crawling from the door to a window, he raised an eye to the sill. The shrubbery was too thick for him to see through. Tucking the MAC-11 to his shoulder, Bolan waited, counting on Anthony's hotheaded nature and inexperience to give him the clear shot he needed.

Seconds dragged by. Then a chorus of yells broke out in the villa, yells that became louder as they came closer. The next instant a mobster thrust his head out a second-floor window and cupped a hand to his mouth.

"Tony! Tony! Your father is dead!"

"What the hell do you mean, dead?" was Anthony's skeptical reply.

"We were chasing that other guy, the one who looks Chinese. He set a booby trap of some kind. As bad as the one that blew up the cars. It took out three or four rooms and set the house on fire."

"What about my father, you idiot?"

"I'm sorry, Tony. He was caught in the blast."

According to the Feds, Anthony Lucca was a prime suspect in fourteen murders, possibly more. He was categorized as a psychopathic personality with no redeeming virtues. But the psychological profile was in error. He had one virtue. He cared for his father, and he proved it by standing up and blurting, "God, no! Tell me it isn't true!" His lapse in judgment had to have dawned on him because he rotated, directly into the Ingram's sights.

The Executioner emptied what was left in the magazine. Replacing it, he went to fire at the gunner in the window, but the man was gone.

Now, while the surviving gunners were in a state of confusion and shock, was the ideal time to make his getaway. Bolan eased on around the guest house, clinging to the shadows until it screened him from view from the villa.

From there it was a short sprint past the shed to the rear wall. The rope used by the North Koreans to scale it still hung on the inside. Since the Ingram didn't have a shoulder strap, Bolan left it there. Climbing to the top only took a few seconds.

A glance showed the villa was burning, with hungry flames arcing from half a dozen windows.

The Lucca Family was no more. But Fang was still alive, and had to be dealt with. As Bolan swung over the wall, he wondered where Fang had gotten to and what had happened to the North Korean colonel.

Something told the soldier he would see both of them again, and soon.

CHAPTER NINETEEN

San Diego

Watching Dr. Sarah Craft work always fascinated Hal Brognola. Her ability to peel away the layers of the human mind, to delve deep into a person's psyche and reveal its innermost secrets, was uncanny. She was one of the top psychologists in the country, her credentials impeccable, her experience extending back decades.

Brognola liked working with people who were the best there was at what they did. Long ago he had learned there was no substitute for excellence. At the Justice Department, at Stony Man, wherever he worked, he surrounded himself with those who were best able to get the job done.

There was an old saying that if you wanted a job done right, you should do it yourself. Brognola liked to rephrase it. When he wanted a job done right, he hired the right person for the job.

Mack Bolan was a prime example. Striker had no peers in his unique realm of expertise. No one could match his level of skill and insight. Bolan was the ultimate best, which was why Brognola called on him time and time again to perform missions no one else could.

Dr. Craft was a lot like Striker. In her sphere of work she had no rivals, a fact she had demonstrated again over the past several hours as she deftly and delicately probed Robert Walker's mind, uncovering the deep, dark secrets concealed within.

Brognola had watched the procedure through a glass partition from an adjoining room. The glass was tinted so he could see them, but Walker wouldn't be able to see him. He had listened as Dr. Craft hypnotized Walker and proceeded to counter the conditioning that inhibited his responses, erasing all the mental blocks someone else had put in place. It was a long, painstaking process, but at last she achieved success, and now she was staring at the window expectantly, waiting for him to join her.

What Brognola had just learned infuriated him. He loved America, loved his country with a fierce passion that explained his life-long devotion to the pursuit and elimination of her enemies. So to discover that Sin Mak-Fang had been chemically brainwashing top scientists and others to extract America's most closely guarded secrets set his blood to boiling.

And to think! Based on what Walker revealed, Club X had been in business for over a year. Who knew how much classified information had been leeched from drugged dupes like Walker in that amount of time?

Rising, Brognola entered the next room. "Is it safe to talk?" he quietly asked.

"Safe as can be," Dr. Craft said. "He'll only react to my voice, and then only to direct questions or commands." For all her stature in the psychiatric community, Sarah Craft was only five feet two inches tall and weighed less than a hundred pounds. Graying hair topped a slight but energetic frame. She wore a three-piece outfit, a jacket, blouse and pants in a striking cherry color that hinted at her youthful, playful personality.

Brognola took a seat and studied Walker. The young engineer was lying on a couch, his eyes shut, his chest rising and falling rhythmically as if he were asleep.

"Want me to have him squawk like a chicken?" Dr. Craft asked, grinning impishly. "That's always good for a few chuckles."

"I bet you're the life of every party you go to," Brognola responded dryly.

"Go with me to one sometime and find out. That is, if you think you can survive the night." Dr. Craft winked, and they both laughed. Then she became serious. "Okay, Hal. What do you have in store for this poor young man?" She sighed. "Madame Rhee did a real job on him. I must admit, she's quite talented. But I've removed her conditioning. He's like a blank slate waiting to be written on. So tell me what to write."

Brognola had been mulling over how Walker could best be of use ever since the truth became apparent. "I need to know a few things first."

"Ask away, handsome."

"You need new spectacles, Sarah."

"I'll bet you say that to all your groupies."

Brognola had to remind himself that this was how she always behaved, that she was a frisky teenager trapped in the body of a fifty-eight-year-old woman.

"A little professional decorum wouldn't hurt, you know."

"All work and no play—surely you've heard that one before?" Dr. Craft adopted a sober expression. "But for your sake, you cranky dullard, I'll be as professional as I can be."

"Good. Tell me," Brognola said, glancing at Walker, "is it possible to counter Rhee's brainwashing?"

"Weren't you paying attention? I better have you stay after class. What do you think I've been doing all this time? Planting autoerotic suggestions?"

"No, no, that's not what I meant." Brognola suspected she knew exactly what he meant, but she was feigning ignorance to get his goat. That was another thing about brilliant people. Many had what would politely be termed character quirks. Or, as Craft might say, minor mental aberrations.

When Brognola thought about it, though, he was comforted by the knowledge that geniuses could be as nutty as everyone else.

"Elaborate, if you please," Dr. Craft prodded.

"Can you plant a hypnotic suggestion that will counter Madame Rhee's next attempt to extract intel from Walker?"

"Ah. You want him to resist the serum she injects, is that it?"

"Exactly."

"Then why didn't you say so?" Dr. Craft leaned toward the young man and pursed her lips. "I'll be honest with you, Hal. I can't guarantee success. We have no idea what type of chemicals they use, or how potent the chemicals are. Sure, I can instruct Walker to resist, I can reinforce his will, but whether he will be strong enough to fight off the effects remains to be seen.''

"We have to try, Sarah," Brognola said.

"You have a plan, I take it?"

"I want to send Walker in wearing a wire. I want to catch Rhee in the act so we have indisputable proof and can put her behind bars for the rest of her life.'' The trial would be a media sensation, Brognola imagined, and serve as a stern warning to America's enemies that spying would be punished with the utmost severity.

"You'll be asking an awful lot of our young friend here," Dr. Craft commented.

"What if they frisk him and find the wire? What if he isn't able to resist the effects of the chemical brainwashing?" She paused. "Then there's another factor, the X factor."

"It's your turn to elaborate."

"The X factor is the unknown variable in every situation like this. There is a very real chance that Walker could suffer irreparable harm. The brain is fragile, big man. The tug-of-war between the chemicals and his will might induce psychological trauma or organic damage.''

Brognola came to an immediate decision. "Bring him out of it, then."

"Now?"

"I'll ask him whether he wants to cooperate. If he doesn't, I won't force it on him.''

Dr. Craft fluttered her eyelids. "Has anyone ever mentioned how marvelous you look in your shining armor?''

"Please, Sarah. These sessions are recorded, remember?"

"Don't worry. I can always pull a Nixon." She turned to Walker. "Bob, this is Dr. Craft. Do you hear me?"

"I hear you," the engineer replied in a dull monotone.

"When I snap my fingers, you will awaken. You will be fully restored. Do you understand?"

"I understand."

Five seconds later the deed was done, and Bob Walker lay there blinking like someone who had just stepped from a shadowed nook into bright sunlight. "Dr. Craft. Mr. Brognola. Are we done? What did you find out? Am I going to be arrested?"

Brognola didn't hold anything back. He saw the young man's flush of anger as he related the details of the chemical brainwashing technique. When he was done, when he had explained his plan, he sat back. "So what will it be, Mr. Walker? You can do your country an inestimable service by helping out."

Dr. Craft cleared her throat. "You will also be at considerable risk, Bob. I can't stress enough that you might suffer serious harm. You'll be waging a war inside your head, with potentially grave results. Perhaps you would like time to yourself think it over?"

Walker looked from her to Brognola and back again. "Thank you for your concern, Dr. Craft. But I'd like to do what I can. Helping Mr. Brognola will show everyone I'm no traitor."

"I already know that, son," Brognola stated. "The intel on the stealth sub was extracted against your will. You've committed no crime, no breach of trust."

"Then I'll do it to prove something to myself," Walker said.

"What?" Dr. Craft asked.

"Let's just say that it's the right thing to do and let it go at that, can we?" Walker said. "I'm not a kid, you know. I appreciate your warning. But I have to do this. Come what may."

"Are you certain?" Brognola pressed him. False bravado would jeopardize the whole operation and might get the young man killed.

"I've never been more certain of anything in my life. So do what you have to. Let's get this show on the road."

Brognola gestured at Craft. "You heard the man. Put him under again and plant your suggestions."

Dr. Craft's reservations were apparent, but she didn't argue. "I want you to know, Bob," she said, touching the engineer's arm, "this is a very brave thing you're doing."

A smile lit Bob Walker's face.

Interstate 5, midway between San Francisco and San Diego

FANG WASN'T a superstitious man. Not like his pathetic father, who had always been offering prayers and wearing charms to ward off unseen evil. The display had disgusted Fang, even as a child. It was foolish for anyone to believe in a realm of reality that couldn't be verified with the physical senses.

But after two severe setbacks, after the attack on Diversified Industries in Inchon and now the attack on the Lucca villa outside San Francisco, Fang was beginning to think he was under a jinx. Or, as his father would have claimed, an evil spell.

There had to be a rational explanation, though, and Fang believed he knew what it was. The hit squad sent by the RDEI could only have learned about his link with the Lucca Family from one source—his nephew. Cho-Hee's disappearance was now explained. The men in black had gotten their hands on him and forced Cho-Hee to divulge all he knew.

It saddened Fang. His enemies wouldn't have let his nephew live. Cho-Hee had to be dead, a loss Fang felt deeply. His nephew had been the one individual he truly cared for, the only person he had trusted with all his secrets.

Well, not quite all. Fang had kept a few to himself, such as his Swiss bank account and his château in northern France, his hideaway of last resort. It would suit his purposes better than the Thailand fortress. He carried the appropriate passport and papers on him at all times so that if the unthinkable occurred, if his enemies were closing in and his life was imperiled, he could fly to Europe under an assumed identity and hide out until it was safe to resume business as usual.

After the disaster at the villa, Fang was wondering if maybe the time had come to avail himself of his emergency plan.

Since the RDEI had learned about Lucca, odds were they had also found out about Madame Rhee and Club X. It was possible the hit squad, or those who were left, at any rate, were on their way there now. If Fang had any sense, he would forget his scheduled visit and instruct his driver to head for the airport so he could take the first available flight to France.

But he couldn't.

Classified information on the new stealth sub would be worth its weight in gold. Certain foreign powers would pay anything to obtain it. Fang could practically write his own check. And he needed money, lots of money, to recoup his recent losses. The drug shipment in Yokohama and the loss of his Inchon base had set him back millions. Millions he could recoup in one fell swoop by selling the intel on the stealth sub to the highest bidder.

Fang was trapped by circumstances beyond his control. He needed the intel so badly, he was going to meet with Madame Rhee as planned and be on hand when she administered the special serum to the American. As soon as they were done, he would take the information and leave.

Should the RDEI's assassins show up, Fang would be ready for them. Nine of his men had made it out of the Lucca compound, including the invaluable Kon-Li. Madame Rhee had another seven men at her disposal. More than enough to deal with the curs from the RDEI. Still, as always, prudence was called for.

"Kon-Li," he said.

The giant was gazing out the window of their newly rented limousine at the scenery. "Yes, master?" he responded, shifting.

"I want you at my side from the moment we arrive until the moment we leave. And I want the driver to stay with the limo, ready to leave at a moment's notice."

"It will be done."

"Post extra men at the gate and around the grounds.

No one is to get past them. Make it clear that if they fail me and live, they will wish they hadn't.''

"You should have let me deal with the RDEI's assassins in Inchon, master. The Luccas would still be alive.''

They had heard the news on the radio, of all places, an hourly newscast, reporting that reputed Mob boss Angelo Lucca and his son, Anthony, were killed in what the police were describing as a fierce gun battle with a rival Family at the Lucca estate. More than twenty bodies had been discovered, and more were expected to be found as authorities sifted through the rubble of the Lucca villa, which had been gutted by fire.

The Luccas were gone, and with them Fang's hope of establishing a beachhead in America. A valuable contact had been lost, an important pipeline disrupted before it even began to flow.

"I do not want any harm to come to you, '' Fang told the giant.

Kon-Li's usually inscrutable features betrayed indignation. "Am I to infer that you do not think me capable of dealing with them?''

"Your skill is unsurpassed. Of that I have no doubt. But all it takes is one lucky shot, and all the skill in the world counts for nothing.'' Fang paused. "I have lost my nephew. I do not care to lose you, as well, Kon-Li.''

"I vow on the graves of my ancestors that I will slay the vermin who have caused you such grief.''

"You are not to leave my side,'' Fang reiterated. "Not for any reason whatsoever. Is that clear?''

"Yes, master.''

Fang let the matter drop. Not once in all the years they had been together had Kon-Li ever disobeyed him. He gazed at the scenery himself, at the opulence that was America, confident he had taken all the steps necessary to insure his visit to Club X would be short, safe and immensely profitable.

Interstate 5, just east of San Jose

"WITH ALL DUE RESPECT, sir, I do not see why I had to come along," Soh Bong-Kan groused as he passed a slow-moving pickup. "Thanks to you, I am in danger of blowing my cover. All my years of work will go down the tubes."

Colonel Hin's dislike of the man was growing by leaps and bounds. "Down the tubes, is it? How unfortunate your loyalty to our country isn't as finely honed as your grasp of American idioms."

Soh wheeled the van back into the proper lane. "My loyalty has never been questioned. I have proved myself on many occasions." His annoyance bubbled to the surface. "For you to suggest otherwise is an insult."

"If your loyalty is all you claim, then stop complaining," Hin said.

"But this is madness! You are the only one of your unit who is left. What can you hope to accomplish? Sin Mak-Fang is bound to be on his guard."

"It will make no difference. I was ordered to terminate him, and I will accomplish my mission. By myself, if need be."

"Then do so, and let me return to San Francisco. You dragged me off before I could call in sick for tomorrow. My employer will be upset when I do not show up.''

"I am sure you will think up a suitable excuse," Hin remarked. "I need you more than your American employer does."

"For what? You still haven't said."

"I cannot be in two places at the same time."

"Who can? So?"

The man's attitude was grating on Hin, taxing his self-control. He would never tolerate such rank insubordination from a soldier under his command. And while, technically, Soh wasn't in the military anymore, the man still held rank and still answered to men who were. "I need someone to distract Fang's cannon fodder while I go after Fang himself."

"You expect me to engage them in combat, sir?" Soh's anxiety was transparent.

Hin's disdain reached new heights. "No. You would not last ten seconds. You are so out of shape, so out of training, it would be like putting a whale in a shooting gallery."

"I resent that, sir."

"Resent it all you like. But keep your resentment and other personal feelings to yourself from now on, or Fang's men will be the least of your worries."

Soh, fuming, scowled but held his tongue.

"The plain truth, Major, is that you sicken me. But you have your uses, and one of them will be to plant an explosive charge that will lure most of Fang's men from his side, reducing the opposition I must face." Hin arched an eyebrow. "Do you think you can do that, Major Soh, without blowing yourself up?"

"My skills might be rusty but they are intact, sir,"

was Soh's testy response. "Just tell me what you want me to do, and it will get done."

"How comforting to hear," Hin said. "Fang doesn't know it yet, but his hours on this earth are numbered."

San Diego

ARNOLD'S BAR AND Grill was located on F Street, not far from Horton Plaza. The moment he entered, Mack Bolan spotted the big Fed seated at a corner table. Brognola waved, and the Executioner weaved among the tables to take a seat across from him. "Couldn't we have met at the federal building?"

Brognola resumed reading a menu. "Yes, we could have. But I haven't eaten all day, and I doubt you have, either." He motioned at the small, quiet restaurant, which was half of the establishment. "Arnold's is open twenty-four hours and serves some of the best steaks this side of Montana."

Few people were eating, which was perfectly normal at three in the morning. Bolan unbuttoned his trench coat but didn't remove it, not with the Beretta snug under his left arm.

"Okay, let's order and get down to business," Bolan suggested.

The waitress took their order, then returned with coffee.

"Now then," Brognola began, "we're all set to go. I'll have a dozen agents staked out a couple of blocks away. At a signal from you, they'll go in and mop up."

"What was that you said on the phone? Something about using Walker to snare the others?"

Brognola detailed his plan, concluding with, "If all goes well, you'll be in and out before Fang knows what hit him. Walker will gather all the evidence I need to convict Rhee and her cronies. And we'll put Club X out of business, permanently."

Several aspects of the operation didn't appeal to Bolan. For starters, it had to be conducted in broad daylight. "Why not have Walker wait until after dark to go see Madame Rhee?"

"As much as I'd like to, we can't. She instructed him to report to her the minute he's done with the blueprints. He figures that will be around four, and he might have told Rhee as much when she questioned him last. Any later, and she might become suspicious."

"Why use Walker at all?" Bolan quizzed. The engineer was an amateur, and amateurs had an unfortunate habit of getting themselves killed.

"Putting Rhee behind bars is just as important as nailing Fang. I want a clean sweep, Striker." Brognola upended the sugar container over his coffee, adding enough to make a hummingbird giddy. "Having Walker wear a wire is crucial."

"You do realize, don't you, this whole thing could blow up in your face?" Bolan mentioned.

"I'm counting on you to see that it doesn't."

The big Fed was asking a lot, Bolan mused. But if he thought it best, then so be it. He had to accept the special problems a daytime insertion posed, and deal with them. "How many civilians do you estimate will be on the premises?"

"Hard to say, that early. Madame Rhee has a stable of fifteen girls, maybe more, but most work at night. Walker says the most he's seen in the afternoon has been eight or nine. Add in about half a dozen johns. Oh, and Rhee has a housecleaning staff of three, two women and an old man."

"How much opposition?"

"Walker was a bit fuzzy. He has a hard time telling Orientals apart, but he guesses ten or less."

Combined with Fang's men, that made upward of twenty gunners, definitely a force to be reckoned with.

"If it's any consolation, Walker never saw any hardware. They either only pack handguns, or they have the heavy artillery stashed away."

After what Bolan had seen at the Lucca villa, he wasn't leaving anything to chance. He would go in loaded for bear. "Let's suppose a worst-case scenario. Who gets Walker out if things go wrong?"

"Until you signal my men to move in, you'll be the only one in any position to help him," Brognola said. "And before you rake me over the coals, yes, Walker knows he's walking a tightrope with no safety net. In fact, the kid seems to be looking forward to it."

"Does he have a death wish?"

"No. I'm not quite sure why he's doing it. I'm just glad he is."

"Will he be armed?"

"No. What if they frisk him? Planting a wire on him is risky enough. Don't worry, though. We have all the bases covered. Everything will work out fine. This one is as good as wrapped up."

Bolan recalled Brognola saying the same thing to him in Yokohama. It came under the heading of "famous last words."

CHAPTER TWENTY

Bob Walker had never been so scared in his life. Or so excited. He drove from Omnitronics, Incorporated, to Club X in a strange tingly daze, amazed he was actually going through with it. He had worried he might chicken out, might change his mind and refuse to help Brognola. He'd considered doing so dozens of times in the past several hours.

Intrigue. Enemy agents. The threat of death hanging like a cloud.

Walker grinned as he turned onto the street where Club X was located. Never in a million years would he have thought anything like this would ever happen to him. To have a real-life adventure of his own, pitting his wits against Madame Rhee and that other guy the Feds had told him about—what was his name?—oh, yeah, Sin Mak-Fang.

Walker liked that name. It had a ring to it. It was fitting for someone who headed a criminal empire. Much better than, say, Egg Foo-Yong. He giggled at his little joke, then remembered the Feds could hear every sound he made. "Sorry," he blurted. "Just thought a funny."

Embarrassed, he resolved to act more mature. Whoever was listening in would think he was an idiot. "I sure hope this wire is still working properly," he remarked. "I'm counting on you guys to bail me out if the going gets rough."

He shut up. He could see the wall now, and the wrought-iron gate. In broad daylight the place seemed more run-down than he'd envisioned it. The yard was untended and overgrown with tall grass and weeds. This time, when he braked, he saw where the gate guards always popped out from. There was a tall pine to the right of it, the trunk wide enough for a man to hide behind.

So for once Bob wasn't startled by the guard's sudden appearance. "Caught you this time," he said, grinning. "And here I thought you materialized out of thin air."

The Koreans knew him on sight by now. This one admitted him without comment.

Walker wheeled on up the drive, the tingling in his arms and legs growing worse. "Why am I tingling like this?" he asked himself out loud, then wanted to kick himself because the Feds were probably wondering what he meant. "I'm a little nervous, is all," he explained. "Don't worry. I can do this. No problem."

Parking, he got out and scrutinized the building. He'd never noticed before the peeling plaster, the sagging gutter on the roof, how the whole place was in bad need of some paint. "How odd," he said. "I guess we only see what we want to see, huh?"

Squaring his shoulders, Walker marched toward the entrance. Halfway there his mouth went dry and his knees began acting as if they wanted to buckle. Halting, he took a deep breath and muttered, "Here I go. Man, what have I gotten myself into?"

WALKER SAW EVERYTHING with new eyes. The ladies sprawled on the sofas and chairs didn't seem quite as lovely as they usually did. Lines creased their faces, and when they smiled at him, it was mechanically, as if they did it because they had to. There was no warmth, no real friendliness. And the heavy fragrances they wore were more stifling than stimulating. "I see the harlots as they really are," he said under his breath.

Madame Rhee was on a stool at the bar. Smiling broadly, she came over with her arms outstretched. "Robert! How good it is to see you again!"

Walker recoiled a step, struck by the wicked gleam in her dark, glittering eyes, and by the serpentine sway of her body.

"Robert?" Madame Rhee said, stopping cold. "What is the matter? You look as if you've just seen a ghost."

"Sorry. I'm fine." Moistening his lips and mouth, he added, "I was thinking about something else."

"Do you feel all right? You seem a little pale. And you're sweating."

Walker thought fast. "I might be coming down with something. My boss said the same thing to me." Of course, that had been days ago, but she didn't need to know that. He snickered at how clever he was being.

"What is so humorous?" Madame Rhee asked.

"A movie I watched last night," he fibbed, his stomach started to do the jitterbug. He had to be more careful or he would blow it.

Madame Rhee pressed a hand to his forehead. "You feel warm to me, Robert. You might have a temperature. Perhaps you should come with me to my office. I have herbs that can help. And there is someone there I would very much like you to meet."

"After you," Walker said, and followed her. It was strange, but all his senses seemed to be enhanced. His vision was clearer, his hearing sharper. When they entered her office, he realized right away there were three lurking shapes in the shadows. But he ignored them for the moment and concentrated on the bald man seated at her desk, and the giant beside him.

"This is Mr. Sin, an old friend of mine," Madame Rhee said, then motioned at the chair Walker always sat in. "Have a seat, why don't you? He has something important to discuss with you."

This was the moment of truth. Fear twisted Walker's gut as he willed his legs to move. He sensed the men in the shadows closing in the second he sat down. Iron hands gripped his arms, pinning them in place, and straps were applied. Playing his part, he exclaimed, "Hey! What is this?"

"Don't be alarmed, Robert," Madame Rhee said. She looked behind him, and nodded. "Inject it now, Kim. We don't want to keep Mr. Sin waiting."

Walker felt a stinging sensation at the base of his skull, then liquid fire engulfed his brain. The room spun and swirled. Fleeting nausea racked him. He started to feel his consciousness slipping, just as it had to have happened on previous occasions when the chemicals were injected. But this time something new happened.

To Walker, his mind seemed to be in the center of

a vast black void that was steadily contracting. All rational thought was on the verge of blotting out when a tiny voice in the core of his being urged, "Resist, Bob! Resist!"

Walker struggled against the black tide. He imagined himself trapped in a room with the walls closing in, and pushed against them with all his might. He could do it! he told himself. Push!

IN THE SPECIALLY outfitted truck two blocks away, Brognola heard a man with a deep voice ask, "What is happening? Why does he keep saying *push* over and over?"

"I do not know, Mr. Sin," Madame Rhee replied. "He has never done this before. It is almost as if he is resisting the serum."

"That is impossible," Sin Mak-Fang said.

Brognola reached for the headset to pull it off. He had to get Walker out of there.

Then he heard Madame Rhee.

"Look! He's stopped! The chemicals have taken hold!" She had to have moved closer to Walker because her next question was much louder. "Robert, do you hear me?"

"I hear you."

Madame Rhee laughed. "All is well, Mr. Sin. Occasionally, the serum produces erratic effects, but they never last long."

"Then begin extracting the information," Sin Mak-Fang ordered. "My time here is short, remember?"

"As you wish."

THE EXECUTIONER TURNED the corner at Arnhurst and Vine, his hands shoved into the pockets of his trench coat. Over a low wall on his left he could see the roof of Club X, partially hidden by trees. He was at the rear of the property, on a quiet side street. A few cars lined the curb. A cat was nosing in a flower garden across the way, the only sign of life.

Bolan walked to the middle of the block. Pausing, he scanned the homes on the other side to verify no one was watching, then he coiled and leaped straight up, hooking his forearms over the top of the wall. Levering his legs up and over, he dropped into high grass and reached under his trench coat.

In addition to the Beretta and the Desert Eagle, the soldier had brought a Mini-Uzi fitted with a shoulder strap and a Wilson Arms suppressor. Silent stalking was the rule of the day. Brognola didn't want a battle royal to break out in the middle of a residential neighborhood if it could be helped. Unfolding the metal stock, Bolan slowly rose.

Fang was supposed to be on hand for the brainwashing session, according to a phone tap the Feds had on Club X, so Bolan expected lots of guards. Yet he didn't see any. Paralleling the wall, he glided to the left, toward a belt of heavy brush that would afford him the cover he needed to reach the house.

Bolan had only taken a few steps when he nearly stumbled over a body sprawled facedown in some weeds. It was a North Korean, a guard whose throat had been slit from ear to ear.

Someone had already penetrated the property, and it didn't require any great deductive reasoning to guess who. Bolan remembered the colonel's cryptic comment at the Lucca estate, something about knowing all of Fang's secrets. Evidently, the officer had been referring to Fang's visit to the brothel.

Frowning, Bolan moved on. The colonel's presence compounded the danger to Robert Walker. Should a firefight break out, Walker might be an incidental casualty. Or Fang might deliberately have Walker slain in the belief Walker was somehow responsible.

Rustling in the brush brought Bolan to a stop. A dark-clothed figure appeared, but it wasn't the colonel. Another guard was making the rounds, an assault rifle cradled in his arms.

Bolan froze, letting the unwary gunner come closer. The man was gazing toward the house instead of along the wall, his interest grabbed by something Bolan couldn't see. Suddenly, the guard jammed the assault rifle to his shoulder to shoot. Bolan was quicker. A stroke of the Uzi's trigger resulted in the gunner flopping backward like a stricken goose, and collapsing.

Bolan straightened and glanced toward Club X just in time to observe a black-clad figure vanish around an oak tree.

The figure wore a ski mask.

"YOU ARE DOING fine, Robert. Tell me more about the integrator for the cloaking system," Madame Rhee was saying when someone pounded on the side door of the delivery truck. Brognola let one of the agents answer it. He didn't want to miss a word of what was going on in Rhee's office.

Brognola couldn't tell if Walker had been able to resist the serum. The man's voice had the same flat inflection it had when Dr. Craft hypnotized him. Apparently, Madame Rhee was satisfied all was going as it should, and that was all that mattered.

The agent who had answered the knock tapped Brognola on the arm. "Sir? You should take a look at this."

Removing the headset, Brognola moved to the door. Two other agents, Henderson and Grimmel, were outside. They were supposed to be on the roof of an apartment building cater-corner from the Club X lot, keeping an eye on things. Each had hold of an overweight, slovenly Korean who was trying hard to put on a brave front, and failing. "What's this about?"

Henderson handed over an orange backpack. "We spotted him placing this along the north wall, sir."

Brognola flipped the unzipped flap back. Inside was a timer and enough C-4 to blow apart an armored car.

"We stopped him just as he was about to set the timer," Henderson reported.

The Korean mustered a smile. "I told them I just saw it lying there and wondered what it was, but they didn't believe me."

"I don't believe you, either," Brognola said. "Who are you? What were you up to?"

"Nothing at all," the Korean said. "If you insist on holding me, I demand to see a lawyer. I know my rights under American law."

Inside the truck, the agent who was monitoring and recording the goings-on in Madame Rhee's office called out, "Sir! You should give a listen."

"Now what?" Brognola said.

"I think I just heard shots."

BOLAN WAS THREADING through the trees faster than he should in order to overtake the North Korean colonel before the officer reached the house. Without warning, he came on another slain guard. This one had been garroted with a slender wire.

The house was sixty feet ahead. Bolan looked up and saw the colonel dart around a corner. It wouldn't be long before he found a way in, putting Robert Walker's life in grave jeopardy.

Bolan hastened on, surveying the vegetation. A maple tree had to be skirted, and as he went past he heard the crunch of a twig. It saved his life. He whirled, and a gleaming knife that would have been buried in his back missed by a handbreadth.

The guard holding the hilt skipped in low and fast, slashing again and again. He had a pistol in a shoulder holster but had relied on the blade instead, maybe because it was quieter.

Bolan, backpedaling, started to level the Uzi. He felt his left heel snag on something, and tripped. An exposed root was the culprit; he saw it as he fell onto his back.

Sneering, the guard pounced, leaping onto Bolan before he could recover. The man's knee gouged into the soldier's chest as his free hand sought his victim's throat.

Bolan let go of the Uzi to seize hold of the guard's right wrist as the knife arced toward his ribs. With his other hand he pried at the fingers encircling his neck. His attacker was wiry but strong. Locked together, they rolled from one side to the other, neither able to gain the upper hand.

Bolan was keenly aware that other guards could appear at any second. He bucked upward and succeeded in partly dislodging his adversary. The man clutched at the trench coat to keep from being tossed off, then thrust the knife at Bolan's neck. Wrenching his head to the right, Bolan avoided having his jugular opened.

The guard hissed like a viper, then drove a knee at the soldier's groin.

A last-instant swivel of his hips spared Bolan, but the knee rammed into his inner thigh and spiked piercing pain through his whole body. Gritting his teeth against it, he surged up onto his knees.

The Korean tried a head butt next, driving his forehead at Bolan's nose. It missed, connecting with Bolan's ear when he jerked aside.

A second later, over the guard's shoulder, the soldier spotted another gunner, strolling along casually, as yet unaware of them.

Bolan had to end it, and soon. Tearing his right arm from his enemy's grasp, he gripped the Uzi and angled the barrel so the muzzle gouged into the man's gut. He had only to tap the trigger once. Stiffening, the guard opened his mouth to cry out, but Bolan clamped a hand over it and lowered the convulsing body to the ground.

The other man heard something. He looked toward them, only to have his left eyeball explode as his cranium was cored from front to back.

The delay had proved costly. Bolan sprinted to the rear of the house, but the colonel was long gone. Moving in the same direction the officer had, Bolan rounded a corner and spied an open window under an awning.

Ducking low, the soldier crept to the shoulder-high sill. No lights were on, but enough sunlight streamed in to reveal it was a bedroom. Empty, too, from what Bolan could see. He swung the Mini-Uzi behind him, grasped hold and pulled himself up. As his chest slid through, a hard object was jabbed against his temple.

"This is getting to be a habit, Sergeant."

Bolan froze, unsure whether the colonel would regard him as ally or foe. "We need to talk," he whispered.

The colonel stepped back but didn't lower his weapon. "Climb on in," he said softly. "I do not want any of the guards to see your legs sticking out and sound an alarm." He held out his left hand. "First, give me the Uzi."

Bolan had no choice but to comply. As he sank onto his hands and knees under the window, the officer stepped back, slinging the Mini-Uzi over his own shoulder.

"So your people knew about the brothel and Fang's visit today, too? I should have expected as much."

"Give it up," Bolan said.

"Be serious."

"I'm not alone. Federal agents have the house under surveillance and will be closing in at any moment."

The colonel shrugged. "Let them. By then I will have done what I came to do and be on my way. As long as they do not try to stop me, I will not harm any of them."

"Let us deal with Fang," Bolan said. "He's on American soil. I'll tend to him, and the Feds will arrest everyone else. Case closed."

"It is not that simple, I am afraid."

Thanks to the ski mask, Bolan couldn't read the man's expression and thus had no clue what he might be thinking. "Why not? In Inchon you let me live so one or the other of us could deal with Fang."

"That was then, Sergeant. Since Inchon all my men have been killed. I owe Sin Mak-Fang. He is mine, and mine alone."

"That's not very professional."

"On the contrary, Sergeant, I am being totally professional. My orders are to terminate him. In this I have failed, twice, but I will not fail a third time. Here is where it ends, one way or the other."

Bolan gauged the distance between them and decided he couldn't reach the officer without taking a slug or two, if the other were so inclined. "It doesn't have to be this way. You can slip back out that window and be gone before anyone is the wiser. The Feds will never know."

"You would keep it a secret?" The colonel was silent a bit. Then he slowly pulled the ski mask off and tossed it onto a nearby dresser. "I thank you, Sergeant, for the consideration you have shown me. I, Colonel Hin Bo-Kee, salute you." Tapping his heels together, he did just that, executing a crisp salute. Then he backed toward the door.

"It's still not too late to change your mind, Colonel Hin."

"Do not try to stop me, Sergeant. Do not attempt to interfere in any way. I, and I alone, must kill Sin Mak-Fang. Take my advice and stay in this room until it is over. It would upset me greatly to have to hurt you." Hin peeked out, nodded once at the soldier and slipped into the corridor.

Barely ten seconds later gunfire rocked Club X.

BOB WALKER WAS DOING what he had always secretly longed to do. He was involved in a thrilling escapade. His wits, his cleverness, were all that stood between him and an early grave. And he loved it.

Walker had been spouting nonsense to Madame Rhee, making things up as he went along, providing information as worthless as a baby's scribble. But Madame Rhee didn't know that. She was having it recorded, on video and on a cassette recorder. It was enough to make him laugh but he dared not or they would catch on to the ruse.

The only problem was that Walker's body felt drained of all energy, an effect of the serum, he figured. Mentally, he was almost as fatigued, but at least the sickening sensation of being sucked into a black void was gone.

"You are doing fine, Robert," Madame Rhee said. "Tell me more about the integrator for the cloaking system."

Careful not to show any emotion or alter his flat tone, Walker responded, "The integrator is essential to the entire system. Without it, the cloaking device will not work. It is housed in a titanium-lined box for maximum protection."

"Tell me how it works, Robert," Madame Rhee became specific. "Tell me exactly how the device functions."

Walker started to reel off more technobabble, but the bald guy Brognola had warned him about, Fang, his name was, was growing impatient and interrupted him.

"How much longer will this take? I have a flight to catch in an hour."

"My utmost apologies," Madame Rhee answered, "but you wanted all the information this young fool has. The new systems he was granted access to are quite complicated and—" She fell silent when Sin Mak-Fang gestured.

"Why did the American stop just now?"

"Stop?"

"Yes. You told him to tell you exactly how the integrator device works. He started to, but he stopped talking when I did. Why?"

Walker realized his mistake before Madame Rhee did. She was so accustomed to bowing and scraping around her lord and master that what he had done appeared perfectly natural to her.

Fang elaborated. "Anyone under the influence of the serum must obey every command their control gives them. He should not have stopped until you told him to."

"That's right!" Madame Rhee turned her full attention to Walker. "Can it be he is faking?"

"It is easy enough to find out," Fang said. "Loosen one of his arms. Then order him to bite the tip of a finger off."

Walker suppressed a shudder. He tried to convince himself they wouldn't really go through with it, that no one could possibly be so cold-hearted, so brutal, but at a snap of Madame Rhee's fingers, the man called Kim stepped forward and unfastened the strap securing Walker's right wrist to the chair.

Madame Rhee's eyes were boring into him as if she could see right through him. "Can you hear me, Robert?"

"I hear you."

"Put the middle finger of your right hand into your mouth, between your teeth, and bite off the end of it. Right this instant."

Terrified but not knowing what else to do, Walker inserted his finger in his mouth. Now he had two choices—either bite it off, or free his other arm and try to escape. He tensed to reach for the other strap.

That was when the door burst open and the room exploded in violence.

CHAPTER TWENTY-ONE

Colonel Hin Bo-Kee didn't know which surprised him more, the twinge of regret he felt at his treatment of the American, or the thrill of anticipation that coursed through his veins at the prospect of confronting Sin Mak-Fang.

Hin knew the sergeant would try to stop him. When he'd glanced out the window to make sure none of the guards had seen him enter and had instead seen the sergeant coming around the corner, he had flattened against the wall. The American was after him, and it could only be for one reason, to talk him out of going after Fang.

Hin couldn't let that happen. The smart thing to do would have been to kill the sergeant outright. That was what he had been trained to do in situations like this. Anyone who stood in the way of a mission being performed was to be eliminated. It was as basic a rule as any Hin lived by.

His superiors would be shocked to learn he hadn't. They would be outraged that he'd had the sergeant under his gun and hadn't squeezed the trigger.

But Hin couldn't bring himself to do it. He had grown to respect the man, to see that, to a large degree, they were very much alike. Ideologies aside, they were soldiers first and foremost, consummate professionals, men devoted to ideals, so devoted they were willing to die for those ideals.

As Hin shut the door to the bedroom and turned, he put the American from his mind and concentrated on his prey. The rush of excitement he felt was unusual. Killing was a job to him, no more, no less. He had been ordered to terminate scores of people over the years, but never, not once in all that time, had he felt so much as a flicker of emotion. He killed coldly, dispassionately, as he had been taught to do. For him, putting a bullet into a human brain involved no more feeling than swatting a fly did for others.

Yet Hin couldn't deny he felt great relish at the thought of slaying Sin Mak-Fang. Sin was a traitor in the first degree, an embarrassment to his country and to the Party. But more than that, because of Sin, Hin had lost all his men, all those fine troopers he had diligently trained and nurtured as if they were his own sons.

Hin couldn't wait to reach Sin Mak-Fang. In his haste he ran a few yards to a corner and stepped partly past it instead of looking first. As a result, a guard strolling down the hall spotted him and went for a weapon.

The officer was quicker. He unleashed a burst from his assault rifle, then sped past the riddled body. He had a layout of the building filed in his mind, a layout provided courtesy of Sin Cho-Hee, who had visited Club X on two occasions, once when it was originally set up and again when Madame Rhee obtained especially important intel. Cho-Hee had drawn a sketch of the floor plans before he died, smearing the paper with his blood.

Shouts erupted from various quarters. Racing around another corner, the colonel nearly collided with a pair of buxom women in scanty attire. They screamed at the sight of him but didn't get out of his way. Petrified, they stood rooted like granite cows, so he plowed through them and on toward a certain door just ahead.

To the rear a cannon boomed. Or what sounded like a cannon. Hin suspected it was the American's side arm, the Desert Eagle the sergeant had been wearing, the sound amplified by the narrow halls. From the sound of things, the American was involved in a fierce battle.

The colonel grinned. While the sergeant kept the guards occupied, or vice versa, he would tend to Sin Mak-Fang.

On the left was the door Hin had been making for, the door to Madame Rhee's office. Throwing caution aside, he burst in. He was afraid that Sin Mak-Fang might escape through a window or by some other secret means, as the renegade had in Inchon. But no, as he barreled into the shadowy room, he beheld the object of his quest seated across a desk.

Immediately, Hin brought the rifle to bear but others were rushing toward him and he had to dispose of them first. He shot a man on his right, another on his left, then sighted down the barrel at a woman who had to be Madame Rhee. Before he could fire, though, from out of nowhere a blow to the side of his neck felled him like a crippled ox.

Whoever had hit him had known just where to

strike. Hin's nervous system was aflame. He tried to rise but his body refused to obey. His assault rifle was ripped from his grasp, and the American's Mini-Uzi was taken. He heard Madame Rhee cry out, and glanced out of the corner of an eye.

"Listen! There are others! Club X is under attack! What do we do?"

"Stay calm, for one thing," Sin Mak-Fang said. Remarkably composed, he slowly rose. "You and your husband must retrieve the master disks from the computer room. Meet me at the special place in three minutes. Go."

The woman and another man hastened on out. That left Hin alone with the traitor, a young American strapped to a metal chair, and one other, the one who had struck the pressure point in his neck, the giant his superiors had warned him about, the living weapon called Ruy Kon-Li.

Sin Mak-Fang came around the desk and leaned against it. "It seems RDEI assassins pop out of the woodwork wherever we go. Kill him, Kon-Li. Take a minute or so. Make him suffer. Make him suffer horribly for all he and the other RDEI maggots have cost me."

Hin saw the giant bend and reach for his collar. Willing himself to resist the fading pain, he lashed out, kicking the giant in the shins, sweeping Kon-Li's legs out from under him even as he shoved up and retreated a few paces to give himself room to maneuver. He adopted a cat stance.

The giant was rising, an ugly scowl marring his features. The scowl deepened when Sin Mak-Fang chuckled.

"You are becoming sloppy, Kon-Li. No one has ever knocked you off your feet before. Perhaps it is time you were put out to pasture." Fang sobered. "Do as I commanded. Kill him. Now."

Hin had a Type 67 silenced pistol in a shoulder rig but he didn't go for it, not with Kon-Li so close. It would never clear leather. Based on all the stories told about Kon-Li, Hin expected him to be a formidable fighter, but he wasn't without skill in that regard himself. He had taken up tae kwon do at the age of eleven and was now a master. In the whole Korean army, only a handful of men could match his skill at unarmed combat. He braced for the giant's onslaught.

Swifter than thought itself, Kon-Li executed a flying kick from a standing start, a kick so swift and so powerful that Hin was sent crashing against the wall before he could think to defend himself. He adopted a horse stance, his body rigid as steel, but he had barely set himself when the giant was on him again.

As they fought, as the colonel delivered a flurry of foot and hand blows and countered the few Kon-Li delivered, he learned another of life's important lessons: there were masters, and then there were *masters*.

The giant avoided all of Hin's swings, thrusts and kicks with ridiculous ease. Blocking, shifting, ducking, sliding, Kon-Li demonstrated he was worthy of his legend.

Hin had the impression the giant was toying with him, that Kon-Li was testing him to see how good he really was. And he wasn't the only one who noticed.

"Quit holding back," Sin Mak-Fang snapped. "We don't have all day for you to indulge yourself."

Chastised, Kon-Li changed from defensive tactics

to offensive moves. He tore into Hin like a human whirlwind, a whirlwind with lightning reflexes and steel arms and legs.

Hin tried to ward off the blows, but for every one he blocked, two got through, and each hit inflicted searing anguish. Every strike was precise, to a pressure point, to where exposed nerves rendered a man most vulnerable.

The colonel's left leg went numb, then his right arm. Tottering, he did what he should have done much sooner, he grabbed at his pistol. But he had to use his left hand, his right was useless, and with his left he was much slower. His fingers barely touched the grips when the giant's foot caught him full force on the sternum.

Hin's second lesson of the day was that there was pain, and then there was *pain*. His chest seemed to collapse in upon itself, his ribs shattering and splintering like so much kindling. The impact slammed him against the wall. As he slumped into a sitting posture, blood oozed from his mouth and nose. He tried to rise to continue, but a wave of weakness washed over him.

He saw Kon-Li step in close and elevate a rigid right hand for the coup de grâce.

"No," Sin Mak-Fang said.

The giant glanced back.

"Let him linger. Let him suffer. Let him die knowing he failed, that I live on, to expand my empire to all corners of the globe."

Kon-Li lowered his hand, then smirked at Hin. "You were good, assassin, but not good enough. No one is my equal. No one."

The chatter of an SMG down the hall made Sin

Mak-Fang stiffen. He pointed at a window. "We need to leave, quickly. Break it out."

Obediently, the giant walked around the desk, picked up the heavy chair as if it were weightless and carried it over. He set the chair down so he could rip off the curtains and cast them aside, then he lifted it clear over his head and hurled it as effortlessly as if it were made of air.

Hin struggled to stay conscious. He had a wet, salty taste in his mouth, and every breath he took seared his lungs with torment.

Kon-Li used his hands to bust out the few pieces of glass that remained, then stepped back so his master could climb through ahead of him.

Sin Mak-Fang seemed to be struck by an idea, and stopped. "Free the engineer and bring him with us. We might have need of a hostage. And later, if all goes well, we can take him to the marina and question him. I still may acquire the information I need on the stealth sub."

Hin watched as Kon-Li stalked to the metal chair. The young American resisted for all of two seconds. A short chop to the neck was all it took, and Kon-Li threw him over a shoulder.

By the window Sin Mak-Fang glanced at Hin and smiled. "Had I the time, I would cut off your head and send it to your superiors as a warning. They need to learn that I am a power to be reckoned with. They court my wrath at their peril." Gripping the jambs, Fang began to pull himself through, but he couldn't resist one final taunt. "Maybe I will go to the trouble of learning where they bury you so I can spit on your grave."

The colonel attempted to curse the traitor but all that issued from his mouth was more blood.

Laughing, Sin Mak-Fang departed. Kon-Li was right behind, the young American dangling like so much limp laundry.

The colonel would have given anything to be able to leap up after them. He would have given anything for the opportunity to empty his pistol into the giant and then torture Sin Mak-Fang until the renegade begged for mercy. He would have given anything. But all Hin could do was groan.

THE EXECUTIONER DREW the Desert Eagle as he crossed to the door. He poked his head out and spotted Hin vanishing around a corner to his left. Before he could give chase, however, a startled shout to his right warned him of two guards who were unlimbering pistols of their own. He ducked back as lead thunked into the door.

Bolan swung out into the hall again, adopted a Weaver stance and banged off two rapid shots. He nailed one of the gunners but the other darted into a room. And as Bolan skipped backward, yet another guard appeared, this one armed with an SMG.

Autofire ripped into the jambs, the walls, the floor. The new arrival was spraying rounds as if there were no tomorrow, the trademark of a novice at lethal craft.

Whirling, Bolan ran to the window. Engaging the guards in a gun duel would be counterproductive. They could keep him pinned in there indefinitely.

The soldier's main concern now was to reach Bob Walker and get the young engineer to safety. And if, along the way, he put an end to Sin Mak-Fang's criminal career, so much the better.

Once in the sunlight, Bolan sped along the house to the right. Yells let him know the perimeter guards were converging to find out what was going on. He spotted one, off through the trees, but the man was running toward the front gate and didn't see him. In order not to give his location away, Bolan didn't fire.

Around the next corner was an unlocked side door. Bolan crouched just inside to let his eyes adjust. From the direction of the gate SMGs crackled like firecrackers; from the sound of things, a firefight was underway.

Brognola's boys had arrived, Bolan guessed, but it would take them a while to overcome the stiff opposition and fight their way to the house. By then Walker might be dead.

Bolan had never seen the engineer, but Brognola had provided him with a description, and a diagram of the interior of Club X as best Walker remembered it. Madame Rhee's office was straight ahead.

The soldier jogged down the corridor. As he passed a door on his left, it flew open and out stepped a Korean in the act of loading an SMG. At a range of less than a foot Bolan fired the Desert Eagle. The Korean was jolted backward as if an invisible sledgehammer had slammed into him.

Women were screaming out in the lobby. To the north a heavy-caliber weapon boomed. And the skirmish at the gate was still in full swing. Bedlam was the order of the day, and Bolan didn't intend to be caught up in it. He saw Rhee's office, and slowed.

The Desert Eagle extended, Bolan sidestepped to

the open door, then darted in primed to cut loose. Only there was no one to shoot. Two bodies were on the floor, but Madame Rhee and Sin Mak-Fang were gone. Worse, there was no sign of Walker.

Bolan almost missed spotting the figure slumped in the gloom along the wall. Warily, he sidled over, and when he saw who it was, he dropped onto a knee and gripped the other's shoulder. "Colonel Hin?"

The officer's eyelids fluttered open and steadied. His jaw and neck were darkly stained. When he spoke, his voice rasped like sandpaper on metal. "I was hoping you would find me."

No wounds were apparent. Bolan started to rise, saying, "I'll let the Feds know you're in here. They'll get you to a hospital."

Hin's hand snatched the soldier's wrist. "Do not bother, Sergeant. I am not long for this life. Ruy Kon-Li has seen to that."

"I need to go look for someone else," Bolan said, by way of explaining why he couldn't linger. "But I'll be back."

"The engineer?" Hin said faintly. "He is gone."

Bolan squatted again. "Gone where?"

"Fang took him out the window." Hin sought to say more but a coughing fit prevented him. When he could speak again, he did so in short bursts, gasping for breath between each one. "As a hostage. Kon-Li carried him off."

Bolan hurried to the window and looked out, but Fang and the giant were nowhere around. He doubted they would get very far. By now the Feds had the property surrounded. He started to lift a leg over the sill.

"Sergeant! Wait! I must tell you something important—"

Bolan ran back to the North Korean. "Tell me what?"

Hin attempted to speak. He made inarticulate sounds, his eyelids fluttering, then he slumped lower, too weak to do anything. After a bit he marshaled his strength enough to mutter bitterly, "Be careful of the giant. So quick. So strong. His hands and feet are like sledgehammers."

"I've got to go after them. What were you going to say?"

"Say?"

"You said it was something important."

"Oh." Gritting his teeth, Hin looked up. "Almost forgot. So woozy. So weak. Can't think straight."

"Tell me, quickly," Bolan said, afraid the North Korean would succumb before he could get it out.

"I heard—" Hin began, but couldn't finish. Gasping loudly, he gripped his side and nearly doubled over.

A blast shook the front of the brothel, and a woman's shriek wavered long and loud, to end in a pitiable whine.

"Do you have any regrets, Sergeant?" Hin asked unexpectedly.

"Who doesn't?" Bolan said, wishing the officer would get to the point.

"Have you a wife? Children? A home?" Hin gazed across the room, his eyes acquiring a wistful aspect. "I regret not marrying. There was a woman once. But I thought she would hamper my career."

Bolan didn't respond. His personal life was just that,

and he rarely discussed it, even with those closest to him. As for his regrets, he had learned to balance them against the greater good he was doing. The sacrifices he had made to wage the Everlasting War were costly ones. He wouldn't deny that. But he had decided to make them of his own free will. No one forced him to. So when his time came, the only real regret he'd have was that he didn't have enough time to put every kingpin of crime, drug lord and tyrant out of business.

"Have you ever wondered," Hin said, his voice terribly weak, "what waits on the other side for men like us?"

"Now and then," Bolan admitted.

"Some say when we die, that is the end. Others say we live on. Soon I will know."

Hin smiled. "I will send you a postcard."

The pad of rushing feet spun Bolan toward the doorway. A North Korean in a suit, one of Fang's men, rushed in, shouting in Korean for his master, unaware Fang had fled. On spying the two men, he jerked up a pistol.

Bolan emptied the Desert Eagle into the man. Ejecting the magazine, he inserted another, and in the process, a familiar object on the floor caught his eye. Sliding the Desert Eagle into the holster on his hip, he reclaimed the Mini-Uzi.

"Sergeant?" Hin said more faintly than ever.

"I haven't left," Bolan said.

"Who turned out the light?"

The lamp over the desk was still on, and shafts of sunshine streamed in the window. Bolan squatted beside him. It wouldn't be long now. The soldier listened but heard no sounds from the hall. The firing out by the gate had died down, which was a good sign. "What were you going to tell me?"

Hin began wheezing, his chest heaving like a bellows. His mouth moved but no sounds came out. Then he made a visible attempt to marshal his waning strength. "I haven't told you yet? Slipping—"

"Do it now," Bolan said.

"Lean closer. Little breath left."

Bolan did as the North Korean requested. "I'm listening."

"Fang. Heard him—" The officer began trembling from head to toe, his limbs limply flailing the air.

"Heard what?"

"He said—taking engineer—to a marina." Colonel Hin Bo-Kee suddenly sucked in a deep breath, arched upward and flung a hand toward the ceiling as if reaching for something only he could see. His fingers closed on empty air. Melting onto his back, his arm fell to the floor at his side with a thump. His wide eyes stared blankly upward.

The Executioner closed them and rose. He had delayed long enough. Too long. But the information about the marina might prove helpful. Hurrying to the window, he paused as he stepped over the sill to gaze at the lifeless figure. Then he slipped out into the welcome sunlight.

THE OFFICE Hal Brognola had commandeered in the federal building in downtown San Diego was Spartan by comparison with his office in Washington, D.C., but it had an extra chair into which Mack Bolan sank after filling a paper cup at the water cooler. "How much longer?" he asked.

Brognola shrugged. "Your guess is as good as mine. Do you realize how many marinas there are in San Diego? Cross-referencing them with Club X and Sin Mak-Fang's known fronts will take time."

Bolan glanced at the wall clock. It had already taken five hours, and every tick of the clock was another precious second out of Bob Walker's life. If the engineer was even still alive. Once Fang pried the stealth sub info from him, the young man's life wouldn't be worth a hill of beans.

"I still can't believe Fang got away," Brognola said. "I had agents stationed on all four adjacent streets, just outside the walls, to keep anyone from slipping through our net. Yet Fang and that giant of his waltzed off as if they were invisible."

Bolan had been listening to his friend grouse about it since arriving. He downed the water in two gulps, crushed the paper cup and tossed it into the waste can.

"One of the agents must have turned his back at the wrong moment," Brognola remarked. "That's the only explanation I can think of."

"How soon before the cleanup crews finish up at the brothel?" Bolan idly asked to change the subject.

"Oh, midnight at the earliest. All the bodies have to be bagged and sent to the morgue. They'll make a sweep of all the rooms, but it won't be until tomorrow that they'll get to go over the place from top to bottom with a fine-tooth comb." Brognola linked his hands together and stretched. "The only bright spot in this whole miserable mess is that we nabbed Madame Rhee and her husband, Kim. We also got our hands on a couple of computer disks that have turned into a treasure trove of information. We're learning enough about Fang's operation to put a major crimp in it even if we don't catch him.''

''Has Rhee agreed to cooperate yet?''

''No. We've offered her limited immunity if she'll tell us where Fang took Walker. But all she does is laugh in our faces and go on and on about how her master is the cleverest man alive, and how we can never catch him, even when he's right under our noses. If ever there was a case for legalizing the rack, this is it.''

Bolan shared the big Fed's irritation. Walker had placed his life in their hands, had trusted them to see that no harm befell him, and they had let him down.

''By the way, we contacted the North Koreans and offered to turn Colonel Hin's body over to them. You'll never guess what they said.''

''They disavowed any knowledge of him and claimed he wasn't a North Korean citizen.''

''You're psychic. Maybe you should set up one of those phone-in networks. I hear there's big bucks to be made.''

At a knock on the door they both turned. A female agent stuck her head in and waved a sheet of paper. ''Your instructions were to bring this to you immediately, sir.''

In his eagerness Brognola didn't wait for her to enter. He leaped up and grabbed it from her hand. After a cursory glance he grinned and declared, ''The cross-referencing paid off. Fang has a marina out at Mission Bay. Lock and load, Striker. This time we take him down for good.''

CHAPTER TWENTY-TWO

It was fitting, the Executioner supposed, that his conflict with Sin Mak-Fang should end where it began, by the sea. He had first learned about Fang at Hideo Koto's warehouse on Tokyo Bay. Now here he was at Mission Bay, half a block from the Seaside Marina, the one the Feds believed was linked to Madame Rhee and Club X.

It didn't look promising. The marina office was as dark as the night.

By Bolan's watch it was half-past ten. The dock was lined with moored craft, pleasure boats, mostly. On one a man was reading by lantern light. On another a college-age crowd was listening to rock music. At the end of the dock a pair of fishermen guzzled beer while waiting for nibbles.

Bolan walked along the pier and gazed out over the ocean, acting as if he were just out for a late stroll. At the last moment, as he came abreast of the office, he angled over to it and stood to one side of the door. Sliding a hand under his trench coat, he gripped the Desert Eagle.

No shouts of alarm or shots rang out. Cautiously, Bolan peered through the glass. To the left was a counter; to the right a lot of fishing tackle and boating gear hung on a wall. More gear filled neatly arranged shelves.

"What are you up to, mister?"

A boy of eight or nine stood at the corner of the building. Sticking a lollipop into his mouth, the boy sucked on it with loud slurping sounds.

"I was hoping to find someone here," the soldier said.

"Never anyone this late. Ever."

"Know that for a fact, do you? You must live nearby."

"Nope. Come here a lot with my dad. We go out on his boat." The boy extended a finger. "That's him there."

Bolan stepped to the corner. The boy was pointing at the man reading the book. "Have you ever met the person who runs this marina?"

"Mr. Lee? Oh, sure. He's real nice. He gives all us kids suckers." The boy held his up. "He gave me this just this afternoon."

"Is Mr. Lee an Oriental?" Bolan asked. It was possible the manager was another Korean, maybe hand-picked for the job by Sin Mak-Fang or Madame Rhee.

"I think my dad said he's Catholic, like us."

Bolan tried hard to suppress a grin. "What does this Mr. Lee look like?"

"Well, he's real old, maybe thirty or forty. He has yellow hair and a yellow beard. And a great big gut, like a basketball, that shakes when he laughs."

"Thanks," Bolan said. He didn't sound like one of Fang's men. On the surface, at least, the marina seemed legit. Why, then, did Fang own it? He thought of Eureka, and the guns smuggled in from the passing ship, and wondered if the marina was a cover for the contraband operation. It would be simple to take a boat out to pick up illegal merchandise. On a whim Bolan strolled toward the two fishermen.

They were in their sixties, their tackle boxes open beside them, a six-pack of beer half gone. Both looked up and one grinned, showing a gap where two of his upper front teeth had been. "Howdy, mister."

"Having any luck?" Bolan asked.

"Not tonight yet, no," the oldster said, "but you should have been here night before last. I caught me one as long as your arm."

"In your dreams, Horace," the other fisherman promptly said, and winked at Bolan. "Don't believe a word this old buzzard tells you. Every fish that ever got away from him was the size of Moby Dick."

"Screw you, Arnie," Horace responded. "You're just jealous because all you ever catch are minnows."

Bolan smiled and gestured. "This seems like a nice, quiet marina. I was thinking of renting a space for my boat."

"You'll like it. Quiet as can be," Arnie said, "except for those damned kids and their godawful music. But they don't come down all that often."

"Much go on around here at night? A lot of coming and going?"

Horace shook his head. "No, sir. It's not rowdy like some marinas." He paused. "The only one who goes out fairly regular at night is the Dragon Lady and her bunch."

"Who?"

Arnie answered. "We call her the Dragon Lady.

Don't know her real name. She's Japanese or Korean or something like that. Once a month or so she takes out her boat to do some night fishing.''

"Is her boat here now?"

"That's it right behind you," Horace said. "Dragon Lady is about overdue to go out again. Not that they ever catch anything. Most pitiful bunch of fishermen you ever did see."

Bolan turned. Madame Rhee's craft was a vintage motor yacht sixty feet from bow to stern. It could hold a lot of drugs or guns, or both. At the moment the cabin was as dark as the marina office. "Anyone paid it a visit today that you know of?"

"Nope," Horace said, "and we've been fishing since noon."

"Why are you so interested?" Arnie asked.

A tug on Horace's line spared Bolan from having to concoct an excuse. Horace yipped for joy and whipped back on his rod, then started reeling in the line like a madman. The rod bent under the pressure as the fish resisted.

"I got one! I got one! I got me a monster, Arnie!"

"Give it some slack, you idiot!" Arnie bawled. "Let it tire itself out before you—"

The sharp snap of Horace's line ended the contest. Horace was dumped onto his back and lay there cursing a blue streak.

Arnie looked at Bolan. "See what I have to put up with? Twenty-two years we've been fishing buddies, and he still doesn't know the first thing about how to reel one in. A big old fish could be dangling right under his nose, and it would still get away from him."

Right under his nose. The phrase reminded Bolan

of what Brognola had said about Madame Rhee, how she bragged that Fang was the cleverest man alive, and that the Feds could never catch him, even when he was right under their noses.

Bolan also recalled how perplexed Brognola had been by Fang's escape, since agents had been posted on all four sides of the property. Escape hadn't just *seemed* impossible. It *was* impossible.

And suddenly Bolan knew. If not the specifics, at least the truth. Whirling, he raced up the dock. The two fishermen called after him, but he had no time to lose. Brognola had mentioned that the Feds would wrap everything up by midnight. He had to reach Club X by then, and it was already close to eleven.

Bolan hoped he was right, for Bob Walker's sake. It meant the engineer was still alive.

But he had to hurry.

THE FEDERAL AGENTS WEREN'T through until after one. By then only four were still on the premises. They closed and locked the front door and climbed into a car. At the front gate they braked to trade small talk with two uniformed members of San Diego's finest. At last they drove off.

The Executioner watched the policemen string yellow tape across the front of the gate. It warned the general public the site was a crime scene.

Once they were done, the pair slid into their cruiser and departed.

Quiet descended. A stiff breeze off the Pacific rustled the leaves and grass, but otherwise the grounds were as still as a cemetery. From his vantage point in the crook of a tree inside the walls, Bolan waited. For what, exactly, he couldn't say.

The hidden elevator in Inchon had demonstrated that Sin Mak-Fang planned for every contingency, including a way out if forced to beat a hasty retreat. But guessing what Fang had come up with at Club X was impossible.

The minutes dragged by. Five became ten, and ten became twenty. Bolan began to think he had erred, that his insight was wrong, that by now Fang was miles away, safe from the long arm of justice.

Then the soldier heard louder rustling than the breeze could cause, coming from a patch of shrubs fifty feet away. The whole patch was shaking as if from an earthquake. It rippled, it swayed and separated from the earth, rising up into the air.

A canvas tarp was being pushed back from over a wide hole. The camouflage was excellent. Whoever had painted the tarp and attached the artificial shrubbery had done an outstanding job. Even in daylight it had seemed like a natural part of the landscape.

Out into the starlight clambered Ruy Kon-Li. There was no mistaking that gigantic lean frame. He surveyed the vicinity, then bent and reached back into the hole to drag out the bound and gagged Bob Walker.

Sin Mak-Fang climbed out on his own. His bald pate shining dully, he brushed off his jacket.

Bolan quickly descended. Staying low, he moved toward the driveway and palmed the Desert Eagle. A bush at the asphalt's edge was big enough to conceal him. He had no sooner hunkered than Fang and the giant came walking down the drive as coolly as could be. Walker was draped over the giant's right shoulder. He was struggling, but in vain.

"Behave yourself, my young friend," Sin Mak-Fang chided, "or the few hours of life you have left will be spent in more misery than need be." Fang smoothed his tie, running his hand over the diamond stickpin. "We're taking you to a marina, then on out to sea where we can question you without fear of being interrupted. Tell me what I need to know and we will get along nicely. Refuse, and you will suffer as few ever have."

Walker tried to talk, but whatever he said was too muffled by the gag to be understood.

"Easy or hard, without any pain or with more pain than you can imagine, it's up to you," Fang said. "And when we are done, how you die will depend on how cooperative you have been. I can make it quick with a bullet to the brain, or I can have my associate gut you and throw you into the water for the sharks to feast on. I did that once in Korea, and you should have heard the fellow scream."

They were close enough now. Rising, Bolan centered the Desert Eagle's sights on the crime lord. "Your gutting days are over."

Sin and the giant halted.

"Put Walker on the ground," Bolan commanded.

The engineer twisted to see him, relief bringing tears to the young man's eyes.

Kon-Li looked at Fang, who said something in Korean. Then Fang did the worst thing he could have; he smiled.

"Well, this is a surprise. We meet again, American, and here I thought you had died in Inchon."

"Have him put Walker down," Bolan repeated. "Slowly." He couldn't shoot, not with the lower half of Walker's body slanted across the giant's torso. A head shot might bring Kon-Li down, but if it didn't kill him instantly, Walker still might come to harm.

Fang didn't do as he'd been instructed. Instead, he calmly folded his arms across his chest. "I'm curious. How is it you were waiting for us? How did you figure out about the camouflaged hole? Did you use a heat-seeking device? Infrared? What?"

"You couldn't have escaped, so you had to still be here, somewhere." Bolan inched to the right for a better shot at the giant. "It was that simple."

"Nothing in life is ever as simple as it seems," Sin Mak-Fang said. "Take this situation, for instance. It would seem you have the upper hand but you really don't. I advise you to lower your weapon."

"Not on your life."

"What about Mr. Walker's life?" Fang spoke in Korean again, and suddenly Kon-Li had Walker by the throat, holding the engineer in front of him as a human shield.

Bolan turned to marble.

"The problem, you see," Fang continued, "is that you clearly care whether the young man lives or dies. To me he is a means to an end, nothing more. And while valuable, he is expendable. So unless you want to see him harmed, you will lower your pistol and step away from it."

"All that matters to me is keeping you from leaving," Bolan bluffed.

"Is it, indeed?" Fang's smile evaporated. "Let's

find out, shall we?'' He barked an order at his body-guard.

Kon-Li's rush was so swift that even though Bolan was expecting it, even though he was braced and had the Desert Eagle extended, he was almost caught off guard. He skipped to the right but Kon-Li shifted, keeping Walker between them, then hurled Walker as if the engineer were a rag doll.

Walker slammed into Bolan and they both went down, Walker on top, thrashing and squawking. The Executioner pushed him off and surged upward, but he was barely off the ground when the giant reached them. A foot flashed, connecting with Bolan's right wrist, and the Desert Eagle skittered down the drive.

The soldier threw himself backward, away from those deadly feet and hands. The blow had numbed his forearm. He grabbed for the Beretta left-handed while ducking under another kick that would have caved in the side of his skull. As he jerked out the pistol, the giant jumped into the air and spun, the heel of a foot smashing the Beretta from the Executioner's grasp. It went skittering off in a different direction than the Desert Eagle had.

Fang was laughing. He had every confidence in his bodyguard, and every reason to have such confidence. ''I warned you, American,'' he taunted. ''Now I will have him kill you slowly so I can savor your humili-ation.'' In Korean he addressed Kon-Li.

The giant had dropped into a crouch, his hands poised to strike, his features empty of emotion.

Bolan had no illusions about how he would fare. He was skilled at unarmed combat, extremely skilled, but he was no match for a killing machine like Kon-Li.

Few were. A glance over his shoulder showed where the Desert Eagle lay. He spun and sprinted to reclaim it. He sensed the giant had overtaken him a heartbeat before a foot hooked his ankle, tripping him, and iron fingers speared into his rib cage.

Tumbling, Bolan landed hard on his back, his breath gone, his ribs aflame. He pushed up into a crouch, surprised the giant made no move to finish him off. Instead, Kon-Li circled him like a cat circling an injured canary.

"Any regrets, American?" Fang asked, the very question Colonel Hin had posed before he died. "Do you regret meddling in my affairs? Do you regret thinking you could best me?"

"The only thing I regret," Bolan responded, "is having to listen to you flap your gums."

"That is easily remedied."

Fang motioned, and Kon-Li came in fast and furious, raining blows, a bone-shattering barrage no one could withstand for long.

Bolan didn't try to. He zigged to the left, he zagged to the right, he ducked, he dodged, he weaved, always staying one step ahead of the giant. It wasn't a pace he could sustain for long, though. He knew it and the giant knew it, so when he abruptly slowed, Kon-Li took it for granted he was winded and slowed to deliver a fatal blow.

Bolan didn't stand there awaiting the chop of Kon-Li's axlike hand. He didn't seek to avoid the death strike. He did the last thing the giant or the crime lord would expect him to do. He attacked.

Hurtling forward, his shoulders down low, the Executioner flew at Kon-Li as if tackling an opposing quarterback. He lifted the giant clear off the ground and slammed him onto the asphalt, then drove his fist into the North Korean's groin.

Kon-Li was endowed with enormous strength. He was solid muscle and bone, as powerful as any man alive. But he had the same weak spot all men did. And now he doubled over, his hands clasped over himself, sputtering through clenched teeth.

It was only a momentary reprieve. Bolan glanced about for either of his pistols, registering too late the rush of movement behind him. Brawny arms encircled him, pinning his own to his side.

"I will enjoy killing you personally," Fang hissed in his ear. Fang wrenched sharply to the left, and down, seeking to ram Bolan's head into the ground.

Bolan was able to shift and absorb the stress on his shoulder. As Fang struggled to raise him to try again, the soldier snapped his head back, once, twice, three times, pounding it against Fang's face. He was rewarded by the crunch of cartilage and a vehement oath.

Fang's grip loosened, allowing Bolan to push loose and rise.

The crime lord was now down, but the giant was rising. Kon-Li was no longer the cold, detached engine of destruction. Rage animated him. Baring his teeth as if they were fangs, he sprang.

Bolan barely had enough forewarning to avoid the initial flurry. He dipped at the knees, then leaped to the right, to the left. A stony heel whisked by his face. Fingers like railroad spikes narrowly missed his neck, clipping his shoulder. For seconds that stretched into eternity he evaded the giant's death blows, which only served to incense Kon-Li more.

Not once did Bolan go on the offensive. He wanted the giant to think he couldn't muster much of an offense, that when it came to hand-to-hand combat he was woefully inept, so that when he did make his move, when at long last he ducked under a swing and then surged upward, lancing the tips of his rigid fingers into the base of the giant's throat, it was so totally unexpected that it caught Kon-Li flatfooted.

The giant automatically assumed a defensive stance, a back stance, but suddenly he commenced to wheeze and gasp, his face turning scarlet. He raised a thickly callused hand to his throat as if in wonderment.

To the right lay the Beretta. Bolan feinted, throwing a punch he never intended to land, then shifted in midswing toward the pistol. Taking two long strides, he dived for it even as Kon-Li galvanized into action and streaked toward him, bent on vengeance.

Bolan snagged the Beretta on the roll. Flipping up into a combat crouch, he triggered off a burst as the giant crossed the intervening space, fired again as the giant hiked a hand to strike, fired a third time as the giant folded at the waist, and a fourth as, on his hands and knees, Kon-Li reached for him with clawed fingers.

The soldier immediately rotated to cover Fang, but the mastermind wasn't there. An inky shape was speeding off toward the north wall, bounding like a goat over bushes and other obstacles.

"I'll be right back," Bolan shouted to Walker, and gave chase.

Fang was incredibly fleet of foot and rapidly pulled

ahead. Once he got over the wall, he could lose himself in the dark streets and alleys beyond.

Bolan didn't fire, not yet. He had no idea how many rounds were left in the magazine, and wasting them might prove costly. Pouring all he had into running, he threaded through a last cluster of trees and spied his quarry.

Fang never stopped, never slowed. He came to the wall and flung himself upward with outstretched arms. Clutching the top, he pressed his shoes flat against the bricks and pumped higher. For several seconds his body was silhouetted against the glare of streetlights on the other side.

Sinking onto his left knee, the Executioner took aim.

Fang looked back to see if Bolan was still after him. At the Beretta's bark, Fang arched his spine and opened his arms wide as if he were about to dive off a diving board. Instead, he keeled backward and fell with a loud thud.

Bolan raced up to the wall.

The North Korean was still alive but couldn't rise. Eyes frantic with fear, he looked up and pleaded, "Please, no! No!"

"Yes." Bolan pressed the Beretta's muzzle against Fang's forehead.

"Wait! I have money! Lots of money! In a Swiss account! Half of it is yours if you will let me live! Get me to a hospital and I promise you, I will make you a rich man. What do you say?"

The Executioner thought of Hin, Bob Walker and Fang's countless victims.

He let the Beretta answer.

**A journey through the dangerous frontier
known as the future...**

JAMES AXLER
DEATH LANDS®
Zero City

Hungry and exhausted, Ryan and his band emerge from
a redoubt into an untouched predark city, and uncover a
cache of weapons and food. Among other interlopers,
huge winged creatures guard the city. Holed up inside
an old government building, where Ryan's son, Dean,
lies near death, Ryan and Krysty must raid where a local
baron uses human flesh as fertilizer....

James Axler

OUTLANDERS®

DOOM DYNASTY

Kane, once a keeper of law and order in the new America, is part of the driving machine to return power to the true inheritors of the earth. California is the opening salvo in one baron's savage quest for immortality—and a fateful act of defiance against earth's dangerous oppressors. Yet their sanctity is grimly uncertain as an unseen force arrives for a final confrontation with those who seek to rule, or reclaim, planet Earth.